ALSO BY RACHEL HOWZELL HALL

AND NOW SHE'S GONE

RACHEL HOWZELL HALL

A TOM DOHERTY ASSOCIATES BOOK
NEW YORK

AND NOW SHE'S GONE

A Forge Book
Published by Tom Doherty Associates
120 Broadway
New York, NY 10271

www.tor-forge.com

Forge® is a registered trademark of Macmillan Publishing Group, LLC.

ISBN 978-1-250-83351-8

Our books may be purchased in bulk for promotional, educational, or business use. Please contact your local bookseller or the Macmillan Corporate and Premium Sales Department at 1-800-221-7945, extension 5442, or by email at MacmillanSpecialMarkets@macmillan.com.

First Edition: September 2020
First Mass Market Edition: January 2022

Printed in the United States of America

0 9 8 7 6 5 4 3 2 1

To Gretchen, Jason, and Terry
Hey, look at us . . .

One need not be a chamber to be haunted,
One need not be a house;
The brain has corridors surpassing
material place.

EMILY DICKINSON

SHE
HAD
TO
LEAVE

She had to do it.

She had to glance in her rearview mirror.

Because a black SUV was rolling up behind her.

Closer . . .

A black SUV with the green Range Rover medallion on the left side of its grille.

Closer . . .

The truck stopped inches away from her car's rear bumper.

The sound of music reached her first—Notorious B.I.G., "Hypnotize."

Shit.

Maybe her worry was irrational. It wasn't like she was on an abandoned road. She was on the west side of Los Angeles, and there was a sports equipment store over there. And a Taco Bell over there. There were storefront windows that promised *Pho! Massage! Comic Books!*

Didn't matter, because right at that moment, she was the only woman in the world.

But the man behind her wore familiar-looking aviator sunglasses and—

This truck could be his.

Shitshitshit.

Whenever she spotted a black Range Rover, the hair on her neck and arms shot up like straw. In this city, that meant she was a scarecrow four times ‎ day.

She was trembling now, panic sizzling throug‎ her blood. She fought it, shallow breath by shallo‎ breath, until she could take deeper breaths, until h‎ fear huddled in that safe place behind her bladd‎ She kneaded her mind to remember any tiny det‎ that would tell her this was not the truck. Like . . .‎ yellow pine tree air freshener hung from the mirr‎ Like . . . A white scrape on the fender's black paint.‎

No luck.

She was boxed in—car to the left of her, car to t‎ right, cross traffic and red light before her. In the cros‎ walk, an old lady inched from one curb to the oth‎ curb.

What if he tries to open my back passenger door‎ I'm sitting here?

The doors were locked.

What if he tries to break a window?

Then she'd . . . blow the red light, try her damne‎ est not to hit the old lady in the crosswalk, but if s‎ had to hit her . . .

No. She wouldn't let him walk up on her aga‎ like that.

The driver removed his sunglasses.

Those eyes . . .

She squinted at the image in the rearview mirr‎ "That's not him."

Those eyes . . .

Too small. Too spaced apart.

He was not the man who had promised to kill h‎ Not this time.

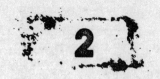

2

Los Angeles was a city of skies—and everyone in the city now sweltered beneath a dirty-blue sky. Later in the evening, that same sky would turn rose quartz and then, in the morning, Necco wafer orange. Because the marine layer, exhaust from cars and refineries, and brushfire smoke reflected the sun. It was a murder sky, killing four million people slowly . . . slowly . . . molecule . . . by molecule.

But Grayson Sykes wouldn't die on this eleventh day of July because of that killer sky.

She planned to end her day with dollar tacos and strawberry margaritas with her coworkers at Sam Jose's. They would talk about Zadie's upcoming retirement, Clarissa's upcoming bachelorette party, and Jennifer's "thing" with her husband's chief mechanic.

Gray had no wedding and she was far from retirement. "I just won't eat heavy tomorrow," "Are you serious?," and "I did my steps today"—those were her happy hour lines. The quartet would eat, drink, and laugh; they'd cast lustful glances at men who should've been home with their wives, who should've been working out at the gym, who should've been at the office preparing PowerPoint presentations on midyear fiscal numbers.

Now, though, Jennifer Bellman sat in the lobby of the smoked green glass and metal building where

Rader Consulting was located. Just a hop, skip, and jump away from the magnificent Pacific Ocean, Rader Consulting did it all—from pets to cons. Looking for lugs in all the right places, squeezing into spots where cops weren't allowed to go. No warrants? *No problem.* Need info? *Got it right here.* From background checks to finding long-lost boyfriends. From simple internet searches and deep, dark web dives to, *ahem*, other methods.

The blonde was pretending to read the two-week-old *People* left on the coffee table. One of the primary skip tracers at Rader Consulting, Jennifer sniffed, snuffled, and clawed to find missing deadbeats and debtors. Men saw the hair, the boobs, the blouse that framed those boobs, and they never took her serious enough to keep their traps—or their flies—closed.

Gray asked, "Why are you sitting down here?"

Jennifer bit her bottom lip. "There's a new tech titan on the third floor. Tall, Slavic hotness in a Hugo Boss suit. He needs to know that I exist." A gossip, a ditz, a flirt—thrice-married (and still married) Jennifer could be all that and worse.

The "worse" now walked beside Gray to the elevator bank. "Where'd you go?" she asked.

"Pharmacy."

"No offense, but I don't know *why* we celebrate one hundred percent linen."

"You lost me." Gray pressed the Up button.

"Your *pants*, honey." Jennifer *tsk*ed Gray's wrinkled white linen slacks, then batted her baby blue eyes. "What's that dog with all the wrinkles in its face?"

"A Shar-Pei?"

Jennifer clapped. "That's it! Wrinkles everywhere, like your slacks. They're cute, though. The dogs, I mean." Jennifer and her perfect blonde bob and her perfect high breasts bursting from her floral print Chico's dress. So efficient, Jennifer Bellman. So eager to climb and so eager to please.

Not really. Jennifer Bellman was a fifty-year-old rottweiler in cocker spaniel cosplay.

The two women entered the elevator together. Gray's eyes burned—Jennifer wore enough perfume to scent a small country. At the end of the day, Gray always smelled like marshmallow and vanilla.

"Oh," Jennifer said. "Nick's been drifting through the building looking for you."

"He texted—he just gave me my first *real* case."

Jennifer clapped. "No more looking for lost Chihuahuas! Cheating husband?"

"Missing girlfriend."

The elevator doors opened to the second floor.

"You're gonna need help," Jennifer said. "I'll be right there to guide you. My first bit of advice: when all else fails, cry. Tears make people feel sorry for you, and they'll tell you anything you need to know just to shut you up."

White-haired Zadie Mendelbaum stood at the breakfast bar clutching a soft pack of Camels and a bottle of Dr Pepper. A career of squinting at records had frozen her face into a mask of narrowed eyes and an upturned nose. She also had a pack-a-day habit and exquisite hobbit-size hands. She'd worked at Rader Consulting since its establishment, seven years before, and was always proud to boast that she was "employee number one."

The old woman reminded Gray of one of her foster mothers. Naomi Applewhite also had a Dr Pepper addiction, but she smoked hard-pack Newports while sucking peppermints. Gray had stayed with Mom Naomi for seven months. Two weeks before starting eighth grade, Gray had been snatched out of that depressing Oakland apartment by Child Protective Services and placed into a girls' home. No explanation given. Whenever Gray smelled smoky mint or cloves-black licorice almonds, she thought of Naomi Applewhite. Which, now that she worked with Zadie, was all the time.

"Went on break without telling me?" Zadie followed the two women into Gray's office.

Gray dropped her purse onto the credenza. "About to start my first missing person case."

"Congrats, honey," Zadie said. "How you feelin'?"

"Excited. Nervous. Nauseous."

"Like a virgin at a prison rodeo?" Jennifer asked.

"Never been to a rodeo," Gray said. "So . . . *maybe*?"

"You'll do fine." Zadie pointed at the pile of books on the corner of Gray's desk. "Looks like you've been studying."

For two years, Gray had worked as a contractor for Rader Consulting, writing reports, transcribing recordings, and *much, much more!* Now, though, she wanted to be a private investigator. She'd read handbooks, attended community college courses, shadowed Nick for two weeks, and watched YouTube videos featuring investigators on the job. She'd even immersed herself in mysteries written by Hammett, Chandler, and Mosley. Nick promoted her, placing her on his license until she'd be eligible to apply for her own in three years. And then he'd given her a case: finding Cheeto, a stolen Chihuahua.

"Sounds simple," Gray said. "Find the guy's girlfriend. I shouldn't fuck it up too much."

"You obviously haven't met you," Jennifer snarked.

Gray plucked a sheet of tissue from the box on her desk. "I have, and I'm actually the best report writer here." She cleaned her tortoiseshell glasses but kept her gaze on Jennifer.

Jennifer offered a saccharine smile. "Totally different skill set. But you'll see that."

Zadie clicked her nails against the Dr Pepper bottle. "I'll always remember my first missing person case. . . . He woke up on Saturday, stayed home while the wife and kids drove to synagogue. He fed the dog, opened the front door. He took his kayak out in the marina, where he 'drowned.' But really, he swam down shore for three miles, where he'd hid dry clothes and a new life and a new name behind a fucking drug dealer's boat."

Gray and Jennifer eyed each other.

Zadie had just described how her husband Saul had disappeared thirty years ago.

"Well, women disappear all the time," Jennifer said. "Some *intentionally*."

Because she'd grown tired of her man, had grown tired of his hands, of that job, of those freaking dishes that kept filling the sink, dishes that no one touched even as their stink wafted through the house. If she wasn't taking the kids with her, she kissed them farewell, took out the trash one last time, and just . . . *left*.

Natalie Dixon, a woman Gray knew once upon a time, had disappeared like that.

Unlike the men who disappeared, women left their egos behind along with their keys, photo identification, and unpaid electric bills. These women may have wondered about their past lives—*What are they doing back home? How are they living without me? Did somebody finally wash those damned dishes?*—but they rarely did more than wonder. They never visited old haunts. They never searched their names on Google or checked their Facebook pages. Unlike most men who vanished, women rarely got caught. They just wanted a new beginning.

Natalie Dixon had also longed for a new life and hadn't wanted to be found. Guilt had gnawed at her spirit, Gray recalled, and that prickly sensation of millions of eyes had pecked at poor Natalie Dixon, and she always worried that the wrong pair would pick her from the crowd.

"Two, three days, tops," Gray said. "That's Nick's estimation."

"I would say use sex appeal to help you," Jennifer said, eyes on her coral-painted fingernails, "but that won't work. Fortunately, you have a great personality. You can talk about books and . . . and . . . movies and . . . politics. Oh, and comic books. Improvise. Make shit up."

Gray cocked an eyebrow. "I'm good at making shit up."

"She's better than you at that, Jen," Zadie said.

"Doubt it," Jennifer sang, with a twisted grin. "I'm a *supreme* liar—Oh!" She pointed at Gray. "Think I'm a bitch now? Skip Sam Jose's tonight and see how evil I'll be tomorrow morning. I can't do Clarissa alone."

Zadie rolled her eyes. "That girl does nothing but yak, yak, yak."

"I'll let you know about tonight," Gray said.

Jennifer slapped Gray's desktop. "Nuh-uh. I've dated enough black men to know that 'I'll let you know' means 'I'm not showing up.'"

Gray laughed.

"You'll see your ex-*marine*," Jennifer sang.

"*Former* marine," Gray corrected.

Hank Wexler was the new owner of Sam Jose's. Two weeks ago, the square-jawed jarhead with blue eyes and thick salt-and-pepper hair had claimed that the blue-inked Hebrew letters tattooed on his left forearm were Gray's name. Back then, he didn't even *know* her name, not that him not knowing had kept Gray from licking tequila salt off his skin. An hour later, she and Hank had made out in his office—it was like they'd known each other in a former life, so making out so soon was okay. He had tasted like whiskey sours and Juicy Fruit gum. That had been a good night.

"No flaking," Jennifer said now, as she glided out of Gray's office.

"Scout's honor," Gray shouted. "Have a margarita waiting for me."

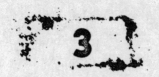

3

Dominick Rader, founder and CEO of Rader Consulting, was not at his desk.

Gray, though, had enough information to start working.

It was two o'clock, and traffic pockets filled with a trillion cars mixed with bursts of highway freedom, and sometimes, *sometimes*, the speedometer on Gray's silver Camry crept toward forty miles per hour. *Zooming.* She rolled down the sedan's windows, then turned up Angie Stone on the stereo, lamenting not being able to eat or sleep anymore cuz of love.

Right then, Gray felt "L.A. fly," a near-native alone in her car beneath that weird-colored, murder sky with those white plumes of smoke to the north, to the east, and to the west of her. One woman in the second-biggest city in America, disappearing in a heartbeat from block to block. No one and everyone knew her in Los Angeles. Some called that a weakness, like color blindness or fallen arches. For Gray, that six degrees of anonymity was Marilyn Monroe's mole or Barbra Streisand's nose.

She kept north until she pulled into the garage for UCLA Medical Plaza, a city unto itself. Anchored by the university, the plaza spanned nearly seven hundred thousand square feet and was filled with outpatient centers, hospitals, and research facilities.

Cardiologist Ian O'Donnell worked in UCLA's Urgent Care department, and Gray met the eyes of patients waiting to see someone about their lungs, their hearts, their mucus. Battered chairs hosted bloody men with bruised knuckles. Diabetics waited for insulin shots and children clutching blankets barked coughs that sounded like gravel trucks. The waiting room stank of phlegm and unwashed bodies, but the carpets were clean and the lights were bright.

At least.

Gray pushed her eyeglasses to the top of her head. She crossed and uncrossed her legs as though she needed to pee. She ignored the tingle and yanking near her belly button—her body knew she needed to be here as a patient—as she scanned the waiting room in search of threats.

Runny noses and runny eyes made her clench. She couldn't get sick again—not even a cold, because colds sometimes masqueraded as stealthy pneumonia with its filled lungs and hacky cough. And then pneumonia led to health questionnaires that requested information she didn't want to share with staff here or at sketchy clinics that passed ibuprofen off as penicillin.

"Next." Behind the registration desk, a black woman beckoned Gray to step forward. She pushed an admissions form toward Gray. "What's going on today?"

Questions, even though she had dry eyes and clear lungs.

And a missing appendix. And minor abdominal pain. And possibly a fever.

"Actually, I'm not here for a medical visit," Gray said. "I'm here to see Dr. O'Donnell on business. I was asked to come by this afternoon." She scribbled her name on top of the admissions form, then pushed it back.

The clerk said, "Okay, have a seat over in the chairs. He may be tied up, though. As you can see, we're busy today."

Since Gray would rather wait near blood than perch close to viruses she couldn't see, she selected a seat near an old man holding a saturated bloody towel against his forearm. She winced at him to show sympathy, then found her phone in her purse.

It was time to create a new phone number for this, her first major case as a private investigator. She used Burner, an app that allowed her to generate as many phone numbers as she needed while keeping her personal phone number private. Nick Rader had a number. Jennifer, Zadie, Clarissa, and her other coworkers had a number. Utilities, taxes, her apartment's management office—those shared the same number.

That virgin-at-a-prison-rodeo nervousness crackled through her, and she grinned as Burner generated a new number for the Isabel Lincoln case.

Yee-haw!

She pulled intake forms from her leather binder.

Isabel Lincoln had been missing since May 27 and her birthday was just a day away. She had brown hair and brown eyes. Tall at five nine. There was a butterfly tattoo on her left thigh.

A heartbreaker. That's what Gray's father, Victor, would say about pretty girls like Isabel Lincoln. Big, innocent eyes. Sweet, innocent smile. Long ponytail and *Vogue* cheekbones. The kind of girl you married. A Mary Ann. *You're not a Mary Ann,* Victor would tell Gray. *You're . . . the Skipper.* No-nonsense. Reliable. Resourceful.

Gray reread Isabel's race as listed on the intake form. *White?*

Isabel Lincoln was not "white." Mixed, *maybe*. High yellow, definitely. Isabel Lincoln was as white as Halle Berry.

The second intake form had been completed for a dog with curly chocolate-blond hair. The Labradoodle, named Kenny G., belonged to Dr. Ian O'Donnell and had been with Isabel on the day she disappeared.

"Gray Sykes?"

Gray looked up and over to the door that separated the waiting room from the treatment areas. That voice belonged to a tall, sun-kissed god with dirty-blond hair and swimmer's shoulders that strained beneath his blue scrubs.

"Dr. O'Donnell?" When he nodded, she floated over to him with her hand out to shake. Something quickened and fluttered in her belly—he'd knocked her up by simply standing there.

His eyes peeked at her short, boy-cut hairdo, her Rubenesque hips, and her Victorian bosom, and then his eyes glazed and he stopped seeing her altogether. He finally accepted her hand. "You can call me Ian. I was expecting . . ."

"Nick assigned your case to me."

"Ah. Let's talk in my office."

Past the double doors, past the bleeding and asthmatic, and past the beeping machines, Gray finally landed in Ian O'Donnell's office. It was a clean, ordered space with folders placed on the corner of his desk and pictures of patients pinned on a corkboard. Near the desk phone, there were pictures of Ian holding Kenny G., a picture of Kenny G. wearing a doggie surgery cap, and then another picture of Kenny G., romping on the beach.

Gray sat her bag in the other guest chair, then

noted the one picture of Isabel. In this shot, the sun was setting at Isabel's back and her face was hidden in shadow. Gray could barely see Ian's one-and-only.

Did the nurses they'd passed—the ones who'd gazed at him as though he lit the skies each morning—did *they* believe that Isabel was his one-and-only? *Had* she been his one-and-only?

According to the good doctor, yes, Isabel had been. They'd been so happy. They'd rarely argued. They had plans, ambitious plans—a wedding, then a honeymoon in Barcelona and Pantages Theatre season passes.

"I really thought we were happy." Ian was pinching his bottom lip, and it now looked cherry red and bee-stung. "I just want her to come back home. I want her to just . . . *talk* to me, you know, and explain why she left this time. And why she pulled my dog into all of this."

"You think she's alive and well?"

His hand froze mid–lip pinch. "Of course. The police would've found her and my dog by now if something had happened, right?"

In her mind, Gray shrugged. "Did you contact the police?"

"Yep. End of that week she disappeared. June first."

Gray wrote "June" on the pad, but then the pen stopped writing. She scribbled. No ink. Her pen was dead. She offered Ian an apologetic smile, said, "One minute." She reached for her purse and her nervous hands knocked the bag to the ground. Wallet, hand sanitizer, chewing gum, coins, all of it, clattered out and around the linoleum floor. Gray dropped to the ground and shoved spilled contents back into the handbag. The doctor's stare burned her back and she wanted to cry as she hurried with the cleanup. And, in all of the ruckus, she neglected to find another pen.

Slipping back into the chair, she said, "Sorry," then pushed out a breath. She'd have to remember as much as she could.

He was staring at her. "All done?"

"Yes." She was boiling inside—heat jumped off her skin like flares off the sun.

"Are you okay?" the doctor asked. "You look a little—"

"I'm good, thank you. So . . . June first. What did the police say?"

"They said that she broke up with me, that the text message she sent proved it."

Gray ran her palm across her sweaty hairline. "And what did the text say?"

He swiped around his phone, then set the device before her.

The text had been sent on Monday, May 27:

LEAVE ME THE FUCK ALONE. YOU CAN GO STRAIGHT TO HELL. WE ARE DONE!!!

Gray nodded. "Yeah. Reads like a breakup."

"The cops said that I pissed her off enough that she decided to take the dog, and unless there was evidence of foul play, they had no reason to look for her. I could report Kenny G. as stolen, but they said that reporting could backfire. They think she'll get tired of the dog and will bring him back. They obviously haven't met Kenny G. He's a keeper."

Gray held up a hand. "Let's back up. You said, 'left this time.' She do this a lot? Leave?"

"Are you going to write any of this down?" he asked, eyeing her.

Gray's cheeks burned. "Umm . . ." She pointed to the cup of pens near his computer monitor. "May I?"

He nodded.

She scribbled as much as she could in five seconds. A bead of sweat trickled down her temple but she didn't swipe it.

Ian O'Donnell bent to open a small refrigerator near his desk. He pulled out a bottled water and twisted the cap. "I think you need this."

She caught that bead of perspiration with a knuckle, then reached for the small bottle. As the cool liquid slipped down her throat, the craggy, cranky places in her smoothed and cooled.

Refreshed, she dropped the empty bottle into her bag. "Thank you."

"It's hot out there." He leaned back in his high-backed chair. "So, Isabel leaving . . . Whenever we're in a rough patch—if we're arguing or her friends are being jerks or whatever—Iz—that's what I call her—Iz just gets in her car and leaves. Since we've been together—it would've been a year on the fourth—she's walked off about two or three times. She's gone for a few days and then she comes back, ready to be a grown-up again."

"Where does she usually go?"

"Palm Springs. Vegas once."

Las Vegas used to be a great disappearing town, before the casino owners installed all those surveillance cameras, before sorority girls Snapped and Boomeranged and selfied, sometimes catching random, taggable folks in the background. It was damn near impossible to hide in Vegas now.

Gray asked, "Is it possible . . ."

No ink coming now from the nib of the borrowed pen.

She wanted the earth to gobble her up for good. Since the earth refused to move, she lifted the binder some, so that Ian O'Donnell couldn't see that the words she wrote on her pad were now invisible. "Is it possible that Isabel just didn't want to come back this last time?"

The doctor's green eyes flared. "We have a future together. I'm a nice guy, and . . . and there's her family. I don't think she would've left them to get back at me. No way.

"She's selfish, that's her problem. Thinks only about herself, and part of me wants to . . ."

"Part of you wants to . . . what?"

He pinched his lip.

"You don't think she wants to come back," Gray said. "Why, then, does she need to be found?"

He turned a sad pink. "Because I want my dog."

"Are there other folks I should talk to?"

Isabel's parents, Joe and Rebekah Lawrence; her best friend, Tea Something; her coworkers Farrah, Beth, and Nan; and Pastor Bernard Dunlop.

"Oh," the doctor added, "and one time, this guy Omar texted her while she was in the shower. I took down the number but never called it. Don't know who the hell *he* is."

"Did you read Omar's text message?"

"Nope. Her phone was locked."

"Could you send those numbers to . . ." Gray offered her new phone number, and Ian O'Donnell texted contact information for everyone except the Lawrences.

"I've never met her parents," he said. "Tea's been my go-between in this craziness."

"When was the last time you talked to Tea?"

"I saw her about two weeks ago. She still hadn't seen Iz."

Gray held up the intake form. "On here you

describe Isabel as being white. I'm looking at her and I'm . . . not seeing that. Which means that other people won't see that, either."

"She's biracial. She prefers to check that box instead of the other box."

"The . . . *other* box?"

Ian waved his hand. "I don't see color. She's *human* to me."

Gray's nerves jangled, and she was almost certain that her eyes had crossed.

He cocked an eyebrow. "What?"

Gray jammed her lips together.

"Iz and I . . . we're post-racial, and really . . . Do you act this way with all of your clients?" He sighed at her just like the white boys she'd dated back when Public Enemy and Air Jordans had crossed color lines.

"What questions should I ask her to prove that she's Isabel and that she's okay?"

Ian O'Donnell rubbed his chin as he thought. "What was my first car? What was my first gift to her? And . . . what am I allergic to?"

Ian, Ian, Ian—even in Isabel's proof of life.

"Did you and Isabel live together?" she asked.

"We were talking about her moving to my place, but we hadn't done it yet."

Probably because she smelled the crazy on him and didn't want it to get into her favorite coat. Hard to get the stink of nuts out of wool. Gray had lost many a good outfit that way.

"I helped pay her rent, though," he said. "Since her credit's shot, I hold the lease."

"Where does she live?"

"Some neighborhood. I don't know. I don't go over there a lot. Never went over there before we started dating." He then recited Isabel's address on Don Lorenzo Drive.

"That's off Stocker Street," Gray said. "In Baldwin Hills."

"Sure. I don't know that part of town."

"Tina Turner had a home there. John Singleton, Tom Bradley, Ray Charles . . ."

"Wow," he said, unimpressed. "Anyway, I can meet you there later today."

"Awesome. So, where do you think she went? The desert or the Strip?"

He lowered his chin to gaze down at her. "If I knew that, I wouldn't be asking you for help, now would I?"

She thought of his single nice gesture toward her, the gift of water. One small bottle. Though she was fake smiling, she wanted to lunge across the desk and drive his cheap, dry pen through his golden cheek.

He frowned at her as though she were a child. "Her friends probably think I've done something to her. I haven't *touched* her. I haven't *seen* her, and I would never, ever *hurt* her. Like I said, I'm a nice guy. We're a typical couple. Yes, I'd get mad. Yes, she'd get mad. I'd scream, she'd scream, we'd both scream.

"Our last argument, though? She told me that she hated me, that she'd kill me if she could get away with it, which was unbelievable. I know she didn't mean it, but goddamn, it hurt, hearing that. And then, to take my *dog* on top of that?"

There was a knock on the door, and a cute blonde nurse with Michelle Pfeiffer eyes poked her head in to say, "We need you, Dr. O. It's getting crazy out here."

Ian O'Donnell offered Hot Nurse Pfeiffer a ready-made smile. "I'm almost done, Trin."

A moment passed after the nurse had closed the

door. Then Ian's eyes and Gray's eyes met—his now shimmered with tears while hers remained as dry and flat as all of Los Angeles. Those dry and flat eyes doubted that they were looking upon a man madly, deeply, truly in love.

Because weren't men all madly, deeply, truly in love before they were no longer madly, deeply, truly in love—minutes before they shot up classrooms, sanctuaries, dental offices, or bedrooms? Boyfriends and husbands, baby daddies and one-night stands were always madly, deeply, truly in love. Bloody love. Crazy love. Love-you-to-death kind of love.

Gray was a skeptic, a cynic, an agnostic of love. She believed more in yetis, chemtrails, and human-meat restaurants than in that four-letter word. "Here's your pen," she said now, dropping the doctor's nonworking writing utensil back into its cup.

Ian O'Donnell stood from his chair. "I'd like a report from you at the end of each day. Nick promised that in my contract. Even if it's just a couple of sentences, I want to know your progress. Who you've talked to. What they said. Et cetera."

Gray closed her binder with a pop. "Certainly."

"No excuses. Every day. Do you understand?"

Ian O'Donnell. The hero, the god, the man who healed people every day. The man who probably always got what he wanted from women. He'd expect nothing less from Gray.

Yeah.

He had no idea.

4

Last year, a day before the Fourth of July, Ian and Isabel had a meet cute. She'd slipped in a puddle out in the UCLA Medical Center courtyard. He'd witnessed her fall from fifty yards away, ran to her rescue, and carried her to the emergency room to personally ensure she received immediate care. Two hours later, Ian had returned to his office with her phone number and Isabel had left the E.R. with a broken ankle protected by a soft cast. The next day, they grabbed a prepackaged picnic basket from a gourmet supermarket and headed to the Hollywood Bowl to watch fireworks. They kissed for the first time as canned Ray Charles sang about America, as fiery red, white, and blue pyrotechnic peonies burst in the skies above the city.

Ian O'Donnell shared this story with Gray as he escorted her to the main entrance. "Again: nice guy here."

Gray said, "Aww, that's sweet," but she knew that if she typed "Boyfriend kills girlfriend neighbor says he's nice" into any search engine, or "Husband kills wife neighbor calls him nice," "Husband kills ex-wife neighbors thought he was nice," or any combination of those words, she would get almost six million results. She'd get stories of police recovering handguns the nice guy had used; she'd read stories of paramedics pronouncing the woman's death at the scene. That is, if the nice guy hadn't buried her in a shallow grave, left her bundled in a blanket in the back seat of his truck, or dumped her in a bay, marina, or harbor to disappear her altogether.

Had Isabel Lincoln met her end like this? Was Ian O'Donnell now performing Nice Guy Kabuki because he thought Gray was dumb? Because he thought Gray was awed by him?

If he hadn't been a jerk, she would've been awed, but she wouldn't ever be dumb.

Today. Because Gray had also stumbled through those heady romances with successful and beautiful men who knew just how successful and beautiful they were. She, too, had looked beyond their arrogance and casual disrespect because *ohmigod, look at him; look at me riding in his Bimmer.* She'd *change* him, love him enough so that he'd soften like butter. She'd be the diamond drill bit to his slab of marble. Alas, those successful, beautiful men had never changed. No—*she'd* changed, pushing away friends, pushing away gut feelings, pushing down tears, all to make him love her. *He* had been the diamond drill bit and *she* had been simple hardwood.

Eventually, she had wised up.

And maybe so had Isabel Lincoln.

"We used to see each other for lunch every day," Ian O'Donnell said now. "Before everything went wrong."

"She works close then?" Gray asked.

"At the Alumni Center up on the main campus. She's an alum. Class of 2009. Not me. I went to Brown for undergrad, then Harvard Med, and now I'm here. Weather's better in L.A. than Boston. Girls are prettier, too." He chuckled. "Just kidding. Not kidding."

Gray laughed for him.

She didn't like Dr. Ian O'Donnell, and she hoped that Isabel had left a scorching review of him on Yelp before she disappeared. " . . . *and the tiny-dicked bastard hogged all the covers and ate his ear-wax.*" But liking wasn't a requirement of the job, especially since Rader Consulting's business model was built on the backs of cheaters and scammers, hags and nags.

The doctor and the P.I. exited the medical office building and entered the bright outdoors with its thick, hills-on-fire air and flecked blue sky. One of Gray's laparoscopic scars, left by her emergency appendectomy just six weeks before, burned and hissed beneath the waistband of her slacks, and she took a deep, cleansing breath of that tainted air.

"You know how to get to the Alumni Center from here?" Ian O'Donnell asked.

Gray pointed north. "Just walk that way."

"You know who you're gonna talk to?"

"Farrah, Beth, and Nan."

"If you don't solve this thing by four today, I'll meet you at Iz's place at five. She told me about 'C.P. time,' so not five ten or five thirty. Five sharp. Don't be late. *Please.*"

The nerves beneath Gray's skin crackled. Isabel Lincoln had the nerve to discuss "Colored People Time" with Ian O'Donnell? And then, *he* dared to utter that shit . . . ?

Fifteen years ago, he'd be catching these hands. Alone again, Gray squeezed her eyes shut, waited for the pain in her middle to pass, and wished that she had completed her regimen of amoxicillin, then remembered that she carried in her purse the new refill of oxycodone that Dr. Messamer had prescribed for the pain.

She couldn't find the oxycodone—she'd *just* picked it up from the pharmacy—but she did find a bottle of ibuprofen, 600 milligrams. *Good enough.* She popped one giant pill dry and it scraped along her throat. It was bitter, but then, on days like today, so was she.

I need another pen. "You have to do better than this."

She fumbled through her purse again. After finding an ancient ballpoint coated in stickysomething and strands of hair, she sat on a nearby retaining wall and quickly transcribed her conversation with her new client. Alas, she had only approximations for dates, since she couldn't decipher the gouged scribbles made by the dry pens she'd used in Ian's office.

Maybe it wouldn't matter.

Maybe she'd find Isabel Lincoln before having to rely on a timeline.

She winced, a little cranky, plenty sore, then plucked a small bottle of sanitizer from her battered handbag. As she rubbed gel into her hands, her phone buzzed.

A text message from Ian O'Donnell.

Just making sure you're not lost.

"Seriously?" Gray texted back *I'm good*, and she started her trek to the Alumni Center.

Was Ian O'Donnell always this . . . asshole-y?

Sure, he wanted to know that his girlfriend was okay—but was that out of love and concern? Or was it because she'd made him look bad? Because how *dare* she dump him? And how *dare* she steal his dog?

Gray remembered how Ian O'Donnell had strolled back into the hospital. Lady nurses had waved at him. Men in scrubs had nodded at him. He was the Man.

But did any of them know about Isabel?

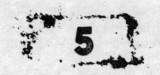

5

The Alumni Center's executive director, Farrah Tarrino, was a plump, round-faced, freckled beauty with big blonde hair. She offered Gray a doughnut as they passed the center's kitchen. Gray spotted a half a glazed in a pink box, along with a half purple-frosted and a half strawberry-filled with its guts seeping out like blood from a stuck pig.

"Help yourself," Farrah said, plucking a halved cinnamon-crumbly from the box. "Workday is almost over; they're just gonna be thrown away."

Stomach growling, Gray selected the halved chocolate-glazed and immediately regretted her decision—chocolate and white linen slacks went together like canned ham and lobster.

Farrah pinched at her doughnut's crumbly top, then squinted at Gray. "I'm sorry. Who are you working for again?"

Somehow, chocolate had already flecked the cuff of Gray's shirt. She licked her thumb, then remembered, *Damn it. I just came from a hospital.* She then finished the doughnut in one hurried bite, wiping her fingers and mouth with the napkin. "I'm with Rader Consulting. I can't say more than that. Client confidentiality."

Farrah nibbled at crumbles. "Guess it doesn't matter. We all want Izzy home safe and sound. Ab-so-lutely.

I'll take you to her desk. It's quiet right now—summer hours. And lots of folks are on vacation." Her panty-hosed thighs swooshed against each other as Gray's mules slapped at the brown-tiled floor. Together, they weaved through the nearly empty cubicle farm and stopped at a double-wide cubby with two worksta-tions.

One workstation's wall was bare. At the other station, sheets of paper covered in sticky notes had been left on the chair, waiting for Isabel's return and review. There were no desktop pictures of Kenny G. with Isabel, nor pictures of Isabel with Ian O'Donnell. A framed picture of the missing woman cuddling an orange tabby sat next to a photo of the same missing woman standing between Clair Huxtable and Lou Rawls look-alikes.

Isabel Lincoln's parents?

Couldn't be. This couple looked like they knew *all* the lyrics to "Lift Every Voice and Sing." They looked like the couple who hoarded petrified copies of *Jet* in the attic and had watched *Soul Train* every Satur-day morning and had attended wedding receptions that ended with the Hustle or the Electric Slide. There was a pressing comb in a drawer somewhere in their house. Because this couple? They were *black* black.

Gray reached into her purse. "Do you mind if I record our conversation? Just so that I have every-thing?" Because of *course* she thought of recording an interview *now*.

Farrah said, "Sure," and Gray pressed Record on her phone's voice memo app.

"Okay," Gray said. "So, Isabel's job?"

"She organizes events for our scholars to meet their benefactors. She organizes board meetings, hosts alumni trips. . . . She's been here for, oh, two years now. But she recently applied for a student life advisor position to work directly with incoming freshmen. Though I'd hate to lose her, I gave her a glowing recommendation."

"Did she ever leave for days at a time?"

"Yes, but she always cleared time off with me first."

"Do you have a list of her days off?"

Back in her office, Farrah tapped at the computer keyboard. "Here we go." She clicked Print and, seven seconds later, Gray had a list of dates that Isabel Lincoln had requested.

December 5–7
March 13–15
May 22–24

The March and May dates . . . Since Gray hadn't been able to take notes, she wasn't sure if those dates matched the dates Ian O'Donnell had mentioned.

Farrah allowed Gray to conduct interviews in a small conference room that reeked of ranch salad dressing and jalapeños. She offered the P.I. a Diet Coke—Gray needed a caffeine boost to power through her third and fourth interviews of the day.

"At first, we didn't think anything was wrong." This was from Beth Sharpe, a tall brunette who wore a silver nose stud. "Isabel told me that she and Ian were heading to Palm Springs for the Memorial Day weekend."

"Really?" Gray's eyebrows lifted. The good doctor hadn't mentioned a trip to the desert.

Gray liked Secret Santa, secret sauce. . . . Secret plans, though, were the best secrets!

Down on the conference room table, her phone blinked, then the screen went dark. She pressed the

Home button, then got the Empty Battery icon. Dead phone.

"Uh-oh," Beth Sharpe said. "Need a pen?"

"I have one." Gray searched through her bag for that stupid, sticky pen. Wallet, ibuprofen, hand sanitizer, chewing gum, coins . . . no pen. "Sorry. We can keep talking," she said, face warm again. "If I need to clarify anything—"

"We can email," Beth Sharpe said, nodding. "So, anyway, Izzy thought Ian was gonna finally propose. Not that she would've said yes. Can I tell you something?" She jiggled her knees, then stopped jiggling her knees, then jiggled her knees again. "This is gonna sound crazy, and I'm kinda glad that your phone died, because I don't know if I want this recorded, but . . . I think Ian took Izzy out to Palm Springs and killed her. I think he buried her near one of those giant wind turbines."

"That's a rather . . . *extreme* thing to say."

"She told me that Ian had a temper and that she'd discovered his big secret. She was really nervous the last time I saw her. She said it could ruin his career."

"And so . . ."

"He knew that she knew . . ."

"And?"

"He killed her."

"And?"

"He buried her body—"

"Beneath a giant wind turbine," the women said together.

Nan Keaton, an older redhead wearing a prairie skirt and cowboy boots, stomped into the conference room before Gray could find another pen. Nan sat with an "Oomph," crossed her arms against her doughy breasts, and kept her jaw clamped like a crocodile on a wildebeest's leg. That kind of defensive body language was known as "She knows something but ain't sayin'."

Gray was already exhausted. "Ian said that he and Isabel ate lunch together every day."

Nan barked, "Ha! She was lucky if it was twice a week. He always had to work, he always had to save *lives*, to *literally* hold people's hearts in his hands. He always told her that if she ever wanted to be a doctor's wife, she'd have to share him with his patients."

"And what was Isabel's response to that?"

"What do you expect it to be?"

"Did she ever think he was cheating on her when he was supposed to be seeing patients?"

Nan didn't respond. She was the type of woman who prayed hard, drank harder, and kept the lights on for her trucker lover or her small-town-sheriff lover or her prodigal son. Tears cried for those men always disappeared into the folds of her weathered skin, but *They still counted, you hear? They still counted.*

"Did you know that Isabel took Dr. O'Donnell's dog?" Gray asked.

Nan snorted. "Does it look like I give a fuck?"

"Looks like you're a dues-paying member of Gives No Fucks Sorority Incorporated, but you should probably know that she kidnapped the man's dog."

Nan harrumphed. "Serves him right."

"Okay, screw the dog, screw Ian. What can you tell me about Isabel's state of mind?"

"She was upset a few days before we all left for Memorial Day weekend."

"You know why?"

Tight jaw and crossed arms again for Nan.

Squinty eyes and acid stomach for Gray. Her neck tensed as she tried to wait Nan out. But she wouldn't win this waiting game, not against a woman who kept the lights on for truckers and prodigal sons.

"I'm sure," Gray said, forcing patience into her words, "that you want us to find—"

"*Us?*" The old redhead scowled. "You ain't the police, and if I'm gonna tell *anybody* anything about what was going on, it's gonna be *them*, when they come to talk to me."

"But the police aren't interested. She's been gone for about seven weeks, right? They're not looking for her because they don't think she's missing. But if you know something, if you know the *truth*, you have to tell me so that I can alert—"

"You think I'm an idiot?" Nan whispered. "You think I'm one of those young things with barely a thought in my head?"

"I think you have *millions* of thoughts in your head, and that's why I need your help."

Nan plucked lint from her cotton blouse and let the fibers float to the carpet. "I don't know who you're working for, young lady, but I *do* know that I ain't gotta say *shit* to you." The old woman chewed on her tongue—she wanted to say something else, because old gals like Nan Keaton liked saying plenty of things.

But just as Gray was about to give up . . .

"Problem is," Nan said, "Isabel ain't all that innocent in this, either. But she did what she had to do, cuz that's us women. Doing what we gotta do to survive. And sometimes? That ain't nice. Sometimes, that ain't easy. But we get to be aboveground for one more day."

A FAIRY TALE AWAITS

Girls' trip!

Las Vegas with Zoe, Jay, and Avery!

Tonight, Natalie thought, the town looked show-girl gorgeous. Fake everything, uh-huh, but shiny and clean and impossibly slick and painted. At noon, thermometers had hit 110 degrees, but once the sun had dipped, temperatures dropped to one hundred. Two hours before midnight, the sky was still bright as the afternoon—neon signs and car headlights, digital billboards and the glint of chrome and brass *everything*.

That night, the girls partied at TRUE in Caesars Palace. After five blowjob shots—delicious concoctions of Baileys, Kahlúa, amaretto, and whipped cream—Natalie stumbled onto the club's VIP deck and right into Sean Dixon, the club's promoter and the most gorgeous man she'd ever met. With close-cut wavy hair and skin the color of Southern pecans, he was a big man who moved like a dancer. Smooth like Cab, smooth like Fred. *Slick*. Yeah, Sean Dixon was *slick*.

He said, "I like your smile, Shorty."

Yeah, okay. Her *smile*, and not the hot-pink dress wrapped tight as sausage skin around her hips and ass?

She said, "Thank you. I like your eyes." Hazel to

brown on cue, those eyes cut her open, right there on the spot, they were that sharp.

He bought her another drink and they talked about everything and nothing. The first black president. The dangers versus the rewards of eating raw cookie dough. Her job at the Oakland Museum of California.

She liked his confidence.

He liked her reference to Marlon Brando hiding in the shadows in *Apocalypse Now*.

Later, the couple escaped to his suite on the eighth floor. He touched her, and she shimmered like silver dust on a butterfly's wings, like golden sunbeams through crystal raindrops. She held her breath as she straddled his waist. Not wanting to burst. Not wanting to release any of the crazy excitement that ricocheted through her veins. Her joy was fragile—a new thing, a rare thing, the finest china dangling from a cliffside.

She was twenty-nine years old and nothing had ever gone her way—why would this?

So she held her breath.

"Stay the night?" Sean asked, after they made love.

Worried, Natalie glanced at the window and imagined her friends wandering the Strip in search of her. And then, in that same window, she saw everything shining like gemstones. The world was so . . . *alive*.

"My girls," she said. "They're probably freaking out."

"It's damn near three o'clock in the morning. They're finished freaking out and now they're in bed with curlers in their hair." Sean laughed and rubbed her arm. "Stay, babe."

She tried to laugh. "You're probably right."

"If you're gonna stress out, though, just call them. Where are you guys staying?"

She grabbed her cell phone from the nightstand. "Circus Circus."

He snorted. "Seriously? That place is ghetto as *fuck*."

Natalie tapped Avery's number. "Sixty dollars a night—can't beat it when you still have student loans to pay." *She* didn't have loans—her parents hadn't needed to borrow—but Sean didn't need to know that.

Avery didn't answer. Neither did Jay or Zoe. So Natalie left a message and then sent a group text. *I'm safe. With Sean at Caesars. See u in the morning!*

That night, Natalie stopped holding her breath.

That night, Natalie shimmered like silver dust and golden sunbeams.

The next morning, she called Avery again.

This time, Avery answered. "Oh, so you decided to let us know you're not dead."

Avery's words slithered from the receiver and coiled around Natalie's neck. But she ignored that tightening and the anger rolling around her gut. "I'll see you guys soon."

After a fifteen-minute cab ride, Natalie slipped into the smoky casino of Circus Circus. Up in the hotel room, her friends said nothing to her, and so she retreated to the bathroom to change into shorts, a tank top, and a pair of Vans. She twisted her long hair into a ponytail while talking herself into confronting her friends.

Just go. Just . . . get it over with.

She stomped out of the bathroom and into the room. Arms crossed, she stood in front of the television. "Are y'all gonna say something?"

Avery, on the carpet, kept flipping through *Cosmopolitan*.

Zoe, on the couch, kept painting her toenails.

Jay, in one of the queen-size beds, pretended to sleep.

Not feeling her feet or her face, Natalie said, "Fine. What-the-fuck-ever. I'll check in with you guys later."

After she and Sean ate breakfast, they played slots and then walked along the Strip. Later, they held hands as they caught a magic show over at Excalibur. He bought her a Gucci handbag, kissed her again, and then, with a pat on her ass, he sent her back to her friends.

At dinnertime, she returned to Circus Circus.

Thick eyebrow cocked, Avery said, "You just met the man and he bought you a *Gucci*?"

Zoe's fuchsia lips twisted into a grin. "In exchange for ridin' that dick all night."

"Ouch, Zee." Jay's eyes burned into their wayward friend, who was now standing before them with tears in her eyes.

Being called a whore by her best friends? Damn, that hurt. "Can't you be happy that I *finally* met someone?"

He's an asshole.

He's possessive.

Can't you tell that he's crazy as fuck?

None of this was true. They hated that Sean had taken her away from them for one night. One. Night. That he hadn't included them in her magical evening. Jealousy. Like onions and sweat, jealousy stunk up a room.

On Monday's flight back to Oakland, Jay, Avery, and Zoe didn't speak to Natalie.

The quartet reached their apartment across the

street from Lake Merritt. A crystal vase of lavender roses for Natalie sat on the porch. On the card, Sean had written, "Let me show you the world," and had promised to buy her a return ticket to Las Vegas.

Couldn't the girls *see*? Wasn't it *obvious*?

Natalie and Sean were meant to be together.

6

The cardiologist was performing some sort of magic trick, and Gray gave Farrah, Beth, and Nan her phone number in case they had more clues to offer on how to uncover that trick.

Ultimately, though, her job was simple: obtain proof that Isabel and Kenny G. were alive.

But now she stood before the Alumni Center's full-length bathroom mirror, disgusted with her reflection. Chocolate-stained. Wrinkled. Swollen feet. Numb legs. Dead phone. Lost pen. No drugs. Distracting pain. What the *fuck*?

"And I probably have hepatitis from licking my freakin' fingers." She washed her hands and watched as brown grime—*hepatitis?*—swirled into the drain.

It was minutes before four o'clock as Gray tromped back through the tiled lobby and back out into the sticky air. She reached into her bag for car keys and heard the purse's inside lining rip.

She hated this purse and longed for the bags she'd carried back in the good old days. Buttery Givenchy satchels big enough to carry a book, a pair of shoes and a set of keys, plane tickets to somewhere else. Bags like that, though, caught people's attention, and she didn't need women remembering, *Oh yeah, she was carrying that limited-edition Fendi and I remember cuz I had a salad that day with cranberries and I was wearing my red jeans, the ones with the tear in the left knee*. And so, cheap, forgettable purses. The one with her now was a Liz Claiborne shoulder bag, camel-colored, with a black strap, faux leather outside, and (ripped) polyester lining inside. A five-star bag on the Macy's website, now at two stars because it couldn't handle Gray's life just after two years of hard labor.

Back in the car, she connected her phone to the charger—*power again!*—then she texted Ian O'Donnell: *What were the dates she left for no reason?*

Immediate ellipses. Shouldn't he have been staring at chest X-rays? Providing comfort and care to another Mary Ann, this one with a bad ticker instead of a broken ankle? Didn't he have a body hidden beneath a windmill to relocate?

Waiting for his response, Gray found a ballpoint pen in the glove compartment. She consulted Isabel Lincoln's intake form again.

LAST SEEN: MAY 27

Ian O'Donnell responded.

Gone mid-March and end of May

Gray updated her blank notepad.

Isabel had been gone for four days before Ian had . . . *realized it*? Or had he realized it but just hadn't called the cops? According to Farrah Tarrino, Isabel had requested three days off in December—but Ian, just now, hadn't mentioned her leaving then. And they'd been together in December. *Maybe those were just times spent at home?*

Gray listened to her interview with Farrah Tarrino and Beth Sharpe—but her phone had died just before the executive director had started to speak in specifics. Flummoxed, Gray flipped through her two pages of scribbles. "What am I supposed to do now?"

Omar.

She found Ian O'Donnell's text message that had listed contact numbers.

Had Isabel been stepping out on the nice guy doctor with this Omar dude?

Or was Omar just a cousin, maybe, or the service advisor at the neighborhood Jiffy Lube?

Gray dialed the mystery man's number.

Ringing . . .

"Hey . . ." A man's voice. "This is Oz." Were Oz and Omar the same person? "Leave a message." Silence, and then: "This mailbox is full. Good-bye."

Gray swiped at her limp bangs, then swiped at her phone's screen until she found the ORO app, from Rader Consulting's automatic license plate reader contractor.

Anytime. Anywhere. We see you.

Their tagline creeped Gray out, but not enough for her to stop using their technology. She'd set up an automatic tracker on a black Range Rover with personalized Nevada plates (VGSKING), and a red Jaguar, also Nevada personalized plates (CAQTINLV). If either car was spotted by an automated license plate reader in Greater Los Angeles, she'd receive an alert and an image of the car.

Three weeks ago, she'd wondered if ORO's technology was flawed or if those cars had been sold to new owners—but then her phone had buzzed. A rear license plate from an SUV had been captured near the train station in the middle of the day. And for three days, notifications filled her phone's screen—Santa Monica, Westwood Village, Culver City.

Soon, no alerts filled the ORO app's dashboard. But that Range Rover had roamed the streets of Los Angeles for three days.

Looking for Natalie Dixon.

7

At every intersection she crossed, at every traffic light she heeded, Gray sent her eyes searching for English luxury cars. Sometimes she rolled down the Camry's window and listened for the boom of a bass line, for the slurred delivery of a lyric. There was Cardi B. There was Jay-Z. And her heavy breathing—there was that, too. But there was no Notorious B.I.G.

As usual, she made sudden right turns as she drove, pissing off the drivers behind her and forcing the Camry to be more agile than its original design allowed. Gray didn't care, didn't want anyone tailing her. What had Nan said? *That's us women: doing what we gotta do to survive.* Anything to stay aboveground for one more day.

Ian's "love" . . . It was nice to look at, it could resist some damage, but too many rainy days had caused mold to grow and had caused it to warp. Ian and Isabel had a bamboo kind of love.

Gray drove south on La Brea Avenue to Baldwin Hills. The fancy black neighborhood at the top enjoyed views of downtown Los Angeles or the Pacific Ocean. The neighborhood at the bottom, originally nicknamed "the Jungle," but not for Grandpa's racist reasons, also enjoyed some of those views—that is, if the windows hadn't been boarded up or covered in aluminum foil.

There was less congestion in this part of town than the Westside. More brown faces. More Bantu knots and Brazilian blowouts. Barbecue, Baptists, *buñuelos y bebidas*. More Mickie D's and Del Tacos tag-teaming in the Diabetes Hypertension Die-Off.

Isabel Lincoln lived closer to the fancier neighborhood. Here, gray-and-white condominiums on Don Lorenzo Drive sat across from the Stocker Corridor hillside trail. For a so-called white girl, Isabel Lincoln had chosen one of the most colored places to live.

Gray parked south of the security gate.

She was fifteen minutes early.

Her phone chirped: Ian.

You meet her co-workers?

Yes, but I won't have anything to report if I tell you everything now.

He sent a smile emoji.

See you at Iz's condo at five. It's a little hard to find.
Be careful it's rough over there.

Gray had dated "woke" white boys who thought all black neighborhoods were "rough." Dealing with this kind of muted racism—"*Essence* magazine is reverse discrimination," wah-wah-wah—had been an exhausting journey of tight-lipped hostility mixed with astounding sex. . . .

Yeah, she'd do it again.

She found Isabel Lincoln's Facebook profile. The missing woman liked "Keep Calm" memes, Grumpy Cat and UCLA Bruins, *Friends* and Sprinkles cupcakes. The last picture, posted on May 20, had been a tribe photo—Isabel and her friends in a selfie huddle.

The missing woman stood in the back of the pack with her eyes hidden by shades. *The toughest days are easier with your girls in front of you.*

May 17. The orange tabby, Morris, lounged in a laundry basket. The responses to this post were all sad-face emojis, RIPs, and "So sorry, Izzy." No condolences, though, from Ian O'Donnell.

April 6. A group of friends, wine tasting. Glasses of reds, whites, and sparklings. Isabel, not in the shot, had probably taken the picture. *When life gives you lemons, drink wine.*

Relationship status . . . There *was* no relationship status. Hell, there were no pictures of Ian O'Donnell *anywhere*.

Ian O'Donnell's Facebook page, on the other hand, captured a full-blown romance, mostly with himself and, in second place, with Kenny G. His most recent post: a picture of himself speaking at the California Endowment about building healthy communities. Other posts included shots of him and Isabel at an Adele concert. He and Kenny G. on a sailboat, in a convertible Porsche, and sharing an ice cream cone. There was a picture of a UCLA Medical Center billboard that featured Ian.

A simple web search pulled up almost five million results for "Isabel Lincoln," but only two of those—both UCLA-related—could be obviously tied to Gray's missing woman. She consulted the text filled with Isabel's friends and family and selected "Tea." In a text message, Gray told Tea that she was looking into Isabel's . . . "situation" and that she'd like to talk with Tea as soon as possible.

No response from Tea.

Gray climbed out of the Camry to stretch her legs. The sun was still burning trees and hillsides, and sweat sizzled down Gray's spine. She could taste the air—it tasted like ground black pepper and wood chips.

Needing to stretch more, she strolled over to the condominium's gated entry.

Isabel Lincoln's porch was just a few feet from the gate. There were no piled-up newspapers or dead leaves blown onto the welcome mat by the wind . . . unlike the entry gate with its janky lock, now creaking open from the slight breeze. Creaking open just . . . like . . . that.

Gray slipped through the gate, then pulled it until she heard the lock click. Wouldn't want trespassers sneaking through to start trouble. She strolled to Isabel's porch as though she belonged there, then knocked on the front door, because she was polite and maybe the missing woman wasn't missing but was hunkered on the couch with a bottle of pinot noir and a pack of Nutter Butters, streaming *Empire* on her sixty-inch television and being secretly black.

"She ain't there, baby." An old woman with the wide, freckled face of Maya Angelou and the floral housecoat of old ladies everywhere stood in her open doorway across the breezeway she shared with Isabel Lincoln. Judge Judy's televised voice—"*You picked her*"—played from the living room.

Caught, Gray startled, but then she pushed a smile to her face. "Hi! I'm Maya, one of Izzy's friends." She nodded to the door. "She's supposed to be coming back. Her birthday's tomorrow and we're planning to surprise her."

The old lady grinned, and her clouded eyes twinkled. "Sure makes me happy hearing that she's okay. She ain't usually gone this long, just a week or two, but this time . . ."

"You are . . ."

"Beatrice Tompkins."

"Nice to meet you." Gray cocked her head. "Yes, we were all caught off guard with her leaving this last time. Especially since she left upset."

"I can tell when she and her doctor be fighting," Beatrice Tompkins said. "Sometimes I can hear 'em yelling and carrying on like someone being killed. But then, the next day, he come out as nice as pie. Like butter don't melt in his mouth, that doctor. I ain't ever spent more than two minutes with him, but he mean as a snake. I know that like I know day follows night."

Gray rolled her eyes with mock exasperation. "We're not too fond of him, either. We were hoping that she'd finally break up with him for good." She moved closer to the old woman and glimpsed a living room filled with a sofa, an armchair covered in multicolored crocheted blankets, and a modern-day television with its volume up to eight hundred.

"Well, that morning, she had her suitcase and *whoosh*"—Beatrice Tompkins lifted her arms like Superman in flight—"she was gone. Got in that car—"

"*Her* car?"

"No, not her car. *Her* car is still parked back there." The woman nodded to her left.

"So when did she get in this car?"

"That Monday. Memorial Day. She got in a black *truck*, not a car, and *whoosh* . . ." Another Superman.

Gray asked, "Did she have Ian's dog with her?"

"Dog? I ain't seen no dog. He don't seem like the dog type. He treat *her* like one."

"Ha. Not like he treats *this* dog. He treats Kenny G.—"

"Kenny *what*?"

"Kenny G. Cuz the dog's hair is curly like the guy who plays the sax?"

The old lady grunted. "I only started to worry about Isabel when the police came by and asked me some questions. But if *you're* here and she's supposed to be home soon, that means I ain't gotta worry no more."

"What did the cops ask?"

"Oh . . . wasn't nothing about her." She tilted her head and squinted into the distance. "They asked about somebody named . . . oh . . . my memory . . . Lisa, I think they said. If a Lisa lived in the complex. Asked if people I didn't know was hanging around. I told 'em that I didn't know no Lisa and can't nobody get past them gates without a key or a code."

Gray had gotten in without either a key or a code.

"Okay, I'm wrong," the old lady said. "This one man, he was more of a giant than a man, he kept knocking at the gate. One time, somebody let him in, and he knocked on Isabel's door. He knocked on mine, too, but I didn't answer."

"Black guy? White guy?"

"Okay, I'm wrong," Mrs. Tompkins said. "There were *two* men. One was black—he came by last month. And then there was a white man. He looked *I*-talian. He started coming by last week. I didn't answer my door for *him*, either."

"Well, she's supposed to come home tomorrow, but she's being very unpredictable right now." Gray narrowed her eyes. "Did you see the person driving the black truck?"

Beatrice Tompkins pooched her lips. "No. The sun was high. Couldn't see cuz of the shadow. But I ain't never seen that truck before. Other cars, yes, but not that truck. It was one of them ugly-looking things with the big wheels and the metal bars and the loud engine that go *bup-bup-bup*? I was still hearing it ten miles away."

Gray glanced back at Isabel's front door. "I don't see any water bottles or newspapers out. Have any of her other friends . . ."

Beatrice Tompkins laughed. "Ain't nobody else come round here. Not that I can remember. I got a key to her place, so I've been taking everything in. I used to take care of Morris sometimes. You know, feed him, clean his litter box, keep him company whenever she was out of town."

"Poor kitty," Gray said. "She loved that cat."

"Oh yes she did. I can let you in, if you need. She left a message on my machine a few days after she left. She said that you'd be coming by to pick up some mail and her key."

Gray's skin tightened. "Huh?"

But the old lady had already shuffled back into her home. "Took you a long time to come round. Hold on."

Panic exploded near Gray's heart. *She said that you'd be coming by.* What did that mean? "She?" Who? "You?" Who?

"I found the key," Beatrice Tompkins shouted.

A camel-colored man with broad shoulders and a crew cut strolled in from the entry gate. He wore army fatigues and clean boots. As broad as a linebacker, he was several inches taller than Gray, six feet at least. "May I help you?" he asked.

"Kevin," the old lady called out, "that you?"

He kept his gaze on Gray, and shouted, "Yes, Mom. It's me."

Gray offered her hand. "Hi. I'm Maya." She pointed to Isabel's door. "Her friend." The lie made Gray buoyant and light as a balloon. So far, lying was her favorite part of the job.

The old lady returned to the breezeway with three keys on a pink ribbon. To her son, she said, "How you doing, baby?"

Kevin kissed the top of his mother's snowy head. "Mom, you should be resting."

She waved her hand at that. "What you think I been doing all day?"

He frowned. "Just because your hip feels like it's healed, doesn't mean—"

"Boy, hush now." She touched the soldier's chest, then turned to Gray. "I'll let you in."

Kevin glared at Gray and shook his head.

Gray's stomach wobbled, and her open mouth popped closed, then opened again to say, "That's okay, Mrs. Tompkins. Really. Kevin's right—you should be resting."

Her phone wiggled in her hand and she glanced at the screen. *Tea!*

"You sure?" Mrs. Tompkins asked.

Gray met Kevin's eyes—hard, dark, resolved—and glanced at her phone again. "I'm positive." She offered the old woman a reassuring smile. "Thanks so much for helping Izzy. You're incredibly kind."

"I can't wait to see her," Beatrice Tompkins said. "Maybe she'll have dinner with my Kevin. He's been in the army going on fifteen years. He's a sergeant now. He likes fishing and photography and he's the most generous man she'll ever meet. And he's handsome, too."

Kevin almost smiled. "Okay, Mom." To Gray, he said, "Nice meeting you, Maya."

Gray hurried back to her car, praying that Tea Christopher's message would bring her one step closer to Isabel Lincoln.

8

Back in the Camry, Gray read Tea Christopher's text message.

Did Ian hire you? I have nothing to say

Frustration, anger, distrust—each emotion bristled from those nine words.

I don't want her to come back. If you met him you'd know how awful he is.

Gray *had* met him, and now she wanted to drive back to UCLA and yell in Ian O'Donnell's face, *Just leave her the fuck alone!* This was so unfair, so unnecessary, and she was pissed that Nick had given her *this* case.

I told her to move on but now he wants her to come back and I don't so NO I'M NOT TALKING TO YOU. BE blessed.

Gray laughed—*Be blessed*—and that relieved some of the tension in her shoulders.

If Ian was truly an abuser, as Beth had suggested, Tea was probably the frustrated BFF who had stayed up late at night consoling her distraught friend. Tea had probably cried, *I'll do anything for you, Izzy, I don't care. Let's just go. You can't let him do this.* Words that all concerned friends said out of desperation. Words that ultimately fell on deaf ears. Words like:

Well, when is the right time to leave?

Do you hear yourself?

What kind of life is this?

But words? Just distinct elements of speech used with other elements to make a sentence or to form a thought. As concrete as air.

Gray paused before responding, and her fingers hovered over the phone's keyboard. Her body hot again, she watched a hawk circle the sky as she waited for her pulse to slow.

3 minutes, 3 questions. Then you'll never have to hear from me again.

Back at the condos, Kevin was pushing a trash bin to the curbside. Dressed in those fatigues, he looked heroic, strong, like America back in its heyday, America before the Nazis and the anthem and the uranium and the wall and the treason and the porn stars.

Another text, from an unknown number.

Gray read words—distinct elements as concrete as air—that stole breath from her chest. Words that screamed at her from the seven-inch screen.

PLEASE LET ME BE MISSING!

9

Please let me be missing!

Not typical for a missing woman to respond with text messages. One didn't need to be a cop to know that missing women usually communicated via left-behind femurs or ragged fingernails crammed with the scraped skin of their murderers. Not Isabel Lincoln. She was one of a kind.

And now Gray had proof in her hands.

Isabel Lincoln was alive!

Excitement bounced around her chest—she was talking with her target! And doing it on the first day of the investigation!

The text message had been sent from a phone with a 702 area code. Las Vegas.

I promise I will let you stay missing but you have to help me first.

Day was dying in the west, and the dying sun had tinted the sky carnival pink. It was hot in the Camry, and it smelled of yesterday's In-N-Out burger and cold French fries.

Gray saved the 702 number in the "Lincoln case" contacts list, then sent a message to Clarissa, her co-worker at Rader Consulting: *Please find out more re: this number ASAP origin, IP, whatever, thanks!*

And how would Isabel Lincoln respond? The missing woman wasn't Gray's client—Isabel's jerky boyfriend was. Also? How had Isabel found Gray's unlisted number, created just hours ago on a Burner account? Had Tea given it to Isabel?

Kevin Tompkins had finished arranging the trash and recycle bins at the curb and was now picking up litter from the sidewalk. Was he currently on leave? Was he as interested in dating Isabel as his mother was interested in him dating Isabel?

Gray's phone vibrated.

How will u help?

Isabel!
Easier to explain if I call you.
Gray would ask the three questions.
Isabel would answer them.
Her phone buzzed again.

It was a text and selfie from Hank Wexler, the hot bartender at Sam Jose's. He was holding a strawberry margarita.

Your name is on this & something else.

His dazzling blue eyes looked silver, Nosferatic.
Gray's stomach flip-flopped, and the Camry's temperature rose to Jupiter levels.
Then Isabel texted:

Don't want to call. Can be traced. U don't understand!!! He will kill me if I come back. Please drop this!

"I *do* understand." Gray could give TED Talks on "Ways That Life Sucks."
She tapped the phone icon next to Isabel's name.

The line rang and rang. *Don't go. Please don't go.* And she'd barely caught her breath before the phone pulsed against her ear.

I'm not going to talk to u

OK, Gray texted, *have Tea talk to me face to face.*
No response.
Isabel Lincoln had ducked back into her bunker.

THE FIRST

Mrs. Dixon had always been tiny. Malnourished as a baby, she always looked hungry, like food only passed her lips on bank holidays. Standing next to Sean—six three, two hundred ten pounds of college-ball muscle—she was the butterfly to his vulture.

She loved his hands. Loved those beautiful, long brown fingers, crooked from old breaks caused by catching flying pigs. Strong hands.

After checking into their Jacuzzi suite on the twelfth floor of the Bellagio Hotel and Casino, after watching the famous water show from their living room window, Mr. and Mrs. Dixon shopped at Armani, Chanel, and Gucci down on Via Bellagio. At Cartier, he bought her a diamond for her nose.

"Damn." Sean gazed at the stone he'd bought her. "You are fuckin' fly, baby."

A perfect first-year anniversary weekend already, a staycation that would've been the envy of her friends . . . had they known.

As the sun set over Sin City and they ate dinner at Le Cirque, he toasted her. He told her, "You are my life," as the sky turned pink, red, and desert blue. His love was astonishing. White hot. Phosphorescent. His love made Mrs. Dixon close her eyes and look away.

You deserve this. After everything . . . You deserve

this. This man. This joy. This two-hundred-dollar bottle of wine. This lobster risotto. Lift up your head. You deserve this.

Her happiness made her dizzy, Disneyland teacups dizzy—she now knew this feeling, since Sean had taken her to the Magic Kingdom for her very first time. She liked that feeling then—Disneyland would never make her *sick* sick; they loved her—and she liked that feeling now. In the last year, Sean's love had exploded all around her. Like mink-lined shrapnel, his love had struck her in unexpected ways. But she didn't fear it.

She had thought her diamond engagement ring—three carats, princess cut, smaller baguettes on each side, worth two paychecks, she'd been told—made sparks fly out of other girls' eyes. But it had been her simple, sleek platinum band that had sent those bipedal, stiletto-wearing hyenas stampeding and frothing at the mouth. She'd caught the gold ring (well, platinum) and she'd sure as hell celebrate.

And celebrating—that was their (well, *Sean's*) business. And he'd gone all out for her on their special weekend, even though living in Las Vegas had lost its glow. Too loud, this city. The world's toilet, this city, where everybody came to take a dump and live their worst lives.

Tonight, she'd play.

She was Mrs. Sean Dixon.

One year of wearing his name. One happy year flossing that platinum band that, in some types of light, resembled sea foam. One year of wearing designer clothes and pushing a Jaguar. A dream life.

After dinner, Mr. and Mrs. Dixon took a town car to dance at Club Rio, the location of his client's event on this night. After dancing, she took the third position at a blackjack table with a twenty-five-dollar minimum bet. She didn't like playing with such a high minimum, but Sean had a reputation to maintain. No five-dollar shit for his wife. His *wife*.

Since he was a lousy blackjack player (he claimed it was a boring game that had nothing to do with skill), Sean stood behind her chair.

The dealer laid before the little lady in the red and black Betsey Johnson party dress a six of diamonds and a four of spades. The other bettors had numbers, which meant aces and faces had to come next.

The rich, red-faced Texan on her right had been cursed with a ten of diamonds and a three of clubs. So he doubled down on Mrs. Dixon's ten. The dealer slipped an ace of clubs on that ten. Twenty-one! Everyone—except Sean—whooped and clapped.

Texas patted her hand with his pudgy one, then squeezed. "Keep the money, darlin'."

Two hundred fifty dollars. She kept the money. A thrill ran through her. Like she was wine-wasted and owned all the cheese in the world.

Sean glared at her. Didn't congratulate her. Didn't say a word to her after that. He walked in front of her. Wouldn't hold the doors open for her. He was mad.

They returned to Club Rio and Sean danced with stripper-body Chyna—he knew her from back in the day. He bought skinny blonde Anise drinks—it was the first time that they could party without having to work. He found every reason to avoid returning to their table and sharing the bottle of Moët. Prince's "Adore" played—their song—and Sean stayed on the other side of the club, joking with some skank who slouched and couldn't even walk right in her heels.

His silent anger, though, was better than his active anger. Not that he'd *hit* her or anything. Sometimes, it had just *felt* like he would.

10

Pens—I need pens.

Gray pawed through the Camry's center console and found two new ballpoints. She scribbled on a page in her binder—plenty of ink. Then she rolled down her car window and sniffed: eucalyptus and skunk. No scent of ham or bullshit—Ian O'Donnell hadn't arrived yet.

That moment ended, though, as a dark gray Porsche raced in Gray's direction. The convertible swerved into a parking space closest to the entry gate. The blond man behind the steering wheel didn't climb out of the car.

Neither did Gray.

Ian O'Donnell held a phone to his ear.

Gray picked up her own phone—fully charged now—and aimed it in Ian's direction.

"Just ignore him," Ian was saying. "There's nothing that says you gotta answer his text." He laughed that big cannon laugh that men give women while talking on the phone. Extra loud. Overcompensating so that it could be believed, since it couldn't be seen.

"You act like you don't see me all day," Ian continued. "No. . . . Well, she's . . . I know. . . . I'm here now. . . . I know it's not cheap, but I gotta look for her. . . . Ha! . . . Maybe she's transgendered or . . . Her name . . . I know, right?" He laughed again, then looked at his watch. "There you go again with the 'chocolate factory.' . . . Cuz I hate it when you say racist shit like that. I can't believe you're jealous of a . . . Not my type, no. . . . She's not my type. . . . I wouldn't say she's *fat* . . ."

Ian was talking about *her*.

"She's . . . chubby, like what's-her-face from *American Idol*, Jennifer . . . That one. Seriously. . . . Ha! . . . No, you're my . . . I *am* being serious." He flipped down the visor mirror and picked at something stuck between his front teeth. "Yes, I will. . . . Gotta go. . . . She's gonna be here . . . Yes, I'll call you after. . . . Okay. . . . Me, too."

Gray glanced at the time stamp on the phone. 0:00. *Shit*. She'd forgotten to tap the big red Record button.

Ian O'Donnell climbed out of the Porsche. He still wore his blue surgical scrubs—sunshine and honey for some women. He tossed a glance up the street and peered at his watch. He muttered something, then shook his head, frustrated with the chubby, transgender chocolate private eye with the dude's name. At the security gate, he punched in the entry code, then disappeared into the shadows.

Gray whispered, "Be nice," then grabbed her binder.

Outside, the cool air had a crisp bite. A sweet kiss after this damn hot day.

Her phone vibrated as she crossed the street. It was Ian.

Where are U? Been waiting for 10 min now

Liar.

Gray texted, *I've been waiting for 15 minutes*. Defeat a big lie with a bigger truth.

Ian returned to the security gate. "You should've texted me."

Always someone else's fault.

He led her to the same blue door she'd discovered minutes ago without his assistance. "That's a damn long time to stay in your car. Dangerous. It's rough over here."

Right now, eucalyptus trees swished in the wind. No trash, broken glass, or cars on blocks at the curbs. Brown-skinned millennials wearing Lululemon wore buds in their ears as they jogged in pairs or biked in groups. Rough.

"You talk to Tea yet?" he asked.

"Just a text so far, but I can tell that she has very strong opinions about you." Gray paused, then asked, "Oh. Do you know if Isabel took her car when she left?"

"No. It's out back."

The red Honda Prelude sat in its carport, locked and dusty.

"You have the key?" Gray asked.

"Nope."

As they walked back to the front door, Gray asked, "Do you wonder *how* she left, then?"

"Uber maybe? Or maybe Tea drove her somewhere? Doesn't matter—she's gone." He slipped the key into the lock and pushed open the blue door. Cool, vanilla-scented air rushed toward them as he hit a light switch.

"She's still paying the utility bills?" Gray asked.

"No, *I'm* still paying the utility bills. Again: nice guy." His eyebrows lifted as he watched her take notes. "You have pens that work this time. Good job."

Gray blushed, then wrote, "JERK."

The small living room boasted cheap gray carpet,

oak furniture, oak cabinets, and white tile. The blueberry-colored couch looked too stiff to be comfortable, and it matched absolutely nothing else in the room. Not even the orange and yellow throw pillows on its cushions.

The clean kitchen sparkled but smelled of chlorine bleach and the bananas on the counter, which were so shriveled and black that not even fruit flies swarmed around them.

"Do you know if she was injured before she left?" Gray asked. "Like, did she have any cuts or bruises? Sprained ankles or . . ."

Ian shook his head.

"In your opinion—medical, personal—was she . . . suicidal?"

He rolled his eyes. "Tea concocted this story about Iz taking pills before disappearing."

"When was that?"

"The Friday night before Memorial Day. Whatever. It's not true. You just don't *get better* through prayer after taking a bunch of Tylenol PMs. I told Tea to lie better, especially about shit like that. Isabel takes a bunch of pills one day and has the energy to leave L.A. two days later without medical intervention? Bullshit. It's not happening."

Standing this close, Gray could better study Ian's face. There were no scars from a woman's fingernails. No almost-healed bruises beneath his eyes. No cuts on his lips. He was a perfect-looking man with perfect-looking skin.

"This place is tiny, right?" Ian now asked. "It's two stories and still cramped."

"Good size if it's just you."

"So are coffins."

A book of word searches had been left on the couch. A pack of Kool menthols sat on the coffee table next to an empty ashtray. No lighter. No matchbook.

"She smoke?" Gray asked.

"Sometimes." Ian tucked his hands beneath his armpits.

"It's her birthday tomorrow," Gray said.

"Whose?"

Gray looked back at him.

Blank face. Eyebrows not even crumpled. Not even *trying* to figure it out.

She said, "No one's," then sighed, her heart breaking a little more for Isabel Lincoln.

The staircase walls were lined with photographs of Isabel and Ian in happier times. Kissing in front of the Eiffel Tower. Embracing in the turquoise waters of the Caribbean.

"I paid for these quick little trips," Ian said, "and I had more lined up for her. I wanted to show her the world outside of L.A., outside of the U.S. Be her tour guide through life, I suppose. Be there when she saw the Taj Mahal for the first time, or tasted a *real* Italian pizza—with the egg on top? I treated her like a princess, and *this* is what she does?"

But something about those pictures in Paris and Saint Martin made Gray nauseous. And the sweet-sticky words Ian was now pouring down her throat . . . Before today, she'd never swallowed, but, in her effort to "be nice," she forced those words down and offered a sad smile. "The women at the Alumni Center mentioned that you and Isabel were supposed to go away on that Memorial Day weekend. They say that you didn't show up. Is that why she took the pills?"

Ian squirmed. "Umm . . . Again, I don't think she took those pills."

"You didn't mention that trip to me."

"You didn't ask."

"So, what happened?"

He blushed. "I had to work—she refused to accept that. She liked the benefits of dating a doctor but hated me *being* a doctor. This is Los Angeles and we have *a lot* of heart patients and sometimes I need to stay and help out, even when I'm supposed to be having downtime.

"I mean, if she needed cardiac care, she wouldn't want to hear, 'Oh, the doctor is on vacation, miss, you're just gonna have to wait, unless you want this second-year putting in your pacemaker.' I don't *think* so."

Gray said, "I get it," and this time, she did. She'd never needed a cardiologist, but emergency room doctors had stitched her up lots of times. She'd never thought about their wives or their kids or their postponed trips to Borneo as they treated her. Not once.

The steps groaned as Gray and Ian climbed them to the second level. "According to her coworkers," she said to Ian over her shoulder, "you were supposed to propose that weekend."

"Propose? *Marriage?*"

Gray nodded.

He laughed a laugh as real as Parmesan cheese from a green can. "She always expected me to follow this script in her head about what's supposed to happen and when. Month anniversaries. Our engagement. How I was supposed to propose. *Where* I was supposed to propose. I got tired of her micromanagement, to be honest, and so I decided *not* to obey her and to propose when *I* wanted. Which would've been on July fourth, our one-year anniversary. But of course, she was gone by then."

They reached the guest room, which was nearly bare except for a pair of battered sneakers and a large pile of clothes on the carpet. The blinds were closed. The room stank of sweat, other body odor, and that dirty laundry.

Gray and Ian entered Isabel's bedroom. Books, pens, and notepads lay everywhere. The sheets on the full-size bed twisted around an empty gym bag. A thick fuchsia vibrator poked from the linens. Eye shadows, mascara, and lipstick tubes cluttered the nightstand and dresser. Two L'Oréal hair color boxes sat on top of the DVD player.

"Did she color her hair recently?" Gray asked. "On the intake form, it says her hair is a dark golden brown."

Ian didn't answer. He was staring at the vibrator.

Gray cleared her throat, and asked, louder this time, "Did she color her hair?"

"Not that I know of."

The hair dye was Black Sapphire. One box was unopened, the other was empty.

In the master bathroom, there was a black tinge near the bathtub drain.

Gray took a picture of the tub and a few close-ups of the stained drain. "She probably dyed her hair. The proof of life picture will confirm that."

Ian pointed at an Apple Watch sitting in its slim white box. "She left it. I paid out the freakin' nose for that thing."

Isabel had followed the first rule of disappearing: don't get attached to anything you can't leave behind in five seconds. She sure as hell didn't want to be tracked by a fancy location beacon on her wrist.

Nothing obvious in the room belonged to the doctor.

"Did you ever stay overnight?" Gray asked, trying to ignore her need to pee.

"Of course I did." His phone buzzed and he looked at the screen. "It's the hospital. Gotta take this." He headed for the door, then looked back at her. "You do *not* have permission to take anything, understand? I don't want her pissed at me when she comes back."

"So, you *do* think she'll come back."

"Once she realizes she's being stupid, yes, she'll come back." Ian pointed at her. "I just need *you* to help *me* help *her* accept that sooner rather than later."

Gray gave him a thumbs-up to his face and a middle finger to his back. She opened the top dresser drawer. Panties and bras in every shade. Something else glimmered beneath the piles of lingerie, but she left it there and snapped a quick picture instead. In the second drawer, she found T-shirts and yoga pants. Nothing special.

There were framed pictures on top of the bureau— the same picture of Isabel standing between the Lou Rawls and Clair Huxtable look-alikes and a picture of a diverse klatch of women wearing ski gear, with white snow twinkling behind them.

There were no spatters of blood or ripped curtains hanging limp like a woman's wasted-away corpse. Gray heard no screams in this room, but dread still coiled in her gut. *Why?*

In the closet, there were no red-bottom shoes, but plenty of heels, sneakers, and sandals that cost less than a concert ticket. Gray poked around in the darkness until her fingers found something hard, boxy, and cold. "What's this?" she whispered.

"Sorry about that." Ian's face was flushed. "I'll need to leave soon."

Gray stood, then asked, "Would you mind if I . . ." She pointed to the bathroom.

Ian made a face. "Do you really have to? I mean . . . Sure."

She flushed but quickstepped to the bathroom anyway. Completing her chore in less than two minutes, she returned to Isabel's bedroom.

Ian, arms folded, was waiting for her.

"So," Gray said, "quick question: Was Isabel married before? Engaged previously?"

"No. But she's been in bad relationships. She's done far worse than me."

With a shark's smile, Gray said, "The ladies at the Alumni Center said *you* were bad."

He flicked his hand. "I don't care what they think. I have more important shit to do in life than worry about bitter bitches."

"Those past relationships. With the guys far worse than you. Know any of their names?"

He snorted. "Why would I ask for names?"

"You were never curious? She never complained to you about Michael, who used to shave and never clean the sink afterward? Or Paul, who'd clip his toenails in bed?"

Another snort from Ian. "Sorry. Not interested."

Gray and Ian clomped back down the steps and wandered to the kitchen. This time, she noticed a half-filled mug sitting near the range—the inside was stained from evaporated coffee. On a saucer, there was a bagel schmeared with cemented cream cheese.

Had Isabel left suddenly on that Monday morning?

Couldn't have. Mrs. Tompkins had mentioned that Isabel was carrying a suitcase. She'd had enough time to pack. And to dye her hair.

There was a blank notepad on the breakfast counter. There were no specks of dried blood on the oven door. No shards of broken glass or ceramic on the tile floor. No tufts of pulled-out hair beneath the refrigerator vent.

"Morris," Gray said. "How did he die?"

"He ate something."

"Poison?"

"No idea."

Gray squinted at him.

Ian gaped at Gray. "Seriously? Now I kill *cats*? To be honest, I never *saw* Morris. He was always hiding anytime I came over. Iz never asked *me* to watch him, not once." With a trembling finger, he pointed in the direction of Mrs. Tompkins's condo. "You talk to that old busybody and not tell me?"

Before she could respond, he whirled away from her. "Fucking remarkable. And now I'm a cat killer. She steals my dog, but *I'm* the villain. She never cared about Kenny G."

"Did she take care of him at all? Because of your schedule?"

"Please. Kenny G. had a dog sitter most times. Isabel was a flake and she'd forget to come over. I couldn't rely on her. Yes, she'd help out every now and then. That's why she had him on that Monday—she picked him up from the sitter that morning, around ten.

"And Tea is a liar—you should know that before you talk to her again. She's so caught up in the Saint Isabel myth, she can't even *think* straight. Take my advice: only believe ten percent of what she says." He shook his head, then added, "I didn't kill the fucking cat, okay?"

"Okay. I may need to come back here to look at some things."

Ian blanched. "Nick said we were gonna be done by tomorrow or Saturday at the latest."

"Maybe. I'm moving as quickly as I can."

He ran his hands over his face. "I'll try to let you in again, but I *do* have patients."

Down at the security gate, he said, "And yes: it *is* Isabel's birthday tomorrow. I know that. You just mentioned it at a random time. But, of course, you take that the wrong way."

Once again, Gray pushed that synthetic smile to her lips. "Thank you for taking time out of your day to walk me through. I know you're incredibly busy. Is there anything else I should know? Any relevant secrets that could help explain her disappearance? Is there another woman in the picture? Or another man?"

The doctor shook his head. "Other than that guy Omar? No. Nothing. No one."

Gray kept her eyes locked on his.

What about the Big Secret? Or the Hot Nurse? What did you really do on the Friday night of Memorial Day weekend?

Ian O'Donnell dropped back into his Porsche. He zoomed down the hill without tossing her a wave or a nod.

As Gray returned to the Camry, she knew that she'd need to take a closer look around Isabel Lincoln's condo. There was something about that blank notepad on the breakfast counter. And there was something about that tiny key hidden beneath the missing woman's lingerie. And that hard metal box on the floor in the darkest reaches of Isabel's closet . . .

There were big secrets everywhere.

11

Before partaking of tacos, margaritas, and hot Jewish bartenders, Gray needed to stop one more time at the office. And just as she plopped back at her desk, Dominick Rader strolled into her office with slices of pepperoni pizza on a paper plate.

"Finally," she said, "a visit from the big boss." She pushed her glasses to the top of her head, then tugged at her shirt, caring now about the small gaps between the buttonholes and the roll of . . . *her* bulging over the waistband of her wrinkled linen slacks.

Nick's tanned skin gleamed with pizza grease, but even with oil smears he was a gently handsome, forty-six-year-old man who checked every box to describe his ethnicity—his ancestors' ethos of "Love the one you're with" showed in his slanted gray eyes, his full lips, and those sharp, freckled cheekbones.

"I see you've settled in," he said. "Glad you could get an office."

"Let's just say that I know a guy." Seeing him sit there in her guest chair—*her* chair, *her* office—anyway, seeing him there made Gray's breath tumble in her chest.

Outside her office, skip tracers and administrative assistants, data analysts and random consultants huddled at the island in the large kitchen around boxes of pizza. And now the irresistible aromas of Italian meats and oregano-kissed tomato sauce tickled Gray's nose.

Nick adjusted the leather shoulder holster beneath his blazer. "You know, there's pizza out there. My treat." He paused, then added, "You're not on those shakes again, are you?"

"Maybe?" Right now there was a can of strawberry-flavored with her name on it, chilling in the office fridge. "The newsletter said that there would also be beer."

His eyebrows lifted. "On my dime?"

"Yep. Good beer, too."

"You guys are worth it," Nick said with a full mouth. "The best for the best."

"The new H.R. lady's all about employee happiness. *It's no secret that we care about you.* That's the signature line on her emails."

"We *do* care."

"You sent me roses after my surgery. In your official capacity as founder and CEO."

"I did?"

"Cuz you care. It's no secret."

"You should have some pizza. One slice won't hurt. You're recovering. You should eat."

"Pizza isn't penicillin." Not that she'd finished that course of penicillin after surgery.

"I can have them order salad. Rice cakes or—"

"Nick."

He held up a hand. "All right. Chill. Just wanna make sure that . . . you know, we're being all inclusive or whatever. Meeting dietary . . . things."

In March, Gray had been mentally ready for her promotion to baby P.I., but her body? Not so much. And two months later, she'd needed that appendectomy. Before then, she had worked from home but

had tired of reporting the findings of investigations—
she wanted to lead them. Especially cases that helped
women get away from dangerous men. But she couldn't
be an investigator, Nick had told her, if she wasn't in
the building.

She now had an office with a window overlooking tree-lined walkways, and access to a game room
with a Ping-Pong table. Throw in the best coffee in
the building, free pizza, and alcohol—she had gained
another ten pounds from all that, and from skipping
her daily three-mile runs. Dr. Messamer had said that
she could restart her routine in June, but it was now
July, and since then, she'd only run to the bathroom.

Nick started on his second slice of pizza. "You
look good now."

Gray laughed. "Not like a busted can of biscuits,
which is how I usually look?"

"I didn't mean it like that. I worry, okay? You've
been sick, and this job . . . No set schedule. No regular
mealtimes . . . You going to your follow-up appointments?"

"When needed."

"Gray—"

"I don't want to give away more information than
necessary. *You* taught me that. I'm taking my meds
and the doctor said that I'd have pain, that it's normal, that I'm healing." She gave a thumbs-up. "So,
what's up? You checking to see if Ian O'Donnell is
still alive?"

"Can't two old friends just talk for a minute?" Nick
and Gray had known each other for twenty-four years,
since she was fifteen years old. Back then, they were
like brother and sister. They grew up, though, and now
Gray loved Nick *like that*. But he had told her that she
wasn't ready for him. Pissed at his assessment of her,

she'd put their friendship on pause, talking to him only as her employer. *Yes, sir. No, sir. Thank you, sir.* And he had avoided her—no chance meetings in the hallways, no bumping into each other in the kitchen or down in the parking lot.

Back in May, though, they had picked up their friendship like a yellowed newspaper on a battered porch. Just in time for her appendix to burst.

And now, her old friend grinned at her. "I was surprised you wanted to be a P.I., working with people paid to be nosy."

"Yes, and nosy people tell me that you're seeing a biochemist. I'm surprised. I mean, all those brains and random equations in her head. With *you*?"

His smile widened. "And I'm surprised that you care. With you actively ignoring me ninety-eight percent of the time, I mean. So, your case?"

"A doozy."

"Yeah?" Nick crossed his long legs and pinched the crease of his Italian wool trousers.

"He's . . ."

"A jerk? But he's not like the regular jerks who're searching for runaway girlfriends."

"No? Cuz he certainly smells like that kind."

"Well, he's a friend," Nick said. "He patched me up a long time ago. I was thinking of taking his case for old times' sake, but I'm going out of town with . . . with . . ."

"With the biochemist," she said with a slow grin.

He wiped his fingers on a tired napkin. "She's always complaining that I don't take her anywhere. I guess I just don't get it. All beaches look the same. The ocean is blue and wet or green and wet. Every mai tai has that Malibu shit in 'em, and mosquitos are evil fuckers here and everywhere else. Save your money. Stay at home."

Gray placed her chin in her hand. "You're such a romantic."

"Whatever. I'm going out of town, so I can't work the case, and I thought it would be easy enough for you to handle without a lot of supervision."

"He mentioned that he never met Isabel's parents. Do you know why?"

"You ask him?" When she didn't nod, he said, "You should've—that's your job."

Over in the kitchen, glass bottles clanked against other glass bottles.

Nick looked back over his shoulder—more staff had joined the others around the island. "Is that the beer?"

"Sounds like it."

"Want a bottle?"

"Nope. I don't drink beer, remember?"

He glanced again at his camped-out employees. "I remember. I just don't believe it."

"May I . . . say something, now that I have some context? I know this is our job," she said, "but since the beginning of the world, every day begins and ends with a woman dumping a man. This happens on seven continents in over one hundred ninety countries around the world. Also on Pluto."

"Women don't dump this guy."

"Yeah, that's part of my problem with your friend. And why I'd asked not to be assigned male clients."

"You hate him cuz his ego's the size of my dick."

Gray rolled her eyes. "Low-hanging fruit, Nick."

"Hanging all the way down to my knees, baby. To my *knees*." He hopped up from his chair. "How can you sit there when free fucking beers are, like, six feet away?"

"They aren't free," she said, speaking to his back. "You're paying for them."

He darted out of her office to join the mob at the breakfast bar.

How was she gonna say this? That Ian O'Donnell—Nick's friend—was a wife beater?

She pulled the beaded cord on the window blinds until only a slice of sunlight cut across her notepad. She rubbed her temples, pushing at the new headache pinging behind her eyes. Came from not wearing her glasses around Dominick Rader. Came from old injuries that worsened in air-conditioning and high humidity.

Nick returned to her office, clutching two bottles of Flat Tire.

"What part of 'I don't drink beer' don't you understand?" she asked.

He snorted. "These aren't for you, sweetheart. This one"—he held up one bottle—"is my To Go. You been to Kauai before?"

"Not recently." She hadn't left the continental U.S. since 2008.

"That's where I'm taking her. Booked us a suite, and I even got a rental car." He flicked off the cap of his Right Now beer and guzzled half the bottle.

"She must be a genius in the lab *and* in the sack to get you to rent a car."

"So, your first big case. Cool, right?"

"Uh-huh."

"Thought you'd be happier, being sent out into the field, looking for *people*."

She blinked at him. "This is my happy resting bitch face."

"You can handle this, right?" No cockiness in his question. "And yeah, you told me that you didn't want to help jerks find women . . ."

Gray smiled. "It's fine. I help jerks all the time. How many times have I helped you?"

"I'm being serious."

Gray's eyes skipped around her office—the crimson orchid, the Ruscha prints of "Idea," floating in gray, and "The Absolute End," floating in blue. "What if . . ." She found Isabel Lincoln's text message on her phone, then read it to Nick.

He grunted.

She blinked at him. "That's it?"

"Ian isn't that guy."

Her nostrils flared. "Because he's one of your homies, he can't be an asshole?"

"An asshole and a wife beater are two different creatures."

"I know that."

"I thought you did, which is why I gave you this case." He pointed at her. "You need to take two steps back, all right? In this business? Everyone lies. Everyone leaves something out of the narrative."

"Our job—"

"Is to do what we're being paid to do, and in this case, our job is to *what*?"

She didn't respond.

"To *what*?"

"To find Isabel Lincoln. To have her sign a statement saying that she's okay. To have her answer three security questions. To take a picture of the tattoo on her left thigh and of her holding *USA Today*, then hand the picture and statement—"

"And the dog," Nick interrupted. "You're finding the dog, too."

"And if she's scared of him? What, then?"

"Maybe this case is too much for you." He said this more to himself than to Gray. "Maybe it's too soon. Maybe—"

"I can handle it," Gray said, her words hard. They stared at each other until she sighed and said, "I think he wants the dog back more than he wants the girl."

"I think you're right. Just . . . listen to your gut. Get her to sign the damned statement."

"And if she needs our help?" Gray prodded.

He pushed out a frustrated breath. "Then we'll help her."

She scowled. "You sound so dismissive."

He drained his beer. "And you're making this more dramatic than necessary."

"Dramatic," she said, drawing out that one word *dramatically*.

Like when "missing" turned into "she's hiding and doesn't want to be found"? And if Isabel Lincoln didn't want to be found, it may have been because the searcher—Ian O'Donnell—had hit her, kicked her, or strangled her. If she didn't want to be found, it was because maybe he would kill her. Dramatic? Indeed. Possible? Indeed as fuck.

Gray and Nick strolled to his black Yukon. Her eyes burned—the mountains surrounding the Basin were still on fire. That white sun was now the top layer on the City of Angels's five-layer dip of sun, ashes, smog, humidity, and cracked earth.

A Jeep Patriot trailed them to snag Nick's soon-to-be-abandoned parking space. Nick and Gray eyed the woman driving the Jeep, who was now rolling on their heels. The driver saw something dangerous in their faces, and she sped ahead to find another parking space.

"If you can't reach me for whatever reason," Nick said, "call Portia. She'll get you what you need. And Jen can help. She knows things. Zadie, if you don't wanna deal with Jen."

"Got it."

"I'll bring you back a pineapple or a snow globe."

"I can't have both?" As she hugged him, she closed her eyes and inhaled. He smelled like oranges and clean laundry.

"I told you: the biochemist is expensive. And you all are cutting into my bottom line with free pizza and beer." His gun brushed against her arm, and he kissed her cheek with lips still cool from the beer.

Once they pulled apart, she said, "You're gonna come back one of these days married to some random chick with blonde highlights and teeth whiter than all of Maine."

He faked a shudder.

Gray faked a chuckle.

This conversation had been one big lie. Yes, there was a biochemist. But Nick's trip was not vacation. He knew how to find people, and he also knew how to hide them.

The biochemist was going away.

But Gray didn't know that, *officially*. She didn't dare ask. None of this was in the books she'd read or the courses she'd taken. She'd seen other women go away. Hell, she'd researched new places for these women to start a new life.

And if she could prove it was necessary, Nick would help Isabel Lincoln start a new life, too.

HE
HAD
TO
STOP
HER

12

Gray made her way to Sam Jose's, just a mile west, heading away from that copper sun drifting down to the horizon. "I'm a P.I.," she said, smiling at her reflection in the rearview mirror. She was now a helper. No longer a runner, not anymore.

Tonight, Jennifer drove a metallic-turquoise BMW—it was the brightest, slickest car in the Sam Jose's parking lot. Her third husband, Reynaldo, owned a car rental business near the airport, and Jennifer often drove the exotics as advertising. With that paint job and tricked-out engine, the car cost more than $100,000, but any Joe with a decent credit rating could rent it for $699. The red banner plastered to the passenger window screamed, "ASK ME!"

Gray didn't spot Zadie's battered Subaru or Clarissa's tiny Fiat—they'd probably carpooled for the short drive from the office.

Sam Jose's doubled as the archive for all Mexican kitsch in Los Angeles, the "starting over again" place if an asteroid struck Olvera Street. Gray couldn't see her three coworkers past the glares of neon beer signs, multicolored Christmas lights, or dangling maracas. *Dia de los Muertos* this, *Lucha libre* that, sombreros and piñatas in every empty space.

Hank Wexler was shaking a martini at the bar.

Aware that she was sweaty, stained, and wrinkled,

Gray hunched to make herself smaller as she slunk across the cantina's tiled floor.

Hank saw her and paused midshake, ruining what would have been a pretty swell cocktail.

Gray tossed him a bashful wave and mouthed, *Hey.*

Hank tossed her a smile and a "Hey."

"We're over here!" Jennifer's words were slurred—blame the tall glass of Long Island Iced Tea in her hand. "You look like you rode a goat here or something."

"I did. Billy says, 'Yo.'" Gray slid into the booth beside Zadie and studied the fallen margarita waiting on her place setting. "It's damn near melted."

"Next time," Zadie growled, "get here quicker."

Clarissa tugged at her pink-streaked ponytail. "Dude, I'll drink it if you, like, don't want it. I'm not driving—Irving's picking me up." The Chinese American millennial reached for the margarita, but Gray slapped at her hand.

Irving Hwang and Clarissa planned to marry in mid-August. Despite their digging, Clarissa and Jennifer couldn't find one obviously malicious thing about the skinny Taiwanese accountant who now worked in the United States on a visa and loved everything American, including blondes, burgers, and, oh yeah, Clarissa.

"Hank over there says our first round is on the house." Zadie drained her gin fizz, then added, "That man's got it bad for you."

"Just like my bae has it bad for *me*," Clarissa chirped.

Jennifer rolled her eyes. "Oh, *please*. I've met Irving—he is *not* a 'bae.'" She pointed at Gray. "Don't you have another outfit?"

Gray said, "I didn't have time to change."

Jennifer pounded the table. "*Make* time. You wanna look your sexiest, right? And I saw how you tried to sneak in, hoping he didn't see you. So. Next time. Some wipes. Something black, something flattering. More effort, Grayson."

Gray had nothing except, "You're a boozy fount of drunken wisdom, Jen."

"Glad you finally recognize that." Jennifer sucked down more of her cocktail. "I ordered you a salad. No tacos."

"*What?*"

"No gassy foods, remember?" Clarissa said. "You're literally still recovering."

"Remember how you thought you were dying," Jennifer said, "and you collapsed in the bathroom and I came in and found you and it's all because you ate that burrito?"

Gray remembered that delicious burrito she'd eaten two weeks after her appendectomy, and, more than that, she remembered the incapacitating pain that came afterward. She'd gone to a clinic—they said it was just gas. Worse, that same clinic had a data breach days later and thousands of patient names and credit card data had been stolen. That delicious burrito hadn't been worth the trouble.

Zadie swirled the ice in her glass. "Jankowski was looking for you. Something about your W-2 form, now that you're full-time."

Gray tried to stir the margarita back to life. "I haven't filled one out."

Jankowski wouldn't pay her directly anyway. Instead, Rader Consulting paid Renata Dawn LLC, Gray's DBA. She'd asked Nick to explain the setup to Jankowski and guessed he hadn't. *Paperwork.* Nick hated paperwork.

"So, your first case, right?" Clarissa said. "Somebody, like, lost their keys?"

"Did you read the text I sent you about two hours ago?" Gray asked.

"You sent me a text?" Clarissa swiped around her phone. "Didn't know that I should be paying attention. You're actually on a *case* case."

Gray squinted at her. "I am."

"I'll take care of it tonight. Oh. Good news: he's safe."

"*Who's* safe?"

"Hank the bartender," Clarissa said. "I literally ran a background check on him. He bought this place four years ago. Honorable discharge from the Marines ten years ago, after a couple of tours in Iraq and Afghanistan. No kids. Had a wife but they got divorced a year later. He owns a cabin up in Big Bear and a duplex not far from here. He gives money to vets, animals, and cancer research. Two credit cards, a car note, no priors, no college degree, a new refrigerator, and a Husky named Sir. He's, like, literally the perfect man." She sat back in the booth and grinned. "I say go for it. Netflix and chill."

Gray cocked her head. "You did all of this and yet you didn't see my text message?"

Jennifer looked over her shoulder at the proprietor of the best cantina in Culver City. "And if *you* won't get with him, *I* will."

Clarissa gasped. "You're married."

"You'll understand one day," Jennifer said. "Marriage is hard. Right, Zadie?"

The old woman snorted. "You know what *my* husband did."

Jennifer sipped from her glass. "Neither you nor Gray understand just how much compromise is needed in a marriage."

"You've been married three times," Gray pointed out, eyebrow cocked.

"That's three more times than you," Jennifer said. "That's because I *go* for it. What's the saying? Don't talk about it, *be* about it."

Gray chuckled. "You learned a lot of black shit from husband number two, didn't you? And anyway, I plan to 'be about it' with Mr. Wexler over there."

"When?" the trio asked.

Gray blushed. "Tonight. Maybe."

Jennifer and Clarissa high-fived.

"So, what's your case about?" Clarissa asked.

"No, no, no, no, no." Jennifer flapped her hands. "No shop talk. It's time for tacos and sex talk and margaritas."

The four women said nothing for a moment.

Finally, Gray said, "A guy lost his girlfriend, who stole his dog."

Clarissa asked, "Was he cheating?"

"Not sure yet, but I suspect so. I told the girlfriend's pal to meet me here tonight." Gray's eyes skipped around the cantina, looking for anyone resembling a "Tea."

There was a guy with bad facial hair, studying the menu as though it were the Torah.

There were four *Golden Girls* types nursing glasses of white wine.

Other customers watched the Dodgers game on the television over at the bar.

"You told her to come *here*?" Zadie asked.

"That"—Jennifer raised a finger—"is a big no-no. Don't *ever* mix business with pleasure. This place? This place is your *safe* place. Where you can be all that you can be. Cuz what if this Tea likes it and comes back and you can't chill here anymore? So: bad girl." She tapped Gray's hand. "*Bad.*"

"You're right," Gray said. "Stupid idea. Too late now."

"Anyway," Jennifer said, "your client hit her and then she left."

"He hit her," Zadie said, "cheated on her, hit her again, and *then* she left."

"Dude killed her," Clarissa said. "They always do, you know. Like the nut who totally showed up at that lady's school and literally shot up her classroom."

"Or the nut who showed up to the house wearing a Santa suit," Zadie added.

Jennifer squinted. "The one with the flamethrower?"

Zadie frowned. "Where the hell do you buy a flamethrower?"

"Amazon," Gray said. "And this woman's alive. She asked that I stop looking for her."

Clarissa canted her head. "You sure that was *her*?"

Gray's face burned. "I . . . just assumed . . . *Shit.*"

Zadie said, "Don't ever assume anyone is telling you the truth. No need to stress about it now—you're gonna make mistakes."

Clarissa eased an ice cube from her glass, into her mouth. "If that *was* her, and she *is* alive, then she's, like, totally stupid."

Gray clenched the thick stem of the margarita glass. "I wouldn't use that word to describe her—if it *is* her."

"Nuh-uh," Clarissa said, chomping ice. "She's *literally* stupid, cuz, like, why is she texting the fucking hunter? We, like, literally use all kinds of voodoo shit to, like, find people."

"It could be *him*," Jennifer said. "The boyfriend, trying to throw you off the scent. Okay, say he has her phone and he cut her thumbs off to unlock her phone. He boards the dog and now he's pretending to be her. He hires you so that people will think that he cares. And there you go, into the wild blue yonder, talking to her friends and to her family.

"Meanwhile, *she's* in his basement without any thumbs, and cuz he's a doctor he knows how to cut the rest of her up, and then he'll use his buddy's yacht to throw pieces of her into the Pacific, cuz in Hermosa Beach right now there are some great whites swimming around, and so she's eaten by the sharks but he's still, 'Where did she go and where's my dog, blahblahblah.'"

Gray shook her head. "I didn't think of that. Again, you're a fount of wisdom, Jen."

Ernesto, the waiter, dropped off their platters of food: tacos for everyone except Gray, who would enjoy a Mexican Caesar salad drowning in dressing.

"You know," Clarissa said, "the missing lady, like, needs to get a nose job, a boob job, and then fly to Machu Picchu or wherever, cuz you're *literally* gonna find her once I look at her phone number. Sorry I didn't see your text. My personal trainer is being such a brat and—"

"What does your personal trainer have to do with you not doing your job?" Gray glanced over at Hank.

He beckoned her to come over.

The last time Hank had called Gray over, he'd offered her a sip of fifty-year-old Remy Martin. Afterward, they'd slipped into his office and onto his suede couch. For a cool ten minutes they made out like teenagers, with Gray's hand shoved beneath his boxers and his hand shoved beneath her bra. Just as her other hand unbuttoned the fly of his 501s, Alex, the backup bartender, knocked on the office door and shouted that a bunch of college boys from Loyola Marymount had just arrived. Hank had kissed her nose and whispered, "Later?" Gray had nibbled his bottom lip. "Um-hmm."

Yeah, Hank was a Republican, but he kissed like a Democrat, and "later" was "now," and who was she to ignore his efforts to put country before party?

And now, Gray said, "Pardon me, ladies," then eased out of the booth, with her margarita. Wrinkled linen pants and chocolate-stained shirt be damned.

Clarissa shouted, "Be back in time for my bachelorette party."

Gray said, "Ha! Maybe," even though she hadn't planned to attend, because Clarissa's party was in Las Vegas. She hated that place and had sworn never to return.

Over at the bar, she slid her dying cocktail toward Hank's enormous hands. "I'd like a refund, please. I like 'em strong."

"Oh, yeah?" His eyes twinkled with neon light.

"I need it to work me over. Get me shook, you know?"

His smile, those eyes—all of him made Gray dizzy and excited and a little disoriented. Like she had murdered the former Baptist-Catholic-atheist schoolgirl inside of her and now the slutty twin had taken her place, wearing Saturday panties on Tuesday.

"How about . . . something now, and then something later?" Hank asked.

"You're so generous. So . . . dedicated to your craft." She traced those Hebrew letters on his forearm, now tinted by the jeweled reds, yellows, and blues of Lucha Libre and Dos Equis.

L'Shana Tova, Hava Nagila, olé.

"Your friends are looking over here," Hank said.

"Let them look." Her finger traced gimel and resh, letters that did, in fact, start her name.

"No. Seriously."

She glanced back over her shoulder.

A woman stood at the booth. Clarissa was now pointing at Gray.

"New friend?" Hank asked.

"Don't know her." Gray backed away from the former marine, not wanting to look away but knowing that, eventually, she had to. "Text me later?"

He flashed that smile, and those eyes danced as he slid over to take a customer's order.

The visitor at Gray's booth had skin the color of almonds. She smelled like bacon, which wasn't the worst quality in a person. Except for poufy bangs, the visitor's hair lived in long braids. A big girl, she stood about five nine, with shoulders slouching into her arms like a slug. She was melting in her turquoise sweater set.

Gray said, "Hi."

The woman said, "Hello."

They looked at each other for a moment. "Are you Gray?"

"Last time I checked, yeah."

"Isabel told me to tell you . . . She said to tell you . . . Fuck off."

13

Fuck off.

"Is that an *exact* quote?" Zadie asked.

Gray said, "And you're . . . *who* again?"

"Tea Christopher." The woman blinked at the quartet, through her thick-lensed, horn-rimmed glasses. "I don't mean to curse, but I didn't wanna water down what Isabel told me to say. She said it was very important that you knew it was her speaking and not me."

But Gray didn't know Isabel, and she sure as hell didn't know *this* woman, who smelled like breakfast. "Just to confirm: You're *Tea* Tea?" she asked. "Isabel's friend Tea?" *Isabel with the* Vogue *cheekbones and the long ponytail? The Mary Ann with the hotshot doctor boyfriend?*

The woman said, "Not just her friend. Her *best* friend."

Clarissa said hi and then introduced herself, as though all of this was normal.

"You're not hot in that sweater?" Zadie asked.

"I'm fine. Thank you."

Gray had pictured Tea as a tall, willowy blonde wearing Valentino slacks and a crisp blazer. Or the black Tea, with long dreadlocks, an R & B voice, and soulful brown eyes. Behind those bottle-bottom eyeglasses, this Tea had thick, gorgeous eyelashes like a cow's. But there was dried blood around her torn cuticle, she was tall but not willowy, and the sweater set was more "way in the back of TJ Maxx" than anywhere at Neiman Marcus.

The two women slid into the banquette.

"Want a drink?" Gray asked.

The young woman nibbled the hangnail on her thumb. "A Sprite?"

"Sure." Gray scanned the restaurant—no servers anywhere. Even Hank had disappeared. "Someone will be out in a minute. In the meantime, thanks for coming to see me. I know this must be difficult for you."

"I'd do anything for Isabel." Tea went back to nibbling that hangnail.

Gray smiled, hoping that Tea would see she had nothing to fear. "So, how long have you and Isabel been friends?"

"For about three years. I knocked on her door to offer Bible study with my church. Mount Gethsemane over on Crenshaw, by Dulan's? I was surprised when she let me in, and we talked—about the Bible, about her life. The good and the bad. Mostly the bad. She's so beautiful, but she needed more than someone saying how pretty she was. So we prayed, and then I picked her up for church that next Sunday and that was that. We've been inseparable ever since. Until now." She glanced around the restaurant. "Is there food?"

Gray wanted to say, *Nope, no food at a Mexican restaurant. Only sombreros and empty piñatas.* Instead, she said, "Umm . . ." and finally spotted a waitress near the kitchen.

Tea ordered that Sprite, along with a flauta, a chimichanga, and a beef *torta*. "I haven't eaten all day. And then, after work—"

"What do you do?"

"I'm a communications associate at a theater arts

nonprofit. We put on plays and readings, teach makeup arts, that kind of thing. I'm responsible for newsletters and the blog."

This young woman was so well-spoken. Not a "like" or a "yup" or a "I can't even" in the five minutes they'd spent together.

"After work," Tea continued, "I had to stop at church, and then I came here, so I haven't eaten dinner yet."

Gray waved a hand. "It's no problem."

"Is Grayson your real name?"

Scalp tight and smile frozen in place, Gray nodded.

Tea closed her eyes and whispered. After ending her prayer with "Amen," the woman took a deep breath, slowly exhaled, then opened her eyes. "I just want the Holy Spirit to guide me, cuz the words that are about to come out of my mouth are mine, not Isabel's. And I also prayed for you, Miss Sykes, that *you* do the right thing, that God guides your investigation. Okay?"

"Okay."

"There are a lot of reasons Isabel left, and Ian is the cause for all of them. He hurt her so bad—*physically* hurt her—that she can't even move her arm all the way—"

Gray held up a hand. "Dr. O'Donnell *abused* her?" *Just like she'd thought.*

Tea blinked her cow lashes. "Am I speaking Greek?"

"Like you, I want the words coming out of both of our mouths to be clear. What you're telling me is . . . explosive."

"I know."

"When did he hit her?"

"The last time was in April."

"Did she take pictures afterward?"

"Maybe. Probably." Calm, Tea folded her hands atop the table. "You saw him today?"

Gray nodded.

"On Valentine's Day, Isabel cooked for him, since it was their first Valentine's together. She bought this special outfit and everything. Decorated the condo. Totally romantic. He was supposed to come over at seven that night, but he didn't show up. Eight o'clock and still no Ian. He called her at ten, claiming that he had to take his mother to the emergency room."

"Was he lying?"

"He *said* that he had called Isabel and had left messages . . ."

"But?"

"*But* Isabel was so upset that she didn't hear her phone ring. Knowing Ian, though, he probably lied and didn't leave any messages but then blamed her for not picking them up. He did stuff like that all the time. Make her think that *she* was the crazy one."

Sadie returned to their booth, holding a tray filled with dinner plates. To Gray, she said, "This is for you. From Hank." She set down a margarita and a note scribbled on a napkin.

"*You licked it so it's yours.*"

Gray's face warmed, and she didn't dare look over at him, out of fear she'd *kaboom!* and leave pieces of herself all over the piñatas and sombreros.

Across from her, Isabel's best friend was whispering a blessing over her meal. Then Tea grabbed the bottle of Cholula and dumped about thirty cups of it onto her torta. "Did he tell you about Memorial Day weekend?"

"A little, but her coworkers told me that she was upset on that Friday."

"You went to the Alumni Center?" Tea asked, eyes big.

"Yeah. They were very helpful."

"Isabel and Ian had been arguing all week. They were supposed to go out of town that Friday night. He didn't show up, though. So, remembering what he did on Valentine's Day, Isabel drove to his house. He lives over by the Farmers Market, off Fairfax." Tea took a big bite of torta and meat tumbled from the bun to the plate. "Anyway, she knocked, because he never gave her a key, even though he has keys to her mailbox *and* to her front door. So he answered but wouldn't let her in. That's when she saw one of his nurses—"

"Blonde?" Gray asked. "Pretty? Looks like Michelle Pfeiffer?"

"Uh-huh. You meet her?"

"No. She popped in his office while we were talking."

"Well," Tea continued, "Isabel saw her—her name's Trinity—standing in his bedroom door and—" Tears shimmered in Tea's eyes and beaded on those magnificent eyelashes. "She was so upset, cuz she knew for sure now that he was cheating on her. She shouted at him, and he slapped her, right there, in front of his other woman, then kicked Isabel out.

"She called me around ten, eleven o'clock that night, and I'm listening to her, and I'm saying to myself, *She doesn't sound right*. She was talking slow and strange. I drove over to her place, and the door was unlocked, and so I went in, and there she was, on the bathroom floor, and there were pills . . ." Tea covered her mouth with her hand to tamp back a sob. "Pills everywhere."

Gray's ears warmed and she put a shaky hand atop Tea's trembling wrist. "So, she tried to commit suicide? Ian says—"

"I know what Ian says," Tea snapped. "She wouldn't let me call nine-one-one. She wouldn't let me take her to the doctor—especially since *he* probably knew all the emergency room docs in L.A. She told me that if God wanted her to live, she'd live. So I just sat there with her, and I prayed that He'd save her, and I prayed and hoped that she hadn't taken enough pills.

"She made it through Friday night. Was sick, though, all Saturday and Sunday. It was God's will that she survived."

"And then she left on Monday?"

Tea nodded.

According to Mrs. Tompkins, Isabel had climbed into a black truck that Monday morning.

"What about her family?" Gray asked. "What did they say?"

"She didn't tell her parents," Tea said, nibbling shredded lettuce. "She knew that they'd write her out of their will or something if she didn't get therapy, go to rehab, or do whatever happens after suicide attempts. So we kept it secret."

"And her other friends—did they know?"

"*What* other friends?"

"The ones I see on her Facebook page. Wine tasting in Temecula and brunch—"

"Oh. Them. They're not her *real* friends," Tea said, chin high. "They're more for show. For drinking—cuz I don't drink. I don't know them and I don't *want* to know them. They want her to stay with Ian. For his money and for his status, for all of the material things he gives her. Isabel could never admit to them . . . to women like *that* . . . that she's . . . that Ian's . . ."

Gray nodded, understanding. "Do they know that she's gone?"

Tea shrugged.

"You haven't told them?"

"No. They're not worried about her, either. They don't miss her. Not one of them has reached out to me and she's been gone all of June, most of July, and her birthday is tomorrow, and they're busy drinking and smoking weed and sleeping around. They're partly responsible for Isabel's depression. She was becoming like them—her soul was conflicted."

"So, you told Ian that Isabel tried to kill herself. And he said . . ."

"He said, 'She can't even die right.'"

"You heard him *say* that?"

"No. That's what he texted."

"To you?"

"Yes."

"When?"

"Like, a few days after everything happened."

"Isabel was long gone by then."

Tea nodded.

"You were still in contact with her."

Tea nodded again.

"But Ian didn't think anything was wrong . . ."

"Until around June first. That's when he contacted the police. He tried calling her, but she wouldn't answer. He went to her place, but she was gone. Then he claimed that she stole Kenny G. *That's* why he hired you. He doesn't care about *her*—he just wants his damned dog."

"Speaking of the dog . . ."

"Isabel always took care of him, cuz of Ian's schedule. He's as much her dog as his."

"But he *bought* the dog, Tea. He probably pays the license for the dog, and I think you're right—he cares more about the dog than about her. But she has to give him back. I can arrange for a swap. Or *you* can retrieve him and bring him back."

"I'll ask Isabel, but don't hold your breath." A tear tumbled down Tea's cheek and she dabbed it with a knuckle. "She knew that he didn't care. She knew that he wanted her dead, and she decided to leave—for good this time."

Gray's insides were pinballing. *Wanted her dead?* "He told me that she's left before."

"And he'd always sweet talk her into coming back. And when the sweet talk failed, he threatened her into coming back."

"How did he threaten her?" Gray fought back tears. Maybe Nick had been right. Maybe it *was* too soon for her to work a case like this.

"He said . . ." Tea traced her finger through the lettuce and cheese debris on the table. She was overheating in that sweater set and perspiration trickled down her temple. "He said that he'd hurt somebody she loved. At first she didn't believe him, but then he poisoned her cat."

Gray's lungs tightened. Ian had denied any involvement in Morris's death. "How?"

"The vet found rat poison in Morris's system. Isabel had no choice but to euthanize him."

"How do you know that Ian . . . I mean, cats always get into shit. Morris could've found . . ." She stopped speaking, since Tea kept shaking her head. "Okay, so he *maybe* killed the cat."

"We *know* that he killed the cat."

Gray sipped the margarita, not really tasting it. A good thing, since she hated tequila. She loved martinis—dirty, pink, Gibsons, and vespers. But she'd abandoned that life, and those cocktails.

"Listen, Tea. I understand everything you've just told me, and I'm so sorry that Isabel's in this situation. But I can't just tell Ian that she's fine, that Kenny G. is fine, and that he should just move on. I'm gonna need proof."

Tea squinted at Gray. "What *kind* of proof?"

"Specifically, a picture of Isabel holding tomorrow's newspaper, a picture of her left thigh, a handwritten statement that says she's okay, along with answers to three security questions. And I need Kenny G. to be in the newspaper picture."

On a napkin, Gray jotted down these instructions, along with her email address. "Quick question: Did you give Isabel my phone number?"

Tea folded the napkin into a small square. "I did. I thought she should know that he was trying to find her, and that he hired you."

The Corona sign threw weak gold and blue light over the empty plates. This case reminded Gray of the shredded cheese and lettuce scattered all around the table. She wanted to ask Tea about the black truck and the early-morning ride—and she wanted to ask about Omar, especially—but her gut told her to wait.

"So, do you know where she is?" Gray asked instead. "Does she need anything? Money or a plane ticket . . ."

Tea shook her head. "Everything about Ian is a lie. He didn't love her. He was never *in* love with her. And if she ever comes back, she's gonna tell the California Medical Board everything, about every punch and kick she took from him. They're gonna revoke his license."

"The police—"

"We never called the police. Calling the police would've made Ian angrier."

In some cases, restraining orders fed the beast instead of tamed it. Sometimes, restraining orders offered a sense of false security when it was only a paper shield. As though an asshole who had shoved, kicked, beaten, and strangled his lover would follow and respect the *law*. And then there was this: violating a restraining order was a *misdemeanor*. A bug bite, not even from a Zika-infested mosquito. What rhinoceros was scared of a common mosquito?

Isabel not going to the law for protection?

Gray understood that more than anything.

"Isabel's fine," Tea said. "She has money, she has a gun, and she has . . . *me*."

Isabel had a *gun*?

Shit.

Nick thought Ian O'Donnell didn't seem violent enough to warrant a weapon, but Gray also knew better than that. They *never* seemed violent enough . . . until it was too late and their knuckles were already dripping with blood.

UNFORGETTABLE

It was their first anniversary, and for the third time that night, Sean danced with Georgina, the Brit with bad bangs who was over corporate accounts at SD Promotions. And now Mrs. Dixon knew that she'd have to say *something*, and she knew that he'd glare at her like he'd glared at her on the day after her birthday, just two weeks before—the birthday he'd forgotten.

An argument on their first freaking anniversary.

Back in their suite, Mrs. Dixon set on the bed a bucket of quarters that she'd won from playing slots. She'd played alone. Her nerves were tight by then, snake-in-the-grass tight, monster-in-the-closet tight. "Was I supposed to tell him, *No, thanks, I'll pass on taking two hundred fifty dollars?*" she finally asked her husband. "What should I have done?"

Sean didn't respond. He cracked open a can of Coke from the bar, then poured that and two mini bottles of Jack Daniel's into a glass. He swirled the mixture with his pinkie and kept his hard eyes on the window overlooking the Strip.

"Sean," Mrs. Dixon pleaded, "please answer me and stop pouting." Her resolve to be "right" had folded over and it was hard for her to breathe and plead at the same time.

But she knew now: even though this moment hadn't

been *Indecent Proposal*, that's *exactly* what she should have done. No one had offered Sean a million dollars—and she never would have slept with the Texan anyway. Still, she apologized. "I'll never do it again, okay? *Sean*. It was harmless fun, I would've—"

He rushed toward her, veered at the last moment, and slapped the bucket on the bed. Quarters exploded like tiny grenades around the room. "How do you think it made me feel," he shouted, "seeing my *wife* whore herself out like that?"

She stepped to him, the daughter of a Bureau man who had told her to never take shit from anybody. Nostrils flared, Mrs. Dixon shouted, "Who the hell are you calling a *whore*?"

Sean growled, "I know you better *step* the hell away from me, *bitch*."

She put her hands on her hips. "Or what?" That was the daughter of a public school teacher, who'd told her that bullies didn't like to be challenged and would pull back if they were.

But Sean didn't retreat. He grabbed her arm, grabbed it so hard that she gagged from surprise. She tried to pull free from his grip, but his fingers only tightened. He reached with his other hand and clutched her throat and she could barely let out a cry of surprise. Then he shoved her and she flipped back over the couch and splashed into the Jacuzzi, coming to a stop with a bone-breaking bang.

That moment was like . . . like . . . one of those tornadoes spouting over Illinois, randomly dropping, all dark, mean, and sudden.

Sean didn't speak. He just gaped at his wife, a wet mess now, struggling and slipping out onto the carpet. And then, he . . . *left the room*. No "Good-bye," no "I'll be back." He just . . . *left*.

The fall hadn't broken any of her bones, but it had broken plenty of other things.

Mrs. Dixon cried as the city beyond those floor-to-ceiling windows shimmered and sparkled. *Magic! Loose slots! Girls! Lobster!* She spent the night searching for quarters, a diversion from the sudden mess in her life. She winced with every pull of breath into her lungs. Pain ricocheted from her eyes to her tailbone to the web of skin and cartilage around her ankles.

She had no one to contact. Her friends hated Sean, and over the year, Mrs. Dixon had stopped calling Avery, Zoe, and Jay. She'd still been invited to birthday parties, cookouts, and Zoe's engagement dinner, but her friends' lives were so . . . *different* from hers. Avery and Zoe still lived in Northern California, and Jay lived in North Vegas, twelve miles away from Mrs. Dixon's home in Summerlin. It had become the longest twelve miles in the history of the earth.

Cleave to your husband. Faye had, even after Victor's death, which led to her own death.

Mrs. Dixon's mind worked frantically until it found memories of Faye and Victor, rest their souls. Victor had been an FBI agent in San Francisco's field office, and Faye had been his public school teacher wife. They hadn't been violent toward each other, not ever. A stable and loving environment. Black excellence. *It's what we expect from you.* That's what Faye and Victor always told her.

But this—sprawled out on a chaise longue in tears? This wasn't black excellence.

Do something. That's what Dad would have told her. Mom would have folded her arms, cocked an eyebrow, and said, "Well?"

Mrs. Dixon crept down to the closest coin collector in the casino and converted those quarters into cash—another seventy-five dollars for her rainy-day fund.

Back in the room, she wrote the first entry in the Tiffany leather journal that Sean had just given her to celebrate their first anniversary: *The night did not go well.* She could still smell her fear, his breath, and those quarters. Tears slapped at the words on the page as she chronicled the push, the cut that resulted from biting her lip during the tumble, and Sean's disappearance. The pain from all over her body gathered in her right hand as she wrote in great detail, preserving the moment like a lepidopterist pinning down a Sapho longwing butterfly. As Dr. Underhill had told her throughout her therapy, journaling relieved the pressure, caused her thinking to slow, squeezed at the fear. And soon she had filled those pages with her fears, along with dates, descriptions of how Sean had hurt her, and the threats that he'd made.

Any time she wrote in that journal, she'd hide it in the secret pockets of her designer handbags or beneath the false bottom of the waste can in her bathroom. She'd think, *This is ridiculous*, but she never stopped hiding it. All day she'd write, since she had no job—he didn't want her to work. She scavenged and saved any money she found in his clothes, in the washing machine and dryer. Sometimes the money jingled. Sometimes, if she lucked out, the money folded. And the rings—she always had Faye's rings and her rings just in case. . . .

But on this night, just a year married, she hadn't thought that far ahead, and only one page of that fancy leather journal had been filled.

Around three in the morning, Sean returned to their suite.

She pretended to be asleep.

He didn't breach the bedroom's doorway. No, he just stood there, his shadow growing loud and long. Finally, he retreated, and then . . . music. Luther Vandross on the stereo. The *hell*?

Mrs. Dixon lay with one foot on the ground as Luther sang about the time when she played her sweet guitar. She didn't know what to think. Sean wasn't *like that*. Obviously angry, cartoonishly possessive. He hadn't been drunk, which would have made sense. She'd seen that sort of anger before. She'd been slapped, pushed, pinched in those hard times. Always on display, that kind of violence. And she cried in bed as Luther Vandross, her favorite crooner, sang strange-sounding love songs from the other room.

This couldn't be Sean.

No.

That's what she told herself the next morning as she stood, puffy-eyed, in front of the bathroom mirror with light that, just the day before, had made her look glamorous. That light now made the cut on her lip, the tender purple bruise around her right bicep, and the matching bruise at her kidney appear uglier and meaner than they were. Yeah, the light did that.

Sean came into the bathroom and stood behind her. He met her eyes in the mirror's reflection. "We got a little carried away, huh?" He wore 501s and his favorite V-neck sweater over a white T-shirt. Nice Guy uniform. He swiped his hand across his beautiful face.

A teardrop tumbled down Mrs. Dixon's cheek. That was the only movement on her body.

Watching that teardrop fall made anger flicker in Sean's eyes. "I . . ." His nostrils flared.

Barely breathing, she tore her gaze away from his. She grew rigid as his breath scorched her ears. *What was he about to do to her?*

He said, "I'll never touch you like that again. Okay?"

His words traveled like a giant pill scraping her throat and leaving behind a bitter taste. She swallowed whatever it was, then whispered, "Okay."

He grasped her shoulders, then kissed the top of her head. "I don't deserve you. I know that. *You* know that. The world, including dude last night, knows that, and I let it get to me. You're incredible, Mrs. Dixon. You take my breath away, and I'm gonna make it up to you."

He'd said almost the exact collection of words once he'd apologized for forgetting her birthday last month. *I'm gonna make it up to you.*

This morning, he kissed the bruise on her arm. "Get dressed. We'll eat breakfast and then we'll go shopping, okay? And I was gonna surprise you, but . . ." He grinned, bashful all of a sudden. "I got us tickets to see Copperfield tonight. You love Copperfield. So . . . Okay. Let's get going." He winked at her reflection and patted her butt.

Mrs. Dixon tensed beneath his kinder hit that was still a hit. Even after he'd left the bathroom, she stayed there, in front of that magic mirror, with that diamond in her nose. Flawless. But those bruises were getting uglier as blood continued to spill through broken veins beneath her skin. She didn't want to see that ugliness, not on this, her first anniversary.

So she pawed through her makeup bag, moving aside eyeliner, lip gloss, mascara, a tampon, moisturizer, sharpener, cotton swab, tweezers . . . *Ah. Here.* And she twisted the cap off the bottle of liquid foundation, and she dabbed a perfect drop on her finger.

14

Tea ordered dessert, then asked Gray to promise she wouldn't drag Isabel back to L.A.

But Gray hadn't been hired to drag anybody anywhere. After watching Tea consume churros and ice cream, and after paying the bill, she walked the woman out to the parking lot, to a scraped-up green Altima with its rear window lined with thousands of troll dolls.

The sun had set and all light came from hundreds of headlamps and brake lights that buzzed east and west on Jefferson Boulevard. It was time to join the fray.

"Just ask Isabel to send the few things that I need," Gray told Tea, "and I'll pick up the dog from wherever she decides, and then we'll be done. Promise."

"I'll do my best to convince her," Tea said. "Thanks, Gray. Be blessed."

Back in the restaurant, Jennifer grabbed her purse from the banquette she'd shared with Gray for just six minutes. "So much for us not working tonight."

"Don't worry," Gray said. "*You* didn't work. And it couldn't be helped."

"*You* told her to meet you here," Jennifer pointed out.

"Rookie mistake," Clarissa said.

Jennifer slipped her arm through Gray's as they strolled to the exit. "Productive?"

Gray glanced back at the bar. Hank was pouring beers for the college kids. "She claims that the boyfriend used to beat Isabel."

"What's that in your voice?" Jennifer asked.

"I'm just not sure why Nick gave this case to me. I mean, I get it, but . . ."

Jennifer squeezed Gray's arm. "If you don't want it, I'll take it. And you can go back to doing what you do best. What was that again? Typing?"

"Typing *and* proofing," Gray said. "Anyway, Isabel should be sending proof of life tomorrow and I will have solved my very first case. Yay, me."

With that, Gray climbed back into the Camry and started her twisty, five-extra-miles drive home. Her route was a centipede, a tableau of red ribbons, a bullet ricocheting through a 503-square-mile corpse. No black Range Rovers or red Jaguars reflected in her rearview mirror. And that made her think about her promise not to drag Isabel Lincoln back to Los Angeles.

Because the truth was this: every nine seconds, a woman was battered in America. Over ten thousand women were killed by their current or ex-partners every year. America—the *world*—had a woman problem, and there was not enough money in Warren Buffett's bank account to compel Gray to contribute to those statistics. If it came down to that, to dragging Isabel back to Los Angeles, she'd hand the case over to Jennifer and apologize to Nick.

Do unto others.

15

Just five years ago, Beaudry Towers had been one of the swankiest places to live in downtown Los Angeles. Apartment units either boasted northern views of the Dorothy Chandler Pavilion and city hall or southern views of downtown skyscrapers and the bulk of south Los Angeles. The Towers had a swimming pool and patio space that sparkled. Trees and shrubbery had been regularly trimmed and tended.

But then real estate barons constructed fancier apartments that boasted better views and grocery stores on the ground floors. Beaudry Towers became the neglected big sister left to fend for herself. She hadn't been downgraded to "dump" yet, but she was a gurgle away from being "down the drain." And now her tenants left grocery store circulars on the sticky linoleum. Worse, they wedged squares of cardboard between the latch and the strike plate of the security door that separated the mail room from the elevator bank.

Gray was glaring at one of those stupid wads of cardboard now.

"I know how you feel." That came from Mr. Shrewsbury, the gray-haired widower who also lived on the seventeenth floor. "I'm tired of assholes leaving their shit. And *that*."

With a stiff brown finger, he pointed at the door. "Why am I paying for a secured building when they allow horseshit like *that*? Makes no gah-damned sense."

"We're supposed to be getting new keys," Gray said.

"*Again?*"

She tossed the cardboard wedge into the trash can. "Third new key since Christmas."

"Did you hear? Folks broke into this door again this morning. Probably the same ones who tore off the entire mail panel two weeks ago. Stole some checks and gift cards."

Gray pulled sales papers addressed to "Resident" from her own metal box. For the last three years she'd had her real mail—like the income from renting her parents' home in Monterey Bay—sent to a UPS Store P.O. box a mile from Rader Consulting. She also kept old important things in that same box: keys, legal papers, cash.

"Maybe it's time to move," she said to her neighbor.

Mr. Shrewsbury held the security door open for Gray. "Don't know about you, but I can't afford to move. I've been here forever, so my rent's still lower than most people's."

Like the old man, Gray paid only $1,800 a month for her one-bedroom unit.

They were trapped.

And so she and the widower chatted about the day's air quality as they rode up to their luxury-living cages on the seventeenth floor. They chatted about management's decision to change out carpet for hardwood. They chatted about the new *creperie* on the ground level, and then about air quality again. Shouting good night, they retreated to different parts of the seventeenth floor.

Mrs. Kim, the ancient Korean woman in apartment

1715, had cooked something that smelled like musk ox. In apartment 1710, Jessica and Conner, a twee hipster couple with suspect income, continued to ignore the pink notices that Towers management had taped to their door.

A five-gallon bottle of water sat at unit 1708, Gray's apartment at the end of the hall.

As she pulled the bottle across the threshold, her refrigerator coughed and rumbled its *Welcome home, honey*. Gray yelped, startled at the fridge's mini explosion. Management had promised two weeks ago to fix the freaking motor, but they hadn't.

With the lights off, the dark living room glowed with light from the Department of Water and Power across the street and from diffused light that moved like pollen from cars snaking along the freeway.

Purple sky. No moon. Cars, cars, cars jamming the 101 and 110. Always alive. Always fast. The freeways that never slept. It was never, ever completely dark in downtown Los Angeles, even during blackouts. Closing her eyes—that was the only time Gray saw darkness. And quiet? Never quiet. Even with thick, double-paned glass, Gray still heard traffic hum, helicopters roar, and the city rumble, wild and nonstop.

The air conditioner clicked on and the vertical blinds shifted with the new breeze.

Over on the couch, her phone buzzed in her bag. Isabel.

Tea said she saw you

Gray's hands shook. *Yes*. She didn't know what else to say, she wanted to say so many—
You don't know me but I am here for you

Once, we were in his car on the 10. Going to some
fancy dinner. Honoring his greatness.
Don't even remember what I said
And he kept one hand on the wheel
Punched me in the head with the other.

Tears stung Gray's eyes. *I'm sorry.*

Can you do me a favor?
Just write a statement and sign it. I'll ask Tea to pick
up the dog.

Can't

Why do I have to jump through hoops???!!! I haven't
done anything wrong!!

I know I'm sorry

Are you????

Gray typed *Yes*. And she stared at her phone, waiting for Isabel's response. For minutes and more minutes, she stared and waited.
Nothing.
Finally, she sank to the couch and pushed out a
long breath.
Her phone buzzed. A text message from Hank.

Home yet? I could come there or you could come
here

The smile on her lips lasted a second before it
waned. She wasn't ready to leave the view or this

quiet yet. Thursday had been a day of unexpected noise and unexpected lies. Thursday had forced her to think way too much about her past. And that thinking made a ribbon of hot pain twist from her navel to her right side.

Pain—the only expected event.

Hank would help her relax, and now she thought of him, of his hands working their way around her body. She thought of his kisses across her back—and his hardness, she thought of that, too. All of it made her feel light as cotton.

But then it would be over, and he would fall asleep, and she would lie awake next to him with her eyes on the ceiling and—

No. Don't. Deal with it when, or if, you get to it.

She held her middle, stepped over to the moody, tree-trunk-looking abstract painting that hid a surveillance camera. Though her apartment was only nine hundred square feet, she still didn't want anyone entering it without her knowledge. But as she viewed the video, she saw that no one had entered. There'd only been one knock on the door, announcing the water bottle's arrival. Unless he was the Fly or Spider-Man, no man (or woman) could sneak in through the windows. Even firemen, with their tallest ladder, couldn't reach her, not here on the seventeenth floor. No one could enter except through the door.

Finally, she texted Hank—*home in 10 minutes, come here*—and included her address. She rarely invited guests to her home, but if shit was going down, she'd rather be on her territory than his. There was a Glock in the nightstand drawer, a hunter's knife beneath the couch cushions, a can of Mace in the medicine cabinet, and an ice pick in the potted fern in the solarium. Besides, Clarissa had performed a background check and Hank wasn't problematic and he probably wouldn't require her to use any weapon on him other than her killer sex appeal.

She said, "Sex appeal," aloud and chuckled. Amused, the Skipper stripped the yellow pillowcases from the pillows and replaced them with black. Then she changed the white sheets and the white comforter on the bed for the black sheets and the black comforter.

The bottle of Ketel One vodka was calling her from the ice cube bin in the freezer. The refrigerator coughed again, and Gray heeded the call. She shuffled to the bright white kitchen, made brighter by the painting of bright yellow dahlias. She found the five-pound bag of rice in the cupboard, dug through it to find a stainless steel shaker and a single martini glass. Behind the cans of broth, refried beans, and diced tomatoes, she found a jar of jumbo green olives and a small bottle of vermouth, and she made a perfect dirty martini. A treat now, she allowed herself just one bottle of vodka a year since she'd adopted tequila as her public profile liquor, the official booze of Grayson Sykes.

She closed her eyes as the vodka dribbled down her throat. Her knees sagged and her head fell back. She wanted more. *Needed* more. Only seven olives and a quarter of the Ketel One bottle remained, though, and it was just July. She finished the martini, chomped the two olives, washed and dried the glass and the silver shaker, then hid both in the bag of rice. She shoved the Ketel One back into the ice cube bin, shoved the jar of olives and vermouth back behind the cans of broth, refried beans, and diced tomatoes, then grabbed from the lower fridge shelf one of a million cans of cran-raspberry LaCroix sparkling water, her go-to sober alternative.

Body looser, she grabbed her phone and texted Hank. *Just got in.*

Since her vodka break, nothing had changed on the freeways. Once the Big One finally broke California off from the rest of the continent, once the state fell into the Pacific Ocean, every one of those cars would sink and their headlights would glow in the depths of the sea like phosphorescent deep-sea creatures with strange jaws and bulging blind eyes.

She chuckled—vodka thinking.

Her phone rang.

Nick's picture brightened the phone's screen. He was the only person in the world who possessed her true phone number. But if she had to, she'd burn him, too. He expected nothing less from her. *Don't hold on to something you can't leave behind in five seconds.* He'd taught her that. And then he had added, "Even me."

Phone in hand, she tapped the green Accept button. "Shouldn't you be spooning in Hawaii right now?"

Nick laughed. "You know better than that."

"Yeah, I do."

The biochemist now had a new name and a new job waiting tables and getting paid in cash. She was now hiding her Ph.D. and love of chemistry in a bag of rice and an ice cube bin.

"So?" Nick said. "Feeling better?"

"About the case? Don't know. I still have my reservations."

"Well," Nick said, "he called me."

"Who? Dr. O'Donnell?"

"Yep. Said you were rude."

"Oh?"

"Despite your personal feelings about him, you

need to be respectful, all right? He's a client. He's paying us."

Gray forced down the bile burning her throat, then caught Nick up on the Lincoln case.

"Something's strange," he said.

"Exactly."

"Grayson—"

"But if this guy hurt his girlfriend—"

"Then sniff it out. Get proof. Dive in and grow the fuck up."

"Excuse me?" The spaces behind Gray's eyes creaked with the threat of a headache.

Silence from Nick.

She pictured his tight mouth, his hand balled into a fist.

"If Ian hurt her," he said slowly, "you will find that out. You will see past his blond hair and blue scrubs, and if *she* needs help and protection from him, *we* know how to do that. Something *is* strange with this case, and you've seen strange before, correct?"

Gray nodded, even though he couldn't see her.

"If you need me for *anything*," Nick said, "call immediately. Okay?"

"Yup."

He waited a beat. "We good?"

"You're a national treasure." Her voice sounded shaky.

"And you're chicken soup for my soul. I'll be back in L.A. in a couple of days."

"Okie-dokie."

"You working right now?"

"Nope. I'm about to take a shower and call it a night." She didn't mention Hank.

But Nick was in the business of knowing *everything*.

He probably knew that Hank was just now zooming onto the 405 freeway in his blue Camaro. Knowing that Nick was all-knowing didn't stop Gray from pretending not to know that *he* knew.

Silence, then Nick said, "Good night, you."

She stared down at the crowded roadways and the bright lights. For a moment, she wished that her life had been normal, that Nick had been normal, that they could be normal together, falling in love properly, having babies, vacationing in Oahu, watching *MasterChef* on Wednesday nights and buying Christmas trees on the second Saturday of every December. *If wishes were fishes*, as her father used to say.

Back in her bedroom, Gray aimed the remote control at the television and found *Running Man* on cable. She padded to the bathroom and stripped off the stained silk shirt and wrinkled white linen pants. In the medicine cabinet, she found the still-full bottle of amoxicillin and popped one. She grabbed the new bottle of oxycodone from her purse and shook it as she wondered whether the dull thud in her side required a nuclear weapon.

No. She sat the narcotic on the medicine cabinet shelf and grabbed the vial of Aleve. After taking two, she stared at the diagonal surgical scar on the side of her navel. Small but angry. Yellowing and red hot. *Is that color normal?* And did she want Hank to see it?

"I'll wear a tank top." Then she brushed her teeth, twice—Hank would taste the vodka.

In the shower, lather, lather everywhere, over scars and knots and discolorations. She scrubbed away Thursday until her skin twinkled. She didn't wash her face—didn't have enough time to reapply her makeup. Even though nearly five years had passed, she could still glimpse her right eye, swollen and black. Back then, hiding that eye with inexperienced hands had taken her over an hour, and half a bottle of concealer. Eventually, she learned to use primer first and then foundation to even her skin tone. Once she'd reached pro levels, she harnessed the power of contour powders to make her face look slim and not swollen, and highlighter—she used that for its shimmer and magic. Bronzer made her look sun-kissed, as though she'd lain on a beach for days instead of on her bathroom floor for hours, stunned and scared.

RuPaul was her patron saint, then and now.

Like the other actors in this city, she only scraped off the paint once every light had dimmed and every eye had moved on to witness the next spectacle.

No one had seen Gray without her face in eight years.

Not since her name was Natalie Dixon.

16

The buzz from Gray's phone on the nightstand pulled her from the sleep she'd just found. The digital clock on the dresser blinked five fifty. The world was still as sunlight edged through the bedroom's vertical blinds. No dust motes had arrived yet to swirl in that young, golden light. The soothing scent of her favorite candle—hibiscus, lily, and melon—still lingered.

Gray had slept on her back. *Slept. Ha!* More like catnapped, fifteen-minute snatches of sleep spread over four hours. She'd dreamed a few of those times. Dreamed of driving in an endless desert, dreamed of an icy tornado slamming into Los Angeles and making everything twinkle blue, dreamed of her and Nick eating bright green ice cream out of a tuba.

Hank's arm now lay across her chest, a giant protecting his golden-egg-laying goose. He had been a magnificent lover. He'd easily flipped her upside down, not an easy feat with her weight gain, and he'd easily held her up against the dresser and the wall and above the headboard. If she'd worn an Apple Watch, the OS would have called 911, because her heart rate had soared and had scraped the underside of heaven. There were moments when she could have burst, like her appendix had almost burst before doctors caught it during that nick-of-time CT scan.

Being with Hank had been the most primal thing she'd experienced since . . . discovering In-N-Out's secret menu and eating an Animal Style Double Double with banana peppers, Animal Style French fries, and a Neapolitan milkshake in one sitting. Wonderful and dangerous, and she knew now, like she knew then, that she'd be filled with regret and nausea.

She hurt—a stitch in her side, twinges in her lower back—but she didn't mind taking one for the team, taking one for wellness.

Sunlight, flickering now like candles through the slats, danced across Hank's chiseled face. A perfect and beautiful creature, and in her heart, Gray felt . . . *nothing*. Not one thing. It was like the light now shimmering on his face. There, but . . . not really.

In one of her waking moments, she thought about making breakfast for her guest—but she didn't want him finding comfort here. *Eggs and sausage don't equate to marriage . . . Okay, coffee, that's it,* had been her last thought as she slipped back into another catnap.

Her phone buzzed again from the nightstand.

She thought of ignoring it but then remembered that incoming text messages would dictate her Friday. Isabel Lincoln was supposed to provide proof of life pictures—she could have been sending those now. Tea Christopher could have retrieved Kenny G. Ian O'Donnell may have decided to end this investigation altogether.

In other words, Gray needed to get up and start her day. But it was only 5:52.

Careful not to disturb her sleeping beauty, she reached to the nightstand for the phone.

Hank stirred but kept his arm across her chest, fee-fi-fo-fum. He stilled, then sank back into slumber.

Gray thumbprinted her way into Messages.

Rise and shine babe!

"Who is this?" she whispered.

The text message had been sent to the "Dating" phone number.

It wasn't Isabel Lincoln. Wasn't Ian O'Donnell. Wasn't anyone associated with the case. Not Nick, either. Not on this line.

A new text message slid on top of the first text message.

Been thinking about you all morning. I think about you every day.

And then, a picture.

Somewhere in the universe, her bridal portrait sat on a dining room table. That day, she'd worn a five-thousand-dollar white gown like Grace Kelly's high-necked, long-sleeved, rose-pointed dress. Also on that dining room table, beside her bridal portrait: a silver-slide nine-millimeter SIG Sauer.

That dress was rotting somewhere in a Clark County dump—Sean had poured a bottle of red wine over it during one of their arguments. He hadn't hit her that time, just destroyed the gown, something he claimed was his anyway, since he'd paid for it.

As for the SIG . . . Sean had pointed that gun at her the first time she told him that she was leaving. He had simply aimed it at her. His finger was nowhere near the trigger, but it didn't have to be. The menace of that weapon and its hard beauty had cowed her into stay-ing that night and 365 nights after that.

And now, ice cracked cold across Gray's face. Her skin and muscles hurt. That picture had exploded something deep inside of her. Gripping the phone, she inched from beneath Hank's arm, pulled on her robe, then crept to the living room. She tiptoed out to the solarium. Out in the world, there were cars, cars, cars down there and helicopters buzzing high, high, high in the sky, ready to report traffic on the tens.

She stared at the cars and thought about her and Nick's drive into Los Angeles on the 10 westbound, a transcontinental highway that started in Jacksonville, Florida, and ended in Santa Monica, California. She hadn't come from as far as Florida, but she had been tired and frightened and had resolved to get it right, to smile, laugh, and talk, and to never flinch if someone raised his hand to brush hair from her face or to ca-ress her cheek. She came to Los Angeles to live without fear. Now, here she was, in her haven in the heavens. Tired but not frightened. Flinching sometimes, but not all the time. Sleeping most nights without waking in a sweat.

Progress.

The phone buzzed again.

See you soon

Gray clicked into the Burner app and blocked that number.

See you soon?

How?

Was this a joke? Was this a *threat*?

She needed a pull from that frosty bottle of Ketel

One. Years ago, she wouldn't have hesitated to have a drink. Now, though . . .

Hank found Gray sitting out in the solarium. He had pulled on his boxers, and they had tent-poled in one place in particular—he wanted more of her. But most of Gray had shriveled into hard pellets that needed more than an erect penis to soften. The kisses he left on her shoulder and neck were not working— she kept her hands clutching her elbows.

How did Sean get my phone number?

Had she mistakenly written her number on some public-facing document? Had it somehow been linked to the phone she'd used back then, back when she'd worn his last name? Who had he paid to find her? What database had he used to search for her? When was the last time she'd done a background check on herself?

Because none of this was possible. None of this was *good*.

Sean didn't even *know* her anymore.

If he found her, what would he do? Once, during the second year of their marriage, she'd left him. Six hours had passed before he'd found her at their time-share on Lake Las Vegas. There, he'd fallen to his knees in tears. Begged her to forgive him. Promised that he'd never hurt her again. And she had believed him.

Sean had coaxed her back that time. Would he try to coax her this time? Or would he—

"You okay?"

Hank's baritone made her blink and finally notice him kneeling beside her. "Huh?"

His hands cupped her face. Those silver-blue eyes of his burned with concern. "Everything okay?" He leaned closer to her.

She flinched and leaned away from him.

He frowned.

She thought of vodka, and that made her smile. "Hey. Sorry. I'm just . . . caught off guard. Stupid work thing."

He said, "Ah," not knowing what she did for a living because he'd never asked.

Her smile widened. "Good morning, sunshine."

He peered at her, wary of the sudden switch. Was her cheer real or synthetic? Not knowing that 98 percent of Gray Sykes *was* synthetic, his face relaxed. "Good morning, beautiful." Then he leaned in to kiss her.

And Gray let him. And she let him touch her neck. And she let him caress her breasts and tweak her nipples. She let him take her in the solarium, in the sturdiest chair in the world, for all of the 110 and 101 freeways to see. And she played the part of the wanton woman, and the soldier and the vamp came together as the city awakened to the roar of helicopters and the crunch of fender benders.

Hank had to skip breakfast. "I need to hit the road," he said, pulling on his blue jeans. "Supply run to Northridge before traffic gets too crazy."

Gray's abdomen hated her for the theatrics out in the solarium. Still, she made a disappointed face—but not so disappointed that he'd change his mind. "You sure?"

Hank offered a muted smile. "Next time?"

"At least take a cup of coffee?"

He accepted her travel mug of Peet's House Blend and another kiss. He didn't ask if they'd do this again. He didn't say "See you later." They would get to that bridge—that is, if that bridge didn't get washed out by other things to do and other people to see.

As she closed the door, alone again, Gray was cool

with that committed noncommittal. She had plans anyway, like . . . walking over to her rattling refrigerator. All she had to do was reach for the freezer door handle and just . . . One sip. That's all she needed to smooth herself out. Sex in the solarium had fixed 70 percent of her frayed nerves, and the remainder could be remedied in less than five seconds with a cold drink distilled from 100 percent wheat.

Bad habits.

Sean had inspired the drunk in her.

She did a quick check on ORO for his license plates. No recent sightings of that SUV or sedan, but he could have rented a car. Borrowed a friend's car. Hired a car service . . .

Gray closed her eyes and took a deep breath. Then another. She tugged the door handle, the bottom one, and grabbed a can of LaCroix from the shelf. She popped the tab and guzzled half right there in the kitchen. The tingle of carbonation felt good on her tongue and she poured the rest of the can into the sink, ready to start her day.

Sober.

Good habits.

But she was sick of running, holding her breath, always, *always* watching her back.

In the bathroom, she took the antibiotic and a single oxycodone and resolved to visit a doctor on Sunday if the pain continued.

This time, as she showered, Gray scrubbed her face. Almond-colored makeup ran down her legs and swirled into the drain. She scrubbed behind her ears, because she painted that place, too. Her face felt so light and so clean, and she thanked her ancestors for skin that didn't flare with pimples, because damn, she'd be a giant zit by now.

Drying off, she studied her reflection in the steamy mirror. The naked woman standing there . . . the Skipper, who, once upon a time, had been as small as Mrs. Howell. Her attitude—that had been the biggest thing back then. According to Sean, her attitude had been the cause of chaos, the source of all that screaming and all that hurt. That's when the drinking had started. That's when the weight had come. *A fat slob*. That's what Sean had called her. That's what she had also believed . . . back *then*.

She also saw reflected in that mirror . . . scars, tiny ones, horrific ones, usually spackled and hidden for sixteen of the day's twenty-four hours. The scar beneath her lip had been made by his car key. The sickle-shaped one on her jawline had come from his fingernail. Each scar had grown larger and more violent, like tornadoes on the Fujita scale. Back then, she had pushed each violation away with "It's not that bad," to "It looks worse than it is," until the blood and the glisten of torn muscle and skin could no longer be ignored or covered with a simple bandage. He'd apologize, then present her with a gift that she readily accepted.

Yes, Gray knew firsthand about men who could turn charm on and off like a beer tap. Love letters and expensive sea salt caramels one day, spit-flecked lips and bugged eyes two weeks later. And Nick knew that Gray had firsthand knowledge about dangerous men, and he'd still given her this case.

Was this some sort of test?

Gray shivered now, not from the cold of being naked.

No.

She shivered because Sean had her number then.

And he had her number now.

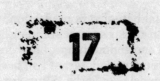

17

Gray ate scrambled eggs and toast for breakfast, chased by two cups of coffee. The oxycodone was working and fuzzy numbness spread across her abdomen. Feeling . . . *right*, and dressed now in a pink linen pantsuit (no one ever expected bad shit from a chick wearing pink linen), Gray sat at the breakfast bar and opened her laptop.

Clarissa had emailed her a list of databases to use as quick-search resources. Gray clicked on PACER, which stored case and docket information from federal, district, and appellate courts across the country.

PACER gave nineteen results for "Isabel Lincoln" in California alone.

Gray scanned the results. "And none of them live on Don Lorenzo Drive."

She clicked into Google.

Ian O'Donnell had no criminal record. On his LinkedIn page, past hospital administrators said that he was "dependable," and an "invaluable member of the team."

Still, all of this goodness, light, and education didn't mean that Ian O'Donnell had never smacked his girlfriend. It simply meant that no one had ever *charged* or *arrested* him for doing so. And he was a physician—he probably knew where to hit and how hard to hit to prevent Isabel from bruising.

Mom Naomi had always pinched the webbing between the toes of Gray's foster sister—Cherie said that pinching hurt more than hitting. Pinching had never left a long-lasting mark.

"Ian O'Donnell could be a pincher," Gray said now.

Or a bottom-of-the-foot beater.

Or maybe he liked shoving.

Maybe he humiliated Isabel instead.

Broke her favorite things.

Kept her from seeing friends.

Wrecked her in places that couldn't be seen on an X-ray.

A message from Clarissa.

Found 702 number. emailing you a profile of the person paying for the phone.

Isabel's mother, Rebekah Lawrence. Lived on Fifth Avenue in Inglewood. No social network accounts. One email account.

Not a lot of information, but at least Gray now had an address to visit.

Even though there was something sinister and nasty lingering beneath his request to find his girlfriend, Ian O'Donnell expected results by today, and all Gray had was a text message plea to be left alone, sent from someone else's phone.

"One last thing." She dialed Omar's number again.

And again the man didn't answer, and his voice mail box was still full.

She emailed Clarissa. *Could you find anything on this phone number? Thanks!* She paused, then added: *this one, too.* She sent the number possibly belonging to Sean Dixon.

Get going. She grabbed from the kitchen utility drawer a pair of disposable latex gloves that she used to touch chicken, and then she banged out the door.

The city was alive now. The sun and the sky were a crisp, ashy blue, and there'd been only one car accident on her drive down Crenshaw Boulevard. More than that, there were no ORO alerts, nor were there Range Rovers and Jaguars in her rearview mirror. Gray's phone stayed dark—still no texts from Tea, Isabel . . . or Hank. By now, he should've sent a *Damn, last night was da bomb* text, but he hadn't. That stung her ego some. Morning-after texts were simple courtesy.

Even though he left just three hours ago?

Yes, the Skipper determined, even then.

18

As Oleta Adams sang about life being a long, flat road, Gray split her attention between making a right turn off Arbor Vitae onto Fifth Avenue and eyeing any car that followed her. Sean Dixon's *Rise and shine* message had kick-started her day of paranoia, and although no ORO alerts had scrolled down her screen, that didn't mean he hadn't come to Los Angeles to confront her. *See you soon.* A threat and a promise, and the day would be long with over-the-shoulder checks. And wondering, *How did he get my number?*

Inglewood was home to Rebekah and Joseph Lawrence as well as the fabulous Forum, the Los Angeles Chargers, and an under-construction football stadium. For now, it remained an affordable middle-class neighborhood with Toyotas and Hondas in some driveways and beat-up Regals and Eldorados in others. Kids enjoying their summer break tossed footballs or performed wheelies on their bikes. Their parents, dressed in suits, nurse's scrubs, or bus uniforms, brushed ashes off their cars' windshields or sipped from travel mugs while gossiping with neighbors. Full steam ahead for the American Dream.

And there were witnesses—Sean wouldn't pull something with so many eyes.

Right?

Gray craved simpler living, like how she sometimes craved Twyla Tatum's meatloaf. Another one of Gray's foster mothers, Mom Twyla had the cheekbones of a gazelle and wore bright fuchsia lipstick that always stained her teeth. She could cook, with meatloaf being her specialty. But then, Gray remembered, that meatloaf had always given her the shits afterward.

Gray slowed, the closer she got to the middle of the block, and she parked a few feet away from the Lawrences' driveway.

A quick glance in the rearview mirror. No Sean and no English luxury cars.

Rebekah Lawrence was beautiful—that was Gray's first thought, as the older woman opened the passenger door of a gold Cadillac. A dead ringer for Clair Huxtable, with that feathered hair and those wise eyes. Rebekah Lawrence didn't deal in nonsense, not wearing that no-nonsense lilac pantsuit. She was the type of woman who could spot a lie coming from a mile away and would not hesitate to drag anyone in her driveway—for truth, justice, and the American Way—for all the neighbors to see.

Gray nestled her leather binder in the crook of her arm and walked toward the army-green ranch-style home with its brown shingled roof and neat white trim. She smiled.

Rebekah Lawrence said, "May I help you?" as Gray had opened her mouth to say, "Good morning." The older woman's voice was low and slow, the kind that asked you to fill out the form, *correctly* this time, and to come back *prepared*, or else she would make you do it again, all day if need be, and *I ain't got nothing but time, sweetheart.*

She reminded Gray of her forever-mother, Faye. *Nothing but time, sweetheart.*

"You're Rebekah Lawrence, yes?" Gray asked, closing in on her. "How are you today?"

"Depends on the next ten seconds."

Gray smiled wider. "It's no big deal. I'm just here to check on your daughter. To make sure she's okay."

Rebekah Lawrence cocked her head. "I need you to say more than *that*. You are . . . ?"

Gray handed the woman one of her new business cards.

Rebekah's eyebrows furrowed as she read aloud: "'Grayson Sykes, Private Investigator, Rader Consulting.' My daughter is fine. I just saw her on Sunday."

"That's good to hear. Has she been living with you?"

"Yes, for the last month." She squinted. "Who hired you?"

"Can't say, Mrs. Lawrence."

"I'm just confused, is all. I don't like being confused."

"Understandable. My client seems to think that your daughter has run away."

"Is that illegal now? She's a grown-up and can go wherever she wants."

"My client thinks she was under duress at the time and is concerned about her safety."

"She wasn't under duress on Sunday, and as far as I'm concerned, she's not missing, nor did she 'run away.' Not in my opinion, and I'm her mother."

Which is why the police had not become involved.

"Wait . . ." Rebekah Lawrence held up her hand. "I know who hired you, and . . ." She pressed that hand against her forehead. "Please tell him that we're working on it, okay? We're not rich people. I mean, we do okay, but ever since Joe's stroke . . . We have a lot going on right now."

Gray offered a comforting smile. "I hate piling on, but could you do me a small favor?"

"Maybe."

"Could you take a picture of the dog and Isabel holding today's newspaper?"

Confused eyes from Rebekah.

"Sounds ridiculous," Gray admitted, "but it's just so that I can show my client that—"

"The *dog*? And . . . *Isabel*?"

"Yes." When the older woman didn't speak, Gray said, "Sorry, I wasn't clear. I assumed you only had one daughter. Isabel."

"I have *two* daughters. And I thought you were talking about *Noelle*."

"No. Isa—"

Rebekah Lawrence was slowly shaking her head.

And the two women stared at each other as the neighbor's sprinklers clicked, as a passing Jetta boomed rap from its janky stereo, as an airplane thundered above their heads.

Rebekah Lawrence reached for her bag in the passenger seat of the Caddy.

Gray dug into her battered Liz Claiborne.

They both thrust pictures at each other.

Gray's picture was of the Mary Ann with the long ponytail and *Vogue* cheekbones.

Rebekah Lawrence's two pictures were of a pig-nosed, light-skinned woman with facial piercings and violet dreadlocks and another woman, with the same nose, darker skin, wearing a Princeton sweatshirt. Neither woman was Isabel. Neither woman had been in the wine tasting tribe pictures on Isabel's Facebook page or in the pictures around her condominium.

Had Clarissa given her wrong information? Was

there another Rebekah Lawrence who had borne a baby girl named Isabel?

"Do you know this woman?" Gray asked, holding up Isabel's picture.

Rebekah Lawrence gave a decisive nod. "Yes. That's Isabel."

"But she's not your daughter?"

"No. She's Noelle's friend." She held up the picture of the woman with the facial piercings. "Noelle stays with Isabel sometimes. I believe they met over at UCLA."

"Ah. Got it." This was a case of the Black Family: lots of play aunties and play cousins and everybody calling every older woman "momma" or "auntie." Growing up, she'd had "play family." Nick Rader— decades ago, he was like a brother to her. Even within her foster families, "Auntie" Charlene had been Mom Twyla's best friend. She'd bathed in Chantilly perfume and smoked skinny brown cigarettes. Charlene had always carried plastic-wrapped caramels in her purse and called Natalie "Li'l Bit" like that was her name. Auntie Charlene had helped Mom Twyla buy purses, jewelry, and cheese with money that the state had paid Twyla for fostering.

"Is Isabel okay?" Rebekah Lawrence asked now.

"We're hoping so. Do you know anything about Isabel's parents?"

"No clue."

Gray now wanted a copy of Isabel Lincoln's birth certificate. "When was the last time you saw her?"

"Maybe a few months ago. March?"

"How was she acting back then?" *Shit. I should be recording this.* Too late.

"She reminded me of a wounded bird," the older

woman said. "She's older than my daughter—Noelle is twenty-five and aimless. Always in trouble. Always running. A bit . . . *slick*, know what I mean? That's why I thought *you* were a process server or a bill collector."

Rebekah Lawrence sighed. "Kids these days are a bit slick. I'd hoped that she'd grow up some, since Isabel seemed so adult, but then Noelle met this *thug*, and he just made her worse. She and I had a big blowup about money and that's when she started living with Isabel. She stayed away for a few weeks, but she came back here. Now she's living with that boyfriend."

"Speaking of boyfriends, do you know Isabel's boyfriend, Ian O'Donnell?"

Rebekah Lawrence blinked at her. "Why would I know *him*?"

"He told me to talk to you."

"Talk to *me*? Why?"

"Because he believes you and Joe are Isabel's parents."

"I have no idea why he'd think *that*."

"Maybe she considers you to be like a mother to her?" Gray offered. "There's a picture of you two on her desk at her house and her job."

"I don't know her like *that*. I don't know Ian Whoever-he-is at *all*. And I really need to get to work right now."

Gray asked for Noelle's phone number.

"I'd rather have Noelle call you. But let me try to get her on the phone right now." Rebekah Lawrence dialed her daughter's number.

Gray watched a black Range Rover roll toward the Lawrence house—*Not Sean; not with that cheap, bubbled window tinting*—and listened as Noelle's phone rang . . . and rang . . . Finally, a female voice told the caller to leave a message. And so Rebekah Lawrence left a message.

Gray thanked the woman, turned to leave, but turned back again. "Who in your family handles phone service?"

Rebekah Lawrence sat her purse back on the Cadillac's passenger seat. "Noelle does. Phone, internet, and all that. To tell you the truth, Miss Sykes? It's all Greek to me."

Play moms. Missing women. Confused boyfriends . . .

Gray sighed. *It's all Greek to me, too, Clair Huxtable.*

LOVE, LOST

On the last Saturday of the month, Special Agent Dominick Rader stood on the porch of 787 Lyndon Street in Monterey, California. In his arms, he held bags filled with eggs, bread, and paper towels—and since Natalie was home on spring break, he included a box of Cap'n Crunch with Crunch Berries. He smiled at the college senior, his gray eyes bright even as the smell of death rolled past him and mixed with the hopeful aromas of evergreens and the Pacific.

Natalie was always thrilled to see Dominick Rader. He always brought light into the house, brought light into her heart. Nowadays, the Grayson house needed light from all sources.

Cancer killed everything.

Natalie's mother, Faye, was still sharp in her sky-blue knitwear, but a little heavier from stress and a diet of fast food. On this morning, she met Dominick in the hallway. "You don't have to do this, Dom. It's such a long drive down from the city."

"I don't mind coming, Mrs. G.," Dominick said. "You and Vic would do it for me." Then he followed Natalie into the kitchen and together they unpacked the groceries. He removed the empty carton of eggs from the fridge. Changed the old box of baking soda and replaced it with a new box. He whistled as he worked, usually Nirvana, sometimes Pearl Jam.

After he and Natalie straightened the kitchen, she led him to the master bedroom, the source of that smell of decay. That's where he found his boss, Victor Grayson, now a whisper of himself at sixty years old, a brown-skinned husk of a man, lost in a hospital bed.

"Looking good, sir," Dominick said.

"Always," Victor answered, his voice still strong. "Nat and Faye are good nurses."

Seven years before, Faye and Victor Grayson had adopted fifteen-year-old Natalie Kittridge. Since then, Faye had taught their only child the art of conversation, ways to spot a liar, how to manage a bank account, how to make a proper martini, how to make a proper pitcher of lemonade. Faye had regularly taken Natalie to the library and to bookstores, and before Victor's diagnosis, they often ate in restaurants that utilized several pieces of flatware.

Natalie had learned that there were "everyday" plates and special occasion plates with scalloped edges rimmed in gold. She had become the proud owner of pink razor blades and a separate kind of lotion for her face. *Her face!*

She'd been a Baptist, an Adventist, an Episcopalian. She'd been a vegetarian and a carnivore. An independent and a socialist. She had believed in science in May but, by Christmas, was a believer in herbs and Mercury in retrograde. Like most kids in foster care, she'd lived as a chameleon until Faye and Victor Grayson rescued her.

The Graysons saw that she was a bright kid, eager to learn, not scared of much. They put her in a club soccer team and enrolled her at a girls' school. They gave her a bedroom, a giant box with sea-green walls. The big bay window was true to its name and she spotted the Pacific Ocean *right there*. And she could decorate her room however she wanted. Posters of Michael Jordan, New Edition, and Janet Jackson covered her walls. She filled her tall bookcase with Tom Clancy, Stephen King, V. C. Andrews, and Jackie Collins. There was a lock on the door that she'd stopped using on her fiftieth night in the Graysons'—no, *her*—home. "This is *your* house," Faye always told her. "You have nothing to fear here."

The men who had visited the Grayson house were as tall and muscular as the men who'd visited Mom Twyla's home. These men carried guns, too, and they also cursed. But these men talked with her new father about presidents and rule of law, amendments and old Scotch whiskey. They were a different flavor of dangerous, and Natalie's nerves knew the difference.

She had listened and performed and excelled, to please Victor and Faye more than anything. She graduated high school with gold cords around her neck and a full scholarship to Cal State, Fresno. All of this to keep them from changing their minds about her and dropping her back at Casa Del Mar Group Home. But they'd kept her, and they'd legally adopted her. The Graysons loved her.

It had been a good life.

Even with the drives to doctors' appointments and nurse visits, Faye hadn't stopped being Natalie's mother. She never sweated and never swore, even now. Her outfits were still the color of flames on weekdays and the colors of Atlantis on Saturdays and Sundays. Freckles still danced across the bridge of her caramel-colored skin, even though her cheeks were often wet with tears.

Victor couldn't perform daddy duty now, but before his sickness he had taught Natalie self-defense and weapons, chess and justice. He had been a big man, six five and as thick as the trees surrounding their home. His hair, when he'd had it, had lived in a black man's crew cut, and his eyebrows had been tangled tufts of fishing lines.

Yeah, a good life, until . . .

On this morning, Dominick Rader gave Victor a shave, changed his catheter, and emptied his bag. Then he sat in the armchair beside the bed and told tales about the latest Bureau fuckup, about this girl Allison and that girl Vanessa. He whispered details that neither Natalie nor Faye could hear in the living room. Both men roared with laughter, though. Laughter was good.

Once Victor had fallen asleep, Natalie joined Dominick on a drive for burgers.

"You're exaggerating." His eyes bugged at the college student seated across from him.

Natalie shook her head. "They played for six hours straight. No seats, all standing. I swear I got a contact high, there was so much weed smoke in the air. I will never, not ever, listen to a George Clinton–Parliament album ever again, you can't make me, no, I won't do it, not after last Saturday night."

Dominick swirled French fries through a puddle of ketchup. "I didn't think you were into P-Funk like that."

"I'm *not*." She took a big bite from her burger. "Not like *that*. Six fucking *hours*?"

"Lemme guess: you went because of a guy."

Natalie blushed. "He likes horns. Parliament; Tower of Power; Earth, Wind and Fire . . ."

"And after?"

"And after, nothing happened. I stood for six hours and I didn't get a hug, didn't get a kiss, didn't get one damned thing. Fucker."

He cocked an amused eyebrow. "Obviously not."

They laughed big, like he had laughed with Victor. Just a normal college student with her father's favorite FBI agent.

He drove Natalie back to Lyndon Street, where healthy green trees shot up, up, up into an impossibly blue sky softened by sea salt and the everlasting roar of waves. Before driving back up to San Francisco, Dominick checked on Victor. Then he hugged Faye and walked with Natalie back to his Ford.

"It means the world to him," Natalie said, tears bright in her eyes, "you visiting him like this. You're like a son to him."

He watched the swaying branches of the pine trees. "Twice a month doesn't feel like it's enough. It *isn't* enough."

She smirked. "Because you have so much free time."

"I know. Still . . ."

"It's not gonna be long now." Those words were sludge in her throat. "Mom wants me to go back to school, since I'm graduating, but I have a feeling it'll be a turnaround trip."

"You'll call me?"

"He's making me memorize your number."

"Forwards and back?"

"Yup."

"I'll be here," he said, meeting her gaze. "Always."

Gray's mind clicked back to her visit to Isabel Lincoln's condo. Those clothes on the floor of the spare bedroom—did they belong to Noelle Lawrence? Were Noelle and her thug boyfriend somehow involved in Isabel's disappearance?

Gray didn't know, although she *did* know that Rebekah Lawrence was tired of her daughter's nonsense. Trouble still followed the put-together woman like the stink of wet trash on her designer pumps. Despite the Cadillac and the expensive purse, the pantsuit and the hair, Rebekah Lawrence was still dealing with hood shit—all because of Noelle. And now, Noelle's friend Isabel, the stable one, had disappeared and some random P.I. had showed up at her house?

"Hood shit," Gray said.

The sun was high and heat spiked through the Camry's windows. Not only had Gray *not* talked to people from yesterday, she had added another name to her list: Noelle Lawrence.

And despite Black Family, it was still strange that Rebekah Lawrence didn't really know Isabel even though her picture now sat in the missing woman's condo and workplace.

One more glance at ORO—no recent notifications—and Gray sped out of Inglewood.

Mount Gethsemane AME Church was known for

its rocking services but also for its location—across the street from the best soul food restaurant in Los Angeles. Dulan's on Crenshaw had been a blessing on those nights when Gray needed comfort food. The kind of food Miss Francine, another one of her foster mothers, had cooked. Miss Francine specialized in yams thick with butter and brown sugar. Tart collard greens speckled with gifts of cubed ham. Smothered chicken that singed tongues and filled bellies.

Pastor Bernard Dunlop had consumed plenty of pork chops and black-eyed peas. The large man wore many-gemmed rings on both thick ring fingers, and a cross as big as a stop sign dangled from a gold rope around his thick neck. He had a nice smile, though, which told Gray that she could tell him *anything* and that anything she told him, he would personally take to God in prayer. He had done that for Isabel Lincoln even though he really didn't know her.

"I do know she's a friend of Sister Tea's," he said, stirring Splenda into his cup of tea. "They met right after Tea's parents died in a car accident, back in 2017. Both she and Sister Isabel came down during an altar call once, after I'd shared a word about freedom in truth from the book of John, eighth chapter. How Jesus forgives and encourages us to walk from darkness into the light. *'For if you do not believe that I am He, you will die in your sins.'*

"Sister Isabel was taken with this message, and she just . . . *wept*. I understood why Sister Tea was crying, and I admit, I thought that Isabel was in an illicit relationship and that my words were getting to her. I'm not here to judge, though. I'm just God's usher." He reached for the plate of cookies on the coffee table. "Help yourself. You look like the cookie type."

"Cookies, doughnuts, ice cream . . . I'm trying

to cut back, but . . ." Gray took an oatmeal-raisin cookie. Who was she to deny delicious desserts offered by one of God's ushers?

"Isabel came down to the altar a few more times after that," Pastor Dunlop continued. "Once, I talked about victory and making it through the valleys of despair—she cried during that. And then I preached about finding a path out of turmoil and to peace. She fell apart again, and while I consider myself a talented speaker . . ."

He tapped the spoon against the cup's rim. "There was something happening with this young lady, and so, afterward, I pulled her aside and offered to pray with her. She accepted my offer, and . . . well . . ."

"Yes?" Gray sipped from her own teacup.

His eyes dropped to his hands. "Sister Isabel confided in me. She told me that she was being abused. I wasn't *shocked* by the allegations per se—the church, unfortunately, is filled with forgotten women, women who've never once been treated right or treated with dignity. No, I was shocked once she told me about *who* had abused her. Her boyfriend, a *doctor*. She told me that he had forced her to deny her blackness, too, and even worse than that, he threatened to kill her. She told me that no one would ever believe her if she spoke up. And then she told me that all of this was her fault."

The teacup in his hands was shaking. "And then she lifted her shirt and she showed me a bruise, here . . ." He touched his left rib cage. "Said that he'd slammed her into the dresser. And then she showed me finger-shaped bruises on her left bicep. When she was showing me this, there was this . . . *look* on her face. *Defiance. Pride.*"

Gray wanted to drop her head, which was heavy

now with memories of bruises that had discolored her own body. She remembered the shame as nurses had iced her injuries and stitched the bloody, raggedy parts of her back together again. She'd never felt proud in those moments. Or defiant. Not ever. Not even now, years later.

What was there to be proud of? That she'd *survived*? Roaches would survive a nuclear war—they certainly didn't deserve a parade.

Cancer. Tsunamis. Plane crashes. That shit came out of nowhere, and *those* people, *they* survived. She'd known that Sean was a vicious asshole with quick hands and a heart filled with mercury. *Danger, danger, danger* had always sparked off him, and once upon a time, that had made her wet and willing. And stupid—she'd been so fucking stupid. And to avoid her culpability, to keep from thinking about her stupidity and his violence and her fetish for his violence, she drank. And she stayed drinking. Maybe not drunk. Not all the time. But always drinking. All the time.

She didn't sense those sparks with Ian O'Donnell, not that she was the ultimate Abuse Hunter. Still . . . not a single spark?

"Did she ask you to do anything?" Gray now asked Pastor Dunlop. *Like help her with the big secret, the one that would destroy Ian O'Donnell?*

"I asked her if she'd told the authorities. She said that they'd never take her word over a doctor's. She didn't want a restraining order, either—we all know that TROs and police can exacerbate the problem."

"So?"

"*So*, I prayed with her, asked the Lord to protect her. I wanted to do more than that, but she stopped coming to church at the end of May, and Tea stopped coming about two weeks ago." Pastor Dunlop's shaky hand covered his mouth, and those warm eyes filled with tears.

Gray touched his arm. "She's okay. I've been texting with her. I'm thinking that she left to avoid the worst. But I'm hoping for the best, too, okay? You keep praying. You stay faithful."

Because some women *did* make it out alive. Some women *did* successfully escape. Yeah, they *survived*. And despite Gray's reluctance, despite her disdain to consider herself as such, she—*they*—were survivors.

20

It was now moments away from eleven o'clock and Dulan's had not opened yet. So Gray returned to the Camry and to Oleta Adams pressing her to just get there if she could.

Back at Isabel's condo, filled trash cans still lined the curbs, and a black, late-model Chevy Malibu was parked where Gray had parked yesterday. The only other spot available was on the condo side of the street, in front of a beat-up Saab with Arizona plates.

Kevin Tompkins, the good soldier, exited the security gates. Today he wore blue jeans and a butter-yellow polo. He looked up and down Don Lorenzo Drive and then jogged to a gray Honda SUV parked behind the black Chevy. He lifted the rear gate, grabbed a Target bag from the cargo space, then wandered up the block. He stopped at a trio of trash bins in front of the next condo development over. He threw cautious glances up and down the street again, then opened the lid of the middle bin and shoved the Target bag deep into its mouth.

Nonchalant now, Kevin Tompkins strolled, *la-di-da*, back toward the entry gate shared by Isabel Lincoln and his mother.

"What's in the bag?" Gray wondered aloud.

Blood rushed like fizzy water through her veins. This was unrelated to Isabel Lincoln's case, but who didn't like a good mystery? She'd always been the nosy kid, the Negro Nancy Drew. Maybe not asking *Why?*, but always wondering, always suspicious, always finding out . . . Like "finding out" that Mom Twyla and Auntie Charlene were girlfriends in the romantic way, kissing and hugging when they thought no one was around. Like "always wondering" why she'd been abandoned by the two people who'd created her. Like "always suspicious" of every person she'd ever met, including Nick, including herself, including Faye and Victor, who had finally adopted her and had saved her from the system.

What is in that freakin' bag?

Her curiosity was jonesing to solve this mystery. But then she heard the worst sound in the world. A sound that heralded the beginning of the end as soon as you needed to retrieve something from a trash bin that's about to be emptied. That's the sound she heard several blocks behind her—and a glimpse in the Camry's mirrors confirmed: a blue and white trash truck on its way down the hill.

Kevin Tompkins smiled as the truck slowly made its way down Don Lorenzo Drive.

What the hell did he toss in the bin?

Whatever it was, he needed it gone. And he now stood in front of the entry gate, waiting for it to disappear.

Not yet. The truck had two more stops, and it growled as its metal claw snatched a bin from the curbside.

That Target bag can't be good. Cuz why is he waiting for that truck?

A gun? A bloody knife? Arsenic? Counterfeit dollar bills?

The security gate opened. Mrs. Tompkins, wearing a pink and purple floral housecoat said, "Kevin, if you ain't gonna do it—"

"Mom," he snapped, turning away from the trash truck. "I told you—"

"And I told *you*," she said, wagging her finger at him. "It's broken and I'm missing my show cuz you don't wanna stop what *you* doing."

"Can I get five minutes? Just five minutes?" He glanced back to the truck.

The truck wasn't moving. The trash guys were shooting the breeze with an old man wearing a one-piece jumpsuit.

"You're being an asshole right now," the old lady warned. "Actin' just like your daddy."

Kevin Tompkins didn't move from his spot.

"Boy, don't make me ask you again."

"Mom." He threw another glance in the truck's direction—the truck was growling again. "Fine." He stomped back through the gates.

Gray could see the soldier lingering in the walkway.

The truck was now at the end of the block.

Mrs. Tompkins's front door slammed shut. Kevin had gone inside.

Gray opened the door and slipped out to the curb. She peeked over the trunk of her car.

Kevin and his mother were no longer outside, but it wouldn't take long for the soldier to fix the television.

Crouching, Gray darted from the Saab to the 4Runner, the Volvo to the Fury. It was hot—ninety degrees already—but the anxious scooting from car to car was the culprit behind her sweaty armpits and the chilled trickles of perspiration down her backbone.

The trash truck was so close that she could smell the old meat, the spilled beer, the rotten diapers. She jammed to the middle bin just as the truck pulled to a stop in front of it.

"Lemme guess," the trash guy said to her. "Accidentally threw something away?"

Gray flushed. "My daughter threw out a bag that . . ." She winced as she touched the middle bin's handle and dug in deep to pluck out the Target bag.

Nauseous, she backed away as the truck's metal claw grabbed the bin from the curb.

The contents in the Target bag shifted. Papers? Magazines? What could be inside? Whatever it was belonged to her now—that was the law. She didn't head back to her car, didn't want Kevin to see her with his trash. Instead, on feet she could no longer feel, she tromped up the block and rounded the corner.

She needed to wash her hands.

She needed to peek into the bag.

Dueling directives kept her mind racing as she happened upon a pocket park, one of those swatches of green frequented by seniors doing tai chi and new moms blowing bubbles at their gurgling babies. And those things were happening now, as Gray slid onto a bench. She took a deep breath and opened the bag.

On first glance, she saw nothing special. In context, Kevin had guarded this bag as though it had been the last black market kidney in a world filled with deathbed diabetics.

A closer look: two pairs of silk panties, a tube of lavender and eucalyptus lotion, a black hair scrunchie. There also were crumpled papers that had been torn from a spiral-bound notebook and filled with words written in blue ink.

> *You are beautiful and you have a beautiful spirit. I love you. That sounds creepy coming from someone you barely know but I can't stop thinking*

Thinking what? The author hadn't finished the sentence or the sentiment.

The second note, this one in green ink, read:

> *Isabel why haven't you responded to my letters?????*

The third note, block print, black ink:

DEAR ISABELLE, TIME IS RUNNING OUT. YOUR SILENCE BRINGS ME SO MUCH PAIN. I WILL DIE FOR YOU. THESE ARE NOT IDLE WORDS. IF YOU KEEP IGNORING ME I DON'T KNOW WHAT I WILL DO TO YOU OR TO ME.

YOURS TRULY,
K.

Gray's hands were shaking, and she'd stopped breathing. And now the sun was too bright, and now the new mothers were ghosts and the slow-moving seniors were wisps of moving air.

Was Kevin Tompkins stalking Isabel?

Were these silk panties hers?

More important than that, how had he *left* Isabel when he last saw her?

Germy and weak-kneed, she tromped back to Don Lorenzo Drive.

Kevin Tompkins's Honda SUV was gone—he had probably left thinking that his cache of scary shit was now on its way to a landfill, gone forever.

He didn't know, though.

A ghost had found his cache of scary shit and his problems were only beginning.

21

The day had been full of unsettling surprises—Sean's text message, then unsettling surprises one through six—and it wasn't even noon yet. That's what Gray was thinking as she plodded back to Isabel Lincoln's condominium. That, and then, *Who the* hell . . . ?

A white guy was now banging on Isabel's front door with one meaty fist while the other fist hung at his waist like a rump roast. He was an English bulldog come to life, stuck in an ill-fitting blue suit. He looked moist and sticky, like he smelled of beer and bananas.

Gray crept past the gate, tiptoed to the end of the block, and slipped back into the Camry.

If Bulldog didn't exit from the security gate, that meant he'd been let in. *But by whom?*

If he *did* leave, well, why had he come here in the first place?

She stowed the Target bag beneath the front passenger seat, then checked her phone's charge—80 percent. She aimed the camera lens at the gate, being sure this time to press the red Record button. She stated the time, the date, and all that she'd observed up to this point on this, the twelfth day of July. Then she shut up and waited to see what Bulldog would do next.

Fortunately, she didn't have to wait long. The man stomped out of the gate with a phone to his ear. He tromped across the street, then climbed into the black

Chevy Malibu. Still talking on the phone, he started the car's engine, but he didn't drive away.

As he sat there, Gray scribbled down his license plate number, then called Clarissa.

"Hey," the younger woman chirped, "I'm about to find the Omar number—"

"Awesome. I'm doing surveillance and I need you to run this plate for me right now."

Seconds later, Clarissa said, "2008 Chevy Malibu . . . registered to . . . Stuart Ardizzone."

"Can you run that name through, please?"

"Run it where?"

"I don't know—whichever database tells you shit."

"Umm . . ."

"Lady's choice. I'll be in the office in a couple of hours."

"Oh! I made reservations at that French restaurant? Bardot Brasserie at the Aria? We can go there for my bachelorette—"

"Sounds good. Gotta go. See you soon."

The Malibu made a three-point turn in the middle of Don Lorenzo Drive, then sped past Gray's Camry. He didn't even look in her direction.

But she saw more of him—his unfortunate underbite and a cauliflower ear that looked as meaty as his hands. With that ear, he could've been a cop or a boxer. He may not have been Stuart Ardizzone—could be just driving the man's Malibu. Whoever he was, he obviously didn't know that Isabel Lincoln hadn't entered or exited that condo since May 27.

Should I follow him, or . . . She sat there, clutching the steering wheel, not sure what to do next. She'd had a plan, but now, with Bulldog's arrival . . . More than a minute passed while she sat there, wondering. And then the question of whether to follow the mysterious man no longer mattered—he was long gone.

Mrs. Tompkins didn't like the looks of the man at all. The old woman had come out to the breezeway as soon as Gray closed the security gate.

"You see that guy who just left?" Gray asked her.

Mrs. Tompkins nodded. "He kept banging on the door like she would be off in there."

"Izzy would never hang out with a guy like that. You ever see him before?"

"Once. Week before the Fourth of July. I ain't like the looks of him then and I don't like the looks of him now."

"Have you noticed any other strange people dropping by?"

"Oh . . ." The old woman rubbed her chin. "There's the girl with purple braids—she used to stay with Isabel from time to time."

Noelle Lawrence had purple locks.

"She came ringing my doorbell after she tried to get into Isabel's condo. I ain't open my door, not with her looking all crazy, with them things stuck in her lips and her nose and all them tattoos . . . Ugh." Mrs. Tompkins frowned. "She could've come in here and stabbed me. Nuh-uh."

Was *Noelle* supposed to claim the mail Mrs. Tompkins had kept for Isabel?

The old woman was shaking her head. "I can't even understand how Isabel had her living off in the Gardners' place anyway. They used to argue, too, and Isabel kicked her out."

"When was the last time the purple braids lady come by?"

"Maybe a week or two after Isabel left. Looking crazy like always."

"Anyone else?"

"I already told you about the other man. The big, black, rough-looking one. He knew better than to knock on my door." She sucked her teeth. "All of a sudden, I'm seeing all these shady-looking people around here."

"And when was *that*? When the big black dude stopped by?"

"A week after the purple-haired girl came round."

Had that been Noelle's thug boyfriend?

"Anyone else?" Gray asked.

"Nah. I try to stay outta people's business."

Gray offered an apologetic smile. "I hate to be a bother, but could you let me in? I—"

"Of course, Maya." She reached into her housecoat and plucked out two wrapped cough drops, a neatly folded handkerchief, and that pink ribbon holding three keys. "Just give 'em back to me later. One of those is the mailbox key, another one is the house key, and the third one . . . I don't know what the third one's for. Anyway, don't lose 'em. I'd hate for her to think that she can't trust me. Oh. Before I forget." The old woman ducked back into her condo.

Gray stood in the doorway.

A talk show blared on the television.

Mrs. Tompkins pushed the Mute button on the television's remote control. "Kevin *just* fixed it for me right before you came, so I don't wanna turn it off. He's a good son."

A good son and a pervert.

"That was nice of him to do. He come by whenever he's in town?"

Mrs. Tompkins pawed through a sideboard drawer. "Oh, he ain't posted anywhere right now. I'm glad, cuz he can take care of me, like sons are supposed to take care of their mothers. Them ex-wives of his ain't never understood that. But he knows—his momma *always* comes first. That's how nice boys are. Where is that . . . It's in here somewhere . . ."

Nice boys. Boys who would never hurt a fly. Boys who were always misunderstood, who fell head over heels for the wrong tramp, the slut after his money, the whore who attacked his manhood. Nice guys—like Ian O'Donnell—who just happened to be in the wrong place at the wrong time and *bam!* That Jezebel *made* him hit her, *made* him steal or kill or . . .

That's what Sean's mom had thought. Sean could do no wrong in Loni Dixon's eyes. Bruises had been a result of thin skin; cuts came from moving away at a strange angle; threats were just words. *Stop being so sensitive. Be lucky. You got a nice car, a nice house, and he comes home at night. You don't even have to work a job. Don't call me again with that nonsense.*

And so it was with Mrs. Tompkins and her nice boy Kevin.

"They never liked us," the old lady sniffed. "The ex-wives, that's who I'm talking about. Jesmyn, his first wife, was an awful, awful woman. Drank a *lot*. And the other one . . . Oh, what's her name? Kelly, Kelsey . . . That one *worked*. That was always her excuse. 'I'm *working*, Kevin. I'm *tired*, Kevin.' She was *lousy* is what she was. She stopped speaking to me and Arnie back when he was alive. That was fine with me." She lifted her chin and poked out her bottom lip.

"So, is Kevin single now?" Gray asked.

The old lady stopped her search and smiled. "Why? You interested?"

Gray shrugged, played coy.

"You ain't like them at all. See, Jesmyn, she was only with him for his military benefits, and the other one, she kept nagging him about how come he ain't been promoted. She never gave him a chance. And she was jealous of me."

"Izzy mentioned Kevin a few times."

Mrs. Tompkins flicked her hand. "Now, I like Isabel, but she's something of a tease." She piled envelopes on top of the sideboard. "Isabel would smile at him—I seen her do it—but then, she'd tell him *No, I don't wanna go to this* or *No, I don't wanna go to that.* He'd send her flowers, but she'd bring them to me, tell me that it was sweet of him to do but that she didn't wanna send him the wrong message. But then, the next day, she'd go back to smiling at him and then turning him down. He just wanted to take her to dinner."

"Could it be Kevin's mistake?" Gray asked. "That her smiling was just being polite?"

The old woman glared at Gray.

What was the thought? On dates, a man worried about the woman rejecting him and the woman worried about the man killing her?

Gray had been polite to men who'd thought that her smile meant "blow job." Men had thrown bottles at her for not responding to their catcalls, or they had dumped Special K into her vodka tonics when she had responded *No, thanks* and had turned the other way. Men told her all the time to smile, and when she didn't smile, they called her a bitch.

"Sometimes, men don't understand," Gray said now, those words making her gag. "Unfortunately, they get in trouble for simply not understanding."

The old woman's eyes shifted to the muted television. "This one girl dropped the charges against Kevin, but only if he gave her some money. He met her up in Washington. He ain't mean her no harm. It was all a misunderstanding.

"See . . . he was in her apartment—and what kind of girl lives alone anyway? Anyway, he was in her apartment and *she* says that he was trying to steal some of her . . . *personal items*. But Kevin told *me* that he'd stayed there overnight before and that he'd left some of his clothes, and so he was only looking for them."

Gray's mind screamed, *Your son's a liar! He's a stalker! A panty thief!* "I can see where there'd be a misunderstanding."

"All she wanted was his money."

"How much did he have to pay her?"

"Around six thousand—oh." Mrs. Tompkins swiveled to the foyer. "It's over there." She returned to the doorway and pulled from the doorknob a grocery bag filled with mail. "While you're here, let me give you . . ." She handed the bag of mail to Gray. "You can go through and sort it all out. I've been collecting her mail since she left."

"I'll do that today. Izzy texted me this morning. She got held up and won't be back until Sunday or so. It's her birthday today and some friends of ours surprised her with a quick trip."

Frowning, Mrs. Tompkins plopped down in a chair. "Oh no. Kevin's gonna hate hearing that. He's been looking forward to seeing her." A pause, then: "You happen to be going over near Fox Hills Mall today?"

"Maybe."

"Could you take him his lunch? I forgot to give it to him. He works at the recruitment center, the one over by the food court? I'd drive over, but my hip . . ." She winced and rubbed her left side. "I shouldn't be driving."

"Anything to make it easier for you. You've been so helpful. Oh . . . Somehow, Morris came up in my last conversation with Izzy. She just started crying her eyes out. I never found out how he died. Did I hear that he was poisoned?"

Mrs. Tompkins sighed. "I feel just awful about that. We was having rodent problems, and I told Kevin to put out some poison to kill 'em, and somehow Morris got into it and . . ." She clutched the front of her housecoat. "I told Isabel that I was sorry. Gave her money for it. Two thousand dollars, even though Morris wasn't no purebred, just an old orange cat. But I felt just awful about it."

So . . . Ian O'Donnell didn't kill the cat after all. But Isabel had told Tea that he had. *Why?* To make him sound worse than what he was?

"You know what else I'm supposed to give you?" Mrs. Tompkins shuffled back to the kitchen, plucked an envelope from beneath a refrigerator magnet. "A friend—I'm guessing that's you—was supposed to pick this up way back in June. It got here but ain't nobody asked me for it. I didn't wanna put it in that bag with the other mail. Looks like it got a check inside."

Gray studied the envelope—JCI Insurance Services—then said, "I'll be sure that she gets it. She probably called JCI looking for it."

"Must be nice, not having to worry about money coming in. Just make sure she gets it."

"Oh. I'll be sure. I'll let her know." *And that's when I'll meet her for sure.*

Money always pulled people from deep, dark spaces.

22

Beatrice Tompkins reminded Gray of Mom Naomi, the ancient senior citizen who'd fostered little Natalie only to keep food in the apartment. Natalie's two-month-long presence in that stuffy, overheated unit meant milk, bread, and grits. The orphan got a toilet that worked, and the old woman got round steak and orange juice. Over warmed Hostess fruit pies, the orphan would listen to the old woman read from the book of Daniel. He'd overcome adversity, walked through fire, went from prisoner to the second in command. Naomi had prophesied that, one day, Natalie would be Daniel. "From vic*tim* to vic*tor*," Naomi had said. "Just you wait."

Gray stuck Isabel's house key into the lock.

Am I a victor now? Sneaking into people's houses?

The condo still smelled of bleach and bananas. The only sound was the steady and smooth hum of the refrigerator. She slipped on the latex gloves and then held her breath as she flipped the light switch.

Empty couch.

No Isabel.

At the small dining room table, Gray opened the grocery bag from Mrs. Tompkins and sorted through Isabel's mail.

Gas and light bills addressed to Ian O'Donnell, thirty days past due.

July *Vogue* to Isabel Lincoln.

Coach sale postcard to Elyse Miller.

Offer from T-Mobile to Rebekah Lawrence.

Mail Boxes Etc. promo card to Elyse Miller.

Honda Financing bill to Ian O'Donnell.

There was a greeting card, but its envelope didn't have a postmark. Her address had been written in green ink by a familiar hand—Kevin Tompkins's hand. Unlike the notes he'd written and tossed, the soldier hadn't been able to snatch back this card in time.

Mail check complete, Gray crept over to the bottom of the staircase.

It was dark up there.

Gray swallowed—she wasn't supposed to be here. Isabel hadn't given her permission. Neither had Ian. She glanced at the front door and thought about slipping on the security chain. But then if someone *did* try to come in but was blocked from entering, they would know *for sure* that someone was there.

She climbed the stairs and was trembling by the time she reached the second story. She crept past the guest room and reached the master bedroom. Before entering, she listened . . .

Her booming heart . . .

The quiet hum of a healthy fridge . . .

She hustled over to the closet and reached in the corner, beneath the darkness and the dresses and winter coats. Her hand hit hard steel and she pulled the object to the light.

A metal lockbox.

She found the tiny key beneath the bundles of lingerie.

Outside, a door slammed.

Gray's breath caught in her chest and she froze.

Footsteps tapped against the pavement.

Hinges on the entry gate squealed.

Bam! The gate.

Footsteps echoed through the breezeway.

A door slammed close.

But it wasn't Isabel Lincoln's door.

Gray stuck the key into the lock.

Click.

There was a Social Security card ending in 6303, for Isabel Lincoln. There was also a birth certificate and pictures showing a bruise beneath Isabel's left arm, a purpling lump on her forehead, another bruise beneath her black eye, and a cut on the inside of her lower lip.

Gray groaned. Who'd done this, Ian or Kevin?

Both. Maybe Ian had beaten Isabel. Maybe Kevin had rescued Isabel. But once she rejected Kevin, he had killed her. Maybe.

Gray scanned the birth certificate. Christopher and Hope Walters Lincoln listed as parents. She took pictures of the birth certificate. She took pictures of the Social Security card and those snapshots of Isabel's injuries.

Searching in the bottom of the lockbox, Gray's knuckles brushed against soft plastic.

It was a sandwich baggie filled with . . .

Fluffy tufts of brown hair and fingernail clippings.

She peered back into the box. There was another bag, also filled with hair and fingernails.

"If I took this . . ." she asked aloud. *What would I do with it?* No clue. But she'd let her imagination roam as free as a buffalo. *Something good*, that's what her mind would find.

Gray put the lockbox back into the closet and the key back into the drawer. She stopped again in the bathroom. Yes, that *was* a black ring around the bathtub drain. She opened the medicine cabinet—orange vials of oxycodone, Demerol, ibuprofen, tubes of masks and creams and a bottle of Tylenol PM with the childproof wrapper still intact. Unopened.

Tea had said that, in her suicide attempt, Isabel had taken all the Tylenol PM.

Either Isabel had tried to overdose on a different bottle or . . .

"It didn't happen," Gray said. Just like Ian O'Donnell had said.

She crept back to the hallway, then slunk back to the staircase.

What was that?

She cocked her head to listen.

Scratching . . . somewhere . . . above her?

Eyes on the ceiling, she took one step down, then another, then paused.

No, the scratching was . . . in the *wall*?

Rodents. Mrs. Tompkins had mentioned using rat poison. That's how Morris had died.

Gray returned to the breakfast counter and to that blank notepad. She flipped through it and came to a page toward the back.

BZE 11:55 12:30 12:55 AA
10:25 DEL UA 6:00

Flights? Was "AA" American? "DEL" Delta? "UA" United?

But what's BZE? And when had these notes been made? And why had Isabel kept hair and nail clippings in a baggie?

Gray didn't know, but she *did* know the reasons behind the pictures of Isabel's injuries. Part of a victim's safety plan, pictures of abuse played a crucial role in a plea to a judge for a new name without a public hearing. "*He'd kill me if he found me,*" with receipts. The judge, seeing the bruises in color, would be compelled to keep the victim's new identity a secret.

"I need to leave," she whispered.

Mrs. Tompkins was probably looking out her peephole to see if Gray had left to take Kevin his lunch.

And now Gray was also peeping out the peephole.

The breezeway was empty.

She hurried back to the Camry and threw herself into the front seat. She glanced in the rearview and side mirrors. Don Lorenzo Drive looked abandoned.

She plucked her phone from her bag to search the internet.

What is "BZE"?

The search icon circled. There were barely two bars of reception here. Finally . . .

BZE . . . Philip S. W. Goldson International Airport. Belize City.

23

Isabel was supposed to fly to *Belize*?

But the young woman must have abandoned her original, ordered plan to leave Los Angeles. That's why she hadn't taken those pictures or her birth certificate. No time. Harried and frightened, she'd thrown clothes into a suitcase, her heart banging in her throat as she rushed to the black truck and raced away, pulse still banging around her body as the plane taxied down the runway and landed, hours later, in Belize City.

Maybe.

But as Gray pulled into a parking space at the mall, a part of her kept shaking her head.

Why didn't she believe this story?

Because Kevin Tompkins may have killed Isabel and could be posing as Isabel right now.

The Armed Forces Career Center was steps away from Panda Express. From broccoli beef lover to proud marine in less than twenty yards.

After her mother's funeral, Gray had flirted with the idea of joining the air force—Victor had been an airman before joining the Bureau. She'd visited a recruiting center like this one and had sat across from a stern-looking white man with Charlton Heston's jaw. He had pontificated about patriotism, commitment, and courage, and he'd thought she'd do best in the army, that it would be easier for her because, you know, test scores and education. But then she'd shown him her history degree from Fresno State, and then her high scores on the Armed Forces Qualification Test. She was qualified to join whatever-the-hell service branch she wanted. Which was, ultimately, none—her feeling of being lost and alone had become her "normal" again.

What would her life have been like had she joined? Would she have a flyboy husband named Jake? A son, Zach, and a daughter, Faye? Stars on her shoulders? Ribbons on her chest?

Inside the recruitment center, there were no future soldiers standing in front of monitors that showed a video of hard men jumping out of big planes.

Kevin Tompkins, dressed now in fatigues, spotted Gray standing in the doorway, and his eyes widened in surprise.

Gray smiled. "Isabel's friend Maya, remember? Your mom asked me to bring you this." She held up his lunch bag.

He shook his head. "Oh, no." He took the bag from her. "Thank you."

She pointed at one of the computer screens. "The test is digital now?"

"What do *you* know about *that*?"

"I got an eighty-eight on the AFQT."

He lifted an eyebrow. "And?"

"*And* I changed my mind."

He waited for more.

She shrugged. "The end."

Gray followed Kevin as he strolled back to his work space behind a short cubicle wall. "I'm sorry she forced you to come here."

"No problem." There was a bottle of Coke on

his desk, a bag of barbecue potato chips, and an unlocked cell phone. "I was headed here anyway. How long has she been living there?"

Kevin said, "Since 'ninety-two. She and my dad had a house farther up the hill, but when he died, she decided to sell and get something smaller. With me being sent all over the world, I wanted her to be around people. The Gardners kept her company, but then they moved to Arizona and rented out their condo. Isabel arrived, and . . . She was heaven sent."

Was?

Gray said, "I'm grabbing lunch at Wokcano. Wanna join me? You can pretend to eat your mom's lunch and save it for tomorrow."

He sat in his chair. "Thanks, but no."

"Okay, no garlic." She settled into his guest chair.

"Can't."

"Uncle Sam won't let you leave?"

He laced his fingers across his belly. "I can close for lunch, if I want."

"So, come with me. Share a wonton."

"I don't wanna send the wrong message . . ."

"That . . . *what*?"

"I'm . . . *involved*."

Gray cocked her head. "It's lunch, not *sex*. Not that there's anything *wrong* with sex." The idea of it—sex with Kevin Tompkins—screeched out of her like a distressed peacock. But then she did what women do and found the sultriest smile in her bag of tricks.

His eyes remained flat and uninterested. "I'm involved with Isabel."

"Huh?" For real: *Huh?* Nothing Gray had seen or heard indicated that Isabel was interested in this man.

"We're on the D.L., since she's with the doctor. *Officially.*" He searched Gray's eyes, then added, "I hope you understand," since he'd found not one mote of understanding there.

She nodded. "Have you talked to Izzy lately?"

"It's been a few days."

She squinted at him.

He sensed her skepticism. "We've texted back and forth, I mean."

"It's a special day today," she said, remembering the missing woman's birthday.

"It is." The soldier tossed her a smile—he had no clue.

On the desk, his cell phone chirped. He swiped at the screen as the front door opened.

Young men were filling the center.

Kevin stood from his chair. He said, "Excuse me," to Gray, then shouted, "I see future soldiers." He marched over to the small group, leaving his phone right there on the desk.

She grabbed the phone before it could fall asleep. As Kevin Tompkins talked to the young men about military benefits, Gray swiped through his digital photo album.

A far-off shot of a bedroom window and a woman wearing pink panties and a purple bra.

And another shot—the young woman now wore yoga pants and was bending over to retrieve something out of her yellow VW Beetle.

Gray kept swiping as Kevin Tompkins extolled the virtues of being servicemen. And then she found them.

Pictures of Isabel Lincoln, in various stages of undress, standing in her window or on her patio, or at her car, or in a parking lot. There were also photos of an erect penis and Kevin's blurred face in the background.

Out front, Kevin Tompkins said, "You gentlemen interested?"

Two young men shouted, "Sir, yes *sir*!"

And as he set the future recruits at computer stations, Gray found that woman's smile again and forced herself to walk to the exit and wave at Kevin Tompkins. "See ya later."

Kevin smiled back at her. "Thanks again."

Gray wandered back to her car. From stalking to kidnapping to murder—easy jumps. Her phone buzzed. She clenched, prayed the next text hadn't come from Sean.

Or Kevin. Or Ian . . .

She exhaled. It was a message from Isabel.

Miss Sykes?

I'm here.

Who do you work for?

Rader Consulting. The sun had sucked all the cool air from the Camry, and now sweat trickled down Gray's spine. *Were you and Kevin Tompkins involved?*

Over by the white Subaru, gulls fought over a discarded hamburger bun. Over by the blue Chrysler LeBaron, a mother struggled to collapse a baby stroller. Down on Gray's phone screen, ellipses bubbled . . . bubbled . . .

Ugh no!! Did he say that??

He hinted more than said straight out

No!! He's DISGUSTING!

This wasn't Kevin.

You said you can help me
But I don't want a male detective helping.
I don't trust men anymore.

Gray said, "*Gurl*," then texted, *Got it but you have to confirm that you are you.*
This time, no ellipses. This time, no response.
Gray had nearly reached Playa Vista and Rader Consulting when her phone buzzed again.
An email with two attachments from IL@yahoo. com. The first attachment was a scanned letter dated Friday, July 12.

> *Ian, I meant what I told you back in May. I don't want to be with you anymore. I'm tired of screaming. I'm tired of crying. Tired of your hands on my body. I don't want to be there anymore. I don't want you to find me. I AM OKAY. I AM ALIVE. It is now 12:47 p.m. PST on Friday afternoon. Here are the answers to your questions:*
>
> > *Hyundai Sonata*
> > *Black lace lingerie*
> > *The truth and shellfish.*
>
> *Here is a picture of me holding today's USA Today. Please call her off. You and I have secrets—let's keep them that way. Go in peace.*
> > > *Izzy*

Gray parked in the first space available, then tapped the second attachment.

It was a picture of Isabel standing in a tiled entry-way with a *USA Today* to her chest. She was somewhere tropical—there were palm trees and a ribbon of blue water behind her.

In the background, there was a digital sign. The words . . . The Westin . . . Princeville . . . Isabel Lincoln was in Kauai, Hawaii.

During one of their better months, Gray and Sean had stayed at that resort.

Gray tried to zoom in to read the paper's headline but couldn't. Then she compared the answers in Isabel's email to the answers Ian had provided. All correct. Isabel wasn't dead. Kevin Tompkins hadn't killed her—he wouldn't have said Ian had been allergic to "the truth." That answer could only come from a pissed-off ex-lover.

Proof of life was now in Gray's hands. She could now report to the doctor that his ex-girlfriend was alive and okay. Her job was done.

But Isabel hadn't sent a picture of Kenny G. She hadn't sent a picture of her butterfly-tattooed left thigh. In this picture, Isabel's hair was still golden brown, not the black of that L'Oréal box. And it was now one o'clock in Los Angeles. In Isabel's email, she'd stated that it had been 12:47 p.m. PST on Friday afternoon. Even the email's time stamp in the header said "12:49 p.m. PST."

But it *couldn't* have been 12:49 p.m. in *Hawaii* on *this* Friday afternoon. On the island, it was only 9:47 *a.m.* on Friday *morning* Hawaii Standard Time.

And she'd said, "12:47 p.m. PST" and "afternoon." This picture was a lie.

SHE
WOULDN'T
STOP

24

Yes. This picture that Isabel Lincoln had just sent was a lie.

Bits of disinformation or . . .

Gray stared at Isabel Lincoln's email—that time stamp, especially. The answers *were* correct, answers only the missing woman would have known. But where the hell was the dog? And if she were truly in Kauai, why wasn't the time stamp in Hawaii Standard Time?

No, Gray couldn't help this woman disappear. Not until she knew the truth.

This case was far from over.

At this time of day, all of Rader Consulting was chewing on something. The hallways smelled of luscious ripe strawberries, char-grilled hamburgers, and French fries drowned in vinegary-sweet ketchup.

Gray popped her head into Jennifer's office. "Hey, ladies."

The blonde and Clarissa were pulling California Pizza Kitchen boxes out of a bag. "I *told* you she was coming in," Clarissa said to Jennifer. To Gray: "We got you lunch."

Gray shouted, "Ohmigod, you are the *best*." She pulled one of the last items from the bag. "A *salad*." She gaped at her coworkers, then reached into the bag again for a packet of . . . "What the hell is *this*?"

"Light balsamic dressing," Jennifer said.

"No!"

"We're being strong for you," Clarissa said. "You made us promise, remember?"

Gray groaned as she settled in a guest chair.

Jennifer had switched from botanical oils in her diffuser to sugar-and-spices-scented oils, and now her office smelled like a 3 Musketeers candy bar. Pictures of her and her slick-haired third husband, Reynaldo, crammed the credenza alongside faux Tiffany lamps, scented sachets, and dishes filled with powders, pearls, and gems.

"Since it's too early for margaritas . . ." The blonde grabbed cans of LaCroix from her mini fridge and handed one to Gray. "Day's almost over. You got tired of spooning with your hot soldier and decided to earn a living?"

"He's a hot *marine*," Gray corrected, mouth filled with romaine lettuce.

"Get your swerve on, dude," Clarissa chirped.

Jennifer sliced her Hawaiian pie with a fork and knife. "So? Details?"

Clarissa plopped down to the rug. "And use lots of adjectives."

"And strong verbs," Jennifer said with a wink.

Between bites of lettuce and sips of carbonated water, Gray offered highlights of her late night with Hank. Playing connect-the-dots with her tongue on his scars. How every part of him had been engineered for her hands, for her mouth, for every part of her, and how tears had rolled back into her ears so many times, she was either drowning or going deaf. How she'd shivered and sweated so much that she believed that she'd either caught the flu or was going through the change. He was like the El Niño rains and she was a forest after a ten-year drought.

Jennifer shook her head. "I hate you."

"Dude," Clarissa said, "you *always* have the best sex."

"He is so *hot*," Jennifer said.

Clarissa sighed. "My Irving is . . . rich. Not just rich, but Irving's family was one of the richest in Macao. They'll have money forever."

Jennifer said, "You don't think he's sexy?"

Clarissa said, "The struggle is real." She pulled out her cell phone from her shorts pocket. "Wanna see my American dress? I tried it on this morning." It was cigarette-smoke white with enough tulle for six wedding gowns.

Gray gasped. "Gorgeous."

"And the red one for your Chinese wedding?" Jennifer scrutinized the photo, looking for something, *anything*, to criticize.

Clarissa said, "Still in pins."

"Oh," Jennifer said. "I booked our rooms at the Cosmopolitan."

The scar near Gray's navel throbbed—either the oxycodone was wearing off or her body was preparing to revolt. Because was she *really* gonna step foot in that city again?

Clarissa shoved Gray's leg. "Stop. Don't do that."

Gray blinked at her. "Don't do *what*?"

"Like, you're literally clenching your teeth and staring into space. You're thinking of skipping my weekend, and you can't do that." Clarissa's eyes filled with tears. "C'mon, Gray."

"Don't you have ten other girls going?"

"Five. But I, like, want *you* there, too. Come. *On*."

Gray forced herself to smile. "I'll be there. Cross my heart, hope to die. Time to work."

With that, the women finished their lunches, then

Jennifer and Gray grabbed legal pads as Clarissa grabbed her iPad.

"First of all," Gray said, "today is this poor woman's birthday and she's spending it how? Either running around the world or being dead."

"Sucks to be her," Clarissa said.

"Worst birthday ever," Jennifer said. "Eating gas station hot dogs. I'm talking about me, not this Isabel chick. But that's another story—"

"For another time, yes." Gray told them about Rebekah Lawrence (*Not the momma*) and Kevin Tompkins (*Mega perv*). She showed them a shot of the note she'd taken from Isabel's kitchen counter (*BZE*), the hair and nail bag (*Ew!*), and pictures of the pictures of a battered Isabel Lincoln (*Shit*). There was the envelope from JCI Insurance Services that Gray hadn't opened—a federal crime to open other people's mail—and the possibly fictional suicide attempt (*Tylenol? Lightweight*). *Why?* And there was this sketchy picture of the missing woman in Hawaii, but not a picture of the missing Labradoodle. *Where's Kenny G.?* She didn't tell them about Isabel's request to be disappeared—not everyone at Rader Consulting knew about *that* off-menu item.

"But I don't need you to tell me the whys and how-comes," Gray said to Clarissa. "I need you to get me any data that will help lead me there."

"Basically, do Gray's job for her," Jennifer snarked, eyebrow cocked.

Gray said, "Isn't data mining *her* job?"

"I don't mind," Clarissa said, shaking her head at Gray, then nodding at Jennifer.

Gray held up her hand. "No. Wait. I'm sorry. If I'm being—"

"It's okay," Clarissa said.

Jennifer smirked. "Poor girl. She'll say anything to get you to Vegas."

Gray frowned. "Seriously—"

"No." Clarissa pointed at Jennifer. "Stop. Now. For real." To Gray, she smiled. "I'll find as much information as I can. No problem. I swear. Oh—Omar Neville. I got an address. He lives close. I'll email it to you. And that second number you asked about . . ."

Sean's number. "Uh-huh?"

"Came from a burner phone. Sorry."

"Thanks, Clarissa," Gray said. "And I won't flake. I'm going, okay?" *Shit. Crap. No.*

Back in her office, the red voice mail light on her desk phone glowed. "Hi, Gray. It's Liz Jankowski, over in H.R. I have a quick question about your—"

Gray hit seven—message deleted.

What was she gonna do about Isabel Lincoln's proof of life picture?

Gray dialed Sanjay's extension. The resident graphic designer didn't pick up, so she left a message asking that he call her back as soon as possible. Then she stored Kevin Tompkins's discarded Target bag and Isabel's baggie of hair in a banker's box she'd labeled "I.L. stuff." She kept Isabel's keys in her purse and wondered about the lock belonging to that third key.

"Omar Neville . . ." According to Google Maps, he lived in Leimert Park. Not far. She'd stop by his apartment on her way home.

Gray logged into another people-finding database to do some more digging.

"Natalie Dixon" now lived in Chicago, somewhere on the East Side. She'd donated three hundred dollars to a food bank and had been thanked in the charity's annual report.

She was also registered at Bed Bath & Beyond for a December 7 wedding.

She'd just been buried alongside her dear husband, Raymond, of fifty years.

A "Natalie Dixon" also lived in thirty cities throughout California—and none of them lived in downtown Los Angeles or worked in Playa Vista.

She was still a ghost—*digitally*. So how had Sean found her number?

Her office was cool, and so quiet that the rattle of Vicodin in the emergency vial she kept in her desk drawer startled her. She shoved one capsule into her mouth and chased it with the rest of her LaCroix. Soon the drug would yank her, and the wet ache near her navel would dull and the world would be as good as it could be until the drug wore off.

"Soon" came, and her cheeks felt like a wool skirt with a silk lining. She was ready to feel nothing, just that fuzzy smoothness, and she closed her eyes and ignored the busy quiet of Rader Consulting. Her breath slowed and soon her abdomen numbed, and she heard herself softly snoring. For a perfect moment, she existed in a perfect, peaceful place.

But then her desk phone rang, and the abrupt noise ended this delicious respite.

She offered a groggy, "Hello."

"Miss Sykes, I need to talk to you," the woman on the other end of the call said. "It's important . . . I'm Dr. O'Donnell's big secret."

25

Victoria Avenue was lined with apartment buildings and Spanish-style duplexes and houses built before World War II. The scent of trimmed rosebushes and honeysuckle mixed with marijuana and fried chicken. A soft breeze rustled the boughs of the magnolia and pine trees, and Gray could hear both the echoes of African drums coming from the drum circle at the park and the laugh track from *The King of Queens* coming from behind Omar Neville's roommate, now standing in the doorway of the duplex.

"Yeah, Omar ain't here." She was a caramel-colored woman with an acne-scarred face. Her fuchsia work-out clothes were dark with perspiration.

"Do you know what time he usually gets home?" Gray asked.

"No idea. Not his secretary. Just his roommate."

"What's your name?" Gray asked, smiling. "I'm Maya. Hi."

"Toyia." She had the biceps of a weight lifter and the high ass of a stripper.

"Sorry that I'm bothering you, but Omar is dating my friend." *Why not?* "And she was in a car accident just a few hours ago. We've been trying to call him, but his voice mail is full."

"Yeah . . ." The front door creaked wider, and a Yorkie poked her beribboned head around Toyia's ankle. "He's working out of state right now, and he's not taking *anybody's* calls. Believe me, I've been trying to get him—rent's coming up in two weeks."

"Yikes. That's a little stressful. Maybe I can call his boss? I wouldn't insist except that she's not . . . doing well and I'd hate for him to find out on social media. Who does he work for?"

Toyia squinted at her.

"It's really important. She may actually . . ." Gray made her eyes fill with tears and she made her smile crumple and, eventually, one teardrop gained enough mass to tumble out of her right eye and down her cheek. "I can't even say the word. I'm not ready to let her go."

Toyia pulled her phone from a pocket in her leggings.

Gray swiped at her manufactured tear—a great tip from Jennifer. "I really appreciate it. I wouldn't ask, but . . . And I'll give you my number, too, just in case he calls."

"Allan Construction," Toyia said, finding the number on her phone. "They're building houses in this little town three hours south of Vegas. They're behind schedule, so Oz is ignoring everything except work. But if his girl is hurt . . . What's her name again?"

"Isabel Lincoln. I think they met at the Cork." *Why not?*

Toyia shrugged. "He meets *everybody* at the Cork. Omar is knee-deep in women, no offense to your friend."

Ian O'Donnell was also knee-deep in women.

And women like Trinity Bianchi were rarely nurses. No, women like Trinity Bianchi *sent* men to the emergency room—and to the grave. Gray had thought of her as Hot Nurse Pfeiffer because of her smoky blue eyes and lips stung from telling toxic lies. She had the kind of body that didn't need double Ds or a big ass to stun. She had the walk of a woman who had tromped over broken hearts and had never slipped, not even once.

Trinity Bianchi grinned at Gray, now seated on the bench outside of Café Fletcher. "I knew it was just a matter of time before we chatted. So I just figured . . . Get it over with, right? Rip that bandage off and deal with the truth."

Gray said, "Sure."

"Wise of me, huh?" Those smoky blue eyes twinkled with self-satisfaction, the only setting for eyes like hers.

Gray said, "Sure," again, and then, "Shall we?"

Café Fletcher had a resident cat named Michonne. The male bartenders wore man buns and the women wore flannel shirts and jeans shorts. The cocktails were twelve dollars and none of the appetizers on the menu cast shadows.

Gray's first thought: *What the fuck kinda place is this hipster bullshit?*

Patio diners vaped, and massive plumes of their alt-smoke billowed from mouths too sensitive for meat and peanuts.

She and Trinity snagged a table out on the patio.

The nurse ordered a vegan passion fruit mojito.

Gray ordered Pellegrino with lime and spotted the revolver inside the nurse's handbag.

"This is my favorite spot." Trinity plucked a kale chip from the basket left by a waitress.

Tiny knives plunged into Gray's heart. *What the fuck kinda place* . . . She avoided kale chips—there wasn't enough cheese or salt or butter or oil or cocaine in the world to convince her to enjoy alt-chips. "So . . . you and Ian O'Donnell."

Trinity crunched the kale chip. "That one's easy: we're lovers."

Gray cocked an eyebrow.

Trinity watched for more reaction. When Gray didn't give her any, the nurse rolled her eyes. "If you knew that, then why are we here?"

"*Why* are you lovers?" Gray asked. "That's why we're here."

"Same old, same old. *She doesn't understand me* and *We've grown apart.*" Trinity hid a smirk in the pink iciness of her cocktail. "Also, Isabel's a gold digger. An Olympic champion of gold diggers."

"Says Ian?"

"Says Ian, says me." She leaned across the table. "Look, I get it. Every woman wants to land a doctor, for obvious reasons, right? Well, Isabel was more obvious than the rest of us."

"How?"

"She'd make him buy her expensive clothes. She'd open credit lines under his name, like the Nordstrom card and the Best Buy card. They'd eat at expensive restaurants on *Wednesdays*. Who eats at Providence or Mastro's or JiRaffe on a *Wednesday*? And her little getaways? She'd pay for them with his card. Or her card on his account. When he'd catch her, she'd turn it around and tell him that it was *his* fault that she needed to leave and so it was only right that he pays."

"Is that how he knew where she'd go? Cuz it would show up on his statements?"

Had Ian paid for the trip to Kauai . . . or wherever Isabel was hiding?

"And she's dangerous," Trinity said. "She's unpredictable. Like a wounded dog."

Isabel was also a black woman dating a white man, and just yesterday evening Gray had overheard Ian's conversation about the "chubby transgender P.I. with a man's name"—the conversation during which Trinity, presumably, accused Ian of dipping into the "chocolate factory."

"Isabel's dangerous." Gray nodded at Trinity's purse. "Is that why you're packing?"

The nurse said, "I have a conceal carry license. She scares me. Her eyes . . . There's no emotion in her eyes, no flicker of *anything*."

Ugh. Dangerous. Unpredictable. Scary. Lacking emotion. Common adjectives used to describe black women.

Trinity continued, "And, one time, she showed up at the hospital."

"Yes, I'm told that she knew about you and Ian. And wouldn't she have that right to show up at the hospital since *she* was the girlfriend? And yeah, I would wild the fuck out if my boyfriend was sleeping with his nurse. It may not be a good look, but I would show up at the hospital ready to box. Just being honest. Woman to woman, over kale chips and cocktails."

Trinity stared at the melting ice in her glass.

"There are rumors that Ian beat her," Gray said.

Trinity's eyes widened. "That Ian *O'Donnell* beat—*What?*"

Gray sipped her mineral water and kept her gaze on the woman seated across from her. "You seem shocked."

Trinity finally blinked. "That's the most offensive thing I've heard today. Ian may be a jerk in some ways, in *many* ways, but he'd never, *never* . . ."

The nurse folded her arms and her fingers gripped

both elbows like vises. "The man volunteers at women's shelters all around the city. He pays out of his own pocket for plastic surgery for abused women who can't afford it. He *hides* women from their boyfriends and husbands and baby daddies who storm the E.R." She dropped her voice, then added, "He helps women disappear. That's how he knows your boss."

Hot air rushed across Gray's face. "So, Ian's one of Rader's . . . *consultants*?"

"For almost seven years now."

And that's why Nick had insisted that Ian . . . why he told her to take two steps back . . .

"Tell me about these." Gray showed Trinity the pictures of Isabel's injuries. "This happened in April. And to be honest, I thought *these*, not *you*, were his big secret."

Trinity pointed at Gray's phone. "She's saying that *he* did *this* to *her*?" The nurse's eyes couldn't grow wider. Her skin couldn't get paler. True horror racked her face—she wasn't faking this terror, this distress. "It's a lie. She's lying. She's a liar."

"Why would she lie?" Gray swiped through the pictures again. The bruise above Isabel's left kidney . . . the gash above Isabel's right eye. That wound alone would've needed . . .

Gray's chest tightened. That wound alone would've needed *stitches*. At least ten.

"I don't know why she's doing this," Trinity said. "I don't know why she took Kenny G. To get back at Ian for *me*? Because she's evil? I don't know. I *do* know this: Ian O'Donnell . . ."

She pointed at Gray's phone again. "He isn't that guy."

26

Back in the Camry, Gray found Tea's Facebook profile.

There had been one picture of Isabel, added on April 28, taken on the steps of the Baldwin Hills Scenic Overlook, two days after Ian had allegedly beaten Isabel.

Gray zoomed in on Isabel's face, tighter on her right eye.

No bruises. No scars. No signs of new stitches. No signs of any type of trauma. Barefaced; no makeup. A pretty girl without the paint. Eyebrows on fleek.

Gray studied the proof of life picture that Isabel had emailed her. A picture she knew was a piece of shit. The time zone . . . If Isabel had escaped to Hawaii four weeks ago, or even three days ago, her phone's clock would have switched from Pacific to Hawaii time.

So who mocked up the picture? Isabel?

Or maybe it still was Ian O'Donnell behind this, eager to prove that his ex-girlfriend was alive and to end his business relationship with Gray and Rader Consulting by sending that faked picture. *See? Nothing's wrong—and the P.I. found nothing wrong.*

Gray's phone buzzed in her hand. Ian O'Donnell's number sent the missing woman's picture to the background.

"Hey," the doctor said. "Tea just texted me. She said that Iz responded? When were you going to tell me?"

"Well, I wanted to confirm—"

"You need to come over," he said. "I'm home. You can show me the picture and then we can end this. We're done."

"But—"

"No. *Now.* Thanks." He spat out his address.

Twenty minutes later, Gray reached Ian O'Donnell's neighborhood, a block lined with jacarandas. This late in the season, a few bright purple flowers still clung to their branches. Like Gray had clung to this case. He stood in the doorway, wearing Adidas trainers, a gray Harvard T-shirt, and black slip-on sandals. He said, "That took forever."

"Traffic." The usual excuse for tardiness in Southern California.

Ian's living room boasted lots of light and bleached wood floors. A comfy couch and pastel throw pillows, a coffee table the color of driftwood. Chill. Relaxed. A room she wouldn't have picked out for the so-not-chill man standing beside her.

"Anything to drink?" He strolled to an airy kitchen the size of Gray's entire apartment.

"Yes, please. Anything would be good." She wandered the living room, pausing at the mantel and the pictures of Ian and Isabel at a black-tie event, Ian and Isabel shaking hands with Stevie Wonder, Ian and Isabel parasailing. Those frames were dust free, unlike the pictures of him and an older blond couple who had his eyes and his jaw. Or the six pictures of Kenny G. on surfboards and sailboats. Either he'd dusted Isabel's pictures and forgotten to dust the others or he had just placed those pictures on the mantel before Gray's arrival.

Ian offered her a glass of white wine. "Hope you like Viognier."

She said, "Perfect," and it was.

He settled in the armchair with his own glass of wine.

Gray sat on the love seat. She closed her eyes as the wine scoured a throat thick with ashes and anxiety.

He said, "So? How was your meeting with Rebekah Lawrence this morning?"

"More on that in a minute. Have you heard the name Kevin Tompkins before?"

"No. Who is that?"

Gray told him about the soldier's claims that he and Isabel were secretly dating.

Ian flicked his hand. "Isabel is a lot of things, but she's not crazy enough to date . . . *that* guy. And army, so his checking account isn't big enough for her."

Gray chuckled, because if a broke Navy SEAL was standing naked in her bedroom . . . *Money?* What was *money?* Sometimes women craved something more than big dollars.

She handed Ian her cell phone with Isabel's email on the screen.

His eyes pecked at the words there. "She answered correctly."

"What are the secrets she's referring to?"

"Not really your concern."

"Then this won't be over. As long as she has something on you . . ."

"The picture. She send the picture?"

"Tap the attachment."

He squinted at the image. "That's Isabel. And that's

USA Today. Maybe my dog is at the groomer's, or at a boarding facility." He handed the phone back to Gray. "Anyway, I guess that's that. She's alive and wants nothing to do with me." He looked tired—red-rimmed eyes, sallow skin, gnawed fingernails.

"Don't you want me to authenticate the picture?" Gray asked. "Don't you want to know for sure if the dog is okay?"

He set his wineglass on the coffee table. "She'd never hurt him. She loved him almost as much as I did."

"It wouldn't be a problem—"

"She answered correctly, Ms. Sykes. What difference does the picture make? She's in a tropical paradise and she's obviously happy. And Kenny G.—he's okay. I know he is."

Gray cocked her head. Why did he want to end this? "This picture can't be."

Irritation spiked from the doctor's eyes. "Pardon?"

"This can't be Isabel standing here holding today's paper." She hoped that he didn't leap over the coffee table to strangle her and then bury her beside his other big secret.

Maybe I shouldn't have drunk the wine. Maybe he poisoned it and I'm already dying. Since it was too late now, she went on to explain the discrepancy between the email's time stamp and the time Isabel had mentioned in the words she'd typed.

"I'll confirm that what I'm saying is correct," Gray said, "but I'm pretty sure. Also, her hair in the picture isn't black and she didn't send a picture of her tattoo or a picture of the dog."

He covered his eyes with his hands.

"Dr. O'Donnell," Gray whispered, "there's something else."

He groaned, then let one hand fall from his face.

Gray told him about the allegations of abuse.

"She's lying," Ian said, his voice quavering. "Never. Not ever. My mother was abused. She had heart problems because of it, and she . . . I . . . Nick Rader, your boss, and I . . ."

"Why is she saying that you hit her?"

"Trinity. When did she say this happened? That I . . . did that to her?"

"Late April was the last incident."

"The *last*? She's saying that I hit her *regularly*?"

"She thinks you're capable of killing her."

He placed his head between his knees. After a moment of deep breathing, he looked out at her. "If I showed you something . . ."

"Everything is confidential—that is, until we go to court, if necessary."

"I . . . recorded us." His Adam's apple bobbed. "*With* her knowledge, of course."

Her skin prickled. She knew what *that* meant. "Okay. Let's see what you have."

What Ian had was a recording of him naked, a tattoo of an X over his heart, golden skin, tight abs. There was naked Isabel, kneeling on a bed, flawless skin from there all the way to there. No blood, no bruises. In the background, there was a sixty-inch television and Rachel Maddow reporting that April day's breaking news.

Face burning, Gray asked, "May I have a copy? Again, this is all confidential." She'd be fine if she never glimpsed another minute of this recording.

Ian tapped a few keys and *whoosh*, the video landed in Gray's inbox. "It's Tea. She's the one who puts all these thoughts in Isabel's head. Tells her that

I'm abusive and mean and . . . I know I gave you Tea's number. Maybe I shouldn't have. I know you've already talked to her, but maybe . . . Don't trust a word she says."

"There's something else."

"I don't know if I can hear any more."

"Rebekah and Joe Lawrence aren't her parents. They're not her stepparents. They're not related at all." Then Gray told him of her conversation with Inglewood's Clair Huxtable.

Ian frowned. "What do you mean, she doesn't know me?"

Gray told him that Rebekah Lawrence was the mother of one of Isabel's friends.

"Noelle?" Ian said. "I don't know a Noelle and I never saw anyone living in the condo."

"Do you know the names Christopher Lincoln or Hope Walters Lincoln?"

He shook his head.

"They're on Isabel's birth certificate," Gray said. "*They're* her parents."

Ian grabbed the wineglass from the coffee table. "Maybe she was adopted."

"Maybe. Do you want me to keep working?"

Ian rolled the cool wineglass against his forehead. "This is crazy. This is nuts." He took in a deep breath, then slowly released it. "I was thinking about something you asked me yesterday. Shit—was it just yesterday? About her ex-boyfriends."

Gray said, "Okay," then took a long sip of Viognier.

"She told me about this one guy, Mitch. He owns a furniture store off of Venice Boulevard. Spoiled her sometimes. Smashed her head in, the other times. Sounded like a jerk."

"I'm also trying to reach Omar. Anything else?"

"Slicked-back hair. Lots of jewelry. All about the machismo thing, but the Russian version. We drove by there once, so that I could get a look at him."

"I'll talk with Mitch, then. See what he knows, find out when he talked with her last. May I ask . . . if you weren't with Isabel, where were you on Memorial Day weekend? Really?"

Defiance shone in Ian's eyes briefly before it vaporized. "I was with Trinity Bianchi."

"Your nurse."

"We stayed at the Four Seasons in Newport Beach."

"Do you have proof?"

"Credit card bills—it was a very expensive weekend. I'm sure there's closed-circuit TVs around that hotel. And there's Trinity. You can ask her—but her word is as good as mine, right?"

Secrets and lies screamed out of Ian like bottle rockets and barn owls. Secrets and lies had led to Gray being hired to find his girlfriend. He wasn't who he said he was. Neither was Isabel Lincoln. But then again, who was?

Stricken, Ian said, "I didn't *touch* Isabel. Not like that. Not even in some sexual BDSM thing. She didn't leave because I hit her or because I tried to kill her. I know that for a fact."

"Why did she leave then?"

"She was threatening to tell the board about Trinity and me. About an . . . episode in one of the treatment rooms late one night. Either I paid her fifty K or she'd do a *Gone Girl* and fake her death, leaving all evidence pointing to me. She said she had bills, and if I didn't pay up she'd make me pay in other ways. I couldn't figure out which bills she had left, since I'd paid almost every bill she had, including rent. Her name is on the application as tenant but I'm fucking on the hook for everything else."

"So, basically, it's your apartment."

"That's what the Gardners told me."

"And did you pay the fifty grand?"

"All cash—and I have a bank record, because I'm not *that* stupid and it's a lot of money. . . . I left it on the counter in the condo. But she never responded. I texted her to make sure she received it. No answer. So I worried—about the money, yes, but she took my dog and . . ."

He scrubbed his face with his hands. "I just want her to stop. I don't want to keep paying her. I want my dog back—that's really why I hired you guys. Fuck her—she could drop off the face of the earth, but I'm scared she's gonna keep blackmailing me and I need it to stop. I'm hoping you find her and that Nick, you know, convinces her to leave me the fuck alone. You probably don't know this, but Nick can be . . . persuasive."

"The cops—"

"I don't want the cops involved. This is my reputation. My career gets destroyed because I started seeing someone else? Isabel and I, we weren't even married. And when I *did* try to break things off with her properly, in March, she lost it and left town, but then she came back with bruises and I worried that she hurt herself because of me . . ."

The two sat in silence until Gray asked, "May I have the condo key and your permission to touch and take what I need? Since your name *is* on the lease."

He worked the key off his key fob and handed it to Gray.

Now she had all the keys to the condo. No one could enter except through her.

"If I continue . . ." Gray said.

"I'll keep paying your rate. Just get my dog back and make all of this stop."

27

Gray was exhausted now, and buzzed from delicious white wine and the last breaths of lunchtime Vicodin. She had one more hour left in her, an hour and a half at most, before her internal clock hit midnight and she turned into a pumpkin.

Sitting in traffic, she was too irritated to listen to Oleta, Angie, or even Jill. She didn't want to hear about lost love, found love, found faith, lost faith. She wanted to get to that damned place, to finish this damned case, either by standing over a body or by sitting across from one.

The evening brought with it cool breezes, and the sky swirled with colors of tangerines and pomegranates, eggplants and lemons. She was hungry, and her fridge at home was filled with diet shakes. Neon signs lining La Brea Avenue suggested burgers, chicken, and poke.

No, she didn't want any of this.

Fifteen minutes later, a young black man with sleepy eyes spooned oxtails and gravy into a foam carton. "Your first side?" he asked.

A line snaked across the rust-colored tile floors of Dulan's. Squirming kids, exhausted nurses, and starving men wanted their protein and three sides. Cobbler, too, but only if it was fresh.

Gray stood at the front of that line and her eyes

darted from the steaming steel pockets of glistening collard greens and the colorful medley of corn-
tomatoes-okra to the creamy orange of macaroni and
cheese. At the register, she added a tub of peach cobbler to her bill because, today, she had earned every
sugary cinnamon bite. She deserved the soft crunch of
crust after having received a faked proof of life picture. Those buttery, melt-in-your-mouth peaches, no
longer fruit but more of a memory of fruit, were rewards for peeking through Kevin Tompkins's album
of peeping tomfoolery. Every calorie she ate would
replace a smidgen of the soul she'd lost since meeting Ian O'Donnell and the people associated with this
case.

And Hank. *Fucker.* Not a text, not a call. Nothing. She'd eat *both* corn muffins to cloud her feelings
about *that*. The six thousand calories and countless carbohydrates would slog down those feelings,
mute her hatred and resentment, quiet the "Girl, you
was *used*" drag queen that sometimes perched and
preached in her head.

The bottle of Viognier that she purchased from
the fancy downtown grocery store would help it all
go down like a queen's feast. No LaCroix at queen's
feasts.

Her phone rang right as she buckled her seat belt.
Wasn't Nick. Wasn't Hank. It was definitely work related, and she'd already accepted that being a private
investigator was not a nine-to-five gig. And so she answered.

"Hey, it's Bruce Norwich, over at Allan Construction." The man sounded out of breath and phlegmy
but strong enough to haul a beam of wood across his
back. "Looks like you called a few hours ago. Sorry
for getting back to you so late."

Glad that she had answered, Gray explained that she was working a missing persons case. "And Omar Neville's name came up, but only as a friend. He certainly hasn't done anything wrong. It's just that we can't find someone he knows."

Bruce Norwich barked a laugh. "You taking more clients? I haven't seen Oz in weeks."

"He's in Nevada, isn't he?"

"He was *supposed* to be, but he never showed up. I waited two weeks for him to come, but nope, no Omar. No word from Omar. No nothing from Omar. So I fired him last week—not that he knows that."

"He didn't pick up his last check?" Gray's face had numbed, and now she couldn't feel the words vibrating off her lips.

"Nope. Someone else signed for it."

Gray grabbed a pen from the center console and a napkin from the bag. "You know who signed for his check?"

"Uhh . . . Lemme look . . ."

She closed her eyes as Bruce Norwich flipped through the pages of a ledger. "Here . . . I found it. So . . . his wife picked it up. Yeah. Says here, Elyse Miller. You should probably call her—she'll know where he is."

Gray sat in her car, gaping at the cars racing up and down Crenshaw Boulevard. Unblinking. Unmoving. Until: "Who the *fuck* is Elyse Miller?"

28

The aroma from Gray's bag of soul food trumped whatever musky creature Mrs. Kim was now sautéing behind her apartment door. The hipsters were blasting Macklemore, and "Good Old Days" echoed through the hallway. Gray thought she'd already hated Jessica and Conner at full capacity, but tonight . . .

A sticky note had been taped to her door: a delivery down at the security desk. *What now?* A certified letter from the IRS about being audited? A collections notice from Columbia House Records from 1992?

Her phone rang.

"Are you Gray?" a young woman asked.

Gray said, "Yep, and this is . . . ?"

The caller took a deep breath, then pushed out, "This is Noelle Lawrence, Isabel's friend. You talked to my mom this morning."

Gray paused in her step, then unlocked her front door. "Hi. Thanks for calling—"

"Listen. This whole thing with Isabel is just . . . crazy, and—" A car horn in Noelle's world honked and honked.

"Do you know where she is?" Gray dropped the bag of food on the breakfast counter.

"Yeah. Well . . . kind of. It's complicated. She used to have me do some shady shit. Last time I asked, she sent somebody—Oh, fuck. Hold up."

Gray said, "Noelle—"

"Can't talk right now," the young woman whispered. "Come to the Grove tomorrow. No, go to . . . Phillips on Centinela. Like around six. Gotta go."

The dial tone hummed in Gray's ear.

Down in her building's lobby, Melvin the guard sat behind the security desk. He had a tiny head and a heart as big as a golden retriever's. "Something special came for you today."

"I have no idea what it could be."

"Best kind of surprise." He took the notification from her, then waddled back to the storage room. A few seconds later, he returned with a crystal vase of lavender roses.

Gray clutched her neck. "They're *gorgeous.* You sure those are for me?"

"Your name, your roses."

From waking up to text messages from Sean to the Hank-hatred that she'd clung to all day . . . All of that was now shoved off a cliff by the dizzy joy twirling inside of her like Julie Andrews in the Swiss Alps.

Back in her apartment, the refrigerator's humming was scratchy, like it had caught a cold. Ignoring it like management had ignored her request for a new fridge, she set the vase on the dining room table.

The flowers had already made her house into a home. Those flowers warmed up the part of the couch that had rarely hosted another's rear. Adding to that, the aromas of soul food and gravy now sloshing at the bottom of the plastic bag reminded her of home cooking. Mom Naomi's meatloaf with that ketchup topping. Mom Twyla's fried chicken legs with those burn spots here and there.

Maybe Gray would eat at her tiny—no, *intimate*—dining room table. Use one of her nice wineglasses, a stemmed one instead of a tumbler. Maybe she'd listen to Luther or Maxwell or that old D'Angelo album she'd played all the time back in the day. Maybe she'd do all of that instead of sitting in her place on the lived-in side of the couch, in front of the television and the Netflix home page.

She plucked the bouquet's card from its envelope.

You take my breath away.

Typed. No signature.

Hank—he'd said the same thing to Gray last night. He'd said it again before he'd left her apartment this morning, as the sun kissed the sky.

How had he guessed that lavender roses were her favorites, in this life and in her last? She took a picture of the arrangement, then texted the former marine. *They're beautiful!!*

Gray moved the vase to the coffee table as ellipses from Hank bubbled on the phone's screen. She checked the ORO license plate reader app—no alerts—and security video from her doorbell camera—no visitors except for Melvin placing the delivery notice on her door.

She hadn't received flowers from a lover in years—living by the five-second rule meant there was no room for others. Hank Wexler, though, had managed to sneak through.

Her phone vibrated.

U trying to make me jealous?

Huh? I just wanted to thank you.

For?

The flowers dude

Phantom crows dropped frozen pebbles into her belly.

The fridge clattered again.

Her phone buzzed, and she startled as though a gun had gone off an inch from her ears.

I didn't send those. Sorry. Didn't think we were there yet.

Cheeks burning, she typed, *Oops,* with a blushing face emoji.

More frozen pebbles filled her belly. With stiff fingers, she texted Nick. *Hey! Did you send me something today?*

As a thank you for taking the Lincoln case? As a—

No I didn't

Ian O'Donnell didn't know Gray's home address, so he couldn't have sent . . .

Gray's stomach cramped from all those cold stones, *because who* . . .

Oh. *Oh.*

He found me.

Sean had not only found her phone number, he had also found her address.

Shit.

She plopped down on the couch. Hugging her knees to chest, she sat there, as still as a possum under threat.

Now what?

The old Gray would've texted Nick her distress code—43 57—then grabbed the already packed Louis Vuitton backpack—a Christmas gift from Nick—that she kept in the back of her closet. A blue Honda minivan with plates that led to nowhere, sent by Nick, driven by a mom type with a bad ponytail and high-waisted jeans, would have picked her up in the lowest level of the parking garage. Gray would have hidden on the floor of that minivan, among the crushed Goldfish crackers and *The Very Hungry Caterpillar*. Her eyes would be closed as the Honda wheezed on its climb up the Hollywood Hills or Topanga Canyon to a safe house. She would have stayed there until Nick moved her somewhere else. Again.

Gray had changed her adult life already because of Sean Dixon, all because of a young woman's natural desire to be loved, all because she'd had mercy that night and didn't end him when she'd had a chance.

Now she grabbed her Glock from beneath the pillow on her bed, then grabbed the vase of perfect lavender roses. Her heart, scarred from nearly four decades of living, pumped electric blood through her body as she snatched open the front door.

She looked up and down the hallway, hoping that Sean Dixon stood there with a smug smile on his face, with his Jim Beam eyes widening as the Glock lifted in one smooth motion, pointed in his direction.

But no one stood in the hallway.

Gray left the door open, hoping that Sean would pop in and "surprise" her from the shadows. *Heeeere's Johnny!* Then she could shoot him and claim that he'd been trespassing and had invaded her home. That's what she hoped for as she slipped into the trash room and pulled down the chute's handle. She dropped the vase in and down it went, sixteen stories, fifteen, fourteen . . . until a crash, then silence.

Somewhere, a door hinge squeaked.

Gray strained every muscle in her body to hear . . .

Voices, male, deep, floated down the hall and into the trash room.

She stepped back into the hallway.

Alone.

No one stood at her door or at the emergency exit.

Back in her apartment, she stood in the doorway.

The fridge grumbled.

She crept to her bedroom.

The comforter on the bed—that dip in the middle. Was that always there or . . .

Into the bathroom.

She slammed the shower curtain to one side.

Empty.

She peeked into her closets.

Empty.

No one was here.

Nauseous, she closed her eyes. *Breathe. Just breathe.*

The red numbers on the nightstand clock glowed 10:02, and the refrigerator rattled, and it was as it was every night . . . except she could still smell the faint scent of those lavender roses.

The old Gray would have never eaten that peach cobbler. No. Tonight, Gray enjoyed her hard-earned meal but drank only one glass of Viognier. She could have eaten more, drunk the bottle to commemorate My Abusive Ex Found Me Day. But he didn't deserve any of her fought-for binge.

Still . . .

How had Sean Dixon found her?

Did he have someone following her again?

After dinner, she cleaned her gun and remembered those Sunday afternoons when she'd done the same with Victor Grayson. Then she made sure that knives remained in their designated spaces around her six hundred square feet. And she made sure the Mace in the medicine cabinet sat beside vials of pills, mouthwash, and Chanel No. 5—the perfume, not the cologne. Then she drank cans of LaCroix. Sober. Steady. Tired of his shit. Tired of *this* shit. Couldn't even get properly drunk on a night she deserved to be wasted.

Sean had fucked up, this time.

No more running.

She'd find his spy and kill that person. Then she'd find Sean Dixon, but she'd let him live long enough to realize, to understand, and to accept that he would die by her hand. And then she'd kill him. And this time she'd shove mercy through the holes she'd put in his bloody chest.

AN OLD FRIEND

Two months before Natalie had graduated with a B.A. in history, Victor was diagnosed with pancreatic cancer. It was a nasty, quick disease, and he died a day after her graduation Sunday. Nick had remained at Victor's bedside as Faye had flown down to attend their daughter's ceremony.

Victor Grayson's funeral had been upright, with American flags everywhere and straight spines and somber men, many soldiers wearing uniforms. Faye, wearing black, had clutched that trifolded flag like a life raft. Evil hadn't taken away her beloved—his treacherous body had.

Every federal agent in Northern California, including Dominick Rader, attended his funeral. Victor's small family, the two women he'd left behind, cried and mourned. The younger one hurt but understood that her dad had been in pain. With her diverse belief system as a foster child, she knew that Victor Grayson could be anywhere or nowhere after his death.

It was a Thursday three months later when Faye kissed her daughter's forehead and told her that she wanted to be alone for a moment and that she'd made lasagna for dinner. The heartbroken widow retreated to her and Victor's favorite place, Half Moon Bay, a small coastal town an hour's drive south of San Francisco. Big waves. Good fishing. Perfect sunsets. And as Natalie watched a rerun of *The X-Files* while eating pasta and drinking from one of the many bottles of wine left from Victor's funeral repast, Faye Grayson walked into the cold waters of Half Moon Bay. Surfers found her battered body yards away from a pod of seals.

And so, three months after the first, Natalie Grayson planned a second funeral. Not many agents attended, but Dominick Rader came. Educators, students, and their parents filled the pews. Despite the hundreds that attended, despite the assurances that Faye *had* loved her, Natalie knew and understood the truth—that Faye had loved Victor *more*. She'd only been a Grayson for seven years. That had been enough time, though, to inherit the house on Monterey Bay and to receive insurance and Social Security payments, pension payments, access to bank accounts, a Volvo, a Jeep, and jewelry. She had more than she'd ever had, but . . .

She was alone in the world again.

Natalie sold the Volvo and stored the jewelry, including Faye's diamond engagement ring, in her parents' safe deposit box at a bank in the city. She also kept the house and paid a company to manage renters. Zoe, Jay, and Avery persuaded her to move to Oakland—they lived across the street from Lake Merritt—and so she packed the Jeep and rolled up the highway.

And now, on the seventh anniversary of Victor Grayson's death, Natalie visited a seaside cemetery near Monterey Bay to place yellow tulips on his marker and to place tiger lilies on Faye's marker just a reach away. She tasted tears from crying and she tasted blood from tearing at dry skin on her lips. Her parents had been dead now for seven years.

Felt like a hundred.

Someone came to stand behind her.

She glanced over her shoulder.

That familiar face had always been a grab bag of ethnicities. Today, Dominick Rader looked African American.

"Didn't think I'd see you today, Dom," she said. "It's been a while."

"Wow," he said, that word flat and far from "wow." "You remember my name."

Every time he'd come to their house for dinner, Natalie's belly had fluttered, just like it fluttered now. "Yeah. I remember all of Dad's agents."

"Hunh." Irritation flashed across his face—he'd been more than *just* an agent to the Graysons. "You still living here?" His voice was deep and scratchy, like stones and whiskey.

"No. I live in Oakland. Like you don't already know that."

"And the house?"

"Still mine. A minister and his family are renting it, but . . ." She had spent the happiest years of her life grilling and reading big books on that deck. "I'll never sell it."

"That's good to hear."

Sunlight danced across the steel plate of her father's marker. The salty Pacific rode atop the breeze and her stomach wobbled. Dominick wanted to say something to her, but he was hesitant. And she was impatient. "What is it? Just spit it out."

"Victor and Faye wouldn't be happy," he said. "With you and Sean—"

"I thought I asked you to stop—"

"Nat, come on."

"And we're just dating. And I'm twenty-nine years old. Most people my age are married by now and have a house and a retirement plan. I don't need your advice." She glared at him, frustrated. "Anyway, you don't even know him."

"And here I thought you knew me." He folded his arms.

She glimpsed his holster and badge beneath his jacket. "You *don't* know him."

"I know enough about him to know that your father—"

"Daddy was being *hyperbolic* when he asked you to look after me. He was *dying*, Dom."

On his deathbed, Victor had forced her to memorize Dominick Rader's phone number. Once she recited it without pause, then recited it backwards without pause, he let go and let God.

"Doesn't matter," Dominick said now. "He gave me an order, and I'm following it." He clasped her arm. "Natalie, look—"

"No." She broke from his hold and kneeled beside her father's grave. "Thank you—and I mean that—but I don't need you to look after me. I mean that, too. Just let me be. Please?"

Grief paralyzed her lungs and her breath caught in her chest. Fat teardrops tumbled down her cheeks and plopped down to the grass—her tears were keeping that piece of land green. She bent and kissed the grave marker's cold metal like she kissed it on every visit.

She looked back over her shoulder. "Dom, I'm—"

Dominick Rader was gone.

She was alone again beneath that hot August sun.

29

Grayson Sykes knew that, in the end, it would all be handled—by her, by Sean Dixon, and by her Heavenly Father above. She knew this was chess, and despite Victor Grayson's insistence on teaching her the game, she had remained a mediocre player. Instead, she excelled at Tetris and Centipede, games that threw spiders and bombs at her, quicker and more complicated missiles with each round, until they burned and separated and spiders and blocks covered every blank piece of the screen.

That afternoon, he had stood from his armchair, beer bottle in hand, Polo shirt still tucked into his khakis even though he was home. "Reactionary," her father had said.

"Nimble," Natalie had countered with a smile.

His love was like fresh strawberries and warm socks, and it flowed over her, that love, like clear, clean water over smooth river stones. A daddy's girl. *Finally.*

"Admit it, Vic," Faye said, looking up from her *Essence* magazine. "You lost, dear."

"You suck at Centipede," their daughter had boasted, "and I am the queen."

Victor had kissed the top of Natalie's head, then slid open the glass door. The aroma of brisket from his smoker wafted into the house. "You are the queen of *this*, Nattie. Chess—"

"Yeah, yeah, game of kings." She'd reached for the board beneath the coffee table, the one she had found off of Champs-Élysées, with the silver and blue stainless steel pieces. The trio had eaten crepes afterward—cheese and black pepper for her, lemon for Mom, and ham for Dad. It had been the third full day of their Parisian vacation . . .

And that's what Gray thought about as she fell asleep—her life with Victor and Faye, savory crepes in Paris, Centipede and chess. She didn't think about Sean; she didn't fret about Hank—five-second rule, just another block in her life that would soon disappear like the others. The heavy food from Dulan's and the exhaustion of a nonstop life pulled her down, down, down, and she slept until well into Saturday.

Gray didn't leave the bed even then, because her limbs refused to move. She didn't feel . . . *together*. There was the pain in her abdomen, but her unease was more than that. She dragged herself to the bathroom, popped another oxycodone, then dragged herself back to bed.

Outside, Los Angeles was so bright—it looked too hot to verb in that light. She fell asleep, so tired, and awakened again to watch the sun move across the sky. She listened to fire engine sirens wail over the thrum of freeway music; listened to her refrigerator gurgle like a swamp thing; heard her phone vibrate with texts and calls and emails. She responded only to her body and its needs. *Sleep, relax, let go.* She didn't eat—didn't need to. The soul food had taken care of her daily calorie requirements for the next month.

Finally, Gray turned on the television and found *The Lord of the Rings* on cable.

At four o'clock, she answered one phone call.

"You okay?" Nick sounded guarded, worried.

She sat up in bed as the Ringwraiths surrounded the Fellowship. "Meh. Mental and physical health day." She glanced at her phone's call log.

Tea, Tea, Isabel, Clarissa, Jennifer, Clarissa, Toyia, Tea, Tea . . .

"From the appendectomy," he asked, "or . . ."

"That"—*and narcotics*—"and I just needed a moment to do nothing. This Lincoln case is a dumpster fire caught in the middle of a tire fire, and the heroine needs to regain her strength in order to continue."

"Maybe you should go to urgent care."

"Maybe."

"I'm flying back tonight, but call if you need me before then." He paused, then asked, "You ever find out who sent you the roses?"

Dread—of Nick's reaction, of Sean's resurgence—bundled in her stomach. She rubbed the scar along her jaw. "Uh-huh."

"Who?"

"Take a guess."

Silence. Then, "Who?"

"Sean."

More silence, and then, "You're fucking kidding me."

She rubbed her face and groaned. "Girl runs from boy, boy finds girl, boy sends girl menacing texts and her favorite flowers. Tale as old as time."

"I'll get an earlier flight—"

"Don't. I'm good."

"How did he find you?"

"No idea. I did a search and I can't find the old me. But you know what? It's okay."

"No, it's not. It's *not* okay." His voice had climbed an octave, and she pictured him pacing the floor wherever he was, hand over his eyes then running through his hair. "How can I hide other women if—"

"Nick, calm—"

"This is my fucking *business* model, Grayson. You and Lauren and Christina and . . . and . . . All of you rely on my ability to keep you hid, to keep you safe, and now this fucker is sending you *flowers*? What the *fuck*?"

She clamped her lips. He was right.

"Your gun?" he asked.

She lifted the pillow and saw the Glock nestled there. "Right next to me. She says hi."

"Natalie—"

"Uh-oh. Calling me by my *name* name."

"Sorry. Slipped. This can't—"

"I'm gonna handle it."

"How, *Grayson*?"

"So many questions this early in the morning."

"It's after four o'clock."

"It's morning somewhere."

He took a deep breath and released it. "Listen. Stay with me for a few days. At least until I figure out how he found you."

"You're not in charge of my messes. How many times do I have to keep saying that?"

"I'm only asking for you to stay until I find out how . . . *Shit*."

"I'll think about it." She raked her fingers across her scalp. "I'm kinda itching for a fight, to be honest. Slaying the dragon has always been on my ultimate bucket list."

"Do you understand my concern?"

"I do."

"This isn't a game."

"You're telling me."

"I'm so sorry, Nat," he said. "I should've done better. Guess I got cocky. Guess—"

"Dom," she whispered. "Don't. Evil squeezes into tight spaces. We'll figure it out."

"You're remarkably calm."

"I've been asleep all day." *And drugged.* "I have a gun. I have knives. I have a phone and muscle memory. I'll watch my back. If it starts to get crazy, I will move in again. Promise. I'm not planning to lose my life to this man. I'll go to jail first."

"It won't come to that. I'm still taking an earlier flight home. You have the house key?"

"Yup. I have to do a little work now. Earn my paycheck." She peered through the window blinds at the dusky sunlight turning the hills of Chavez Ravine creamy blue. "Thank you for calling. I feel a little better, to be honest."

And she did. Still, she decided not to do too much today, since today was damn near over. She listened to her voice mails—every woman except Toyia wanted something from her.

Call me back.

Let us know you're okay.

Call me back.

Let me know if you got it.

Toyia's message was exact: "Omar ain't married. I don't know no Elyse Miller."

Gray said, "Fuck it," because Omar Neville wasn't her client. *Not my monkeys, not my circus.* What grown people did in the privacy of their own homes did not concern her. And with that, she pulled on her favorite pair of relaxed Levi's and a soft black T-shirt. After makeup, hair, leather jacket, and black leather

Cons, she went out the door and down into the twilight.

Located off Venice Boulevard, the Helms Bakery District used to be exactly that—a strip of shops, established in 1931, that delivered baked goods to Angelenos all around the city. Now a landmark, that strip was home to fancy furniture stores and restaurants that charged too much—for a couch and for a sandwich. Shalimar sold Persian-inspired decor, from curly-edged accent tables to fussy chaise longues that cost as much as Gray's Camry.

Mitch Pravin, the store owner and Isabel Lincoln's ex-boyfriend, wore a Bluetooth earpiece like the commander of the starship *Enterprise* and twisted impatiently in his scrolled and ornate, built-for-a-shah office chair. His work space smelled domestic and exotic—French fries and paprika.

Gray asked him about his relationship with Isabel Lincoln.

That's when he stopped twisting in his chair to sneer at her. "*Who?*"

She held up the picture of the Mary Ann with the long ponytail and *Vogue* cheekbones.

He flicked his hand. "We never dated."

"Slept together, kicked it, booty call, whatever."

"You don't get it. I didn't *date* her. I didn't *sleep* with her. That *bitch* T-boned my Maserati last year."

According to Mitch Pravin, the accident had happened four months before Isabel met Ian O'Donnell. "And then she tried to talk me out of suing her. Letting her pay me off the books and shit. And yeah, she offered to blow me, so I took her number. She sent me a promissory note . . . Where'd I put that?"

Gray waited, nervous and wanting to chew her

fingernail or rub her jaw scar or pace, but she willed herself to sit and wait and ignore the *pew-pew-pew* now going off around her body.

He opened a drawer and halfheartedly pawed through some papers before slamming the drawer shut. "It said she'd pay me six hundred a month. The first money order she gives me goes through, right? But then the next month? She sends me nothing. So I called her, and she called back, but I was with a customer. I called her again and no answer. She stopped returning my calls, but I kept lighting up her phone all times of night. From March to September, every fuckin' night I'd call, understand? And then I started texting her. Nothing.

"That's when she finally blocks me. The address she gave me, some dump over on Vermont, near USC? A complete lie. She didn't live there. I didn't have any other information cuz how many fuckin' Lisas or whatever live in L.A.? Hundreds. Anyway. You find her, let me know, cuz so help me, I'm coming after her ass."

30

The stalking, violent boyfriend? Wasn't violent. Wasn't a stalker. Wasn't even a boyfriend. He was a *victim. Isabel's* victim.

And now she was gone.

But Gray would find her. Just like Sean had found *her.*

And how had he done that?

Had he used someone like Nick to search for her? Had he somehow obtained her medical records? Always sold and shared, those records, and the janky clinic that had performed her appendectomy looked like it needed some cash.

But she hadn't used her old name at admissions at that janky clinic. Hell, she hadn't used her married name at admissions even when it had been her name *at that moment.*

Back then, she'd only visit shady clinics in Las Vegas, or farther south in Henderson. Hours-long waits. Clinics where iodine was the solution to everything. Blood everywhere, since the staff hoarded bandages like dwarves hoarded gold. Drug addicts shot up while waiting to see a doctor. No ventilation. Every floor was sticky with . . . *something.*

Back then, she'd used aliases for check-in: Kirby Lewis, Keisha Laramie, Karen Larson. Always *K*s and *L*s, always those three names, sometimes scrambled—

from Kirby Laramie to Keisha Larson. There were no Natalie Dixons with a cracked third rib. No Natalie Dixons with twelve stiches above their jawline or lacerations above the left eye. The beaten Natalie Dixon never existed in patient records, and her regular general practitioner never knew that Natalie Dixon had been cheating on him with Dr. Oxley at Canyon Medical Center, Dr. Mendelbaum at Nevada Health Center, or Nurse Anderson at Rapid-Care.

As she healed, those first few days, she'd stay away from Sean and home. She usually hid in a room at Whiskey Pete's in Primm, Nevada. No hot water in the shower. Damp. Red Cross–thin blankets on the bed. She never pressed charges against Sean—and he knew that she wouldn't, and that she'd never cross that state line into her home state. California was as far away as Tasmania, even though it sat five hundred steps away from her hotel room. She'd use makeup to hide bruises that took too long to heal, then hit the road to return to her Spanish-Californian with the silver porch light and the stark, red-bloom succulents, with "Next time, I'll leave for good" on her lips, just like the now-dry blood that would come alive in the next quarter, her own red bloom, so stark in the wasteland of her life.

But she'd taken pictures of her injuries. Nurse Anderson had held the camera, not saying a word, just using a finger to move her patient's head to the right or to the left. Those pictures were printed and sent to a P.O. box she'd told Natalie to open. "It's safer there," the old black nurse had told her. "Keep the pictures in there along with some money. Mad money, my momma used to call it. When the time comes, you'll have what you need."

Mad money. Like the kind sitting in an account in

California, bursting with rent payments from her tenants in Monterey Bay.

Sean had always noticed her stitches. He had also noticed withdrawals from his bank account—three hundred dollars—every time his fist crashed at some destination around her one-hundred-ten-pound frame. He knew his wife would be discreet and handle her business.

And she *was* discreet . . . until she wasn't.

After changing her name, Grayson Sykes had used those pictures and identity in her argument to the judge to seal her court records—as protection and to keep the new name secret. And it had worked. With Nick's know-how and Gray's vigilance, Natalie Dixon wasn't in the system anymore.

Years later, she still worried about doctors' visits, that Sean would somehow obtain her records from clinics and the courts. And now that he had found her, she knew she'd been right to worry.

Had Isabel Lincoln, an abused woman, escaped like *she* had?

Maybe.

Except Gray no longer believed that the missing woman was an abused anything. The fake proof of life picture, the banged-up Maserati, the blackmail . . . Gray had no body, and sure, Isabel Lincoln could indeed be dead. But something in Gray's gut told her . . .

And Tea: the way she and Isabel had texted Gray all day, asking if they were done. So desperate to end it. "It." What was It? There *was* something, the It of it all.

Maybe Noelle Lawrence would know some of It.

Phillips BBQ on Centinela Boulevard was nearly invisible—fragrant purple smoke billowed from the smoke pits in back of the barbecue joint. A few

customers waited for their orders on the sole bench—
and none of them looked like Noelle Lawrence.

Gray peered at her phone—three minutes after six
o'clock—then ordered hot links with medium-heat
barbecue sauce, beans, and coleslaw. "And one of
those." She pointed to the sweet potato pie wrapped
in cellophane.

So far off the road of postsurgery restrictions.

After paying for her meal, she retreated outside to
wait. Since she was waiting, she called Beth, Isabel's
coworker over at UCLA.

"Like, what kind of injuries?" Beth asked.

"A busted lip, bruises . . ."

"Hmm . . ." Beth thought for a minute. "Not that
I can remember."

"You have any pictures taken with her in April or
May?"

Beth texted Gray three shots: a scholar reception
with donors and Isabel, smiling, flawless. At Diddy
Riese cookie shop. Close-up of her bare face with
the ice cream sandwich. No bruising or swelling. No
makeup trying to hide bruising or swelling. Taken on
April 28. And the last picture: jogging at the track on
campus. All smiles. No bandages. No stitches.

Gray then called Noelle. The phone rang until voice
mail picked up. Gray didn't leave a message—she
didn't know who had access to the woman's phone.

At seven o'clock, and with no word from Noelle
Lawrence, Gray finished the last bite of sweet potato
pie. Her phone vibrated on the car's dashboard.

It wasn't Noelle.

I don't know why you haven't responded yet.

Isabel.

Ian is a liar.
I can prove it.
He and Trinity are scamming patients. This is all
about insurance
TRUST ME

Gray's heart hammered. *Trust me?*
Something was up, and she was now caught up in it.

31

Trust me?

Isabel was also a liar.

But I haven't proven that yet.

That's because Gray had spent the day sleeping and watching spider monkeys and hobbits and Ring-wraiths *do* things as she did nothing but sleep and watch.

Guilt kicked in—for blowing off most of Saturday, for not answering emails or phone calls. The sun still sat in the sky, and since investigators didn't work banker's hours, Gray drove to work in an effort to move files from one place on her desk to maybe a cabinet or credenza.

"Allow me to either, like, jack up your evening or make it totally better." Clarissa stood on the other side of Gray's desk, iPad in her hands. "First, though, you feeling okay?"

"Stomach."

"Ew. T.M.I."

"You asked."

"What if I told you . . ." Clarissa plopped into the guest chair. "What if I told you that Kevin Tompkins is, like, totally shifty in everything except disappearing Isabel Lincoln?"

"I'd say spill it."

Clarissa launched into all that she'd found. Like

Kevin Tompkins enlisting in 1995. Like how, in 2009, he had been arrested for public drunkenness but found not guilty. He had been charged with trespassing a year later, but the case was dismissed.

"He totally has great credit, though." Clarissa faked a smile and offered a thumbs-up.

"With those dings on his record, how is he working at the recruitment center?"

"Also, he was stationed up in Seattle the last part of May up until July third."

"I'd kinda eliminated him as a suspect," Gray admitted. "I think Isabel is alive and that she's the one texting me. What about Noelle Lawrence? Find anything out about her?"

"Noelle is, like, literally one of those children of the corn," Clarissa said. "If it's something worth stealing, she's stolen it. She spent more of her childhood in juvie than in school. She just got out of *jail* jail back in November and . . . no job, no degree, and *literally* thousands and thousands of dollars in debt."

"She'd said Isabel was up to something."

"Duh. Weren't you supposed to meet her?"

"I left a message and haven't heard back. One more thing: find out if there's a marriage license registered to . . ." She handed Clarissa a sticky note with the names Omar Neville and Elyse Miller. She'd told herself that she didn't care—and she didn't. But Negro Nancy Drew couldn't completely ignore a mystery.

Clarissa tapped at the keys. Her brows crumpled. "No licenses in the County of Los Angeles. Shall I try Orange, Riverside, and San Bernardino?"

"And throw in Clark County—they could've tied the knot in Vegas." She twisted in her chair, eyes on Clarissa.

Finally, the younger woman shook her head. "Nothing. Sorry."

Maybe they got married . . .

Occam's razor. *Simplest explanation. They're not married.*

Gray called Rebekah Lawrence and told her that she and Noelle had connected briefly and that Noelle hadn't called Gray back as promised. Rebekah sighed and said, "That's what she does. Welcome to my life."

Rader Consulting housed the creatives and the geeks on the other side of the floor. Their space had been designed with broad entryways flanked with fancy lights or twisting wreaths of iron. There was a pool table alongside the Ping-Pong table, and that's where Gray found Sanjay, alone, pool cue in hand, not responding to her voice mail from yesterday.

"I was just about to call you," he said. "I'm working today and not coming in Monday."

Gray followed him into his office, where foam cups mixed in with ceramic mugs, magazines, comic books, and design manuals. "So, the picture you sent . . ." He plopped in front of his Mac and brought up on the screen the shot of Isabel Lincoln standing in the Westin Kauai's breezeway. He then threw a bunch of words at Gray, and each syllable chipped away at a nerve and at her patience until she finally squeezed shut her eyes. "Sanjay, ohmigod, stop."

He said, "Sorry," then clicked, and hummed as he clicked. "It's a frontal shot, but the position of her head doesn't match her neck. The face is off. The color's weird—this up here is bright sunlight but this down here . . . Saturation, curves, levels, all of it. Off."

"Could it be two pictures merged into one?" Gray asked.

"Probably."

"Can you unmerge it?"

He made a noise that meant "Maybe."

"Anything else?"

"So, I looked at the metadata to see where and when this picture was created: July twelfth at eleven twenty-two a.m. in Los Angeles."

"Yesterday in Los Angeles? You sure?"

"Yep."

Gray returned to her office. It didn't take long for her to find Christopher and Hope Walters Lincoln in People Finder. Isabel's real parents lived off Central Avenue, not far from downtown. Gray typed one name and then the other into the Social Security database—if she was planning to visit someone one last time before heading home, she wanted to be sure that at least one of them still walked God's green earth.

Christopher Lincoln had died in October 1987, not long after Isabel's birth.

Hope Walters Lincoln died in August 1992, a month after Isabel's fifth birthday.

Talk about dead ends.

She tabbed back over to People Finder for any other relational links.

Nothing came up—the Lincolns had died before computers captured every sneeze and strand of hair.

Isabel had attached herself to random people like the Lawrences—she had become an orphan before her sixth birthday. Maybe she, too, had been trapped in the foster system.

Gray brought the proof of life photo to her computer screen. It had been taken in Los Angeles, a damn big place—503 square miles. *If she created this photo in L.A., where would she do it?* Gray sat still for several moments, and then one name popped in her head.

Tea. The communications associate who designed newsletters.

There were two addresses for Isabel's best friend—one in Idyllwild, California, and one in Los Angeles—Westchester by its zip code, a suburb not far from the airport and just two miles south of Rader's headquarters. The Westchester house had been purchased in 1983 by Zachariah and Bobbi Carpenter, and with their deaths two years ago, Tea had inherited the home. Tea's name was also on the title for the cabin—the schlumpy slug was a member of the landed gentry. Not that it was a fancy cabin with a loft, skylights, and bamboo floors. No. The picture on the website showed a simple A-frame with a redwood deck and a stone fireplace.

"Idyllwild," Gray said. "That's outside of . . ." *Palm Springs. Where Beth thinks Isabel is buried.* Gray scribbled the Westchester address onto her pad. *Later.*

And then her phone buzzed.

Are we done now? You never responded.

It was Isabel again.

Gray's mind raced as she texted, *I've been thinking about what you wrote, about Ian lying and insurance.*

You believe me? I'm so glad.

This could be Gray's final chance to communicate with the missing woman. But if Isabel was with Tea, maybe Gray could catch her before she disappeared again. She waited to send her response to Isabel until she had slipped behind the Camry's steering wheel. Then:

I have one last question for you.

The city was slipping into shadow now, and Saturday night traffic was slowing her charge. Gray held her breath, light-headed even as she drove. She whiffed fried chicken and seasoned grease as she sped past Dinah's and then swerved south onto Sepulveda Boulevard.

No more questions.

Ian said that he gave you a lot of money.

IS THAT WHAT HE TOLD YOU?
HE'S LYING! DID HE SHOW YOU A SLIP FROM
THE BANK OR ARE YOU TAKING HIS WORD??
HE'S MANIPULATING YOU!!

Gray reached Seventy-Seventh Street and waited as pedestrians crossed the intersection before making a right turn. She then drove west, passing grand houses of a high-end Mayberry with oak tree–lined streets and blood-colored front doors. In the golden, dying sunlight, gnats swarmed over wet grass and around the heads of gardeners.

GPS told her that she was less than one hundred yards away from her destination. She passed the Christophers' army-green ranch house and circled the block. She came to a stop three houses up from the Christopher house, neat and proper with rosebushes and brass fixtures. The sounds of this neighborhood reminded Gray of Monterey. Lawn mowers, the crunch of skateboard wheels against asphalt, dogs barking.

Fuck U I don't have time for this.

Isabel's response.

A battered green Altima with trolls lining the rear window whipped past the Camry.

Tea zipped into her driveway but didn't immediately leave the car.

Gray texted—but she didn't text Isabel. *Hey Tea! Thanks for your help. I'd like to take you to dinner as a thank you.*

Tea's head dipped.

Ellipses filled the screen on Gray's phone.

I'm not feeling well, so no thank you.

Then, Tea climbed out of the Altima.

Gray texted Isabel. *I need to give you the keys you gave Mrs. Tompkins.*

Tea stopped and dropped the phone into her bag, then held a second phone in front of her face. Her fingers flew across the screen as she slowly approached the porch. Text sent, she shoved the key into the door lock and entered the house.

Gray's phone buzzed with a message from Isabel's number.

Just give the key to Tea. Be blessed.

Could it have been a coincidence that Tea had just happened to be juggling two phones at the same time? Or had she been responding for Isabel? *As* Isabel? "Be blessed"—that had always been Tea's signoff after every text string, not Isabel's. So for Isabel to say that . . .

Because Tea has been doubling as Isabel.

Sure.

But *why*?

Gray chewed on that as she surveilled Tea Christopher's home. Nick had called to let her know that he'd landed safely and was back in Los Angeles. Gray sent him a picture of her sitting behind the wheel of the Camry. *I'm detectiving right now.* He texted:

I asked a few of my contacts re: Sean. No contracts
from him. Still looking. BE CAREFUL.

Back at the Christophers' house, Tea stayed in, and the residents of the house where Gray had parked kept peeking out of their windows. With a bladder heavy from the strawberry soda she'd drunk while eating her hot link, Gray was fine with abandoning her watch.

The city was preparing for bed, but her mind still whirled with questions. She knew, though, that most of those queries would be answered on the other side of midnight.

Questions like why were there bags of hair and nails in that lockbox? Had those things come from Isabel's hands and head?

Ian O'Donnell, now on speakerphone, had no clue. "That's a little strange, right?"

"Oh yeah," Gray said, now at her office desk on Sunday morning, eyes on that baggie.

The office was nearly empty—not even eight o'clock—and so quiet that she could hear the Keurig machine gurgle as it warmed water for a first cup of coffee.

"And you can't prove that Tea answered that text as Isabel?" Ian asked.

"No, but with the timing, and the 'Be blessed' thing, I just . . ." She shook her head. "Well, anyway, I just wanted to call you, since I didn't send a report last night. One more thing: Do you have a toothbrush that belonged to her?"

Twenty minutes later, Gray met the cardiologist in the parking lot of her office building.

He handed her a plastic baggie holding a purple toothbrush. His eyes were bloodshot and the blond whiskers across his jaw threatened a beard if he didn't shave in the next day. "Doesn't seem like we're close to ending this."

Gray waggled the baggie. "Hopefully, this brings us closer." This case was ivy—uncontrollable and tangled—and right then she was a rat without teeth, unable to bite her way through the dark mess that hid who knew what else.

She hadn't heard from Tea that morning—as Tea or as Isabel. *What now?* Dance in place until the next step presented itself? Or find out whose hair and nails?

Gray turned into a Culver City office park with its planned grass, planned trees, and bland architecture. Even though she'd eaten breakfast, her stomach gurgled. It was worry—knowing that this case was an iceberg but not knowing what would happen to her once she hit it. Because she *was* going to hit it.

Would she survive the impact? Would Ian?

All of Me specialized in Maury Povich–style scenarios. *You are* not *the father of little DeShawnivon. You* are *the father of Little Enchantress.* The DNA testing service took a few days to provide results for paternity questions, and up to four weeks for more detailed forensic results.

Rader Consultants was a regular, pay-on-time client, and now Gray needed something in between quick and accurate. She knew that she couldn't request DNA testing without Isabel's consent—she'd watched a video on YouTube University that had informed her of that. But there were ways around this stipulation. And so she plucked at the root seven hairs from her own head and slipped them into the bag alongside Isabel's. Then she tore two nails from her left fingers, wreaking havoc on a perfect manicure. She dumped those in the baggie, too.

She'd have to sign an informed consent form—and she had a right to sign it, since two of her own fingernail samples were in the baggie alongside two of Isabel's fingernails.

Two reports would be generated—the results of her DNA and the results for Isabel's.

Hopefully.

At All of Me, the pictures on the walls showed

happy families wearing shorts and flip-flops running on a sunny beach now that All of Me had determined that little Kylie was heir to a 2003 Volkswagen Jetta and a rackful of Starter NFL jerseys.

"I thought I was the only one working today." Gray smiled at Dr. Mary Alice Piper.

The older woman peered at Gray over the top of her silver eyeglass frames. "Do you have a reference sample? Buccal swab, blood card, whole blood to compare against?"

"Yep," Gray said, shivering. "Well, kinda. I have *this*." She held up the bag with Isabel's purple toothbrush. "This is almost as good, right? She abandoned it at his house. But her spit's all over it." She waggled the toothbrush bag again.

With a promise from Mary Alice to rush the analysis, Gray stepped out into the crisp July morning. "What next?" she asked the world.

Firefighters continued to battle the blazes around the Basin. Overnight, they'd contained the two fires closest to the city. That meant Los Angeles no longer had a funhouse mirror kind of a sky—wavy, pearly, a trick of light that made you think you could touch the city's ceiling. No. This morning's sky was true blue, with no specks of danger. Imperfect still, just like the city, but the green of L.A.'s feral parrots popped against it, and there was a breeze, and Gray's eyes didn't burn, and the creamy yellow linen pants she wore this morning seemed appropriate, now that the world didn't smell like an ancient Reno casino.

Refreshed. For once, her mind wasn't crowded. A single thought had the space to linger and twist without being run over and smashed into the ground by another. And as she drove, she sang, along with Oleta, "I've Got a Right," with those drums and big horns.

Gray sped east into the sun, notepad on her lap, jotting down things to do for the day—paperwork, in-box. And she'd check off each task, because today the city wasn't burning down, because she wore yellow linen, and because her car had a full tank of gasoline.

Ten minutes later, she swerved into her usual parking space on Don Lorenzo Drive, in front of Isabel Lincoln's condo. Weren't many cars parked on the street. The breeze rustled the leaves of the eucalyptus and magnolia trees and, somewhere, someone had dumped fertilizer onto a bare lawn. Gray didn't even mind the smell of crap in the air. It smelled like victory—if not now, then three weeks from now, as new blades of green poked past the shit that had been weighing them down.

That was her life, and she was way overdue for those victory blades of new grass.

As she crossed the street, her phone buzzed.

A message from Ian O'Donnell about his latest credit card statement.

Came in yesterday's email but I just opened it now.

Sephora in San Diego. Target in Phoenix. Soriana in Cancun.
Did you visit any of these places?

No of course not.

Nothing had changed in Isabel's condo since Gray's last visit—the ugly couch was still ugly. That pack of Kools had remained unsmoked . . .

She wandered from the patio to the kitchen, slow-stepping, taking her time, now that she had permission from Ian O'Donnell to be there. She moved from her spot in the living room over to the staircase. On the fourth step, she stopped and turned her head to the right, to the photograph hanging on the wall.

It was a framed eight-by-ten of attractive women in diverse shades. A freckled redhead, a coil-poufed black girl, a cool blonde, and a chunky Latina. A United Colors of Benetton crew photo taken at a winery. Smiles. Hugs. Glasses filled with zinfandel. Check-box friends who were all beautiful, especially since the near-setting sun was God's Photoshop filter.

Tea wasn't in this picture. Tea, with her "Be blessed," her troll dolls, and her raggedy Altima, wouldn't have fit in this clique. None of them looked like Noelle, either. Not a dreadlock or a tattoo or a facial piercing in this mix.

"Who are you ladies?" Gray asked. "And why haven't I talked to any of you?"

By now, at least one of Isabel's girlfriends would've heard that a private investigator had been sniffing around. At least one would have sought out Gray to tell more secrets. *I heard . . .* and *Did he tell you . . .* over gluten-free cocktails and kale chips.

Something soft, like dust, swirled in Gray's lungs and made her eyes burn. Was it the picture's setting? Oak barrels and grapevines, the sun like pinot grigio in the cool, bright morning and like velvet and heavy chardonnay at lunchtime, and finally like rosé as you stumbled back onto the tour bus, filled with vino and enough shots like these to fill a photo album.

She, too, had friends like this, who had mattered to her once upon a time. Zoe, Jay, and Avery had always told her the truth: *You're beautiful. You're smarter than this. He'll destroy you.* They had stuck by her until she'd stopped returning their calls and had started to avoid those places that had meant so much to her—to *them*. "Once upon a time," she whispered.

Gray had a crew now. Sort of. Jennifer and Clarissa, and Zadie, too. Their friendship mattered sometimes—sometimes, it wriggled inside of her. Affection, irritation, and trust.

Like Tea, Isabel wasn't in this picture, either.

Isabel wasn't in the picture on the breakfast counter—the Benetton crew on the deck of a catamaran with the sun setting behind them. Nor was she in the picture placed on the coffee table in the living room—the crew wearing flannels and hiking boots, circling a giant sequoia. Nor were they in the picture on the bedroom dresser—the crew perched on the bumper of a gray Jeep, shivering in snow, bundled up in goose down.

Was Isabel intentionally hiding from the camera? Had her confidence been shaken by an underarm bruise that was still a little too green? Or had it been the eggplant-colored abrasions on her cheeks and neck?

Gray, too, had stopped taking pictures after Avery's birthday party at the MGM. Sean had *allowed* her to attend, and she'd had a great time. That night, she wore her favorite Betsey Johnson dress—a floral jacquard frock the color of cranberries and soot. After the party, she saw the pictures that had been taken that night and she swore that her aching heart would pop and kill her. She'd had under-eye bags from not sleeping well. The bruises on her biceps had been shaped like amoebas. The cut on her lip had blown through the layer of MAC Film Noir. At least her eyes sparkled with joy instead of with fear and tears. And her smile? Rockets and sunshine.

But bruises and cuts never cared to behave and cared less about hiding.

After seeing that version of herself captured on film, Gray had insisted on holding the camera and taking the pictures. She hadn't said "Cheese" in seven years.

Had Isabel taken on the role of—

No.

Isabel hadn't been hit by Ian O'Donnell.

Gray knew that. Isabel Lincoln was a liar.

Hard to do—not believe a woman—especially since Grayson Sykes, formerly known as Natalie Kittridge Grayson Dixon, *was* that woman.

A PERFECT UNION

"Only the best for my Nattie," Sean had promised her.

And he had kept that promise. Mrs. Dixon now lived in a big house on a cul-de-sac in Summerlin, Nevada. Her *own* house. A *clean* house that still smelled of paint and varnish, wood shavings and plastic wrap. No wails from police sirens or car alarms. No more living next to stinking trash or filthy alleys crammed with dead dogs and dying men, as she had in Oakland.

The Spanish-Californian two-story had a silver porch light and a breakfast nook, a landscape of succulents with red flowers that popped from their thorny bodies every three weeks. The sunsets were the purest golds and blues in the universe, and she could see the far-off glow of the Vegas Strip from her bedroom deck.

A dream.

On this night in July, after two years of living as Mrs. Sean Dixon, she wandered Target with a cart of pasta, olives, and popcorn. A bottle of Gray Goose vodka already sat in the back seat of her Jag. It was a night to unwind—Sean had flown to Macao for a gaming convention, and this time, he'd actually *gone* on his trip and hadn't pretended to so that he could watch her—like the time he hadn't flown to Atlantic City and, instead, drove three cars behind her on Simmons Boulevard. At a red light, he had used his key fob to open the rear passenger-side door of her Jaguar and climb into the back seat. His eyes had been hidden by his aviator sunglasses, but their heat burned through her headrest and his hands around her neck had burned—

"Nat Grayson?"

Stones and whiskey. She turned to that familiar voice.

He wore all black, and his hair was slicked back. He looked more Asian tonight, like a member of the yakuza. He was bigger than before, with muscles like a racehorse.

"Dom!" Mrs. Dixon's spirit shimmied, seeing him in the snacks aisle. She ran up to him and threw herself into his arms. "What are you doing here? *Really*— what are you doing *here*, off the Strip, in a freaking Target?"

He squeezed her tight, kissed her neck and cheeks. "Visited a client and now I'm buying provisions for tonight."

She cocked an eyebrow. "Prophylactics?"

He tapped her nose stud. "No love without the glove."

She gave him a playful shove. "You still a G-man?" She could still feel the heat of his body on her palms and wanted to wrap her body with her hands.

Dominick Rader shook his head. "Last year, I got shot in the shoulder. Right here." He tapped the space near the end of his collarbone. "Damn near collapsed a lung, but . . ." He grinned, shrugged. "Here I am."

"Glad you pulled through."

"Still married?" His smile combined dismay and amusement, *She can't be this stupid* with *Oh my, I think she is.*

She said, "Yeah," and then, "So, if you're not in the Bureau, what are you doing all day?"

"I'm back home in L.A. Started a consulting firm. Locates, surveillance, background checks, that kind of thing. What are *you* doing all day? Last time I saw you, you were working at the museum in Oakland, right?"

"Ha. Yeah. Well . . . I'm living here."

Ducking. Dodging. Squeezing into a protective ball.

Sean had hit her five times and shoved her more times than that. He'd eaten most of the food on her plate, but instead of her losing ten pounds, stress, drinking, and popping pain pills had made her gain twenty. Her dream house had turned into a prison and she now lay awake almost every night, eyes on the ceiling, heart banging in her chest, more scared than she'd been at Mom Twyla's crummy duplex with the knocking pipes, the stinking alleys, and the gnawing rats.

She said, "I'm . . . just living. Helping out with my husband's business sometimes." *And saving every coin and dollar I can find.* Her mad money, jump-started by that Texan's $250 blackjack score, had grown to almost a grand. And those secret rent checks from her house in Monterey—twenty-five hundred dollars a month over the last seven years—had added up.

Dominick's eyes darkened. "You getting over the flu or something?"

"Huh? No. I'm fine."

His gaze kept pecking over her and what she now saw as her normal. Like that extra weight around her stomach and hips. Deep, dark pockets beneath her eyes. Great hair, though. Sean loved her long hair.

"You look incredible." She poked him in the abdomen. "But then you've always been, dare I say, *hot*. And when you wore that badge around your neck?" She flapped at her face and pretended to get the vapors.

"Didn't think you noticed."

"I may be stupid, but I'm not blind."

He kissed her left hand, then peered at her rings. "Can't believe you're married."

"Two years now."

"That long?"

Her skin tingled even as she said, "Yeah. That long."

"Happily?"

"Does it matter?"

"Yeah, it matters."

She pulled her hands back, then tucked the hand heavy with diamonds into her hoodie pocket. "It's fine. We're okay. I'm just . . . getting used to being married." Her head ached with that lie, told so many times now, mostly to herself. She swallowed the lie again and it pinched at her throat and it rappelled down her esophagus, glowing like the poison it was. Yes, her lies were going to kill her one day.

She and Dominick Rader didn't speak as moms passed them, pushing toddlers in carts and strollers. As couples wandered hand in hand down the snack aisle, snatching bags of Tostitos and Doritos off shelves. As normal people did normal things.

"Let's have a drink," he said. "Dinner, if you have the time."

"I'm not dressed for that."

"I can change. I have jeans and a T-shirt—"

"That's okay."

"It's still early. I wanna catch up. See what you've been doing all this time. We can do that over a good meal. I know a guy."

She laughed. "My tale would only stretch through appetizers." She did nothing all day. Sean required that of her. Look pretty, talk pretty, only be interesting if his business clients required interesting conversation. Wit and intelligence were fetishes in this town. More to be ashamed of than sucking noses and fucking chickens. Which, she'd learned, were things.

Dominick tried to smile. "Fine. Let's grab a bag of Target popcorn, sit on the hood of your car, and just talk."

"Dom . . . *Shit*."

A large, bald white dude who worked security at one of Sean's clubs was carrying a basket filled with a roll of paper towels and a liter of Squirt. His eyes had shifted to the shelf in front of him—vacuum cleaners—but slid back to her once he thought she'd looked away. *Mr. Hook*, that's what they called him. Because of his hook head. He'd followed her once before, and later that night Sean had made her see colors.

Dominick Rader was also looking at Mr. Hook. He turned back to her and asked, "That guy following you?"

"It's fine. I know him." Tears were now stinging her eyes. "It's because of the business my husband's in—gangsters and gamblers and gamers, oh my." She tried on a smile. Her mouth lifted—it worked. "I should go."

Dominick moved closer to her and, in a low voice, said, "I'm gonna put my business card over in the aisle with the tampons. Bottom shelf, beneath the first box of Tampax. You take it, okay? Call me any time, Natalie. For anything. You understand?"

She nodded.

He squeezed her arm, and that made her sad, because she'd looked forward to his hug again, to his lips against her skin. But he knew better than to kiss and hug her again—he'd done it too much already. He didn't want to complicate her life any more than he already had.

So they said their good-byes. Then he trundled off to feminine hygiene and she (and Mr. Hook) wandered over to cleaning supplies. She dropped laundry detergent into the cart.

Mr. Hook grabbed dishwasher soap.

I don't need the card. I know his number. Her father had made her memorize it.

In the next aisle, she pulled a pack of toilet paper into her cart.

I should get the card but . . .

Mr. Hook studied trash bags.

How will I get the card and then hide it?

After wandering and debating about whether she should pluck the card from its spot or not, she headed over to feminine hygiene.

That aisle was kryptonite for men like Mr. Hook.

There, on the bottom shelf, was the first box of Tampax. She grabbed that box—not that she needed tampons, after peeing on a stick yesterday, not that she'd need any type of . . . *rescue?* Not with that stick's plus sign. It would be better now with that plus sign. Still, she plucked Nick's card from the shelf.

Nick Rader
RADER CONSULTING

Good decision. He'd changed his phone number from the one she knew backwards and forward. Beneath these new phone and pager numbers, he had written her a note.

Anytime, Nat, and I'll be there.

SHE
FOUND
NEW
DIRECTION

33

As she left Isabel's unit, Gray saw that the English bull-dog with the cauliflower ear had returned and that he had parked his black Chevy Malibu two cars ahead of Gray's Camry. He sat behind the steering wheel and took pictures of Gray exiting the security gate.

Gray froze in her spot and let the gate slam be-hind her. With drums banging in her head, she stomped across Don Lorenzo Drive to the Malibu and said, "Hi."

"How ya doin'?"

The interior of his car was a mess. Cups—from tiny, watercooler size to gigantic megasips—had been crammed into every holder and free space, alongside crumpled balls of foil and wax paper. The stained seats and the torn-off wedges of burger buns asserted that this car belonged to, yes, a slob, but to a slob cop, slob private investigator, or a slob thug. The man himself smelled of weak soap and sadness.

"Why are you stalking Isabel Lincoln?" Gray asked.

"I'm not." He smiled, and Gray thought of the silver-toothed man in *Moonraker*.

Gray snorted. "Every time I come here, *you're* here. Just like a stalker. And now I think I'm gonna call the police."

"Waste of time. I'm a P.I. and I'm working right now. Who the hell are you?"

"*I'm* a P.I. and *I'm* working right now."

He gave her the up-and-down, smirking at her lemony linen. "Your boss didn't tell you to avoid bright colors? You wanna get made? I mean, you already stand out. Cute face, a bit chubby, black, and now you're wearing freakin' yellow?

"Come on, sunshine. They can see you from Calcutta. Some advice. If you *are* a P.I.? Wear black. It's slimming and invisible."

Gray's cheeks warmed. "Says the ugly man parked right in front of the apartment he's surveilling and holding a big-ass 1910 Eastman Kodak in front of his face."

"Ha. Touché."

"What are you P.I.-ing, not that I believe you?"

"Just trying to check on some things, but she hasn't been around. Know where she is?" When Gray didn't respond, he gave her that glinty smile again, then he fished in his trash and found a business card. "This is me. Your turn."

"Stuart Ardizzone . . . JCI Insurance?" She went rigid—that envelope Mrs. Tompkins had handed her last week . . . *Supposed to give this to you. . . .* Gray handed him a business card.

He whistled, and said, "Rader," with a lifted eyebrow. "That's some fancy shit right there. Me and Nick work together a lot of times—insurance cheats, worker's comp cheats, you name it. Does he know you're wearing yellow on a stakeout?"

"I'm not on a stakeout. And why does JCI have you out here, Stuart Ardizzone?"

"Can't say, but I'm thinking it's related." He tossed her card into the pile of seat trash. "So, when was the last time you saw Miss Lincoln?"

"I haven't seen her."

"But you just left her condo." Ardizzone scratched his scalp, sending white flakes to join the bank of dandruff on his polo-shirted shoulders. "You know when she's coming back?"

"Has to be soon. It's not like she has a lot of money to just be gone forever."

"Do me a favor. Lemme know either when she's back or if you find out where she is. I'll give you five hundred dollars for your trouble."

"You think I trust you to pay me?"

"Look at this face." He smiled big and wide and silver. "Would I lie?"

"Yes. That's what we do in this business—lie."

"C'mon, Miss Sykes. I'm with a big outfit. I don't need to lie to *you*. Ask your boss if I'm a straight arrow and he'll tell you 'Hell yeah.'"

"Fine. I will." She called Nick. "So, Stuart Ardizzone?"

Nick laughed. "Went to UCLA with him. I owe him twenty bucks. Why?"

She studied the investigator. That ear, that strained belt buckle, those gorgeous Gucci loafers. "He's sitting right in front of me. Working with JCI on the Lincoln case."

"He being a problem?"

"Just making sure he's being honest."

"*Honest?* Who do you think we are? Captain freakin' America?"

After she ended the call, Stuart Ardizzone grinned. "I check out?"

"Yeah. So, Isabel Lincoln. You think she's scamming you guys?"

"Can't say."

"Fine." She stepped away from the Malibu. "Later, dude."

"Okay, okay. Yeah, she's scamming again. You tell *me* something and I'll tell you something else."

"Deal. I have a few questions first. Easy ones. She have an insurance policy?"

"Of course—that's why I'm here."

"What kind?"

"The whole enchilada—health, life, car."

"Who's the beneficiary?"

Stuart Ardizzone grabbed his iPad from the passenger seat and sent soy sauce and ketchup packets spilling to the mat. He tapped around the screen. "Tea Christopher."

"Really?"

"Yup."

"Isabel use medical insurance to pay for emergency room visits in the last six months?"

"So, that would be January until now? Lemme see . . ." He tapped on his iPad. "Nothing here except a few checkups with her general practitioner."

"She could've paid cash, though. Or visited some random clinic." Like Gray had.

"Yeah, she could've," Ardizzone admitted. "I can tell you this, though: She filed a claim for a car accident last year. Says the guy who hit her didn't have insurance. We paid that. Then there were the medical bills from her doctor—some quack who signed forms for kickbacks. He's in jail for being a kickback king."

"You're gonna love this, then. That guy with no car insurance?"

"Yeah?"

Gray told him about meeting Mitch Pravin, who drove that allegedly uninsured Maserati.

Stuart Ardizzone grinned as he typed into his notes app. "This is good, real good."

"You said 'scamming *again*.' She has a history of this?"

"Last year, she filed a worker's comp claim. Says she slipped over at UCLA—"

"*That's* true. Her boyfriend—he's a doctor over there—he witnessed it. That's actually how they met."

"She says she broke her ankle on the clock that day, on her way to a meeting."

"But?"

"There wasn't no break in her ankle. He signed off on it, though, and said that she had broken it, even though the X-rays were suspect. Didn't matter—she got disability payments."

"She would've had to go to medical appointments to collect disability."

"She saw *him*—I guess the doctor boyfriend—and *he* examined her."

"But *he's* a *cardiologist*."

"Yep."

Gray froze. Isabel's text message. *This is all about insurance. TRUST ME.*

Ian O'Donnell's hands were dirty. *He* had committed insurance fraud. *That* was the Big Secret. The liaison in the treatment room with Hot Nurse Pfeiffer was simply gravy.

Everything about Ian is a lie. Tea Christopher had been right about that, and yet Gray had believed his tears.

Blame the Viognier. Blame his beauty. Blame her willingness to believe a crying, beautiful man plying her with delicious wine.

Gray asked, "How long have you been investigating?"

"Started right before the holiday."

"There's an envelope from JCI on her breakfast bar."

"That's the check for the stolen car."

"Is this the same car wrecked by the accident with the Maserati last year or is this a different car?"

He tapped around the iPad again. "We totaled a 2015 Honda Accord in the accident with the Maserati—gave her eight grand for it. Then she bought a pre-owned 2017 BMW 428 last August, and it got stolen May eleventh, just a few months ago, and we gave her Blue Book for it—thirty-three thousand. That's the check we just sent. That's the check on her breakfast bar."

Gray's belly felt loose and hot and she wanted to sit in the middle of Don Lorenzo Drive.

"So she ain't cashed it yet," Ardizzone was saying. "It won't go through now anyway, cuz we put a hold on the funds. She doesn't know that yet, and I've been coming to see if she's gonna pick it up. How the hell did you get it?"

"The neighbor gave it to me."

"Why would the neighbor give it to *you*?"

"She thinks I'm one of Isabel's friends, and Isabel gave her a key a while ago to take care of a pet. Anyway, the neighbor gave me the house key. And the doctor boyfriend is my client—his name's actually on the lease. He gave me *his* key. So, basically, Miss Lincoln can't enter this condo unless she breaks in or comes through *me*."

Then, Gray told him about the boxes of L'Oréal hair color, the memo pad with flight numbers, and the stolen Labradoodle.

Stuart Ardizzone said, "Jeez."

"Yeah. How much is the life insurance policy for?"

"Half a mil."

"When did she take it out?"

"April."

"For who?"

The silver-toothed man pecked at the iPad, then glared at the sky. "Crap. Connection's gone. Lemme get back to you on that."

"Why would she take out a policy for five hundred thousand dollars and then leave the city?"

"Don't know," Stuart Ardizzone said. "She also upped an older life insurance policy on *her*, for another five hundred K. That's when the number crunchers sent me out."

Isabel Lincoln could be dead, but not by Ian O'Donnell's hand. *Tea*, the sole beneficiary on Isabel's life insurance policy, could have killed her friend and was now impersonating the dead woman through text messages. Tea would also have received the insurance payout for the BMW—that check now sitting on the breakfast counter. Which is why she was juggling those two cell phones. Hers and Isabel's.

Grifter. A red-blooded American grifter.

And Gray had thirty-three thousand dollars' worth of bait.

Stuart Ardizzone raced to talk with Mitch Pravin at Shalimar Furniture.

Gray returned to Isabel Lincoln's condo and opened the envelope from JCI Insurance Services. She held her breath as she pulled out the now-voided check for thirty-three thousand dollars. She laid the check on the breakfast bar, then took a picture of the check and the envelope. She texted the picture to the missing woman and her best friend, along with a message.

Look what I have.

Bait.

I need to meet with one of you so that I can give this to you. I won't leave it just sitting. I won't release it until I get that picture of Isabel's thigh.

Until then, she'd keep the check in Rader's safe.

Gray retreated to the Camry and willed her pulse to slow. Wouldn't be good to have a coronary event while on surveillance. As she sat, she gazed down at her bright lemon pants. Stuart Ardizzone was right—she needed to reconsider her sartorial choices while working a case. Because she *was* staking out. Just like he said.

Too late.

Two hours after she'd left Isabel's condo to sit in the Camry, no one had come or gone. Just sitting there, her head dropped, and once she heard herself snore. She blinked awake—not much time had passed in between these snatches of sleep.

"Do better, girl," she muttered to herself. She could buy cans of Mountain Dew or Red Bull, but then she'd have to pee. Male P.I.s could urinate into a bottle. What did women do?

A text message from Clarissa.

I think this is your guy.

She had included an attachment.

LOS ANGELES MAN FOUND DEAD IN DESERT AREA OF ADELANTO

Gray tapped the link to the short news article. The first image was the driver's license picture of a young, bearded black man.

Omar Neville, 33, was found in an unattended vehicle on Saturday. A person riding an ATV discovered the car and occupant . . . Sheriff Department is investigating . . .

"Oh no, oh no, no—"
The phone vibrated again, but she stared out the windshield instead.
Omar Neville was dead? Why? And who . . .
Elyse Miller. She had to find—
Another vibration. Clarissa again.

U there?

Yeah I'm thinking. I'll contact the sheriff later. Thanks C!

For now, she'd stay planted in the front seat of the Camry, steps away from the janky security gate. She'd wait to hear from Tea Christopher or Isabel Lincoln, wait for that battered green Altima with the troll dolls in the back window to swerve into a space at the curb. Or, better yet, that big black truck Mrs. Tompkins saw on the morning Isabel Lincoln disappeared.

As she sat and waited and expected, sweat poured down Gray's face and back. It was a Sunday in July, and her white silk shirt was nearly transparent with perspiration. The surgery scars in her abdomen throbbed, and she was almost certain that the liquid around them that was making her wound stick to silk wasn't sweat. She found a half-full bottle of water on the car floor, then guzzled it.

Her phone buzzed.

What are you doing right now?

A 310 area code. Los Angeles. *Who wants to know?*

You need to be careful.

Gray's mouth went dry. She glanced at the condos across the street and then glanced in the rearview and side mirrors. No one stood on the sidewalks or in the courtyard. Not many cars were parked at the curb—everyone was still at church or brunch, except for the owners of a white Tesla, a copper Kia, two blue American sedans, Gray's Camry . . . and a black Range Rover.

From her place behind the wheel, she couldn't see the SUV's plates. Couldn't see if anyone sat in the driver's seat. She grabbed her phone and tapped the

ORO app to check alerts for Sean's cars, but the app scrolled . . . *One bar.* "Crap."

She typed, *wrong number. it's obvious you don't know me.*

A picture blinked onto her phone's screen.

3WXA9L2.

The license plate on Gray's Camry. The eucalyptus trees that lined Don Lorenzo Drive. Gray asleep behind the steering wheel.

Her eyes zigzagged around the neighborhood.

No one stood in the courtyard, on the sidewalks, or—

It's gone. Not the Range Rover; it was still parked, and now the car looked dark green instead of black. No, the white Tesla that had been parked on the other side of the street was now gone. She hadn't heard its engine start or its tires crunch against the asphalt.

Was it *Sean*? Had he hired a private investigator that Nick hadn't found yet? Was he—the P.I. or her ex-husband—now driving that white Tesla?

Who is this?? Took forever to type. Gray's fingers had become blocks of ice.

You'll find out soon.

Gray hit the Phone icon to call the texter.

The phone rang . . . rang . . . "The party you have reached is unavailable—"

She tapped End, then, eyes closed, took several breaths. In . . . Out . . . In . . . Out . . .

And Sunday had started out so good. Sunday had started out so long ago.

Hey, Clarissa, Gray typed, *run this phone number please.*

Her phone buzzed again, but not with Clarissa's response.

There was a picture of a butterfly tattoo on a café au lait–colored thigh.

I TOLD U I WAS ALIVE. I need my money!!

Nausea settled over Gray like a heavy, wet blanket, and the world tilted left, then right. That place between *Okay* and *Oh shit* was becoming tissue-thin, and she had just enough time to launch herself out of the car and onto the grassy curbside. Hot. She was too hot. Dehydrated. Not drinking enough water. Not—

Liquified breakfast exploded from her mouth and onto the grass. Her body shook as she vomited, as her stomach yawed and twisted. She gagged and retched as every ounce of fluid poured out of her, and she steadied herself, elbows on knees, as the convulsions softened.

Gray swiped her mouth and nose, both wet and goopy, with the tail of her silk shirt.

A breeze, such a blessing from God, brushed over her, cooling her down some. *You can't sit here much longer—it's too damned hot.* She stayed in the shade. Pain twisted through her nerves and veins, her body hating her loudly now for the sweating, the drinking, the busted appendix, the anxiety. Hating her now for letting it get beaten, never forgiving her for allowing another to destroy its temple, for not finishing those stupid antibiotics after the surgery. And now her body warned her to open her eyes.

She redialed that mysterious number and held her breath.

The phone rang . . . rang . . . This time there was no prompt to leave a message.

"Okay." Her eyes were open, but that curtain of tears blurred. *I'm gonna stop it. I'm gonna stop Sean. Somehow.*

35

Do something.

But on Monday, Gray's new day of rest, she called in sick to work, then drove to the urgent care center a mile from her apartment.

This clinic kept its warped linoleum floors clean but did nothing to fix the busted neon sign hanging on its eaves.

There, Dr. Nazarian saw nothing wrong with her. "Maybe the incision is infected, since you didn't finish your medications." The hundred-year-old physician diagnosed her by only peering at her belly from afar for about a second. Then he prescribed a different antibiotic and more oxycodone before shuffling out of the exam room.

Gray paid for her visit in cash—three hundred dollars—then waited for her drugs at the in-clinic pharmacy. She sat there with near-zero confidence that Dr. Nazarian had properly diagnosed her, but she still held a spark of hope that he had.

At home, she took her first dosages, then climbed into bed.

Do something.

"I'll get him. Not gonna take it anymore," she whispered, as she rehydrated with bottles of Gatorade, Popsicles, and glasses of water, gritting her teeth with every burst of nausea, every stomach cramp . . .

She received one text, from Clarissa, right as she closed her eyes.

> Just got off the phone with travel. No "Isabel Lincoln"
> booked a flight to Belize or anywhere else.
> And that phone number you sent yesterday?
> Burner. Sorry.

Gray tried to feel something—anger, fear, sadness—but she only felt numb. She couldn't live like this. She *wouldn't* live like this.

So do something.

Stop Sean.

Clarissa's party in Las Vegas—she'd stop him then. It would be a trip to remember.

36

The bum check from JCI Insurance Services now sat in Rader Consulting's safe. It was Tuesday night, and Gray found herself working in the office even as the pain in her navel made her squeeze her eyes so tight that a teardrop crystallized into a diamond and tumbled down her cheek. She pushed away from her desk and waited for the sharp twangs to ebb and for her suddenly hot office to cool. She'd medicated earlier in the day—remembering to take her antibiotic, even—but she needed the heavy stuff now.

There weren't many people working at almost eight o'clock. There were more shadows pushing vacuum cleaners than clicking computer keyboards. That meant she could work in silence, work without expecting Jankowski to pop in, helmet hair in place, Stepford wife smile on her lips, steno pad in her hand.

Her mind free to focus, Gray updated logs, files, and clouds with all things Isabel Lincoln. Stuart Ardizzone had left a voice mail message: "*Great conversation with Mitch Pravin yesterday. Thanks for the lead in that. Lemme know if you need anything or heard anything new.*"

The dark outside her office was coming on hard, a December kind of dark, instead of July. The color of night in Los Angeles was milky purple and black, with sparkles of white and red from soaring airplanes and low-flying helicopters.

Not that Gray had been paying attention to the light beyond her office blinds. Her body's clamor had stolen the thunder and she now covered her eyes with shaky hands. Was this pain, months after surgery, normal? Maybe Dr. Messamer had left a scalpel or a cotton swab in her wound before he'd sewn her shut? If she'd had her own tools right then—a scalpel, a knife, a fireplace poker, and a big cold bottle of vodka, Smirnoff even—she would have shoved one of them into her belly just to make the pain stop, or to simply pass out and wait for a cool, silky morphine cocktail administered by doctors who would correct Dr. Messamer's mess.

Maybe the EMTs would drive her to UCLA or Cedars-Sinai this time, hospitals with clean beds, good food, and beautiful doctors—doctors like Ian O'Donnell, who could help her commit insurance fraud for sex. #Goals.

One Mississippi, two Mississippi, three . . .

By fifteen Mississippi, the invisible knife was pulling out of her gut and the twang was lessening to a twinge. Her muscles slackened, her teeth unclenched, and her fists opened into usable things. She was trembling, but then, every minute of the day couldn't be smooth Newport Alive with Pleasure days.

"Where are the freakin' margaritas when you need one?" She pawed through her purse and found the bottle of Percocet. She popped one, then slumped into her chair.

Her office phone chirped and flashed Nick's number. When she picked up, he said, "You rang?"

"I did. Crazy idea." Then she caught him up on

Isabel and Ian, insurance fraud, T-boned Maseratis, and furniture store owners.

Nick didn't speak.

"Hello?" A Perc smile twisted onto her face. "You there? Bored already?"

"Ian walked right into it, didn't he?"

"Men and their penises."

"Empires are built because of men and their penises."

"Rome. Atlantis. The Death Star . . . And Ian was a willing participant in some of this."

"You're on a path. Why'd you call me? To tell me how awesome I am?"

"You're awesome, but also . . ." Gray twisted in her chair. "I wanna check out that cabin in Idyllwild before I talk to Tea. I've been avoiding her."

"Why?"

"Cuz I wanna catch them off guard. What if Isabel's there at that cabin? Or worse? What if Isabel's buried somewhere on that property? And since I don't know what I'll find out there, would you mind tagging along? I know you're doing your own investigation—"

"And every contact I talk to says Dixon isn't their client."

"Could someone be lying?"

"It's possible somebody's working and not saying."

"So?"

"So . . . I'm gonna keep on asking questions. I'm gonna keep on *trucking*."

"Until then, come with me. I'll buy you breakfast. And I'll also put together a fun bag." Wigs, glasses, colored contact lenses, gloves, and scarves.

Nick lived seven minutes away from Rader Consulting and didn't take long to pick up Gray in his

Yukon. She climbed into the passenger seat with opioid electricity razzing through her body.

"I brought you something," he said.

She held out her hands. "Gimme, gimme, gimme."

He placed a plastic bag on her palms. "Okay, open them."

She peeked into the bag. "Aww. You remembered." First, she pulled out the snow globe—palm trees, a blue wave, Santa on a surfboard, red letters that spelled "Hawaii." Then she pulled out the can of Mauna Loa macadamia nuts with pineapple.

Nick had also brought Baby Ruths and Cheetos, Mountain Dew for him, and bottles of Pellegrino for her. "So, where am I going?" He cruised out of the parking lot.

Gray studied his profile. Those cheekbones, his lips . . . Damn.

Did I say that aloud?

She punched an address into the car's navigation system. She popped open the can of nuts, then settled into her seat. She ignored the prickly heat that had killed unsuspecting queens. *Like Cleopatra and . . . and Cersei and . . . was Jezebel a queen?* Gray was also glad that Nick was now playing the Gipsy Kings on the stereo. Dancing music instead of sexing music. Thanks to Spanish guitars, she was now certain that she wouldn't unbutton the fly of his jeans and give him road head. *If he only knew.*

"Only knew what?" Nick asked.

Oops. "Huh?"

"You okay?"

Alert now, Gray nodded.

"What did you take?"

"Nothing."

"Grayson."

"Just Percocet."

"Because?"

"I have a bellyache."

"Maybe we shouldn't—"

"I'm fine. Let's go." She flashed him a smile.

His frown didn't turn upside down.

She licked her finger and stuck it in his ear.

He laughed and batted her hand.

The drive was not an exotic one—Interstate 10 to Palm Springs had never been the public highway that tantalized you with California poppies, ocean views, charming cottages, or even cows, horses, and sheep. No one ever fell in love on the 10 or said, "Ooh, let's take the Ten—we have time." It simply bored you to death with its meth-town Denny's and Del Tacos, places where colored people dared not pee. Better to risk urinary tract and bladder infections than to pee beneath a Confederate flag next to someone with Aryan Brotherhood tats on his bicep or her stretch-marked boob. Gray and Nick did all their peeing at Indian casinos.

Idyllwild sat in the San Jacinto Mountains, forty-six miles from Palm Springs, five and a half thousand feet above sea level. With no lake around, the town's main attractions were the pine and cedar forests and the trails cut between them. Little cabins, a diner, and a fake Bigfoot—that's all there was to see in Idyllwild.

Nick said, "We should come up here this winter. Do some cross-country skiing."

"Never done that. I'm down for a new adventure."

"Not that we have to wait until the *winter*."

"Don't we need snow for cross-country skiing?"

"Well, we wouldn't ski. We'd hike."

"How about October? After Clarissa's wedding?"

"I'll find a cabin."

They rolled past Tea Christopher's A-frame. "When you do find a cabin," Gray said, "just make sure it's bigger than *that*."

Nick cut off the truck's headlamps. "It looks bigger in the pictures." He was comparing the internet results with the dollhouse nestled within a grove of cedars.

A black Ford F-10 truck was parked in the driveway.

Gray rolled down the window and sap-smelling night air rolled past her. The soft rustling of treetops was the only sound, and except for the lights glowing in the cabin, the forest was a glistening black. In the cabin, a shadow moved across the room. Violet-colored light from a television joined golden light from the lamps.

"You see that truck, right?" Gray asked.

"Yep." Nick was already scribbling the license plate number into her notebook. "You bring your laptop?"

Gray's mouth opened, then popped closed. "Oops."

Nick sighed. "Run it back in the office."

Face burning, she said, "The neighbor told me that Isabel left in a black truck."

"She give you the truck's plate number?"

"No."

He offered her the Baby Ruth. "She give you a make and model?"

She took a bite from the candy bar. "No."

"She—"

"I got it, Nick. I didn't say this was *the* truck. I said the lady saw Isabel leave in *a* truck."

But Gray knew in her gut—as sick as her gut was—that this truck *was* that truck.

37

Minutes later, Nick and Gray approached the cabin's front porch. He carried a knapsack filled with a change of clothes and a waistband filled with Beretta. He wore Buddy Holly glasses and had parted his hair like a Silicon Beach tech nerd, which was closer to the truth than he wanted to believe. Gray carried the bag of snacks Nick had purchased for the drive. She'd tugged on an expensive honey-blonde wig she'd named the "Beyoncé" and had popped in green-colored contact lenses. She nodded after Nick whispered, "Ready?"

He knocked on the door.

A man as big and brown as a grizzly bear answered. Coarse black hair poked out and around his gray wife-beater. He smelled of weed and corn chips, and his scowl meant that he didn't like that two strangers stood on his porch this close to midnight.

Nick gaped at him. "*You're* not Andreas. You must be Eric, then."

The man's scowl cut deeper into his pockmarked face. "What the hell are you talking about?" His eyes left Nick's and smacked into Gray's.

She faked a startle. "We're supposed to be Airbnbing with you and Dre. We're the Miyamis. Hi." She stuck out her hand. "Sorry we got here late—traffic."

Big Man didn't take her hand, just glared at her.

"I know, we should've been here hours ago." Nick chuckled, then moved forward to enter the cabin.

"Where you think you going?" Big Man challenged.

"My bad, Eric. We're just a little tired—"

"I'm not Eric," Big Man growled, "and I'm not expecting no guests."

"There must be a misunderstanding," Nick said.

"Sir," Gray said, now squeezing her knees together, "mind if I use the restroom? I've been holding it—I hate public restrooms. They scare me, actually, and—"

"Let me check." Nick rustled around in his knapsack. "The reservation's in here—"

"Who cares, babe?" Gray said, still pee dancing. To Big Man: "I *really* need to go."

"Yeah, whatever, go. Down the hall." Big Man nodded behind him.

"Oh, wait," Nick said. "I have an email with the reservation."

As Nick fumbled around on his phone, Gray quick-stepped past the ancient television set, which was displaying a scene with a bottle blonde spanking a cop handcuffed to the bumper of a squad car. She glanced at the faded green couch and the beaten bookshelves sagging beneath the weight of a trillion DVDs and videocassettes. A bag of Fritos, dead blunts, and a filled ashtray on the coffee table explained Big Man's perfume—even with the pitched ceiling, she was getting a contact high simply by hurrying through the living room.

No porno movie played in the bathroom. But the thought of putting any bare part of herself near any spot Big Man had placed *his* bare parts made Gray's bladder shrivel, making the true need to relieve herself a distant memory.

There was nothing remarkable in the green-tiled room. There was a framed, yellowing picture of the Palm Springs tram hanging above a snow-covered mountain. There was a pine-tree-shaped cake of soap that hadn't melted and looked as new on this day as it had the day the Carpenters purchased it from J. J. Newberry after Jimmy Carter's presidential inauguration.

But there was . . .

"That," Gray whispered.

That was a box of L'Oréal hair color. Black Sapphire, like the box in Isabel's condo. Big Man had a lot of hair, but not on his head.

She lifted the lid on the clothes hamper.

A bloody towel. A bloody white shirt.

She gasped.

The hamper's top dropped.

She froze.

Waited . . . Wondered . . . *Whose blood—*

No pounding fist on the door.

Gray flushed the toilet, ran the tap, then flicked water on the perfect bar of soap. She opened the window—just an inch, just enough to open later. Back in the hallway, she glanced at the ceiling in search of a door that led to an attic, an attic where a woman could hide—or be hidden.

Nothing.

She looked down at the hardwood floor, for a rug that bumped up or sat crooked and hid the entryway for a basement.

There were no tumbled balls of hair. No chew toys. No dog smells. There were no random bits of kibble, nor was there an empty water bowl in a corner.

Back at the front door, Big Man and Nick were still

talking, going on now about the Dodgers' chances of making it to the World Series.

Gray peeked into the bedroom, hoping to spot the Mary Ann with the *Vogue* cheekbones in bed with a book of crossword puzzles on her lap. There was no Mary Ann—just a fuchsia and black Nike duffel bag in the corner of the room and a queen-size bed with linens so funky she could smell them from the doorway.

Smiling, she strolled back to the living room. "Thank you so much, kind sir. I was three minutes away from drowning."

Big Man said, "No problem."

Nick grinned at her. "We figured it out. This is *3871*, not *3811* Pine Cone Drive."

Gray gasped. "I am so sorry, sir."

Big Man flicked his big paw. "These roads get twisty as fuck up here, and there ain't no lights *nowhere*."

Back in the Yukon, Nick took off his Buddy Holly glasses. "See anything?"

Gray took out a bottle of hand sanitizer and squeezed a pool in the middle of her palm. "A box of hair coloring—Black Sapphire, like the box back at Isabel's. There was a woman's gym bag in the bedroom, and . . . there's a bloody towel and shirt in the laundry hamper."

Nick lifted his eyebrows. "Shaving accident?"

"He'd have no head if he'd done that. What about you?"

"His name's Bobby and he has a dog paw tat right here." Nick pointed to his shoulder.

"A dog lover?"

"He's a Blood. You should be brushing up on your gang lore."

"One thing at a time." She paused, then added,

"Why the hell is church-girl Tea keeping company with a Blood?"

"Guess you need to find that out. Shall we stay and see what he does?" Nick was already adjusting his seat to "Sleep."

As Nick slept, that television light in the cabin never dimmed and Bobby's shadow didn't move again. She thought about Sunday's threatening text messages and her life with Sean Dixon. She thought of her succulent garden and her red Jaguar, her subscriptions to *Vanity Fair* and *Glamour*. Had Sean stacked them on the coffee table for her eventual return? Had he sold her car? Before she'd thrown away her iPhone, he'd left pleading voice mail messages begging her to come back home. He'd forgiven her, he'd said, and he chalked it up to both of them being exhausted and taking out their anger and stress in different ways.

Sean's way of dealing with stress and anger usually left her bleeding.

Like the time he'd pushed her down on the second-story deck off their bedroom.

Or the time he'd punched her in the head with one hand while he kept his other hand tight around the steering wheel.

Gray would never forget the time he shoved her so hard that she crashed through the kitchen glass door. That had been a barn burner.

She had come out of their relationship with scars, chipped bones, a spooked spirit, and hearing that sometimes dimmed. More than that, she'd had to forsake her hard-earned name, given to her by a wonderful, infertile couple who'd loved her enough to adopt her.

And now the laparoscopic wound closest to her belly button felt like a fish tugging on a baited line—

the Percocet was wearing off. She thought of waking Nick so that she could pop a pill and take a quick nap. And that need—to take *something* to dull the pain—was slinking back into her life. It was smiling at her, showing its teeth and tail, both edged with the softest, gunpowder-colored razor blades. She had ibuprofen and Tylenol with codeine in her bag. But nothing dulled pain, real or imagined, like Percocet. Full of good intentions with give-no-fucks results. She was on the clock, though, and she needed to care, and the pain wasn't even pain yet. Just a fish tugging on a line.

And she battled like this—*there's pain, no pain, there's pain, no*—until she glimpsed frost on the evergreens. Soon, those branches came alive with red-headed birds and chubby squirrels. God gave her the colors of the forest to wonder at from her foxhole, and sunlight beat against the windshield as it beamed purple-gold across the forest.

38

It was 6:20 in the morning when Bobby shuffled out of the house. Now wearing red jeans, a white sweatshirt, and a red L.A. Clippers baseball cap, he tromped over to the black truck with its gigantic tires, metal bar, and loud engine that went *bup-bup-bup*.

Just like Mrs. Tompkins had described.

This was *the* truck!

Gray elbowed her sleeping beauty. "He's leaving."

Nick sat up like a spark, and his eyes immediately found their target.

The brake lights on the truck brightened and that engine growled as the truck backed out of the driveway and then zoomed down the road.

Gray and Nick hopped out of the Yukon and rushed to the bathroom window she'd cracked. Nick easily lifted the sash, and she climbed through with the grace of a penguin on land. She landed on the wet sink top and grimaced at the slick wetness on her palms before knocking over a can of shave cream.

Nick shushed her, then slipped through the same window as gracefully as every graceful creature, land and sea.

She pointed to the hamper, and then to the box of hair dye on the sink counter.

Nick lifted the hamper lid, frowned, then motioned that they move on.

Golden light danced around the living room, and more dignified viewing now played on the television—an infomercial for a handheld pet hair vacuum. The bedroom was still dark, and that funk still hung in the air, and the comforter and sheets looked as rumpled as they had before.

Gray turned on her phone's flashlight and shined it around the room. The pink and black Nike bag no longer sat in the corner. It was gone.

Nick pulled open the dresser drawers.

Empty.

Gray searched the closet and found a box marked "Ornaments." She opened the flaps and found Christmas bulbs the colors of hard candy. She pawed through the bulbs until she reached the bottom.

A thick manila envelope.

"Found something," she whispered.

Tires crunched the gravel driveway.

Gray and Nick stopped moving.

Bobby?

Nick reached to his waistband and kept his fingers close to the Beretta.

Those tires kept crunching gravel, and then those tires skipped and screeched against the asphalt and that car's engine rumbled and the sound grew fainter . . . fainter . . .

Not Bobby.

Gray pulled out the manila envelope from the ornaments box.

Nick stood guard at the door. "Hurry up, yeah?"

Gray pulled out a Social Security card for Elyse Lorraine Miller. A birth certificate. A diploma from the public College of Southern Nevada, conferred to Elyse Lorraine Miller. College transcripts—from English Composition to Accounting Practices. As and

Bs and a C in Statistics. The final document was a résumé—Elyse had worked at the U.S. Postal Service for five years. Nothing after that.

"Maybe she married rich and stopped working," Nick said.

"Or maybe she got married and wasn't allowed to work," Gray countered.

"I knew a woman in that situation. That it?"

Gray peered into the envelope. "Yep." Then she took pictures of each document.

Tires crunched against the gravel again.

Gray and Nick froze again.

This time the tires didn't crunch back to the road. This time the engine idled, and that idle sounded familiar. *Bup-bup-bup-bup-bup.*

Gray and Nick gawked at each other.

She shoved the papers back into the envelope and the envelope back into the box. After setting the box back into the closet, she followed Nick to the bathroom. She repeated her penguin-on-land routine and clambered out the window just as Bobby opened the front door. She flung herself to the thick carpet of cedar needles, ignoring the sting from landing on pinecones.

Nick slipped through the window and quietly brought down the sash. "You okay?"

She gave a thumbs-up.

They took the long way back to the Yukon and kept their eyes on the ground, in search of newly dug piles of dirt and needles. They hiked through swarms of early morning gnats and towering pines, passing the backyards of other cabins, now alive with the aromas of bacon, toast, and laundry soap. Nick took Gray's hand and they walked longer than they needed, and their pulses matched, if only for two beats or three. Normal. Alone. Adam and Eve on the sixth day.

At a pine tree, Nick stopped in his step.

Gray looked back at him.

They inched toward each other until they stood together with her head at his chin. Being this close to him and being this high up in the mountains made her dizzy.

There was peace here.

Nick's gray eyes sparkled and caught glints of sunlight, and that light danced in her chest. His hands cupped her cheeks and he whispered, "Happy Hump Day."

"Happy Hump Day."

He bent toward her.

She lifted her head.

But then he dropped his head and turned away from her.

Her heart dipped.

He whispered, "I'm . . . We're . . . I want to, but . . ."

Her love for him moved through her body like butterflies dancing in new sunlight.

He wasn't ready.

Was she?

39

Three hours later, after gobbling Grand Slams and chasing her antibiotic with slurps of coffee at an Indian casino Denny's, Gray led Nick into Isabel Lincoln's dark condo. The air was still and hot and the lights no longer worked. The hum of the refrigerator was no longer a sound to envy, since it no longer hummed.

Gray wandered the living room. "Ian probably called the power company."

Nick opened the fridge. "Still cold. So it probably just happened."

Gray returned to the kitchen and to the breakfast counter. She pointed to that name—Elyse Miller—on the Coach sale postcard.

Nick asked, "But who the hell is she?"

"Don't know," Gray said, "but she was married or not married to this Omar guy, who was found dead in the desert, and—*shit*."

She pointed to the front door. "Mrs. Tompkins told me that the cops came knocking on her door back in June. They asked her about someone named Lisa."

"Maybe they asked her about 'Elyse.'"

Gray started to respond, but her phone rang. "Oh, look," she said, with fake cheer. "Tea Christopher, also known as Grifter Number One, is calling." Gray answered. "Tea, how are you?"

"Okay." Just in that one word. The young woman sounded winded. Winded and hurried. Winded, hurried, and harried. "Are you around to talk?"

"Sure. When?"

"Now."

"I'm about to go into a meeting. How about later this afternoon? Say . . . three thirty?" Gray suggested Post & Beam, a soul food restaurant down the hill from Isabel's condo, then ended the call. "I need to change. I stink."

Nick glanced at his watch. "You have time for that?"

She groaned. "No. But I can't stand myself."

"You can . . ." He blushed, then chewed his bottom lip.

She lifted an eyebrow. "I can *what*?"

"Shower at my place. I don't . . . You can . . . I . . ."

She laughed. "I would take you up on that, but I don't have a change of—"

"You do. Still. In your drawer."

Her drawer—third one on the left side of the dresser at his house in Playa del Rey. There, the bare walls were painted white and the teakwood floors were bare. Nick had bought a red suede couch and an armchair since her last visit, and it was the only living room furniture he'd owned in the ten years he'd lived there. But he had a custom bed with high-thread-count sheets and a view of the Pacific Ocean. He'd let her sleep there on her first nights while he had bunked in the guest room.

Gray now stared at that bed—so comfortable that she had sweated while sleeping.

Dressed and fresh in her left-behind pair of jeans and gray T-shirt, she joined Nick out on the deck. She wrapped her arm through his as he sipped from a heavy glass of bourbon. Together, they stared out at the ocean, at foamy waves breaking against the shore. The mist felt good. His arm felt better.

"Why . . ." Nick sighed, then said, "Why are you here?"

She tilted her head to look at him, then found the ocean again. "Uhh . . . cuz I'm meeting Tea and needed a shower since I smelled like old Cheetos and—"

"No. I mean . . . I could've relocated you to Paris or Hawaii, but you chose L.A. Why?"

Because you're here. But she couldn't say that . . . could she?

"Well . . ." She took a deep breath, then slowly released it. "You're the only family I have, you know? The only person who knows who I was, who my parents were, and . . . I know that . . . you care about me, and you still would care if I were in Paris but . . ." She almost smiled. "I can grow safely here. Don't go and get a big head. Well, a *bigger* head."

Nick didn't speak.

Her cheer died. Had she said too much?

"I need to head back," she said, her face suddenly warm.

He drained his glass, straightened and stretched. "Drive one of the trucks."

"'kay," Her skin tingled as she remembered their walk in the forest. She thought about standing on tippy toes now to kiss him, about leading him past that barren living room and to the best bed in the world.

But she waited a second too long, and he turned on his heel and went back inside, where he plunked the empty whiskey glass on the fireplace mantel.

In silence, he drove her back to Rader Consulting and pulled behind her silver Camry. "Get your stuff out of the Toyota. I may disappear the car for a while."

"You know I'm gonna get this bitch, right?"

He brushed her cheek with his knuckle. "She has no idea that somebody just as fucked up is chasing her down."

"*Just* as?"

"*More* fucked up."

"I always try to be number one in everything."

He walked with her to a parked company Yukon and tossed her the key. "You should switch up cars more regularly. People know the woman in the silver Camry."

"Got it." She held up her bag of Hawaiian souvenirs. "*Mahalo.*"

"Bring me a biscuit," he said, "but none of that butter, though. That shit's weird."

"You could come over later and retrieve them."

"I could." Nick squinted at the sun, which was starting its color descent to late afternoon dandelion. In that light, he looked tired, creased, the middle-aged man who had never stopped moving, who kept his brain filled with tasks and changes, plans and escape routes—not for him but for his clients who needed guides from this world to the next. Darkness that could never be navigated—by Gray or anyone—spilled from him, and she would bring him biscuits and the weird honey butter just to make him smile, just to prick a hole in him and see light, even for a second.

LET NO MAN PUT ASUNDER . . .

Some species in the animal kingdom evolve to resemble, behave, and smell like other animals. Ants, for example, are delicious but are dangerous to eat. They're arrogant and confident creatures as they go about their day gathering and stowing food. Jumping spiders mimic ants and sneak unchallenged into their nests. These spiders are never spotted immediately by a colony that numbers in the thousands, and those spiders eat that colony's baby ants.

Chameleons and octopi mimic to survive, too, blending into backgrounds so well that they practically vanish. And it isn't until they stick their poisonous spines into their prey or have stolen eggs from another creature's nest or have gulped another animal whole that the victim finally realizes that the enemy had been there all along, living in its nest, on its piece of bark, or on her couch in her living room, all this time. By then, it's too late.

Mrs. Dixon still drove a red Jaguar. She still lived in a two-story Spanish-Californian with a silver porch light and a succulent garden. She also was switching cell phones every eight weeks because she suspected that her husband was tampering with them. She couldn't prove that he had. If she had taken apart any of those phones, there wouldn't have been anything she would have recognized, that she could have pointed to as proof. No, "Aha! You did this! You're spying on me!" indications.

Sean would have never admitted that he tapped his wife's phone, but he always hinted that he had. He knew things. Points of conversation that he wouldn't have known if he hadn't been listening. "Did Avery tell Martin that she gave her mother ten grand to buy a car?" he asked over dinner once. "Did Zoe change her mind about getting lipo?" He casually dropped these items into conversation, sprinkled these tidbits like caramelized walnuts in a salad.

Each time, Mrs. Dixon gawked at him.

Sean would smile, satisfied that he'd caught her off guard yet again.

And then she would purchase another phone, under names she'd known throughout her life: Twyla, Naomi, Faye. She'd keep the old phone as a ruse. At one time, she was carrying six cell phones in her red Balenciaga bag. Didn't matter, though. Sean only needed her to take a three-minute shower or to go out the front door to accept sandwiches from her neighbors—it only took him a minute to download his Inspector Gadget doo-dad onto her newest smartphone.

On this Tuesday in August, she'd fallen asleep as she had been preparing arroz con pollo for dinner. She'd fallen asleep because that's what pregnant ladies did if they sat still for more than a minute. This time, she awakened to discover that she'd burned the rice.

It was late—that sherbet-colored sky beyond the

kitchen's new French doors (*shatterproof*, the sales-
man had boasted) warned her that she had less than
an hour to maneuver.

Sean would be home soon.

The house stank—the smell clung to the smooth
blue walls and had sunk into the cushions of the slate-
blue suede couches, joining the reek of sadness and
despair that haunted 595 Trail Spring Court.

She dumped the rice and the pot into the trash can
and ordered Chinese food. Orange chicken for him,
kung pao beef for her. She opened all the windows,
then schlepped back to the couch to watch *Special
Delivery*.

At 6:37, the black Range Rover rolled into the garage. She could hear the bass of the stereo and Big-
gie's thick voice rapping over Herb Alpert's "Rise."

Sean entered from the garage. He wore basketball
shorts and Air Jordans and smelled of a woman's perfume. *Anise's perfume*. "What did you burn?" The
first words out of his mouth.

"Chicken and rice," she said, watching television.
"But don't worry. I ordered Chow's."

Sean walked over to the couch. He didn't respond—he was too busy staring at his wife's hair,
styled that afternoon into a short Halle Berry hair-
cut. Finally, he said, "You cut your hair. You look like
a fuckin' dyke." He turned on his heel and climbed
the stairs. The floorboards above her creaked and
the pipes *whooshed* as the knobs on the shower demanded water.

She didn't react to his reaction because she wasn't
surprised. He was a hair freak. But her hair had lost
its luster. Worse, her hair had been falling out.

"It's stress," according to her stylist, Shannon.

"Just start over. I'll cut it and it'll grow back stronger, since you're on those prenatal vitamins—"

"Shh," Mrs. Dixon had warned. "I haven't told him yet." Even at eight weeks.

Shannon only knew about the pregnancy because Mrs. Dixon didn't want to use hair color. And anyway, she planned to tell Sean over dinner that night. She'd tell him, and he'd cry and they'd hug and he'd lift her up and spin her around and they'd laugh because she'd want to throw up from all the spinning and he'd promise that he'd be good, that she wouldn't lose *this* baby, that *this* time she'd make it all the way through.

She wasn't that far along—her breasts had already swollen a cup size, but that was the only difference. Because of nausea and morning sickness, she had lost most of the weight she'd gained from stress and drinking, and now her clothes hung off of her and her cheekbones and clavicles jutted more beneath her brown skin. And her hair—that was different on this day, thanks to Shannon. And her eyes—they were brighter now and flickered with hope.

This one will be a good pregnancy.

No martini tonight. Instead, she sliced a lime and dunked two wedges into her Pellegrino.

"Still drinking that bougie shit," Sean noted, even though he drank the bubbly water with vodka all the time. He put on music for dinner—more Notorious B.I.G. Not the soundtrack she would've selected for this special evening, but what-the-fuck-ever. Anything to keep him happy.

Sean had showered and had changed into trainers and a gray T-shirt. He sat across from her at the breakfast bar loaded with cartons of chicken and beef in various gravies. When Sean wasn't glaring at her hair, he was glaring at the food on his plate.

She wanted to tell him the news—good or bad news, she couldn't tell at this point—but something told her to keep silent and so she did. The food was making her nauseous and sickness now bubbled up her throat. Her head pounded as she waited for the firefight to begin.

He'd sent a few tracer rounds already. *It stinks in here* and *Did you pick up batteries like I asked you to?* and *I don't remember you asking me about paying for your fucking hair*. Since then, the rumble of heavy artillery had moved in on her. She thought about the night he'd thrown glass noodle salad *in her direction*, not *at* her. She didn't want to go through that again, but dread settled on her shoulders as darkness settled over the desert she now called home.

How could she raise a child when she couldn't even keep food in her own belly? When she was almost always scared that he'd . . .

As his silence darkened, she became too scared to think. Even though this was their "normal"—moody silences, glares that could melt wax, levels of tension as thick as igneous rock—it drove her crazy. Being scared that her husband would conduct a one-sided food fight was nuts. That he would even think about throwing food at her was nuttier. That there was a *history* of him pelting her with Asian entrees? Fucking unbelievable.

Once tonight's storm passed, though, she'd tell him that they were gonna have a baby.

They came to the end of dinner. Mrs. Dixon, now a sweaty, hollow mess, focused on the cartons she was plucking from the counter.

Sean grabbed the dirty plates, forks, and spoons.

These plates had been on their wedding registry. Everyday plates. Two-toned in blue and white.

As she moved from the counter to the sink, her feet stopped working and she found herself splayed down on the tile. The left side of her head throbbed with hot and heavy heat. The room tilted as she blinked away sparks zapping white and red before her eyes.

He'd punched her.

She croaked, "Sean," but that one word came out as a bark, since the impact of his size twelve Air Jordans against her abdomen took her breath away. He punched her twice—right ear, right cheek—and snarled, "You a fucking dyke now?" Then he swept his arms across the breakfast counter, sending Chow's Chinese flying all around the kitchen. Breathing hard, he stomped to the door that led to the garage.

Back down on the tile, perfect drops of Mrs. Dixon's blood flecked those empty spaces between grains of rice and spicy peanuts. Those drops were more perfect than the drops that last time, when she'd been thrown through the old glass patio door. She'd been pregnant then, too, and those drops splattered, a Pollock painting mixed with Swarovski crystals.

Tonight, Mrs. Dixon wept as she climbed the stairs, as she passed the room she'd thought of as the nursery, as she passed hanging pictures of Sean and her dancing at their wedding, as she plodded and panted to the bathroom. She slammed and locked the door, then plopped down on the toilet seat. She reached beside her and pulled open the drawer to a wicker chest.

Lotions, creams, soaps, and toners. And makeup. Lots of makeup. Bronzers, highlighters, concealers, correctors, primers, foundations; liquid, liquid powder, whip, mousse, pressed, stick, translucent, oil-free, wet/

dry, satin; honey beige, NW400, cappuccino, almond, nutmeg.

Some were good at hiding scars.

Others were good at hiding bruises.

Some lightened the greens and purples her skin took on in bad times.

Others made her look as though she'd lain out on a Saint-Tropez beach with a le Carré novel in one hand and a Bloody Mary in the other.

Only actresses owned this much makeup.

But then, she, too, was an actress. She'd stood at the mirror how many times, with black eyes and swollen, bruised cheeks. She'd spackle all of this shit over her face while Sean, in another room, would ice his knuckles while sipping Jack and Coke. And then they'd go out.

Smiles, everyone!

Not tonight, though.

She'd wear no makeup tonight.

40

Needing to remain alert, Gray decided against drinking alcohol or taking a pill for the twinges now revving near her navel. It had been a long twenty-four hours, and she needed coffee. Strong, black, and sweet, Sean would say, winking at her. Along with her biscuits and Nick's biscuits, that's what she'd ordered from the cat-eyed waitress—coffee for her and a glass of ice water for her guest.

She sat facing Post & Beam's exit. *Never have your back to the door*, Victor Grayson had told her. *That's a good way to die.* Older couples in leisure wear trickled in for high-priced jerk catfish. The long-cooked greens were delicious but cost more than a decent salad anywhere else. Rum banana bread pudding—okay, *that* was worth the price.

Tea Christopher entered the restaurant right as the server set Gray's basket of biscuits and butter on the table. Today she wore a purple tracksuit with pink trim and busted high-top Skechers. She smelled of sweat, and that odor walloped the sweet aroma of freshly baked biscuits. She plopped into the chair across from Gray. "Sorry for asking last minute for you to come."

The server waited to take Tea's order, but Gray dismissed her with a curt, "That's all."

Unlike their first meeting at Sam Jose's, Gray refused to feed Isabel's best friend. She didn't like nourishing liars and cons on her dime, or Nick's. *Let her savor the glass of ice-cold water against her hot, lying tongue.*

"How can I help you, Tea?" Gray asked.

"You never told me for sure that you were done with the investigation." Behind those glasses, Tea's eyes looked as big as basketballs. "I've been texting you, and Isabel told me to get the check and her keys. Both sets."

"Ah. I'll let you know."

"Know . . . *what*?"

"About the keys, the check, the investigation being done."

"She told me that she sent the picture of her tattoo."

"What about the picture of Kenny G.?"

"But . . ." Tea canted her head. "But she sent you Ian's answers to the questions, and she sent you the two other pictures."

Gray snorted, rolled her eyes, and shook her head, just in case Tea still thought for a moment that Gray *sorta* believed her. "You really *do* think I'm stupid."

Tea gripped the edges of the table. "When will you be finished, Miss Sykes?"

"Once I receive a picture that hasn't been manipulated to look like your friend is holding a newspaper while standing in the breezeway of the Westin Kauai. Once I receive a freakin' picture of the man's dog. Not so hard to understand, is it?" The badger in Gray wanted out, and it clawed at her belly and throat.

Over at the bar, a small man wearing a big Dodgers jersey was leering at Gray as he chewed on a straw. He winked at her and smiled to show off his dimples. Then he looked at his wrist to show off his Rolex.

Bad time, bro. Gray scowled at him. Her mood had

turned as black and bitter as the coffee in her cup, the coffee she hadn't had a chance to sip or sweeten.

"I don't understand," Tea said. "The Hawaii picture—"

"The Hawaii picture's *fake*," Gray said, eyebrow lifted.

Tea's lips and cheeks quivered. "But . . . but . . . th-that's the picture she . . . she sent. She sent it to me and she sent it to you."

"You sure *you* didn't send it to me?"

Tea's tear-filled eyes shimmered behind her glasses. "Isabel's alive, and she just wants you to go away."

"*Keep your tongue from evil and your lips from speaking deceit.*" She remembered that verse from Psalm 34—Mom Naomi would recite it to her at least twice a week, usually after the old woman had slapped her. For secular flair, Gray added, "*By a lie, a man annihilates his dignity as a man.*" Victor Grayson had recited Kant to her only once a month.

With a shaky hand, Tea picked up the glass of water. The ice cubes clinked as she sipped.

Gray broke apart a hot biscuit and refused to wince as steam stung her fingers. "Where is she, Tea?" She peered at Tea as she spread honey butter over the biscuit's perfectly flaky bottom.

Tears tumbled down Tea's acne-scarred cheeks. "I can't . . ."

"Is Isabel Lincoln alive?" Gray bit into the biscuit, not tasting it.

Tea nodded.

"Where is she?"

Tea shook her head.

"I know shit about you that *you* don't even know about you. You need to tell me."

Tea whispered, "I don't know."

"Is she hiding at the cabin in Idyllwild?"

Tea's eyes widened and the muscles over her left temple jumped. Her lips disappeared as though Gray's words had punched them in.

"See? I know shit. Is she in Idyllwild?"

Tea whispered, "No."

"At your house in Westchester?"

"No."

"Should I bring Pastor Dunlop into this? He asked me to keep him—"

"No."

"Ian didn't poison Morris," Gray said. "Mrs. Tompkins did. And she gave Isabel cash as apology. That's just an F.Y.I."

Tea's mouth moved but no words followed.

"Who is Elyse Miller?"

Tea started to respond, but then she squinted at Gray. "*Who?*"

"Elyse Miller."

Tea blinked at her, then shook her head. "Sounds familiar but I don't know her."

"She has mail."

"Where?"

"At Isabel's."

Tea kept shaking her head. "Maybe she rented from the Gardners before Isabel."

And that's why there's a Social Security card, résumés, and shit at your cabin?

"Maybe," Gray said. "Maybe I'll ask the cops. They'll want to know—"

"I'm telling you the *truth*," Tea said, voice raised. "She told me to do all of that."

"Do all of *what*?"

"The picture—she told me to send it. The text messages—she told me to send those, too."

"How did Isabel meet Noelle Lawrence?" Before Tea could deny knowing Noelle, Gray interrupted with, "Noelle called me and told me many interesting things. She was gonna tell me things about *you* but she disappeared. How did two such different women become friends?"

Tea chewed her bottom lip, unsure of the answer. "Mentoring program?"

Gray shrugged.

Tea said, "Some program through UCLA, I think, for young women who were in jail. Wait. Noelle told you things about *me*? I don't know her. I've never met her, but I do remember Isabel telling me that she stole."

"From?"

"Someone she was with in jail, something that has nothing to do with me, with this."

"Why are you doing—"

"Because Ian hit—"

"Don't lie to me." By now, Gray's heart was moments away from popping.

Tea swallowed her lie, then licked her lips. She frowned, not liking the taste very much.

Gray chewed the biscuit. The honey butter coated her mouth, and she didn't like *that*. Nick was right: weird shit.

"Once she found out that Ian had hired someone to look for her," Tea was saying, "she gave me a list of things to do."

"What happened to the BMW?"

"What BMW?"

"Isabel's."

"She drove a Honda Civic."

"Was the Bimmer Noelle's car?"

"I told you, I don't know Noelle. I don't know what Noelle drives."

"What about the car accident with the Maserati?"

Tea sat up like a beagle. She knew the answer to this question. "Her ex-boyfriend—he kept telling her that she owed him more money. She kept paying him, but he kept jacking up how much the repairs cost."

Pity seeped into Gray's spirit and she gaped at the young woman. A "palooka." Tea was the very definition of the word. "Do you know about the money that Ian left on the breakfast counter right after she disappeared?"

"I took it. She asked me to."

"And?"

"And I . . ."

"And you *what*?"

"I drove to the cabin and left it there. And then I drove back home."

"Are there any pictures of you hanging on Isabel's walls?" Gray asked.

Tea cocked her head, thrown by the sudden change in topic. "Huh?"

"Are there any pictures of you on her Facebook or Instagram—"

"Yes," she said, chin high. "I have pictures of us."

"On *her* pages. That *you* didn't share."

Tea called up Facebook on her phone. She didn't say anything as she tapped and swiped up and up and up, but by the way her shoulders slumped and her face darkened, it was clear she knew . . . and she didn't like the answer.

Gray leaned forward and touched Tea's arm. "She only became your friend to get what she wanted. She wanted that condo and you introduced her to the couple who owned it. She wanted to destroy Ian, so she has you as a witness to episodes of abuse that never happened. She's a liar, and she also tried to pull me into her lies."

"No," Tea snarled. "You don't know anything about me or about her."

Gray stared at the young woman. "Did she take out any insurance policies recently?"

Tea's eyes skirted to look past Gray's head. "Why would I know that?"

"You're the beneficiary, aren't you?"

Tea didn't speak.

"Did you know that she has a separate policy on you?"

Tea's nostrils flared and she furrowed her eyebrows.

"When you die, she's getting paid."

"But I'm *healthy*. I'm not *dying*."

"Maybe. Maybe not." Gray sipped from her cup. "She's not your friend, Tea."

"Yes, she is," the woman hissed. "She misses me. That's why—" Her lips clamped.

Gray's belly jumped. "That's why *what*?"

Tea dropped her head.

"When was the last time you *saw* Isabel?"

"The last Sunday in May."

"And the last time you talked to her? Not a text or a phone call. Talked to her *in person*?"

"The last Sunday in May."

"So you don't know one hundred percent that it was Isabel who answered the questions or even told you to send those pictures? You've only communicated with her via text message?"

Tea said, "Yes," then dropped her head. Her hands

were shaking now, and tears plopped from her cheeks and pebbled on the table.

"And the dog?"

"I don't know."

"She ever mention him in the text messages?"

"No, but she'd never hurt that stupid dog."

"Where did she go back in December?"

Tea shook her head.

"Okay, I'm calling the po—"

"Las Vegas."

"And in March?"

"Las Vegas."

"Why?"

Tea waited and waited—minutes, hours, days, it seemed. Finally: "Don't know." She dabbed a napkin at her wet nose.

Softer now, Gray asked, "What else do you know?"

Tea dabbed the napkin at her eyes. "She told me that she needed a safe place to set up her new life away from Ian. She's going to Belize. . . . That's how she's going to use Ian's money, to start a new life away from him."

Clarissa had confirmed that Isabel hadn't flown down yet, at least under her name.

Tea glared at Gray. "And she's buying a ticket for me, too."

"I wouldn't go. She has a policy on you, which means she may be planning to—"

"He was *beating* her." There was fight in those words. Heat, too. All in. Last stand.

"No, Tea," Gray said. "She was blackmailing him about him and Trinity Bianchi having sex at the hospital, about him falsifying her worker's comp papers at UCLA about—"

"I saw the bruises. Ian knew where to hit her so that it wouldn't—"

"No. She faked those to make you believe—"

"No. He beat her, and she begged me to help her escape. So, that Monday, I drove her to the bus station in my friend's truck, cuz my car wouldn't start, and now she's safe."

The young woman stood from the table. "I don't care what you say. I saved my best friend from dying. And now she's never coming back."

41

Gray retreated to the parking lot as Tea shuffled to the women's restroom.

Not only had the young woman lied, she'd shown herself as gullible.

Did she believe that Isabel was a victim in every situation she'd found herself in?

Isabel had picked a ripe one, and the word "palooka" again floated in Gray's mind, although . . .

Could Isabel be innocent in *some* of this?

Which parts, though?

The living dead part? Caught up in a whirlwind of cons and fraud, the missing woman just might have found herself buried beneath the shadow of a windmill or beneath a soft mound of cedar shavings and pine needles.

Maybe.

It was fifteen minutes after five o'clock, and Gray secretly followed Tea Christopher out of the mall parking lot. The city had been roasted alive; there was not a single drop of moisture in the air. Everything—cars, people, buildings—had been baked until their colors had faded. Los Angeles smelled like tar, fire, barbecue ribs, and weed. Gray stayed four cars behind the young woman as they drove south on Crenshaw Boulevard, crowded now with vendors hawking T-shirts and bundles of incense, crowded with winos on bikes, on foot, weaving in and out of traffic while clutching brown paper bags.

After passing blue landmark signs with "Inglewood" in vertical white letters, Tea—and then Gray—turned left onto Seventy-Seventh Street and into a neighborhood of Spanish-style bungalows with pristine lawns.

Tea zoomed through a traffic circle in the middle of the neighborhood, nearly clipping a teenager on his skateboard.

"What's the hurry, Tea?" Gray asked. But then, in her giant truck, she took that circle at half the speed and nearly hit a jogger.

Up ahead, the green Altima rolled past a stop sign and kept speeding east on Seventy-Seventh. Black folks, standing on lawns glistening with sprinkler water, talked to neighbors, tended to rosebushes, stopped to shake their heads as Tea Christopher raced past.

Another traffic circle, but this time the green Altima navigated through it as though it were made of ice and TNT. The car slowed until it U-turned and parked on the opposite side of the street, in front of a white house with a red ceramic-tile roof.

Gray passed that house as Tea bustled from the curb and past its gates. Gray also made a U-turn but parked two houses back. The old man watering the lawn of that house waved at Gray as though he knew her. She waved back at him and ached with the memories of Summerlin.

Mr. Anthony—he owned a candy store in downtown Vegas and always brought her bags of sweets. Lorraine and Phil always wore matching tracksuits and were always drinking glasses of rosé and bringing over leftover sandwiches from parties they regularly hosted. Chris, Maud, and Shannon—their houses looked exactly alike except for Maud's plastic flamingoes,

Shannon's bird feeders, and Chris's UNLV Rebels flag hanging over his front door.

Everyone on that part of Trail Spring Court knew each other's names. But the neighbors didn't know what Natalie and Sean Dixon had been doing before they answered the front door. Or maybe the neighbors *had* known and decided to keep quiet. Just bring the sandwiches and the bottles of rosé and the jokes and pray secret prayers that Sean wouldn't kill his wife.

Mayberry: the most dangerous neighborhood in America.

Back over at the white house with the red roof, the front door opened. An older, vibrant-looking black woman with a short gray bob greeted Tea. Blind, she held a white cane and wore dark glasses. With that nicely tailored lilac skirt set and those sensible black shoes, she could have been a high school principal or the wife of a civil rights leader. She spoke, and whatever she said made Tea laugh.

A black Ford F-10 roared up Seventy-Seventh Street and into the driveway of the white house. It was *the* black Ford F-10, with those wheels and that metal bar and the engine that went *bup-bup-bup*. The bass boom of that new kind of rap that Gray knew nothing about rumbled from the truck's speakers. Big Man, aka Bobby the Blood, climbed out from behind the steering wheel, clutching his phone along with two bags from In-N-Out and a large drink.

"Boy, you gon' make me go deaf," Coretta Scott King shouted. "Turn that down. I already can't see for nothing."

Bobby still wore the red jeans and red Clippers baseball cap from earlier that morning. *This* man, this *Blood*, lived with a woman who probably hung good

African American art on her walls and knew people who were the first black everything.

He nodded "Wassup" to Tea.

The older woman slipped back into the house while Tea and Bobby stayed on the porch.

An ice cream truck playing "Three Blind Mice" rolled past Gray's truck and she thought of chasing it down and buying every rocket pop in its freezer. Maybe the cold would numb the pain now sizzling around her navel.

The ice cream truck stopped at the end of the block. Kids poured out from every yard and rushed to the truck's window.

Three blind mice,
Three blind mice,
See how they run.

And this case had proven that Gray had been as blind as those mice, even though she knew the answer sat inches away. She'd been looking for Isabel Lincoln and Kenny G. for a week now and had gone in circles . . . unless she'd been going in spirals, which meant she'd be soon coming to some kind of an end.

With the nursery rhyme playing and the *whoosh* of water from the old man's garden hose, Gray couldn't hear a word Tea and Bobby spoke. After three minutes of this, the old man dropped his hose and turned off the water. By now, though, Tea had climbed back into the green Altima and had raced toward the sun.

All of it—the heat, the driving, the noise—had jabbed at Gray's nerves, and she wanted to pop. Instead, she muttered, "Fuck it," then grabbed her binder and hopped out of the truck.

Last night, she'd been blonde and green-eyed, and

Bobby had been high as hell. Today, she had short brown hair and big brown eyes. A different woman.

She knocked on the dusty screen door.

The *clunk* of a lock, the twist of a doorknob, and the creak of hinges, and from behind the screen door Bobby said, "You here to pick up Miss Robertson?"

From the house, the older woman shouted, "Is that my car?"

Gray said, "No," and Bobby shouted, "No, Miss Robertson."

He looked bigger than last night, more menacing in the shadows. He wouldn't hurt Gray with Coretta Scott King floating between her journaling space and the altar to her ancestors.

Gray could smell onions and meat, Thousand Island dressing and mustard. And now she craved an In-N-Out Double Double, Animal Style. She showed her identification card. "I'm Gray Sykes and I'm hoping you can help me."

Bobby took a bite from his burger. "You a cop?"

"No. A private investigator."

"What's the difference?"

"I will never be able to shoot you *and* get away with it."

He laughed, and burger bits flecked the screen door. "I'm eating. Come back later."

Ignoring his request, Gray said, "I'm looking for this woman." She held up Isabel Lincoln's picture, far from the door.

Bobby pushed open the screen door to peer closer at the photograph. There was a flash of recognition—an eyebrow lifted—but then that flame died and his poker face returned. His knuckles were bruised purple and swollen like sausages.

Had they been this way last night?

Bobby said, "I don't know her."

"You sure? Look closer. Take as long as you need."

He didn't. "Nope. Never seen her before in my life. Why you asking me, anyway?"

Gray slipped the picture back into the binder. "Someone told me that you were the last person to see her. And now she's missing. Been missing since late May, early June. And again, according to my source, you saw her last."

He sucked his teeth. "That's impossible. I don't let *nobody* borrow my truck."

Blood rushed to her face—she hadn't said anything about anyone borrowing his truck.

Bobby's eyes narrowed. "Who told you that? That I drove her somewhere?"

"Can't say." *Didn't say.*

He stepped back into the house and let the screen door slam close. "Can't help you."

Too late, Bobby.

You've helped plenty.

42

As Gray stepped off Bobby's porch, her phone buzzed with a text.

You there?

Isabel.
Gray veered into the Big Lots! parking lot. *Yes I'm glad you reached out.* The smell of grease from the Rally's burger place next door wafted through the car vents, and Gray's stomach growled. *I have A LOT of concerns right now. Some things are not making sense! The picture that you sent for instance.*

I know. Been thinking all night. I'll meet you F2F I'll explain everything.

When?

Only if you agree to not talk me into getting back with Ian.

I'd NEVER ask that!

DON'T TELL HIM THAT I'M COMING TO SEE YOU

Isabel sent Gray the address to Verve Coffee on Third

Street. Twenty minutes later, she found herself seated at an outdoor table, one hand wrapped around an iced coffee and the other hand wrapped around her phone. A june bug, bumbly and green, bumbled through the thick air, and the aromas of fresh-brewed coffee and just-baked cinnamon buns made Gray giddy. She was moments away from solving this case, moments away from knowing the truth, moments—

"What are *you* doing here?"

She knew the man's voice, and every organ in her body shattered.

Ian O'Donnell stood at the café entrance. He wore green scrubs today and his golden hair was still wet around his ears.

Gray opened her mouth to say, "Isabel asked," but closed it. She scanned the patio, hoping not to spot the missing woman. "I'm meeting someone here."

"For my case?"

She gave a curt nod, and the phone buzzed in her hand.

"Who?" Ian asked.

She cleared her throat. "One of Isabel's family members. But she doesn't want to see you." She paused, then put glaze on the lie. "For obvious reasons."

The man's eyes softened, and his head dropped. "I understand."

"I'll tell you about it in my report. You should go now."

Ian O'Donnell looked through the shop's glass doors, then looked back at the parking lot. "Yeah. I'll head somewhere else. Good luck." He spun on his heel and hurried back to his car.

Gray watched him, and that earlier excitement had now turned to heavy dread in her belly. She held her breath, then looked at the phone.

HE'S THERE! YOU PROMISED!!

Gray's head pounded as her fingers raced across the phone's keyboard. *I didn't tell him, Isabel! Please believe me!!*

But if she could see that Ian was at the coffee shop, that meant . . .

"She's here, too!" Gray's eyes popped from the white Volkswagen parked at the corner to the yellow cab pulling away from the curb. Dog walker . . . jogger . . . cyclist . . . Where was she? Where was Isabel?

Gray's phone vibrated.

No. deal's off
I have nothing to say to you!

The text exploded like a depth charge, and Gray groaned as she sent a last desperate message. *I swear I didn't tell him!*

But no more words, no more ellipses from the missing woman.

Of all the coffeehouses in the city, Ian O'Donnell had to strut into that one.

Ian came.

Isabel saw.

And now she was gone.

And Noelle Lawrence—she was gone, too, and her mother didn't seem surprised by that. Nor did it seem as though Rebekah Lawrence would hire an investigator to find her daughter. People like Noelle were like herpes—around until they weren't, but never really gone.

And Isabel . . . Was it *really* coincidence that Ian had showed up at that particular coffee shop at that particular time, just when Isabel had agreed to meet?

What were the odds of that happening?

Her phone vibrated again with another text message.

Hey.

Hank. Really? How many days had passed since their night together?

She climbed into the Yukon.

Guess where I am?

Tight-hearted, Gray typed, *Hell? Cuz that's where you can go.* She was over him. Over him like an eighteen-year-old over New Kids on the Block and Impulse body spray, rainbow scrunchies and Beanie Babies.

Don't be like that.

She turned the ignition and jabbed the stereo button. Angie Stone sang about not eating and not sleeping anymore.

Guess where I am?

Hank was now a pebble in her shoe, and he wouldn't go away until she shook him out.

Ok you're behind the bar, making my favorite margarita. She let her head fall back on the headrest and closed her eyes, recalled Bobby's claim about not letting a woman he didn't even know drive his car. What would he do next? Call Tea? Call Isabel? And who had he beaten so bad that his knuckles—

Her phone vibrated.

A selfie of Hank standing in front of the Beaudry Towers sign. He held a bouquet of red roses and a bottle of premium tequila. His eyes glistened like Arctic ice.

See you soon.

"What the *fuck* is he doing at my . . ."

The phone shook in her trembling hands and she hated herself more than she hated him. She'd invited him to her home; they'd *slept* together in her home; he had stayed *overnight* in her home. Of *course* he'd "surprise" her like this.

She was burning on the inside, and that fire was creeping up her chest and down her thighs. She'd burn until the fire consumed her, and then the car would catch and she'd blow up and all of her problems would finally be solved.

Maybe.

See you soon.

But not in this traffic. It was as though every car that had a transmission and an AM-FM radio needed to take a Sunday drive on a Wednesday. Not an inch of free space anywhere. Highways were crammed like a summer day at Disneyland.

Freaking Hank.

He'd showed up unannounced at her apartment building. Was this a normal thing? Men just . . . *showing up*? She no longer had a true reference point for proper behavior, nor did she read romance novels or watch rom-coms. Her last "normal" relationship had sent her careening into California. This kind of "normalcy"? She didn't like this kind, and she'd let Hank know that, especially since he hadn't bothered to call or text her since . . . since . . . Friday morning?

And now, she was stuck on the 10 freeway connector to the 110 North—an Easter-egg-hidden level of hell. Nighttime had clocked in for work, but the sun still gave off enough light to make her squint. Something about this traffic jam was different, and whatever it was scraped the back of Gray's neck.

Her phone buzzed. An alert from ORO.

Gray's breath left her, and her gaze zipped from car to car.

Bored-looking faces. Mouths moving to Adele or Smokey Robinson or Maroon 5. Glazed eyes, some hidden by Oakleys or Ray-Bans.

She tapped the banner to open the alert, but her screen froze and went black.

"You're crashing *now*?" she shouted.

Gray switched lanes to exit. That scraping itchiness still rode her neck, and she looked again in the rearview and side mirrors—behind her, four other cars had also switched lanes.

Because it's a freeway, dummy. And the Seventh Street off-ramp was a major exit.

No one in those cars behind her looked familiar or menacing, and yet . . .

And yet . . . Where is he? Where is Sean? Greater Los Angeles meant he could be way south in Watts or way north in Highland Park.

She pushed those buttons that needed pushing to restart her phone. That kick of panic was not irrational; it was instinct. Fight or flight. She'd heeded its scratchy-itchiness before, and it wouldn't make sense to ignore it now.

The phone blinked back to life.

She tapped the ORO icon, but needed to log in again.

No time.

Gray zipped down the off-ramp and made a quick left onto Enid Place. A tidy side street, Enid's only purpose was to send drivers to the mall's parking garage. Gray didn't go that far; she pulled over to the curb and idled in front of a fire hydrant.

The green minivan that had driven behind her slowly rolled past Enid Place. That car was followed by a PT Cruiser, and its driver kept his head straight. A black Mustang slowed in the intersection. The male driver—she couldn't tell if he was white, Latino, or lighter-skinned black—looked to his left, down Enid Place, slowing some as the Beetle behind him tooted its horn and forced him to go forward.

Mustang Man was following her.

Why? Who is he? What does he want? Is he one of Sean's boys?

That scratching against her skin had turned into clawing. But she couldn't hear her heartbeat, or the shallow breaths pushed out of her mouth. Hollow, that's how she felt. Floaty and dead—numb. And she stared out the windshield, not seeing cars or pigeons or anything, not anymore. Not caring that Nick hadn't found the weakness in his company's armor.

Give up.

Weary. Bone tired. In pain—not even sharp pain, but vague, strange, sad pain.

She couldn't even hide while driving a black SUV in a city filled with black SUVs.

Not good.

Unfair. This was all unfair.

What had she done in this life or a past one to deserve *any* of this?

She wanted to mash the gas pedal and escape through the mall. Race past the Mendocino Farms and the Yara boutique.

And then what?
Why fight anything?
Surrender, Dorothy.

Maybe she *would* surrender. And then it would be over, she'd be dead, and she'd come back a *third* time. Maybe as a duchess or a farmer. A housewife in Kentucky with only laundry and pumpkin muffins to fret over. Maybe her husband would beat her and this time she'd simply accept it and stay until he ended her and she came back a fourth time. And maybe *that* time—

Her phone buzzed with a picture of her taken minutes ago. She'd been driving on the 10 freeway. The photographer had been in a car to her left, driving beside her, knowing that she was behind the wheel of the truck instead of the Camry. This was . . . *nuts*. This was—

The phone buzzed again.

I told U 2 b careful

43

Gray made a right onto Figueroa, not caring if Mustang Man spotted her again. As she stopped to make a left onto Third Street, she saw Hank. He stood near her apartment building's sign, wearing jeans and an untucked button-down shirt. A patient man, he had waited for her for over an hour. Four days ago, that simple act—waiting—would have sent Gray's heart skipping like the slickest stone across her chest.

Today, though . . .

She pulled into her building's dark parking garage. No other car—including black Mustangs—rolled in behind her.

Gray climbed out of the Yukon, and the giant parking lot tightened around her. She hugged bags of Hawaiian souvenirs and biscuits to her chest, and on numb legs, she shuffled outside and to the illuminated Beaudry Towers sign.

Hank said, "Hey."

She tried out a smile, but her lips mangled that attempt.

He pulled her into his arms. He smelled like mint and strawberries. "I thought you'd never get here."

"Traffic."

He pointed to the base of the sign, where a brown paper bag sat beside a bouquet of roses. "I brought wine and Thai for dinner. You'll have to heat it up, though."

With that mangled smile of hers stowed away for future failed attempts, Gray asked, "Why are you here?" Funny—hours ago, Nick had asked her the same question.

Hank shoved his hands into his pockets. "Yeah, I got some explaining to do, huh? But can we go to your place? I need to . . . you know . . . use the restroom. It's been a long afternoon."

And so she let him in. And as he used her bathroom, she put the cartons of mint basil beef, Thai chicken, and steamed rice into the microwave. Then she slipped the bottle of white wine into the freezer for a quick chill.

"That's a fifty-dollar bottle," Hank said, rejoining her.

"Can't wait to try it."

The refrigerator coughed.

Hank said, "You should make management fix that."

She grunted, still not saying much as they took their cartons and the barely chilled bottle of wine into the solarium. There, his plastic fork dipped into her carton without permission. Sean had done that same thing—he'd cut pieces of her rib eye steak for himself or take her last hot wing. Sometimes he'd sip from her cocktail. When she made faces at him or requested that he *ask* first, because that was the polite thing to do, he'd always snap, "I'm paying for it, right?"

Now, Hank's fork in her chicken made her skin blister. *I paid for it, right?*

"You're mad," Hank said, nodding.

Gray cocked an eyebrow.

"I'm not sure you know this . . ." He drained his glass, then filled it with more wine. "When we first met, I thought that I didn't have a chance with you. Doesn't help that I've been married before and it didn't end so good. Obviously."

Gray sipped wine and kept her gaze on her guest.

"It hurt, divorcing Cara, and I . . ." He winced. "I didn't want to hurt like that again. And then I saw you, and everything, the past, it didn't matter." He touched her knee. "You're beautiful, but you're also strong and funny and sexy and . . . *different* now. I made the mistake of letting you in. You're probably saying that, too, but for a different reason—"

Gray said, "Yeah."

"*This. Us.*" He pointed to her and then back to him. "Scared me. I went into this . . . Doesn't matter. I'm sorry. About everything."

Gray's phone rang from the small patio table. Nick was calling.

Hank took both of her hands in his. "I think we deserve another chance."

The wine's effects were dulling her anger. The heat of his hold was pulling her down.

Surrender, Dorothy.

Hank kissed her cheek. "What do you think of Tahiti?"

Gray's heart creaked open. "I hear it's beautiful." She let her fingers scratch his head.

"You've never been?" He almost looked surprised.

"No." Not in this life or in her last.

He came close enough that their noses touched. "Wanna go with me?"

Her mind swirled with confusion, confetti caught in a tornado.

"It's still the summer. We can—"

Someone knocked on the door. The video doorbell app bonged.

Hank and Gray both looked toward the living room. He said, "Ignore it."

Another knock.

The app's feed was too small for her to see who was visiting.

Gray scrunched her eyebrows. "I need to get that."

Hank grabbed her wrist with one hand and used his other hand to hold her knee. "C'mon, babe. Whoever it is will go—"

The hair on her neck and arms bristled. She glared at his hands now keeping her there . . .

One. Two. Three. Four. . . . Five.

She rose from the chair and toppled her glass of wine.

Hank, pissed, sat back in the chair.

"And *that's* why I'm not going to Tahiti with you," Gray said, striding to the door under his angry gaze. She peeped into the peephole, then opened the door.

Nick stood there in trainers and a sweatshirt. "I'm here for my biscuits."

Seeing him made the hard shell she'd just tucked into as thin as silk.

Nick's eyes skipped from her face to the living room behind her. "What's up?" He was pretending that there was nothing to see over her shoulder.

Gray said, "Just . . . dinner."

Nick shook his head. "You're . . . busy, and I was just . . ." He held a bottle of top-shelf vodka and a jar of olives.

"Oh. Yeah. I . . . well . . ."

"Everything good?"

She looked back over her shoulder.

Hank was now standing in the living room. A dick

move, to show off his dick and to let Nick know that this *was* what he thought it was.

Nick squinted at Gray. *You serious?* "I'll let you get back to . . ."

Her face burned, and she wanted to vomit. "Okay. I won't be much longer . . ."

Nick backed away from the door. "Call me later. Got something interesting for you."

"About Isabel?"

He started down the hallway.

"What is it? Gonna give me a hint?"

"Later." He pointed toward her apartment. "Tend to your guest."

Hank was closing in behind her, and her hard shell was regenerating. "I'll call you later."

Nick said, "Yep," then sauntered down the hallway.

Look back. Please look back. She kept thinking that—*Look back*—until her head hurt.

Before turning to hit the elevator bank, Nick looked back at her, smiled, then waved.

She caught that smile and crammed it into her heart with the other smiles he'd tossed her since they'd met, so long ago.

44

Hank's blue eyes and his strong arms with those sexy tats had lost their power over her. And those hard abs and strong jaw? Like expired Children's Tylenol in a smashed bottle.

"Is it because of that guy?" he growled, pointing at the door. "You're seeing him, too?"

"Who I'm seeing is none of your business." Gray crossed her arms, but not because she was angry. She felt . . . *nothing*. Nothing for him, nothing for his spiky words.

His frown set deeper in his face. "Then you need to find yourself another cantina."

She stared at him—if she kept at it, she could freeze him solid. "That it?" She opened the front door. "Go ye into the world and live your ignorant truth, Henry. Thanks for playing."

He stomped past her and out into the hallway. "You—"

She slammed the door.

He kicked it.

She didn't flinch. Alas, she'd expected it. Men like Hank grabbed arms, took food without asking. Men like him asked, "Who's *that* guy?" and "Why didn't you pick up when I called you?" Men like Hank Wexler kicked doors and, sometimes, broke doors down. Just in case this one felt like the Kool-Aid Man, Gray grabbed her Glock from beneath the pillow on her bed.

Someone knocked on the door.

Gray peeped through the peephole.

Tiny Mrs. Kim from across the hall stood there with her hands behind her back.

Gray opened the door and smiled at her gray-haired neighbor.

"You okay here?" Worry etched the old woman's face.

Gray said, "Oh yeah. Just . . . men."

Mrs. Kim tugged at the neck of her T-shirt. "He come earlier. I see him downstairs."

"Yeah, I wasn't home yet."

The old woman scowled. "He with some other man. Big white man. No hair. They wanted to ride up, but I say, *No, you wait*."

Gray's ears chilled hearing that. "A big white *bald* man? You sure?"

Mrs. Kim gave a solid nod. "I don't like either one of them. You be careful."

Back in her living room, Gray logged on to ORO and found the earlier alert. Range Rover plates had been read a mile from Rader Consulting and then near USC, three miles from her apartment. There were plate-reading cameras near Staples Center and also Seventh Street and Figueroa and all around downtown, but there'd been no alerts from those.

Because Sean hadn't been the only one looking for her.

She called Nick. "Sorry about that."

"You don't have to apologize. You're a beautiful woman. You should date whoever—"

"I don't want to be with him. He's gone now. Nothing to do with you."

Phone to her ear, she walked to the solarium with a trash bag and stooped to sop up the wine she'd knocked over. "There was something about him that bothered me."

"Hunh."

"What does that mean?"

"It means *Hunh*."

She dumped the cartons of Thai food into the trash bag. "Clarissa did a background check on him and he came up clean."

"*Clarissa* did a . . . Not *you*?"

She said nothing as her certainty spilled around her like the wine had.

Nick took her silence as *No, not me*, then said, "What's his name?"

"Henry Wexler." She spelled it for him and listened as he tapped at a computer keyboard.

"Sam Jose's, right?" Nick sighed.

Gray said, "What?"

"Henry Wexler worked at TRIBE as a bartender from 2010 to 2013."

Gray's stomach dropped alongside her certainty and she plopped onto the carpet. "Oh, fuck. Are you sure? Oh, shit."

She had been married to Sean and living in Las Vegas, and TRIBE had been Sean's second and most successful nightclub. Located in the Tropicana, TRIBE had pulled in a younger, trendier set with its music, its drinks, and its celebrities. African tapestries mixed with Asian lacquers with a dollop of Native American dream catchers and Celtic crosses. "Just chill" spaces; high balconies; the aromas of sage, spices, and oranges wafting across the dance floor. And there were also great cocktails, mixed by . . .

Nick said, "You didn't recognize him?"

Gray moved her mouth, only to hear it squeak. Finally, she managed to say, "I kept my head down. I didn't meet any man's eyes because I didn't know if he was a . . . spy."

Hank must have been the one to alert Sean. *Hey, guess who came into my cantina? Sure, I got her number. Hey, I have her address, too.* Minutes ago, he'd even said to her, *When we first met, I thought that I didn't have a chance.*

"First met" had meant back in the 2010s.

And she'd let Hank in because he wanted to use the bathroom. The same ruse she'd used in Idyllwild to enter Tea Christopher's cabin.

And the big, bald white man who had wanted Mrs. Kim to let him in, that had to be Mr. Hook, the bodyguard who'd always followed Mrs. Dixon around the city.

"You thinking what I'm thinking?" Nick asked now.

Gray told him her theory as defeat found her again, as its stink clung to her skin. Her life had always been rugged country, with each day starting with "One more mountain." That's where hope ended and happiness started—just over that one more mountain.

"That's why I can't find the P.I. working for him," Nick said. "Because there *is* no P.I."

Gray caught her reflection in the mirror and startled. She had a black cap of hair so dark that all light disappeared there. Her skin looked as pale as black skin could. Thin—her skin looked *thin*. As if she were a ghost or a vampire. That she could see herself at all was the most startling.

"He knows where I am," she whispered.

"I'll come get you."

"No. I don't wanna run anymore."

"Then let me end it. I won't miss vital organs."

"You think I missed on *purpose*?" Gray shouted. "Because I'm *incompetent*?"

Nick didn't respond.

Heat swirled in her belly and spiraled up to her head. "You *do* think that."

"Let me end it, Gray. I've done it before, without hesitation."

She squeezed shut her eyes. "I'm handling it."

"By giving up? You said you'd come here when shit got scary. Well, shit's now scary, and you're just . . . *sitting* there, waiting for this fucker to kill you."

Resignation had settled on her like fog just hours ago. At that moment, resignation had triumphed over her one-more-mountain resolve. It was brackish water drowning the pinkish-red of dawn. *Surrender, Dorothy.* She'd thought that, and Nick knew she'd thought that, and now here he was, willing to kill Sean Dixon himself before letting her die from her surrender.

"I'm not giving up," she said. "It's my fight. I'm gonna handle it."

He said nothing.

"I'm *not* giving up, all right? He will *not* win."

"Natalie—Grayson. *Shit.*"

"I know. This is . . . I know." *And I'm sorry.*

"What do you want me to do?"

"I'll let you know." She forced herself to smile and take in the city lights before her. "I hear Tahiti's nice. We can open up a little bookstore and a coffee shop."

He said, "Sure."

Tears burned her eyes as she thought of returning to Monterey Bay and watching that ocean, drinking wine while reading a big book about Antarctica or the space race as fog slid off the ocean and settled around the hills. Doing that by herself—that was good. Doing that with Nick—that was good, too. But if she succeeded in doing what she'd planned to do, she couldn't return to that house on the bay.

Nick didn't ask if she was okay, probably because he knew that she'd have to be okay, or else. He also knew that she had a gun and would use it if needed.

"I still have your biscuits," Gray said now. "But they're cold and hard." *Just like my heart at this very moment.*

He said, "Yeah. Thanks."

"So, what's this update you have about the Lincoln case?"

Trash bag in hand, she trekked to the kitchen, shoved the bag into the waste can, then pulled open the freezer door. She grabbed the icy bottle of vodka. Right then, she didn't need olives or vermouth or a glass. *Take that shit straight,* that's what Mom Twyla had always said before chugging from the bottle of Smirnoff. An elf with a gut, that had been Mom Twyla. All of her drinking and fried chicken and cheese had made her bloated and puffy. She'd squeezed into her clothes only to have the middle part of her whoopie pie beyond the shirttail and waistband. And she'd offer her foster daughter a sip of Smirnoff only after the bottle was nearly empty. Li'l Bit's belly had burned as the vodka hit it, and little Natalie Kittridge liked how Mom Twyla would smile at her and say, "That shit's *tight,* huh?" Li'l Bit would smile back at her and say, "Yeah." Then she'd try to read the *Vibe* article about LL Cool J or Al B. Sure!, but her mind would keep flopping.

Now, so many years later, Natalie Kittridge Grayson Dixon, aka Grayson Sykes, wanted her mind to flop, and she wanted her belly to warm.

But not tonight. Or on any night that she remained prey to Sean's predator.

"Hassan did something nice for you," Nick said. Hassan was their hacker for hire and guide to all things dark web. His name wasn't Hassan, and Gray wasn't even sure he was a he.

"He got into the Lincoln woman's Facebook account."

Bottle tipped over the sink, Gray said, "That's illegal, you know." The icy liquid swirled into the drain and the fumes nearly made her explode all over the kitchen. A good way to go.

"Yeah, yeah," Nick said. "You want the password or not?"

She grabbed a pen from the utility drawer and tore off a paper towel. "Password."

"Lower case g, r, o, capital O, lower case v, y, followed by the number one."

groOvy1. "Not a secret words mastermind, is she?" Gray dumped the empty vodka bottle in the trash can and hurried into her bedroom. She pulled the beaded cords of her window to push the blinds aside for an unspoiled city view and then settled at her desk. She brought up Isabel Lincoln's Facebook page on her laptop computer.

Nothing had changed since Gray's last visit. Just those wine country posts, the dead cat Morris posts, and—She stopped scrolling. That same wine tasting picture hung on the walls along the staircase at Isabel's condo. The Benetton crew picture, too. No one had been tagged, even though there were fifteen Likes.

Who had Liked it? Cindy Eshelman, Jude Valdes, Beth Sharpe . . .

She said, "There's not one Like from the women in the pictures, who were also the same crew in the snow picture, beside the Jeep."

Nick said, "Strange."

Gray brought up Google Images to match faces in the digital world. She uploaded the wine tasting picture, and in less than 0.016 seconds the search engine found a result.

She said, "Oh."

Nick said, "What?"

She uploaded the second picture. "Shit."

"*What?*"

"*Diverse. Friends. Young women. Road trip.*"

"Those are words."

"Yeah, and they're also *tags*. Tags that Getty Images uses to catalog the pictures that I'm now looking at, which came from Isabel Lincoln's Facebook page."

"Huh?"

"The women in the pictures are real. But they're *models*. Stock photography models. The pictures on Isabel's page and hanging in her condo? Those are stock photographs."

She could tell by the silence on the other end of the phone that Nick was gawking at her.

"Morris the cat? His pictures are real, not stock. But the girlfriend shots?" Gray was now grinning as she uploaded each picture from Isabel Lincoln's timeline—the foam star in the latte, the sunrise in Yosemite, the sand castle. Each had come from Getty Images.

Nick said, "You sound delighted."

"Oh, I'm not delighted, but this is pretty good." She moved the cursor to the top of the screen and clicked the down-arrow next to the quick help icon. There was another account profile listed. That second account . . .

"Elyse Miller," she said.

"The name we saw on the mail, and on the résumé, diploma, and Social Security card up in Idyllwild."

"And the woman married or not married to Omar Neville." Gray's pulse revved as though she'd drunk fifteen cups of espresso between snorting twenty lines of cocaine. She clicked on the account for Elyse Miller.

The last comments on that timeline had been posted three years before, on March 27. "Beautiful day . . ." along with a shot of the beach and a puffy-clouded sky.

Where u at, posted by Essence Tucker.

Miss ya girl!! From Val Hutchins.

UR a strait BICH and I hop Ur DEAD!!! From Myracle Hampton.

If Willy Wonka had a black half sister from Oakland, Myracle would be that woman. Red licorice whip hair. Lemonhead-yellow nails. Abba Zaba skin. Hot Tamales lipstick. Terrific contrast to hoping someone—a "bich"—was dead.

Elyse Miller had 378 friends, and none of those posted pictures belonged to Getty Images.

That wasn't shocking.

What *was* shocking: the woman in the pictures was the woman Gray had known as Isabel Lincoln. On this timeline she was younger, a bottle blonde, with multipierced ears and a pierced nose. She liked Hpnotiq and Quarter Pounders and drove a slate-blue Impala on rims.

"This is not a woman who dates doctors," Nick pointed out.

"Just a guess, but I'd say she dates street pharmacists."

Gray's throat tightened, and she forced herself to breathe. Hard to do as she read entries posted by her missing Mary Jane, showing her smoking blunts as thick as sausages and flashing crisp hundred-dollar bills. Gray clicked on the Messenger bubble icon.

Myracle Hampton, the woman who had called Elyse Miller a "bich," had continued her screed in a private message.

WHO DO U THINK U R??? I NEW U WAS A SHADY BICH & I TOLD TOMMY U WAS NO GOOD. DON'T TRUSS HER. HE DIDN'T LISSEN 2 ME AND NOW LOOK. U COM BACK HEAR AND IMA KICK YOUR ASS UNTILL THEIR NOTHING LEFT. TEST ME BICH KEEP RUNNING.

Gray clicked on Myracle's page. Still actively posting. Still actively misspelling.

GUN VIOLINS WAAAY NOT NESSESARY!!! HELP US LORD
GOOD MORNING FBF!

Gray clicked back into Messenger and found a conversation between Elyse and Tommy Hampton, a heavy-lidded, amber-skinned Oakland Raiders fan who looked like he smelled of hot sauce and maple syrup.

-sometimes I feel so stupid and get emotional when it comes 2 u Tommyboy
-You're special to me.
-ur special 2 me E 2
-when r we gonna meet?
-Maybe this picture will help.
-I want more.
-let's meet up. I want to see u f2f!

-when?

-tonight

-Best Western on Embarcadero 9:00

-I'm ready for our first time

-keycard at the lobby

The messages between Elyse Miller and Tommy Hampton stopped on March 26, a day before the puffy-cloud, "Beautiful day" beach post on March 27. There were no indications that they'd met at the Best Western in Oakland.

"Guess they finally slept together and got it out of their systems," Nick said.

"You sound bored," Gray said, still scrolling through the messages.

"Desk work. At the Bureau, I always hated the desk work. That's why I hired you and twenty other people."

"Well, go chase somebody down an alley, then. I'll catch you later."

"Natalie—"

"I'll be careful, Dom. Gun's right here, and I'm completely sober." "Completely sober" also meant no oxycodone and no Percocet. "Trust that I'll call you if shit goes sideways."

He sighed, then said, "Good night."

Gray rose to close the blinds, and pain crackled around her navel. She sat back down and closed her eyes. Waited for the pain to stop.

Beyond her bedroom, the refrigerator coughed and rattled.

She said, "There, there, fridge," as she plucked the ibuprofen bottle from her bag. She popped four, then waited . . . waited . . . inhaled . . . exhaled . . . until . . .

With her body at peace again, she clicked over to Tommy Hampton's Facebook page.

There was a picture of Tommy and a little girl who wore beaded cornrows and had her father's heavy-lidded eyes. There was a page header: "Remembering Thomas Hampton. We hope people who loved Tommy find comfort in visiting his profile to remember and celebrate his life."

The last message had been posted just months ago, on March 26, three years *after* Elyse and Tommy had agreed to meet at the Best Western.

You are missed.

Before that, countless posts:

man, I remember how we . . .

Praying for your family and friends . . .

Thinking of you bro . . .

You're an angel now . . .

Day of remembrance . . .

I won't rest until I get justice for my brother. I know who did it!!!!!

Tommy Hampton was dead.

There were only two short articles on the internet that told of a hotel maid finding Tommy Hampton on the floor of room 321 at the Best Western. A pair of boxers had been shoved into his mouth, a pillow had been dropped on his face, and there had been bullet holes in both the pillow and his forehead. The toxicology report had shown ketamine in his system. Also known as a date-rape drug, Special K, ketamine, made you immobile.

Tommy Hampton couldn't even fight back before he was killed.

Had Elyse Miller killed him?

And if she had killed *him*, then maybe she murdered Omar Neville, too.

Gray searched for any recent news on the most recent dead man, but she found nothing more than the article she'd read days ago.

Myracle Hampton, Tommy's sister, had accused Elyse of killing—

No. She had accused Isabel Lincoln—

Isabel . . . Elyse . . . They were the same woman.

The morning's rhythmic *thump-thump-thump* of helicopter music made Gray open her eyes. She lay in bed, curled into a fetal position, a prim protective ball now being warmed by a V-shaped shaft of light. She blinked and her eyes crunched.

The bedroom smelled like burning forests and car exhaust—after this summer of fire, her apartment's air filters would resemble a honeycomb that had been buried in a mine shaft.

Her phone buzzed from a place within the twisted bed linens. She pawed the comforter and top sheet until she hit something hard and rectangular.

Fucking the help now?

The picture: a selfie of a smiling Hank, with her asleep in his arms.

He sent this last week, piece of shit trying to make me jealous

Gray's breath left her lungs.

Angry tears made those words twist, and she shoved her face into a pillow.

How could Hank betray her like this? How could he—

I told him he could have your fat ass
remember how U hated doing this back in the day

The next picture showed her standing at a gas pump, blocks from Rader Consulting.

Ants crawled over her skin. More tears—hotter, angrier ones—rolled down her cheeks and dropped into the comforter. She swiped at those tears with the bedsheet, then tapped a message on the digital keyboard.

You got me. You found me. I'm here. Now what?
Fucker.

Grayson Sykes wasn't the same woman she'd been five years ago, fake-grimacing at the thought of touching gas pumps, even though she'd grown up touching roach husks and rat corpses. Faking her disgust had made Sean feel manlier, though, and so . . .

No. She wasn't the same woman he had scared with his violence, a woman made meek by isolation. If he wanted her, he could come get her, and he'd die in his attempt to drag her to Vegas or to hell or both. Sean knew Natalie Dixon and had put too much trust in that outdated intel.

To force him fully into the light, Gray typed, *we can meet and u can threaten me to my face just like the old days. U know where I am*

With trembling hands, she burned that "Dating" number and every other number except the one Nick used and the one for Isabel Lincoln's case. She also burned her work number and would give Jennifer, Clarissa, and Zadie a temporary one to use, along with some wack explanation about the need to change it.

Maybe tell them about the breakup with Hank?

Yeah, they'd get that, and they'd understand the need to find another cantina.

Gray kicked away the tangled bed linens and stood on new legs like a wobbly doe. Her mouth tasted funky and metallic, like old blood, and sound danced in her head like Ginger Rogers wearing tap shoes turned up to MAX VOL. She plopped back on the bed and whispered, "Gimme a second, will ya?" and waited for the dancing to stop.

No booze. No narcotics. Yet she still felt like crap.

Gray whispered, "Okay. Now," and then stood without wobbling. One small step for woman . . .

After brushing her teeth and washing her face, she pulled on black slacks and a black shirt, then settled at her home desk.

First, she called Farrah Tarrino at UCLA.

"Is Isabel back yet?" Farrah Tarrino asked.

"No, but I'm hoping you have some news that can help me."

"Maybe. Did I mention that Isabel applied for a job to work directly with the students?"

"You did."

"Did I mention that this role required additional background checks and fingerprinting?"

"You did not."

"Isabel got her prints taken a few days before she left for the Memorial Day weekend."

"Have the prints returned?"

"A while ago, but they've been kicked back to us, and that's why I'm glad you called. I'm going to send you the results."

Farrah's email arrived.

Hello, Ms. Sykes. Here you go. It's strange but the woman in HR told me that these were the correct results.

Gray clicked the attached PDF of the Live Scan report.

> ... in response to your record check ... As of the date of this letter, the fingerprints submitted by applicant ISABEL LINCOLN identified as those fingerprints belonging to ...

Elyse Miller.

She started to type a thanks to Farrah Tarrino, but her phone buzzed again.

An alert from her video doorbell app.

A white guy was standing at her door. He was heroin skinny with dirty-blond hair pulled into a ponytail. His black Metallica T-shirt hung over the waistband of too-big jeans. He looked dead, and Gray could smell him from her bedroom.

She reached beneath her pillow and touched the gun she'd only shot at a range.

She should never have found her way to Sam Jose's.

She'd been so careful for so long. No mail sent where she lived. No long-lasting relationships. No history. Forsaking vodka and nose rings and her *name*. Not visiting her parents' graves. No attachments to anything she couldn't leave behind in five seconds.

Had Sean been searching for her all this time? Or had it been dumb luck that Hank had recognized her and had called him?

It was time to disappear. To become someone else again.

Her mind bristled with the thought of starting over. Since birth, her life had been one big do-over and she was tired of it. At three days old, Baby Girl Natalie had already been grinding. She'd had new starts with every new family or agency that had taken her in. Back then, the only thing she'd kept that hadn't been attached to her by muscle and bone had been her first name. Nothing else had stuck.

And now Grayson Sykes thought of disappearing to her house off the Pacific. She'd never told Sean that she owned anything other than that Jeep—*that* secret, about the house, she'd kept. A part of her had known . . .

Back then, Sean had told her, had *promised* her, that he'd never leave her alone.

Nearly a decade later, he was keeping that promise. *Until death.*

Out in the kitchen, the refrigerator grumbled.

Out in the hallway, the white guy looked at his phone, shook his head, then shuffled away from Gray's apartment. He knocked on the hipsters' door across the hall. Conner answered and said, "Took you forever, man."

Gray's shoulders slumped with relief. Dude had the wrong address.

She slipped the gun back beneath the pillow.

Shaky.

And sober.

SHE
FACED
THE
DRAGON

46

It was one hundred ten degrees in Las Vegas and the sky was a dirty white. The sidewalks were crammed with lobster-red and burned-toast-skinned visitors wearing baseball caps and sun visors. They clutched margaritas in neon plastic sippy cups, beer cozies, and Big Gulps. Cars were everywhere, and where there were no cars, there were busses and trollies.

The town Gray had escaped five years ago hadn't changed.

She had thought about canceling her trip to Vegas. She'd come up with excuses to Clarissa on why she had to remain in Los Angeles.

This Lincoln case just blew up in my face.

You will never believe what Nick needs me to do.

But Gray offered no excuses. She couldn't—not after receiving from the bride-to-be a bouquet of BFF cake pops and a three-hundred-dollar gift card to Target.

And really, the Lincoln case had threatened to boil over, but Isabel hadn't texted again with a picture of Kenny G. or with demands that Gray hand over the insurance check. And Ian arriving at the coffee shop *right then*—that coincidence still bothered Gray. *And*, since Tuesday night, Tea had been hunkered down in her house in Westchester. Gray had called Myracle Hampton as she sat and surveilled Tea, but there had been no answer. No return call, either. So here she was.

Stuck in Sin City.

The bitch was back.

Some good would come from celebrating Clarissa's upcoming nuptials and being one of the girls again. And then there was also something personal, too . . . something *bloodier*.

Gray had thought about things.

She'd taken steps.

Like burning all those extraneous phone numbers and providing her coworkers with a new number. They didn't blink, because new numbers were a part of the game. Since then, she hadn't received a text message from Sean.

Like changing her routes around the city again, no longer driving herself, not even in Nick's cars. Instead, she rode in cars hired from hotels just a half mile south of her apartment.

Like giving Jennifer the Lincoln case, if necessary. Jennifer probably would have finished by now, anyway. With her experience, she would see the links more clearly than Gray.

By Sunday, life would be different for Gray . . . or whoever she'd be by then.

Gray had packed a few things that she could have left behind in five seconds but didn't *want* to leave behind. She wished she could have left that raggedy Liz Claiborne purse, but she had no other handbags. She did pack thin black gloves and those soft jeans she'd washed hundreds of times over four years. She'd packed the signed copy of President Obama's memoir, which she'd read twice and highlighted. *Where there is no experience, the wise man is silent.* She had also

packed that black, yellow, and red handmade man-
dala she bought on a family trip to Panama so long
ago. Irreplaceable things that could again be a foundation for her new start in a new place.

Gray also had made a stop at the safe deposit box
that held her Tiffany journal and Faye's jewelry. She
left the diamonds and took the keys to the house in
Summerlin. She also took her amended birth certificate, which had been issued once the Graysons had
formally adopted her, and fifteen thousand dollars in
cash.

And the black Louis Vuitton backpack that Nick
had privately gifted her for Christmas, she'd brought
that with her, too.

And now the girls poked at her, making ado about
the four-thousand-dollar extravagance with the asym-
metrical zipper and metal studs. "Since when does
Dominick Rader pay us enough to buy Louis Vuitton?" Clarissa laced her calf-high Doc Martens boot,
just one piece of her *Final Fantasy* tutu-leggings-
ponytail ensemble that she'd put together for her special weekend.

Jennifer snorted. "Since when does *Gray* carry designer bags? Was it a *Please take me back* gift from
the Hot Marine?" The blonde looked like she wasn't
traveling to Clarissa's destination, not wearing those
mom capris, espadrilles, and Cartier sunglasses.
WASPy cosplay.

From the front seat of the taxi, Zadie popped open
a can of Dr Pepper. "Since when is it any of your
business how she got the damned thing or why she's
carrying it?" Zadie wore sensible sandals and a gold
sundress. Nana-wear. She smelled of sunscreen and
cigarette smoke.

Gray wore blue jeans and a white T-shirt with no funny sayings or memorable graphics. She planned to blend in this weekend.

Yes, Nick had given her the backpack, and she didn't want to leave it behind because it *was* gorgeous, and Nick didn't spend several grand for "just friends." When she'd first taken it from its dust bag on that Christmas day, she'd imagined the days and nights afterward: Holding hands at the Santa Monica Pier. Going to the driving range and swinging a nine iron as he chose a Big Bertha. She imagined their drives along the Pacific Coast Highway. Kisses—short and sweet ones, and then longer, breathtaking ones. But then, in real life, he'd told her that *they* couldn't happen yet because *she* needed time. So, if she couldn't have him, she'd have his bag, and she clutched it to her chest as their hired car headed north toward the Strip.

No more lobster and sirloin steak for a dollar on the Strip. No more showgirls, either. The hotels in the pyramid, the lion, the castle, the big top, and the needle hadn't changed. Some spots were newer—slick-sided, non-kitschy high-rise hotels like the Aria and the Cosmopolitan.

I'm back here after swearing . . .

Gray's stomach felt waxy and slick. She wanted to vomit. She closed her eyes and waited for the dizzy spell to pass.

Jennifer waggled Gray's knees. "You okay?"

"She's *fine*," Clarissa said. "She's perfect. *This* is perfect. Nothing will go wrong this weekend." The bride-to-be patted Gray's head. "For a minute, though, I totally thought you were gonna, like, flake. We're gonna have so much fun!"

Jennifer found her mirrored compact in her purse,

then applied a new coat of cotton candy–pink lipstick. "And I'll show you all the sights. I know Vegas better than any of you. It's like a second home."

Gray smirked. *Oh, Jennifer.* She *was* happy to hang out and be a girlfriend. Even though she kept her true intentions secret, she would enjoy as much drinking, gambling, and celebrating as she could before retreating underground again like a cicada.

"As a present to *you*"—Jennifer pointed at the bride-to-be—"Nick told me to use the company card for dinner tonight."

"He's paying?" Clarissa said, eyes wide.

Jennifer nodded.

Clarissa screeched.

"That man is a mystery," Zadie said.

"Yeah," Jennifer agreed. "One of those sexy men with mysterious pasts."

Gray said, "Uh-huh," even though she knew that Dominick Rader grew up in Santa Monica with his mom, dad, surfboard, skateboard, and a pit-boxer named Teeny. He'd been valedictorian of his senior class at Crossroads School, had earned his bachelor's degree and JD from UCLA, had joined the FBI afterward, and now visited his parents, both alive and retired in Scottsdale, four times a year.

The Cosmopolitan was big and pretty. "Smooth" was the word Gray thought of. And "bright." Chandeliers and more chandeliers—over bars, over slot machines. And the interior smelled like pastries and fields of flowers. And it all *twinkled.*

Clarissa's five nonwork friends—Kylie, Haley, Kailey, Skylar, and Brianne—were waiting in the hotel lobby. Young women young and perfumed, high-pitched voices, "ohmigosh" and "literally" and "like" and selfies and fake eyelashes . . .

Gray and Jennifer shot each other looks and mouthed, *Wow*.

Each woman had booked separate rooms. "In case we have company," Jennifer said with a wink. "*In case*. Listen to me. I *will* have company."

Clarissa blushed and blinked at Jennifer. "Dude. You're, like, *married*."

Jennifer patted the young woman's shoulder as the group wandered to the elevator bank. "And you're, like, *not*. Which means you wouldn't understand. How do you think I met Reynaldo? Sharing a hymnal at church after my second divorce?" She rolled her eyes. "Come on, Clarissa. Life isn't *Little House on the Prairie*."

Kylie, Skylar, and Brianne blinked and asked, "What's *Little House on the Prairie*?"

As the group rode up to the ninth floor, Clarissa shared her vision of married life. Never going to bed angry. Fidelity until death. Open communication. Clean kitchen. Fifty-fifty everything, even in parenting. The young women said, "Aww" and "So romantic" and "It *is* possible if you try."

The older women held back laughter. Zadie even added, "They're so precious. Aren't they precious, girls?"

Jennifer and Gray smiled, and said, "Oh yeah. Totally precious."

They all gathered in Clarissa's suite before breaking apart—to rest for Gray, Jen, and Zadie; to drink for the young'uns. Clarissa, phone in her hand, rattled off the evening's itinerary. "We're eating at Bardot Brasserie at the Aria at six. We're going to the Cirque du Soleil show at eight, and then we come back here to dance at the Marquee. Okay?"

Gray, Jennifer, and Zadie gaped at her—the *fuck?*—and then said, "Okay," and "Yeah."

Clarissa clapped her hands. "And let's meet back here, dressed and ready for dinner, in . . . three hours. Okay?"

Gray said, "Sure," then trudged across the hall to room 911. After slipping the DO NOT DISTURB hangtag over the doorknob, she took in her surroundings. Marble floors in the bathroom. Soft queen-size bed. From the picture window, she had a view of the entire Strip. All of it took her breath away, and she hated the awe now filling her lungs.

Ten minutes later, she speed walked out of the hotel, caught a cab, then settled in for the twenty-minute drive to Fashion Show mall. There, she entered Sur La Table, a kitchenware mecca that boasted a wide selection of knives.

A sweet-faced brunette asked if Gray needed help.

Gray said, "No," with her attention on the Miyabi cutlery. "I'm good, thanks."

"If you do a lot of food prep," the clerk said, ignoring the no, "this one . . ." She pointed to the Evolution slicing knife. "This one is perfect. Nine and a half inches of steel. Gives you smooth, even cuts every single time."

Gray left Sur La Table without buying the knife. Instead, she sat outside the store and looked for the perfect mark. *There.* Her proxy buyer: a shabby-looking mom pushing a shabby-looking stroller filled with twin redheaded toddler boys. She looked like she needed fifty dollars to either buy a new stroller or to trim the damaged ends of her frizzy red hair.

"That's it?" the woman asked Gray, bloodshot eyes big. "You'll give me fifty dollars to buy the knife?"

"Yep." *Don't ask me why. Please don't ask me* She had thought of a story—her mom was wit in the mall and she didn't want her to see the because it was a surprise gift. Not a very comp story, but the shabby-looking mom of twins ask.

Didn't take long for Gray to possess the knif the woman to collect fifty dollars.

47

It was 5:05, and Gray had an hour before the theater curtains opened again. She spent twenty of those minutes on a power nap, and as she lay in that wonderful bed, she refused to let her mind sprint from the thought of finding Sean to the thought of killing Sean. No, she let her mind take long strokes—Nick, freedom, Nick, food, freedom—until it tired itself out, and soon she felt herself slipping away.

At 5:25, the phone's alarm clock beeped.

Gray popped up, refreshed and ready for a shower. She wanted to stand beneath that perfect blast of hot water forever, but she couldn't. Face painted on, and dressed in black cigarette pants, an off-the-shoulder blouse, and heeled boots, Gray joined her coworkers and the young'uns in Clarissa's room.

Zadie sparkled in her grandmother-of-the-bride sequined shirt and satin pants. Clarissa wore the tiara and veil Jennifer had gifted her, along with another tutu and pink Doc Martens boots. If Zadie looked like the grandmother of the bride, Jennifer could have been the stepmother of the bride in her cut-too-low-for-your-age wrap dress and platform stilettos.

The friends, all eyelashes and baby giraffe legs, wore short dresses and clunky heels. With dewy skin and bright white teeth, they were lovely creatures excited about their future loves and their future lives.

"Okay, okay," Clarissa chirped, flapping her hands. "Picture time!"

Gray inwardly groaned but acquiesced. This could possibly be one of her last moments with the only friends she'd had since before Sean.

At Bardot Brasserie, she devoured wood-grilled bone marrow, lobster bisque, and roasted Mediterranean sea bass.

"You're eating like it's your last meal," Jennifer snarked, though she was not restrained either as she dined on plates of oysters, a gigantic wedge salad, and an enormous rib eye.

"I'm eating like Nick is paying." Gray gasped. "Oh. He is."

Later, from her tenth-row seat, Gray whooped as the divers of *O* did tricks off of diving boards.

Afterward, in the Bellagio's lobby, Clarissa shouted, "Time to club!"

Entering the Marquee, it was as though Gray were stepping on hot coals. She winced at the produced commotion—lasers and loudness, girls dancing on perches. She sipped Kentucky mules and hoped that the bourbon would dull the edges now scraping across her heart and lungs. She squinted through lasers and smoke and searched for eyes that were lingering on her too long.

"You're more quiet than usual tonight," Zadie said. She and Gray were sitting in a booth while Clarissa and Jennifer danced with two gelled blond bros wearing cheap suits.

Gray smiled at the older woman. "Can't remember the last time I was in a club. Guess I'm just trying to enjoy . . . *this*."

Zadie eyed Gray's cocktail. "No margarita?"

"Taking a break from tequila tonight."

"You've been so careful."

Gray said nothing, just looked at the old woman shining in the dark.

Zadie knocked around the ice in her seven and seven. "You two ever gonna just . . . go for it?"

Gray squinted at her. "You missed me with that."

"You and Nick. Your relationship."

Gray sat possum-still and hoped that Zadie would move on to kill something else. But Zadie stared at her, waiting for an answer. Gray said, "Nick's my boss."

"I know who he truly is to you, sweetie," the old woman said. "Who he was to you before Rader Consulting existed. I'm employee number one, remember?"

As though that—employee number one—meant something to Gray.

Zadie sipped her cocktail. "I know that you and Nick are close. Closer than close. And I also know who you are . . . *Natalie*."

48

Zadie kept her twinkling eyes on Gray. She drained her cocktail, then hid a burp behind her delicate hobbit hand. "I know you escaped from this place," the old woman whispered. "I know that Nick helped you do that. And I've noticed that his mood has changed in the last two weeks." She touched Gray's wrist and squeezed. "He loves you."

Gray's eyes clouded with tears. "Who else knows?"

"No one."

Gray slowly exhaled. "Can you keep it secret? All of it? About me. And him?"

"I have all this time, haven't I?" Beneath that club light and with those reflecting sequins, Zadie's eyes looked sharp as razor blades. "I'm old, not stupid."

The air was tight around Gray's head, and the bourbon from her cocktail gurgled in her belly. "Did Nick . . . He *told* . . . ?"

"He didn't have to tell me anything. I did all of your paperwork. You know Nick *hates* paperwork. But don't worry. I'll carry it to my—"

Clarissa staggered back to the booth. Her white veil was now stained with lipstick and grenadine and violated by little holes in the mesh that made it look like a worn mosquito net. "Are you gonna dance?" she slurred, waggling Gray's shoulder.

Gray blinked away her tears. "Nope. Jim Beam is my baby tonight."

Clarissa grabbed the nearly empty bottle of champagne from the silver ice bucket. Just like any dedicated drunk, she brought it to her lips and drank it through the veil.

Gray couldn't care less—about the torn veil or the young bride-to-be drinking from the bottle. There was something more alarming happening: Zadie knew about her, and Nick had never mentioned the old woman's role in Gray's new life.

It was now too loud in here, and too close. People. There were so many people. A weather system was forming over the DJ booth from all the hot bodies and the hotter lights—low fog clung to the floor and clouded above the Exit signs.

"I'm drunk." Clarissa scooted into the booth and placed her head on Gray's shoulder. "I love you, Grayson." It only took a second for her eyelids to droop, and soon she was snoring.

Clarissa's college friends trundled over to the booth and took pictures with the passed-out guest of honor.

Giggling, Gray slipped an ice cube from her mug, then swiped it across Clarissa's nose.

Clarissa snorted awake. "Huh?"

The women hollered with laughter.

Clarissa grabbed her purse from Zadie's lap. "I need to go to bed."

Jennifer waltzed over with her bad-suit bro. He had a buffalo's head and wore as much cologne as Jennifer wore perfume. They'd combust if they rubbed their bare skin together. "This is Dylan," Jennifer said, "and—C'mon, don't tell me y'all are tired. It's only one o'clock."

"We're tired," Clarissa, Zadie, and Gray said.

"We're not," the five young women said.

"Stay with us, Jen," blonde Haley pled.

Jennifer swiveled to face her buffalo-headed date. "Come as a group, leave as a group."

Gray knew Jennifer must have been exhausted.

The quartet wove through the crowds, stumbling past craps tables and old people pulling oxygen tanks. A band in one of the clubs was jamming out "Play That Funky Music," and even though Gray was tired, she couldn't keep her head from bopping to that funky bass line.

Over the music and slot machine noise, Jennifer told them about her new friend, Dylan.

Dylan's only twenty-four, can you believe it?

Dylan's a hedge fund broker, already pulling in a million five, can you believe it?

Jennifer Bellman fit perfectly in this city of secrets, and Gray had already tired of her and the bright lights and the cigarette smoke and the expense. None of that had changed in her time away, and now, more than ever, she yearned to be back in Monterey, out on the deck of the only place she'd ever truly considered home.

Room 911 would suffice for now. It was just as Gray had left it, with the curtains open and the neon lights coloring the dark desert sky. She changed into jeans, a thick hoodie, and a black baseball cap. A pair of platform Chuck Taylors made her an inch taller, and the Elvis Costello glasses hid most of her face. She slipped the Miyabi Evolution slicer into the Louis Vuitton backpack but left her phone on the nightstand—didn't want it pinging off cell phone towers and placing her anywhere except here.

Before opening the door, she peeped out of the peephole.

No one there.

She slipped the backpack straps over her shoulders, then slipped out of the room. She crept to the elevator, strolled through the sweet-smelling, still-crowded lobby, and hailed a cab at the valet in front of the hotel.

"Where to, young lady?" The driver was a dark-skinned man with a broad, flat nose hooked over his mustache. His car smelled of Brut and curry.

"Five ninety-five Trail Spring Court, over in Summerlin."

The cab rolled west, leaving behind the crowds and the lights of the Strip.

Gray thought about Sean's text messages and the pictures he'd sent. With cautious fingers, she pressed on the cheekbone he'd nearly shattered, the cheekbone that still ached anytime the Santa Anas picked up or an El Niño system lingered over California.

Back then, Sean had presented her with the deed to the house on Trail Spring Court. The Spanish-Californian had a ceramic-tile roof, hardwood floors, a formal dining room, a big backyard, and a whirlpool tub in the master bathroom. He hadn't bought it, not yet. "I just got the money together to put a huge down payment on it. I just mocked up this deed in Word."

Natalie's heart had broken. He'd taken her Jeep and sold it without her permission, and now this? She would have liked to have *seen* the house first. Because what if she hated it? What if it wasn't *her*? She'd wanted to tear up that fake deed.

"I can't believe you're crying right now," Sean had said.

She'd stammered, "It's just . . . It's just . . ."

"And what the hell do *you* know about houses?" he had snarled. "You grew up in the fucking ghetto."

Back then, her friend Zoe had asked, "Is your name even on the *real* deed? On the title?"

"On the *what*?" Wide-eyed and beautiful, Natalie had gaped at her friend as though five hundred thousand dollars spent on a house in the desert was merely twenty cents, as though a "title" was a rare Yangtze River dolphin that she needn't care about since it was so rare.

And now she was returning to that house in the desert.

Was she really gonna do this?

Was she really gonna kill him?

The driver stopped at the security gate of the Paseos. "You have an entry code?"

Gray closed her eyes. *Shit.* She hadn't thought . . . "Six one four seven."

The gate creaked open and the taxi rolled past.

Relieved, Gray asked the driver to stop at the beginning of the cul-de-sac where she'd lived. From there, she saw the two-story house that, according to land records, Sean still owned. No one loitered on the sidewalks, not at this time of night, not in the Paseos. Many things had changed in Vegas, but some things—like fancy Summerlin neighborhoods—had not.

The driver looked at her reflection in his rearview mirror. "Want me to wait?"

She peeled off twenties to pay her fare and his tip. "You wouldn't mind?"

"Got nothing else to do 'cept wait."

"I'll meet you at the Chevron back on Desert Foothills."

"That's almost a thirty-minute walk."

"Got nothing else to do 'cept walk," she said.

He gave her his business card. "I'll be there."

"Yep, but if I'm not there," she said, pulling out her set of keys, "or if I haven't called you by four o'clock, just go." She hoped the gas station had a public telephone.

"Got it." He added, "You be careful, young lady."

She passed dark house after dark house until she reached 595.

The property still looked good, thanks to homeowners association demands. Its desert landscaping hadn't changed. Neither had the pink sandstone pavers in the drive and walkways. Her eyes skirted the house's eaves in search of a security or doorbell camera. Nothing. No lights were on.

She gripped the key ring she'd kept in that safe deposit box. House keys, Jaguar key, Range Rover key, mailbox key . . . Calm, even though her heart roared, Gray tugged on the black gloves, then rolled up the sidewalk as though she belonged there. She stepped onto the porch.

Please let this work.

Holding her breath, she slipped the key into the lock.

49

Click.

The key worked.

Surprised, Gray gasped, and electricity zinged through her blood as she pushed . . . open . . . the door . . . and stepped across the threshold.

The foyer was cold and dark. A vampire's lair.

She pulled the knife from her bag, then crept into the living room.

An overstuffed couch and armchair upholstered in a busy paisley pattern, and a just-as-busy floor rug with matching curtains.

No more khakis. No more yellows.

To the fireplace . . .

Framed pictures sat on the mantel: Sean and a pretty Latina who wore lots of eye makeup. A pretty, preteen girl wearing a white soccer uniform. A handsome teenage boy holding a football. Though the kids were too old to be his biologically, Sean was still someone's stepfather. And they were living in Natalie's house.

Sean and Natalie Dixon had never divorced. Not that he needed her to sign divorce papers; published notices in a large-circulation newspaper were enough.

Gray glared at those children.

Fucker. He had ended that dream for her.

Was she really gonna do this?

Hell yes.

She floated to the kitchen, and with a disconnected hand she opened the refrigerator.

A gallon of milk. A carton of eggs. A plate wrapped in foil. Wine bottles. Lunchables. Bottles of Pabst Blue Ribbon. Sean loved that beer. That's why she took the last bottles from the shelf. Opened each. Poured the beer into the sink. Left the empties on the counter.

Fucker.

Did specks of her blood still live beneath the granite island? She'd bled down there, and she'd bled over by the pantry door, too. Once on Fourth of July. Once on the day before taxes were due. And once, that last time, in August . . .

Gray crept up the stairs. The door to the first bedroom was open. She peeked in.

Posters of LeBron James and Russell Wilson. Certificates. Ribbons. Trophies.

The second bedroom was painted pastel purple. Rihanna posters. Certificates. Trophies. An American Girl doll on a rocking chair.

The master suite sat at the end of the hallway. Its double doors were open.

God's hand kept Gray upright as she tiptoed toward her old bedroom. She stood at the threshold until her heartbeat slowed from a gallop to a trot. And then she *looked*.

Fussy paisley-patterned bed linens. Fussy lamps. A chaise. A flat-screen television. A big bed. A pile of laundry sat in the path to the master bathroom. Wasn't Gray's bed anymore, not with all those pillows. Not her bathroom, not with those flouncy towels. Sean's clothes, including the cashmere sweater she'd bought him for Christmas, still hung on his side of the closet, but the clothes on the other side, those heels and belts . . . not hers. The carpet had changed, too. Blue now instead of white. Gray had bled all over that white carpet. Blood was a bitch to get out of white carpet.

She needed a drink.

Gray returned to the living room and sat on the couch. If the pretty Latina came home first, Gray would tell the woman about the stepfather of her children. If *Sean* came home first, well . . . that's what the Miyabi Evolution was for. *Smooth, even cuts every single time.*

Four o'clock came and went, and soon golden light crinkled through the blinds. No one had stepped across the threshold. The car garage door hadn't rumbled.

Gray hadn't moved from her spot on that couch. Gray had thought of nothing and everything and had ignored that voice whispering, telling her to leave. She'd ignored the prickle of her numbing legs and feet, the thud of a full bladder, and the creak of her empty stomach.

The house moaned as the sun's heat warmed wooden beams and ceramic tiles.

At eight o'clock, she finally moved to peek out the living room window.

Across the street, a white woman wearing boxer braids and carrying a Bichon Frise plucked a newspaper from the sidewalk.

"Excuse me," Gray called out as she crossed the street. "Good morning."

The woman smiled at her.

Gray asked about the family who lived at 595.

"They're at Lake Mead," the woman said. "I think they're coming back next week."

Gray let the dog lick her hand as she asked, so matter-of-factly, "Do you know if Sean went with them?"

"Who?" the woman asked.

"Sean Dixon. He owns the house."

The woman's thick eyebrows scrunched. "I'm not so good with names."

"He's tall, a little darker than me. Cute. You'd remember him if you saw him."

The woman shook her head. "I just moved in three weeks ago, and I've only met Precious and her kids, Cayden and Cierra, so . . . Sorry."

The old white guy who lived on the right side of 595—where Phil and Lorraine and their platters of leftover sandwiches had lived until Lorraine's mother in Rhode Island needed live-in help—knew the family, including Sean. "He travels a lot."

No one was coming home today.

Gray whispered, "Shit, shit, shit," as adrenaline drained from her body. Over the two-mile walk to the gas station, she cursed herself. And those three names stayed on her tongue.

Cayden, Cierra, and Precious . . . Cayden, Cierra, and Precious.

There was a public phone at the Chevron, but she didn't call the driver of the curry-smelling cab. In under five minutes, another taxi had picked her up, and the cabbie drove her to SD Promotions. Located in a business park just a stone's throw from McCarran Airport, SD Promotions leased space in a mirrored building. Sean's office manager had crammed Staples furniture into cubicles and offices the size of cereal boxes. Small pods of smokers hung out at the public ashtrays near the turfed pocket park. Administrative assistants in short skirts and cheap heels drank Slim-Fast shakes at the benches close to the parking lot.

Gray didn't know why she'd come here. Was she going to kill Sean at the office? Watch him bleed out on that glass and metal desk he'd spent nearly ten thousand dollars on? The desk where they'd conceived . . . *Faye*. That would have been her name, if she'd been a girl.

The white stenciled letters on the closest parking space read "Sean Dixon."

"Sean Dixon?" the pretty blonde at the reception desk asked.

Gray didn't know this woman, but then, he'd only let her visit the office a handful of times. "The *owner*," Gray said now. "Is he *here*?"

"Let me check." She stood, tugged at her short skirt, and strode toward the offices.

"You can call him from this fancy phone right here, you know," Gray said.

"One minute." The blonde waggled her fingers and disappeared into the cubicle maze.

Gray's eyes flicked from the blown-up photos of staged parties and weddings to the burbling pyramid-shaped water fountain on a coffee table.

The blonde returned to the reception desk, wearing that same synthetic smile. "Mr. Dixon isn't in today."

Gray said, "Okay," but she didn't move to leave.

"Would you like to leave a message?"

"No." She still couldn't move.

The blonde was staring at her. "Anything else, ma'am?"

"Do you know where he is?"

"Uh-huh. He went to visit his wife in L.A."

NEVER YELL "HELP"

Dry-mouthed and barely breathing, Mrs. Dixon dared herself to peek at her panties—no blood. She popped two Vicodin left over from crashing through the glass patio door and receiving stitches for that seven-inch gash. She stood at the mirror—bloody lip and nose—and told her reflection, "I can't take this anymore."

Down in the kitchen, Mrs. Dixon said this again— "I can't. I won't"—then took three long pulls from the vodka bottle in the freezer. It had been six weeks since her last drink.

She kneeled on the kitchen floor to clean up the food. *If he touches me one more time . . .*

The garage door rumbled.

Mrs. Dixon kept scraping Chow's Chinese into one neat heap.

And just as she'd scraped the last peanut into that neat pile, Sean touched her again.

"Touch" was such a pleasant, intimate word. So, no, he didn't "touch." He "slammed" and "punched" and "grabbed." Rice, chicken, and peanuts stuck to her face, her hands, and the undersides of her feet. She pleaded with Sean to stop, to leave, to forgive her for cutting her hair and burning the rice, but he wouldn't stop, so she cried to God, and when *He* didn't respond, she called for Lorraine and Phil, Chris and Maud, and screamed "*Fire!*" and "*Help!*" as his punches and kicks rocked her body.

He wouldn't stop.

She blindly grabbed at the space around her until her hand found . . .

Maybe God *was* listening.

She'd just used that knife to cut lime wedges for her glass of Pellegrino, and now here it was, knocked to the tile along with Chow's Chinese. She wrapped her fingers around the hilt and energy shot from it like Thor's hammer. That electricity coursed through her, and with one push of her knee against Sean's chest, she gained enough space to hold it out before her.

In his rage, Sean didn't see the knife, and he lunged at her.

The blade tore past his T-shirt, broke through his skin, and sank deep into his abdomen.

He shrieked as he clutched his belly. Fear shone in his eyes, black and shiny as beetles.

She kicked him, scrambled to stand, slipping, sliding in rice, blood, tears, and spit.

On the tile, he moaned and writhed in pain.

She stepped over him.

Even then, he couldn't help himself, and he grabbed her ankle.

She shouted, "*No!*" and stomped his hand.

He shouted, "*Ahh!*" and released her.

She ignored his grasping and his hoarse curses, and she prayed that more of his blood gushed out of him and that God would bleed him like the pig he was.

She grabbed her keys from the dining room table and ran to the garage. The door was barely up enough before she threw the Jaguar into reverse and roared out of the driveway. Racing east, toward the Strip, her eyes darted from the road ahead of her to the rearview mirror and the road behind her. It wouldn't be long before he climbed into his SUV and hunted her down.

A half hour later, Mrs. Dixon found herself in the parking lot of the Gold Mine Motor Inn off Paradise Road. The two-story 1960s motel dipped on the edges and was fading before her eyes. It was that rundown and that sandblasted—so tragic, so awfully . . . *bad* that it was almost funny. She sat in the parking lot, shaking now as the adrenaline wore off. She had no money, no identification, no phone. She couldn't go back to Trail Spring Court. If Sean had nearly killed her before she'd stabbed him, he'd certainly kill her now. No, she couldn't go back. But she had no gas in the car and no way to buy any.

Trapped.

Call Dom.

Dominick Rader knew that Sean had been beating her. She could tell that he knew, when they'd bumped into each other at Target just a few weeks before. He'd left his card beneath that box of tampons and had told her to call anytime.

That card . . . Since then, she'd taken it out from the false bottom of her bathroom waste can countless times. The number was different from the number Victor had made her memorize back in college. Looking at this new card, Mrs. Dixon had studied Dominick's new phone number, but she hadn't memorized it backwards like her dad had demanded. And now she glimpsed part of it in her mind's eye.

213 . . .

But the shakes and fear kept her from focusing. Her mind was slippery, and her memory bumped and skidded around "213."

Nighttime here was the color of kitschy neon and

steel. Cars entered and exited the parking lot in a cloud of rusty squeaks and scrapes. Sunburned tourists slurred their sentences as they dragged luggage across the asphalt.

She closed her eyes. *Breathe, Natalie, breathe.* And that's when she saw those seven numbers after 213. She scrounged around her car—seats, carpets, ashtray—and found $1.56 in coins. She hurried to the public phone booth near the lobby entrance. Threw cautious glances at those sunburned tourists, at those parked cars.

Focus.

She grabbed the receiver and deposited a quarter. Punched in the number. Deposited another dime.

Two rings, and a man on the other end said, "Nick Rader."

A sob burst from her gut and she cried for nearly a minute. Once she managed to breathe, she pushed out, "Help me."

"Where are you?"

She told him.

"Get a room, okay?"

She had no money.

"Go in and I'll take care of that."

She told him that Sean had eyes everywhere, that her Jaguar probably had some location device on it, and that he might find out that she was there.

"Don't worry about that. Tell the desk clerk that your name is Alicia Smith. Lock the door. Don't let anyone in except me. If you need a weapon, use the curtain rod or the toilet plunger. Plug in the iron, let it get hot, then use that if you have to. See you soon."

The desk clerk, a bored-looking white woman with frizzy black hair, didn't blink at the fake name, or at the cuts and bruises on Alicia Smith's face, or at the bloodstains as big as sin on Alicia Smith's T-shirt and jeans. She simply handed Alicia Smith a key to room 303 before returning her attention to the iPad on the desk.

Sean would have freaked out if he knew that *his* wife would be sleeping on a bed in a rat hole like this. But fancy hotels like the Sheraton—hell, like the Travelodge—would force her to *be* someone. Not-so-fancy places like the Gold Mine Motor Inn only cared if the customer could pay cash. And that was okay for its primary clientele: prostitutes, johns, and estranged husbands. This Shangri-la welcomed the anonymous with its twenty-nine-dollar-a-day rooms and RCA color televisions.

How soon would Dominick be there?

Would Sean find her first? He always did. And when he did, he would explode, though maybe not immediately. Waiting for him to explode exhausted her. It was like waiting for a single bolt of lightning to strike the tallest tree. It was like waiting for the storm of the century to destroy a weak roof. On those days, she was so anxious, so dread-filled, that she nibbled at herself like a nervous rabbit, chewing through her lipstick and breaking the skin on her bottom lip.

How had she dealt with that all day, every day, for two years and without snapping?

But she *had* snapped. The blood on her clothes— the blood that hadn't come from her—told her that she had snapped.

In room 303, she perched at the end of the hard bed as the colors of the silent RCA television made shadows dance across the walls. Her bladder ached but she didn't dare . . . Because what if . . .

A groan caught in her throat, and tears burned in her eyes, and she sent her attention back to *Matlock*, and then *Murder, She Wrote*, and then *Matlock* again.

Footsteps clomped up and down the walkway outside of her room. Shapes and shadows in the curtains sometimes lingered too long at her window.

Her eyes hurt, but then so did the rest of her. Her bladder was so full that she feared drowning. Fear of catching a urinary tract infection sent her to the bathroom. There, she pulled down her jeans, and that's when she knew: it was over. And as she released her bladder, realizing that it was over, she prayed that Sean had died in a pool of blood just like their baby had. And if he hadn't, she'd make sure that he would one day.

Numb, she returned to the edge of the bed and to *The Andy Griffith Show*. She returned to those lingering shadows and lingering doubts of her worth, back to Dominick's promise and Sean's condition. And just as she thought of leaving the motel room, just as she thought of calling Sean to apologize, just when she'd found her resolve *not* to call him—*Fuck him. Go back and kill that motherfucker*—someone knocked on the door.

Dominick Rader stood there, just as he'd promised.

"I want to leave this place," she told him. "Leave it forever. I need to die."

"You sure?" he asked, as they pulled out of the motel parking lot in his rented Audi.

"Yes."

He would help Natalie Dixon die. It wouldn't be complicated. She had no kids, little credit history, no family. She had a house near Monterey Bay, but Sean didn't know about that. Nor had she told him about her small trust, left by Faye and Victor Grayson.

Natalie had also kept her Tiffany journal in a post office box at the busiest post office in Las Vegas. She'd written in that journal several times a month and, after every Sean Storm, had hidden in its creases pictures of her injuries.

"We'll need that," Dominick told her. "But first we need to get you to a doctor."

During a previous visit, Nurse Anderson at Rapid-Care had offered Natalie her phone number, and now Natalie called her. They met at the clinic, and after performing an ultrasound, Nurse Anderson told Natalie what she already knew. "You miscarried, honey."

Shame and guilt washed over her and she cried into the nurse's bosom.

Back in the Audi, Dominick stared at her with tear-filled eyes as she sifted through the newest pictures of her injuries. "Nat?" he whispered.

"I don't wanna be here. He'll kill me if he isn't dead. I know he will. I wanna disappear."

"You sure?"

She had asked herself this and other questions:

Are you really in love with him?

How could you be in love with him, truly in love with him, if he scares you?

Don't you hate him for embarrassing you, for belittling you, for beating you?

What would Mom and Dad think?

She had never answered those questions honestly. She told herself that Sean's anger didn't scare her. She told herself that she didn't flinch *every* time he raised his voice, even though she had just *stopped* trembling from his last outburst.

If she had answered those questions honestly, she would have had to admit that her relationship with her friends, with the *world*, had changed because of him. She would have had to admit that she'd put up with whatever he did to her, and that she had reasoned it away, no matter how bad it got, all because she had a Cartier bracelet clipped to her wrist, a big house with a succulent garden, and a red Jaguar.

Dominick had asked, *You sure?*

Her bones ached. It hurt to blink.

You sure?

"I'm sure." And she closed her eyes, ready for her change.

50

Las Vegas in the morning was like the hot guy in a dark club who, in the light, had buckteeth, hair plugs, and smelled like a fifties-era bowling alley. Morning Vegas needed to stay in bed until dusk, until the neon and the glass and full-on commitment to the illusion worked best.

The bald cab driver clicked hard candy against his teeth. "It's supposed to hit one twenty today. People gonna be falling out all over the place."

Gray could still see traces of the moon, faint and white, like dissolving foam. It wasn't supposed to be there, that moon. It was supposed to be on the other side of the world. Like her. She wasn't supposed to return to Vegas. But here she was.

Sean was supposed to be here, but he was in Los Angeles visiting his wife, *ha ha.*

No one had walked into that house on Trail Spring Court.

No one's blood was now drying beneath the beds of Gray's fingernails.

You can try again.

Hope warmed her like the sun now warming all of Clark County.

Yeah, I can.

"Here we are." The driver pulled to the curb.

Gray peered out at the motel, which looked as faded and lopsided as it had five years ago.

Tourists on a budget still clattered in and out of the Gold Mine Motor Inn, which now boasted free Wi-Fi. The red Jaguar was no longer parked in that space where she'd left it. Sean had probably sold the car, like she'd sold her engagement ring and platinum wedding band.

Sadness found Gray in the back seat of that taxi, and she wanted to cry. She wanted to kiss that lobby floor and the walls of room 303, her refuge for four hours. *That bathroom. I bled in that bathroom.* Her eyes burned with that thought.

"You wanna get out?" the driver asked.

"No. I'm good." She sat back in the seat, then found that foamy moon again.

Still sucking on candy, the driver pulled into the Cosmopolitan's breezeway twenty minutes after ten o'clock. He reminded Gray to stay out of the sun.

Gray said, "Yep," then paid her fare with cash. Then she slipped into the hotel with its cold, perfumed air, where it was forever seven o'clock in the morning or evening. The chandeliers gleamed, but they didn't mean it. The aromas of bacon and coffee from a nearby restaurant, *that* was true.

Her stomach growled as she moved past empty banks of slot machines and covered gaming tables. Back in her room, Gray texted Jennifer. *U up yet?*

Ellipses bubbled on the screen, and then:

Just now. Meet at Cs for brunch @11.

On the television, Gray found Guy Fieri eating hoagies in New Jersey. She popped her antibiotic—*Good girl!*—and then retreated to the bathroom for a shower. When she returned to dress, she saw that Tea had texted her.

Can we meet? It's very urgent.

Gray responded, *Out of town. Will be back late Sunday.*

At eleven, she met her companions in Clarissa's room. She smelled fresh, looked fresh, and lied about how well she'd slept. Downstairs, they joined the college students, the feathered- and frosted-hair moms, and the NASCAR dads, everyone ready to eat, drink, and gamble.

Gray took all of this in as though she were going to Mars instead of breakfast at a café. *I miss this.* Not the noise or the crowds but the simple living. She missed celebrating her birthday as a Taurus and not as a Scorpio. She missed vodka and signing "Natalie" on triplicate forms and waiting lists at restaurants. She missed "Nat" and "Nattie." She missed *her.* Whoever that was.

If she had succeeded in killing Sean last night, she would never have had the chance to be her again. Now that her fear of Sean had diminished some, she saw "her" standing at the end of a long hallway, waiting on the top of the newest one-more-mountain, ready to reclaim Natalie Grayson once and for all.

Soon.

Today, though, Gray guzzled margaritas as she hooted at the male strippers in *Thunder from Down Under.* Today, she played video poker and got her fortune told. The fullback from the Los Angeles Chargers winked at her. And she clapped as nine red sevens popped onto the wheel of her one-dollar slot machine.

"You are so freakin' lucky," Clarissa said.

"I'd sleep with that football player if I were you," Jennifer said.

"I love it when you smile," Zadie said.

For the moment, being Grayson Sykes was like standing in a clean kitchen as light glinted off the fixtures. For the moment, being Grayson Sykes was like feeling new snow melt on her flushed face. Being Grayson Sykes right *then* felt . . . *good*. And powerful. And meant to be.

Later, she stood in the open window of her hotel room, with the lights of Vegas behind her and the Miyabi Evolution slicer clutched in her free hand. And she took a deep, deep breath, a breath that moved past her lungs and into the molecules that made her, and then she exhaled, slowly, deliberately . . . and imagined killing her forever love.

Before leaving Las Vegas that Sunday, Gray received a text message from Ian O'Donnell. He had received a bill in the mail yesterday from Mail Boxes Etc.

"Looks like Isabel Lincoln's box is in Vegas," Gray explained to her companions.

"So . . ." Clarissa frowned. "We're . . . *stopping*?"

As the taxi sped east on Charleston Boulevard, Gray found the ribbon of keys Mrs. Tompkins had given her—the set that included a mysterious key that Gray hoped would open this mailbox.

Clarissa pouted in the front passenger seat. Her face was swollen from all the alcohol she'd consumed, and her eyes looked like buttons on a rag doll. "I can't believe you're working."

The taxi pulled into a strip mall parking lot with a doughnut shop, a vitamin store, and a Mail Boxes Etc. Cars crawled in and out of parking spaces, and the driver lucked into a spot right in front of the bakery.

"Dude," Clarissa whined, "like, why are we *here*?"

"Party's over, Clarissa," Jennifer said. "I know it's like asking water not to be wet, but stop being a brat." Her skin was flushed—two mimosas and a Bloody Mary had that effect. The all-nighter with Dylan, the hedge fund broker, had also pushed blood to her face.

"I want a bear claw." Jennifer tottered to the entrance of the doughnut shop.

Gray shouted, "Chocolate glaze!" at Jennifer's back. The blonde gave a thumbs-up.

Every Mail Boxes Etc. looked the same—small stations for stationery, bigger stations for packing materials, a long counter, and mailboxes. This kingdom was lorded over by a bored-looking woman wearing glasses and a polo shirt flecked with tape, cardboard, and marker.

Gray approached the clerk with a smile. "I haven't been here in a while and I can't remember my box number."

The woman turned to a computer, then asked, "Name?"

Gray's mind raced. "It could be under my name or my roommate's. I'm Isabel Lincoln."

The clerk's fingers punched at the keys, then paused.

"My roommate is Elyse Miller," Gray added.

The clerk went back to punching keys, then said, "Box three nine one eight."

Box 3918, one of the larger mailboxes, sat at the end of the row closest to the packing tape. Gray stuck the mystery key into the lock and turned. "Yahtzee," she whispered.

On top of the pile of envelopes was a small spiral-bound notebook.

Gray flipped through the pages.

Belize ... Belize City ... apartment in Ladyville $650!! 2bd 1 bath but too close to police
station ... Buttonwood bay? $750 ... Un-
claimed b ... 5k Ermond 501-223-0010

Gray snapped pictures of these pages. *Who is Ermond?*

Some of the envelopes in the box had already
been opened. Like the envelopes from the State of
Alabama and the City of Los Angeles. An envelope
from Live Scan was still sealed—Gray didn't open
it because she already knew that the fingerprints belonged to Elyse Miller. Instead, she looked into the
already open envelope from the State of Alabama.

A birth certificate ... for Elyse Lorraine Miller,
born in Mobile, Alabama, on January 12, 1973 to
Ruth Gaines and Walter Miller.

The manila envelope sent by the Superior Court of
California was thick with legal-looking documents.

PETITION FOR CHANGE OF NAME ...
The Court Orders the name of the birth certifi-
cate OR the current legal name IS CHANGED
TO ...

Isabel Lincoln. Gray's hands shook. She knew
about these types of documents; she had her own set.
But her documents had a SEALED stamp across the
top.

So, who were Hope and Christopher Lincoln, the
people listed on Isabel's birth certificate? Adoptive
parents? Gray's amended birth certificate had become
page two of her original birth certificate. The cabin in
Idyllwild, *that's where the amended certificate was.*
Isabel had separated the pages. It was not an easy

thing to petition for a new identity. How did any of this fit into Isabel Lincoln's disappearance *now*?

Elyse Miller had been born in the south. Did her parents—birth parents?—know where she was? That she was now someone new? Had she changed her name because of Tommy Hampton and his family's threats to kill her?

Gray blinked to clear her head. "This. Is. Nuts."

Good thing she was already packed. Good thing she was already headed to the airport. She couldn't take the knife on the plane to Alabama, but she stood in the middle of Mail Boxes Etc. So she shipped the Miyabi Evolution slicer to her UPS box in Los Angeles. Then she purchased a new notebook and a sparkly purple pen. The ink smelled like grapes.

The taxi smelled of doughnuts and coffee and Jennifer's perfume. Clarissa's face was covered in confectioner's sugar and Zadie had fallen asleep and was now snoring. Gray plucked her laptop from the backpack, which was lighter now without the Japanese knife.

"So, Detective Gadget," Jennifer said.

Zadie snorted awake. She smacked her lips and rummaged through her big purse for another bottle of Dr Pepper.

"*So*, Isabel Lincoln is actually forty-six years old," Gray said. "Not thirty."

"She doesn't look old in the picture," Clarissa said.

"First of all," Gray said, bristling, "forty-six ain't 'old.' Second of all, black don't crack."

Isabel's age changed the dynamic—a middle-aged woman had disappeared, not a scared kitten just starting to "adult." Taking the man's dog had been a gangsta "grown-ass woman" move. Kenny G. might even be dead, since, after forty, women kinda stopped giving a fuck.

Zadie asked, "Now what?"

Gray logged on to the People Finder database. "*Now*, I need to learn more about Ruth and Walter, her biological parents."

Ruth and Walter Miller were alive and living on Till Street in Whistler, Alabama. He worked as a chief mechanic for Mobile County and she drove a bus for Mobile County Public Schools. They were both sixty-eight years old and they were still Negro, just like the clerk had recorded back in 1973, the year their daughter Elyse was born.

"You guys are so *wack*," Clarissa whined, arms crossed. "I shoulda taken a later flight with Haley and *those* girls."

Gray gaped at her. "*Really?* We just spent *how much* on you and—"

"Fucking millennials. I swear," Jennifer mumbled.

"Why are you so goddamned pissy?" Zadie spat.

Anger blew like hot wind around the car. Time to go home.

Clarissa dabbed at her wet eyes. "We came together, we leave together. That's the girlfriend code."

Gray rolled her eyes. "Clarissa, it wouldn't make sense for me to fly back to L.A., then turn around and fly to—"

"You don't have to explain diddly to this girl," Zadie said. "And *you* . . ." She pointed at Clarissa. "You need to grow the fuck up. *Toot-sweet.*"

Jennifer said, "Amen," then enlarged the dick pic that Dylan had sent her. "Did I tell you guys he's uncircumcised? A pig in a blanket. *Yowzah.*"

At McCarran Airport, hundreds of bleary-eyed travelers trudged from TSA to Starbucks to departure gates. Some sat at scattered banks of slot machines while others stretched out on seats and on the carpet. Everyone was over Vegas.

"You sure you don't need me to go with you?" Jennifer asked Gray. "It's not like you know what you're doing in *California*. How will you handle *Alabama*?"

"She's totally right," Clarissa said. "Alabama's, like, another country. And you just found out that you should fill your gas tank every—"

"*Enough.*" Zadie tapped Gray's shoulder and winked. "You know where we are if you need us." She paused, then added, "Well, where *I* am. Heckle and Jeckle here don't have the sense God gave a goat." She smirked at Clarissa. "Sorry, not sorry."

Gray told her friends good-bye and strolled to Delta's ticketing desk. She didn't want to catch the Millers totally off guard, and she also wanted to ensure that they were truly alive and still living on Till Street. So, after she'd purchased a one-way flight, she called the phone number listed for them in the database.

The mechanic had never heard of Gray. He pressed the phone to his chest, then asked someone in his world, "You know some gal named Grayson?" His voice was thick as mucus.

"Who?" a woman shouted.

Gray pictured Ruth Miller at the kitchen sink, curlers in, scarf on, leaning back, head in the doorway.

"Grayson Sykes," Walter Miller shouted.

"Naw."

He came back on the line. "We supposed to know you, Miss Sykes?"

Gray forced light into her voice to say, "No. See. I'm friends with your daughter, Elyse."

Walter Miller didn't respond.

Gray stuck her finger in her ear to better hear his silence. "Hello?"

"Good day, ma'am." Dead air. He'd hung up on her.

Seated way in the back of the plane, near the tiny

bathrooms, Gray wondered more about Walter's reaction. Elyse was a problem child *now*, but how had she been a problem in the years she had lived under the Millers' roof? What pain was Gray about to cause?

The flight to Alabama was a strange one filled with strange people. Seated beside her, a man shaped like a Volkswagen Beetle creaked every time he lifted his bottle of Mountain Dew to his lips. In front of her, a trio of old ladies, their gray hair tinged in violet and blue, shared an endless bag of fried chicken soaked in vinegary hot sauce.

Gray watched an action movie starring the guy from that cool Greek mythology flick, the guy with the abs, but now he was a space scientist or something who'd created a satellite that could reverse climate change or make guacamole or some shit like that.

She landed well after ten o'clock at Mobile Regional Airport. As she exited the plane, her clothes immediately ballooned and purple light flashed across the sky—thunderstorms. Her skin razzed with the *click-click*ing of electricity.

The airport was small—just two floors—and would soon close. The few businesses there—Cruise City Bar and Grille, Hudson News, and Quiznos—had already brought down their security gates. Gray reached Hertz rentals, also soon to close. The clerk handed Gray the keys to a Chevrolet Cruze and so very kindly called the Hilton Garden Inn to see if a room was available.

Hotel reservation made, Gray rushed to the car lot. Her phone vibrated in her back pocket. A text from Nick.

Where'd you go this time???

She settled in the front seat of the Chevrolet. *I found Isabel's real parents! Seeing them in the morning.*

Ellipses, then . . .

Gas. Cash. Keep your phone charged. Be careful.

It was a short drive to the Hilton Garden Inn, and Gray quickly checked into room 216 with its tan Berber carpet, tan walls, and clean towels. She booted up her laptop and found the Millers' address on the internet. They lived seven miles north of Mobile in a house of red brick and wood surrounded by tiny creeks and a grove of tall, thick trees. It would take ten minutes to drive there from the hotel.

With nothing else to do, Gray found *Diners, Drive-Ins and Dives* on the Food Network, then trudged to the bathroom. Wilted and puffy, that's how she looked. That's how she *felt*. Came from straddling two climates in one day.

She washed Vegas and airplane dirt off her body as Flavortown found its way to North Carolina. Clean again, she watched the making of a café's famous onion rings for a minute before deciding she'd heard and seen enough junk for the day. She turned off the television, then slipped beneath the sheets. As soon as she heard the rumble from the sky, she hopped out of bed and pulled apart the window curtains.

Lightning the color of crayons—Atomic Tangerine, Cornflower, and Laser Lemon—exploded against the dark sky.

Los Angeles didn't see many storms, and the chaos terrified and electrified her. The rain burst against the windows like mortars. It was so loud that it became peaceful, and she climbed back into bed. She left the curtains open, and those phosphorescent sky crackles were the last marvels she saw before she closed her eyes.

52

It was a little after eight o'clock on a Monday morning. The rain had stopped, and now golden hot light streamed past her hotel room window. This part of Alabama had found peace again, and butterflies flitted, birds soared, and wisps of steam rose from the few remaining puddles on the pavement.

Five minutes into her drive, Gray groaned and closed her eyes. "It's Monday morning."

The Millers probably wouldn't be home.

Another case of Grayson Sykes leaping before thinking.

Today, though, she lucked out: a gray Dodge Ram truck and a copper Hyundai Sonata were parked in the driveway of the brick and wood house.

The air was loud with the chatter of a million insects and birds, and somewhere hidden in the trees was a creek or two gurgling its way to the Gulf. Dragonflies worked as sentries from the car to the front porch. Gray had never seen so many in her life.

Sean had talked about relocating to Atlanta like the munchkins had dreamed about Oz. But moving had meant starting over again, a small fish in a big pond, even though Las Vegas was one of the biggest ponds for a party promoter.

After triumphing over the creatures that buzzed and hopped, Gray reached the front door. She knocked . . .

waited. Knocked again . . . waited some more. Finally, the door opened, and cool air from the house rolled out to greet her. It smelled of bacon and pressed hair.

The black man standing there wore an untucked denim shirt and clean khakis. "Yes?"

Gray said, "Walter Miller?"

He said yes again, then glanced at his wristwatch.

Gray introduced herself and reminded him that she'd called yesterday.

He grimaced, and the skin across his cheeks thinned.

"I flew out here from L.A. cuz this is important. I really need to talk to you about—"

"Elyse." He looked over his shoulder and shouted, "Ruthie." He kept his head turned away from Gray as they both waited for Ruth Miller to join them.

A woman with ginger-colored skin came to the door. She wore a velour tracksuit and wedged sandals. Her toenails were painted the color of orange soda.

Walter said to her, "It's the woman who—"

"I heard her." Ruth Miller's brown eyes bore into Gray's.

Gray took a step back. "I'm sorry to—"

"Are you?" Ruth asked, eyebrow cocked. "*Really?*"

"I am. My questions won't take long."

Ruth leveled her shoulders, ready to spit fire.

Walter placed a hand on his wife's shoulder.

Tears burned in Ruth's eyes, and she asked, "What do you want?"

"I just need to know where she could be."

The couple simply blinked at her.

Gray rooted in her battered Liz Claiborne purse and pulled out the copy of the birth certificate from Mail Boxes Etc. "You're listed here, yes? As Elyse's parents?"

Walter studied the birth certificate, then handed it to Ruth. "That's us."

Relief made Gray's shoulders drop and her muscles relax. "Okay. Good. It's been a very long July. Tell me where she could be and I'll go there, and I'll stop bugging you. Is she here?"

"She's here," Ruth said.

"Why don't we just take you there?" Walter gazed down at his wife. "Okay?"

Ruth smirked. "Fine. Just let me just turn off the iron and get my phone." She disappeared from the door.

"I can follow you," Gray said. "I have a rental."

"That's probably best," Walter said.

"Please don't tell her that I'm here," Gray said. "I don't want her to run again."

Walter said, "She's done running. I know that like I know there's a God in heaven."

The couple climbed into the Hyundai without saying another word to Gray. Her soul danced with anticipation. She had waited for this moment for almost two weeks now, and here it was. What was Gray going to say to the insurance fraud thief? She had no authority to bring Elyse back to L.A. She'd have to refer the case to the police.

Gray texted Nick with nervous fingers. *Elyse/Isabel is here! I'm with her parents now. Going to meet her.*

Nick typed one word.

What???

At red lights and stop signs, Gray texted Nick, noticing no other cars except one—the copper Hyundai leading her through Whistler, Alabama. After a last *call you later*, she noticed that they'd driven into a beautiful park.

The Millers parked at the curb.

Gray parked behind them and climbed out of the Chevrolet.

Hearses and limousines were parked at curbsides all around the grounds. People wearing blacks, blues, or whites stood at gravesides or marched in clumps to burial sites. Dragonflies buzzed here, too, and their iridescent wings caught the sunlight.

The Millers walked east.

Gray frowned, and called out, "Excuse me . . ."

Walter glanced back at her. "C'mon. This is the best place to meet her. She's over here, waiting for you."

Ruth took Walter's hand.

The trio wound through headstones and markers in an older part of the cemetery. Someone had planted an American flag at Clyde Irby's grave. Someone had stuck pinwheels on Vera Armstrong's marker.

Another minute of walking and then the Millers stopped. Ruth slipped into her husband's arms. He kissed the top of her head.

Gray came to stand alongside the couple. "May I ask the obvious question?"

Ruth said, "Thought you wanted to meet our daughter."

"Ah. Yes. I get it." Since Elyse was on the run, she'd wanted to meet Gray in a safe place, a sacred place. *Sanctuary.* She glanced around the park, eager to meet the Mary Ann she'd been chasing since July 11.

Ruth Miller handed Gray a picture of a pretty little girl with ribbons in her hair. The toddler clutched a sand bucket filled with water for the castle she was building. *A Mary Ann in the making.*

"She's still beautiful," Gray said.

A liar, but still beautiful.

The Millers were staring at her.

Gray canted her head. "I'm . . . missing something."

"Sweetie . . ." Ruth Miller smiled at Gray, but it wasn't a pleasant smile. This one held contempt and pity, "Bless your heart" mixed with strychnine. She stooped beside an oxidized grave marker, then stroked the letters. "Our daughter is right here. *This* is Elyse."

ELYSE LORRAINE MILLER
OUR LOVING GIRL
JANUARY 12, 1973–SEPTEMBER 22, 1975

53

Minutes had passed, and Walter Miller was leaning against the Hyundai. He lit a cigarette as Ruth pushed a piece of Nicorette from the blister pack. More cars had rolled into the cemetery. More dragonflies glided over to greet them. The swampy sun had embraced them all.

Gray stopped shaking and made it back to the cars at the curb. She'd taken pictures of the burial site, but she knew that her shaking hands had made those shots blur. She fumbled in her bag again for the birth certificate. "This *is* you, correct?" She pointed at the signatures there.

Walter said, "Yep, that me."

Ruth said, "And that's me."

"But Elyse . . ."

"Died forty-six years ago," Ruth said. "We were vacationing at the beach. It was a gorgeous day, but the waters didn't know that. Elyse was pulled under, and Walter and our friends . . . They found her, but she'd drowned. We buried her here and . . ." This time, Ruth pulled a document from her purse, and offered it to Gray.

STATE OF ALABAMA—BUREAU OF VITAL
STATISTICS
Elyse Lorraine Miller, female, black, single,
age 2 years, 2 months, ten days. Date of death

September 22, 1975. Cause of death: drowning. Place of burial Walnut Hill Cemetery.

The mortician's signature was the last piece of information listed on the death certificate.

Hollow inside, Gray pulled her phone out of her
bag and found the picture of the woman she'd been
searching for, the Mary Ann with the *Vogue* cheekbones. "Do you know her?"

Ruth and Walter stared at the photograph. He
shook his head. "This the woman who says she's our
daughter?"

Gray nodded.

Walter extinguished the cigarette on the thick sole
of his boot. "We don't know her." He pointed in the
direction of the grave marker. "But that's our daughter right over there. *That's* Elyse Lorraine Miller, and
she's dead."

Gray told them the story about a doctor, a dog,
birth certificates, and insurance policies.

Anguish washed over Ruth and she crumpled into
her husband's arms.

Walter waggled his head as his eyes blurred with
tears. "Indignity after indignity," he said, then buried
his face in his hands.

Gray's legs felt like soggy tissue paper as she stood
there watching the weeping couple and understanding the horror of all that Isabel Lincoln had wrought.
"I'll do my best and alert the authorities." That's all
she could offer them.

Gray climbed back behind the wheel of the Chevrolet Cruze and watched the Millers' Hyundai slowly
wind its way back to the entrance. Then she stared at
the endless green interrupted by tombs, gravestones,

and mourners. There were butterflies. There was sadness. And decay—there was that, too.

Isabel Lincoln was Elyse Lorraine Miller, but not
really, since the *real* Elyse Lorraine Miller, born in
Mobile, Alabama, on January 12, 1973, had died
more than forty years ago.

So who was "Isabel" before the legal name change?
Before she'd stolen the identity of a two-year-old
drowning victim? It had been 1975. The age of computers hadn't fully arrived at state governments, and
public records hadn't been digitized back then. A
toddler had drowned, the coroner had said, "Fine,"
the funeral home director had signed and issued the
death certificate.

Ghosting. Isabel Lincoln had claimed an existing
identity—Elyse Miller—and had obtained a Social
Security card. Since Alabama and California didn't
share information, neither state agency had cross-
checked to see if there'd been a death certificate issued for a black child in Alabama. And because the
real Elyse Miller had been a baby, she'd had no credit
history.

Like cons around the world, *this* con had found
the chink in a state bureaucracy's armor, request-
ing an out-of-state birth certificate for a baby born
in 1973, drowned in 1975, someone with no credit
history and who hadn't been issued a Social Security
card because, back then, Social Security cards weren't
automatically issued to newborns.

Isabel Lincoln had started a whole new life using a
life that had barely begun.

"If she wasn't Isabel at birth, and if she wasn't
Elyse Miller at birth . . ."

Then who the hell was she?

The car's interior had grown sticky and hot. Gray rolled down all four windows and a breeze rolled through. Outside, a crew of ladies dressed in Mardi Gras colors strolled arm in arm toward a parked Escalade. Someone was humming "His Eye Is on the Sparrow."

Gray returned to Elyse Miller's Facebook page and that last message to Tommy Hampton, from his sister Myracle, on March 26, just months ago. *You are missed.*

In her latest Facebook post, Myracle Hampton sported fuchsia hair and enough gold to finance an Ivy League education. Beneath "About," she'd posted that she worked as a parking enforcement officer in Oakland. There were selfies of her in uniform and hat, standing at her little white Prius on streets throughout the Bay Area. She'd listed her phone number, and on the second ring, she answered. Her simple hello spoke of a century of smoking unfiltered cigarettes chased by shots of Hennessy. And now it sounded like she stood at the busiest intersection in all of Oakland.

Gray gave Myracle Hampton an abbreviated version of the Isabel Lincoln–Elyse Miller story. How Gray had flown to Alabama and discovered that the real Elyse Miller was dead—and had been dead more than she'd been alive.

"So you're saying," Myracle Hampton said, "that bitch is *still* leaving victims behind."

"You think she killed Tommy?" Gray asked.

She snorted. "Hell yeah, she killed Tommy, and the cops think so, too. He was in that hotel room for three days. *Three! Days!* That bitch stole his watch, stole his phone, stole cash he had taken out of the ATM. She'd used a fake name to reserve the room, too. Janet

Jackson. Are you fucking *kidding* me? Ain't nobody suspect nothing?"

"May I send you a picture?" Gray asked. "I just wanna confirm that we're talking about the same woman."

Seconds later, Myracle Hampton said, "Uh-huh. That's her. Tell me where she at. We can end this *real* quick."

"Yeah. See. That's the problem. I'm looking for her, but I can't find her. It doesn't seem like she and Tommy dated long."

"I ain't never met her face-to-face," the woman said. "All Tommy told me was that he couldn't make my daughter's birthday party cuz he was meeting some girl named Elyse at the Best Western. He was always doin' shit like that. Never thought it would get him killed, though. Stabbed, maybe. But dead? Nuh-uh."

Gray asked, "How did they meet?"

"Hell if I know. Tommy was a big-ass nerd who played video games all damn day and worked on fishing boats at night. I didn't know her. Don't nobody in our family know her, and I doubt that Tommy really knew her. But he always fell for bad girls. This time, I guess he fell for the *worst* girl."

Gray could only say, "Yeah. I'm so sorry about that."

"I *do* know that there ain't no statues of limitations on murder, know what I'm saying? And I'm glad you trying to track her—Hey, you know what? Hold on."

In Myracle Hampton's world, footsteps tapped at pavement. A creak of a door and then a slam. Quiet. "Okay, that's better. You need to call the detective in charge of Tommy's case. I ain't talked to him in a few months—he got sick of me cuz I was blowing up his phone sixty times a day. His name is Jake Days. He ain't found that bitch yet, but he still hella cool."

Gray scribbled Detective Days's number into her notes. "I'll do my best." The second time saying this in less than an hour. Those promises were all gathering in her belly, and their frayed endings were twisting around her lungs.

When had Isabel Lincoln requested a copy of Elyse Miller's birth certificate?

Alabama Department of Public Health kept all vital records—birth, death, marriage—and that office was located more than 150 miles away, in Montgomery. Anyone could request a copy of a certificate, but to obtain a certified print, that person needed to have legal authority and be able to verify their identity. Isabel had known the answers to those questions.

She texted Clarissa, hoping that the millennial had forgiven her. *Hey! Do you know anyone in Social Security?*

The women wearing Mardi Gras colors had reached the Escalade and had joined hands. The one in gold turned her face toward heaven and prayed for peace, joy, and favor. Words poured from her lips and rode on the breeze sweeping through Gray's car, and Gray hoped that she'd been infected by this prayer and that God would grant her peace, joy, and favor, too.

Clarissa texted:

Burt Polasek info attached. AND YES I'M STILL MAD.

All Gray cared about was the time in which Elyse Miller had requested a replacement Social Security card. Gray read Burt Polasek the number from the picture she'd taken of the card found in the cabin up in Idyllwild.

Burt tapped and pecked at a computer keyboard. "Looks like she requested a card a while ago, twenty-five years ago—Oh."

"What?"

"We issued an entirely new number," Burt said, "because Elyse Miller never had an old number. She didn't have to *replace* anything."

"Right," Gray said. "Because the real Elyse Lorraine Miller had been a two-year-old when she died in 1975, and her parents probably hadn't thought that their toddler needed a number then."

"Uh-huh . . ."

"How did she find that poor little girl's identity in the first place?"

"Scouring newspaper obituaries and Social Security death annexes," Burt Polasek said. "It takes some skill, but it happens all the time. A dead baby is the perfect identity to steal."

"Did she have to explain her request for a Social Security card?" Gray asked.

"It says here"—Burt Polasek tapped keys—"she never had a physical card and she needed one for college."

"And she did *what* to obtain a physical card?"

"All she needed was a certified birth certificate and a form of identification, like a driver's license."

"So she got a copy of the birth certificate for Elyse Miller, used it to get a driver's license as Elyse Miller, and used all of that to get a Social Security card as Elyse Miller."

Burt said, "Probably."

"Has she paid into the system as Elyse Miller?" Gray asked.

"Yes, she worked under that name, but then . . ."

"She had her name legally changed. I know that she's now Isabel Lincoln."

"Ah. Okay."

"Any background on this?" Gray read off Isabel's Social Security number as one plump raindrop and then another struck the Chevrolet's windshield.

Burt tapped the keyboard again. "Isabel Lincoln started paying Social Security five years ago. And according to our system—*Wait*. What Social Security number do you have?"

Gray repeated the number.

He said, "Hmm."

"What?"

"Her address?"

"Forty-three forty-three Don Lorenzo Drive."

"I have an address on Seventy-Seventh Avenue in Inglewood. Her parents are . . ."

"Christopher and Hope—"

"Lincoln, yes. They're dead. But, according to my records . . . so is Isabel."

54

How was Isabel Lincoln *dead*?

Ice filled Gray's veins. "And how long ago did Isabel die? I don't understand."

Burt Polasek said, "Well ... *technically* she's still alive, but she went missing in 'ninety-five. She was fifteen. Since her body hasn't been found, she was declared dead."

"Another child," Gray said, shaking her head. "That address in Inglewood ..." Bobby the Blood lived on Seventy-Seventh, in that red-roofed white house. "Can you check to see if there's a Robert living there?"

Burt Polasek tapped ... and tapped ... "Yep. There's a Robert Engler at that address. The owner is Isabel's aunt, Ruby Robertson. She's receiving Social Security benefits and Engler is her caretaker. He's receiving benefits as well."

"Caretaker?"

"She's blind."

"I know," Gray said, "but I'm having a hard time believing that Engler is ..." She sighed.

Raindrops the size of melon balls now smacked the car. Thunder rumbled across the sky, but Gray didn't startle. The rain was melting her anxiety, but it had done nothing for the burning tightrope snagged around her navel. She needed something stronger than ibuprofen, but all she had eaten was a bagel, and she was still working.

And Sean Dixon was still out there somewhere, eyes on her.

Blame Isabel Lincoln—or whoever the hell she was.

"Isabel's real," Gray said, nodding. "And not real."

She was as real as Gray and as not-real as Gray. But then, was Gray "more" real being Natalie Grayson or Natalie Dixon? Was she more "real" being Natalie Kittridge, the girl who'd dissociate and go to that place in her head every time a foster brother or play uncle touched her? Every time Mom Twyla poured just a little vodka into her Kool-Aid? Was she more "real" every time Child Protective Services pried her hands from the leg of a kitchen table in a hovel somewhere in Northern California? Was she more "real" as the married woman with blood pooling in her cupped hand or her blood splattered on chrome or mirrors or car seats or cabinets or staircase bannisters?

Natalie Dixon hadn't been hit since she'd become Grayson Sykes.

Natalie Kittridge hadn't suffered from ringworm or yeast infections or an empty belly since becoming Natalie Grayson.

During those few moments in her life—being a member of the Grayson family—she'd laughed and ached, fucked and prayed.

So. Which version of her was more real?

Gray sat in her car at Walnut Hill Cemetery for over an hour, and she still needed to find a flight back to California. The inside of the rental car had cooled from the sudden storm, and as the weather system moved north, dragonflies and butterflies danced over the graves of babies, brave men, and beautiful women. New families dressed in whites, blues, and blacks had come to watch a thousand-plus dollars disappear six feet beneath the earth.

Isabel Lincoln was real. As real as the blue butterfly flitting near Gray's open window.

And Gray would find her, and make her pay—for stealing money, for stealing the innocence of a little girl named Elyse, for probably killing Tommy Hampton, for possibly murdering Omar Neville, for—

Gray's phone buzzed. A new email.

Your ALL OF ME results are back!

Gray's clammy hands itched. She'd forgotten that she'd left the purple toothbrush, as well as hair and nail samples, with the DNA diagnostics lab almost two weeks ago.

Person one's ancestry compilation was 89.7 percent sub-Saharan African, 7.5 percent European, 2.3 percent East Asian. A variant had been detected for macular degeneration, but no variants detected for Alzheimer's or celiac disease. Person one had 1,102 DNA relatives on All of Me.

She tapped the link to the second report.

Person two was 64.3 percent sub-Saharan African, 31 percent European, and 4.7 percent East Asian. Person two had 766 DNA relatives on All of Me.

This second report must have been Isabel's; Ian had not thought of his girlfriend as "black" because of that 31 percent European.

Person two had a second cousin, Danielle Sledge, in Raleigh-Durham, North Carolina, and Alicia Kelly, a first cousin in Oakland, California. There were other DNA relatives, but Alicia Kelly was the only first cousin listed.

Gray called Jennifer.

"Hello, stranger. Clarissa's still pissed at you."

"And I'm still *So what*. Listen." Gray told her about Isabel Lincoln's DNA results and the emergence of a first cousin. "So I need an address and phone number for this Alicia chick."

"Got it." Jennifer's fingers clicked the keyboard. "That Dylan guy I met at the club? I ran background on him and guess what? He sells *knives*. Here you go." Then she rattled off an address on Seventy-Second Street in Oakland. "And here's a phone number." She rattled that off, too.

"Can you look at something else?" Gray asked. "Can you find out if she traveled to Belize as Elyse Miller? Clarissa did a search already on the Isabel Lincoln name."

"Lemme check and I'll get back to you."

"Thanks, Jen."

"You coming home anytime soon?"

"Home is where the heart is."

"I don't think Nick will like hearing how much you're spending."

"He authorized all of this," Gray said.

Jennifer snorted. "That's a lie. I know Nick better than you do, don't forget that. And I know he's a tight-ass when it comes to the company Amex, especially after Saturday night's dinner."

Gray said, "Hunh."

"Let me know if you need me to run interference. I have a special touch with him."

Gray rolled her eyes. "I'll let you know."

Her stomach growled—she still hadn't eaten a decent meal today. Breakfast had been a bagel from the hotel's tiny kitchen. It was raining hard and nonstop by the time she found a small, sketchy diner off Wolf

Ridge Road. It was the kind of greasy spoon with greasy windows, old framed photographs, whirling ceiling fans, and "World Famous Fried Chicken." The waitress, a short, thick black woman wearing squeaky shoes and a name tag that said "Lottie," led Gray to a booth near the back and handed her a sticky menu.

There was just one other customer. On the other side of the diner, an old black man sat in a booth near the jukebox, which was now playing "The Great Pretender" by the Platters. His hands cupped a mug of coffee.

Gray ordered chicken-fried steak and grits—she didn't make either dish at home. She found the Percocet vial in her bag and shook one out. This was the best kind of food to take with pills. As she waited for her meal, she flipped through her phone and found the notebook pages she'd photographed at Mail Boxes Etc.

Belize . . . Belize City . . . apartment in Ladyville $650!! 2bd 1 bath but too close to police station . . . Buttonwood bay? $750 . . . Unclaimed b . . . 5k Ermond 501-223-0010

"Right," she whispered. "Who is Ermond?" She dialed the number. How far ahead or behind Alabama was Belize time?

The line rang . . . rang . . . "Yeah." The man sounded as though he'd run to the phone. "Ermond Funeral Home," he said. "Weh di go ann?"

Kriol. Crap. Gray said, "I'm sorry?"

"Da how yudi du?" the man asked, slower.

Gray said, "English?"

"Yes, how may I help you?"

"May I speak to Ermond, please?"

"I am Ermond."

Gray cleared her throat. "You and I talked maybe a few days ago?" She glanced down at her notes. "About unclaimed . . . five thousand?"

"Yes. You get the hair? You get the nail? I take 'em and you get the body nobody want. You get the det' certificate, too. People come, cry and sing, that's extra. Cash only. I can do cremation—very nice service. Very nice. When you come down?"

Her hands were shaking. "Next week?"

"Good. Got a good one for you. Car accident. Nobody can tell what's what. A shame."

"Sounds . . ." Gray swallowed. "Sounds good. Your address?"

"Off Western Highway. Belize City. You can't miss it."

Was Isabel Lincoln buying an unclaimed body from a funeral home in Belize?

If so, who was she planning to pass off as dead?

"The hair and nails," Gray said. "Proof for the death certificate and insurance company."

She was planning to pass *herself* off as dead. The woman with the official name change from Elyse Miller would be "dead."

But what was her endgame?

"Insurance," Gray whispered. "Half a million dollars. *That's* the endgame."

Lottie returned with food as well as a thick steak knife and extra napkins. "Enjoy, baby."

Gray loaded her bowl with sugar and butter, just like Mom Twyla had eaten her grits. Better than the salt, pepper, and cheese grits that Mom Naomi liked.

When she was bites in, a man slipped into her booth and sat across from her. He grinned at her, and his whiskey-brown eyes glinted like stars. "Since when did you start eating grits?"

Gray's belly dropped, and her bottom half warmed.

Otis Redding sang about trying a little tenderness . . .

"You're crap at looking over your shoulder." Sean Dixon plucked the saltshaker from the holder. "I've had someone tailing you for a week now. He was standing in line behind you in Vegas when you bought your ticket to fly down here."

"*Squeeze her, don't tease her . . .*"

Sean smiled. "You should already know this, *Mrs.* Natalie Dixon: I will *never* go away. And you can call yourself by some other name, but you will always be my wife. 'Til death do us part, baby. 'Til death do us part."

55

Panic burst around Gray's body, but she couldn't move, couldn't speak.

Sean Dixon was now shaking salt into Gray's bowl of sweet grits. "I watched you waddle"—he moved the shaker from her grits to her cup of coffee—"around a cemetery today. What was *that* about?"

Gray wanted to throw that coffee in his face. She wanted to scream, *Get away from me!*, but she couldn't move.

He sat the saltshaker down, reached across the table, and laid his hand atop hers.

She whispered, "What do you want?"

"I wanna make it right between you and me. How can I do that?" The veins in his eyes were red and wild, crisscrossing each other like highways on a map. "Don't you want it to be the way it was? Friends again? Lovers again? I mean . . . looking at you *now*, it's obvious that no one wants you. I loved you when you were a buck five. I'll love you now, fat ass and all."

Lottie's squeaky shoes announced her arrival. She set a menu and glass of ice water in front of Sean. "You want something, sugar?"

Sean said, "Nothing for me, thanks."

Gray tried to pull back her hand.

Together, they watched the waitress shuffle back into the kitchen.

The old man nursing the coffee shuffled out into the rain.

The jukebox clicked, and Stevie Wonder sang, "*I never dreamed you'd leave in summer . . .*"

Sean held their clenched hands against Gray's cheek. So cold, his hand. So familiar against her face, that hand. A sob was growing in her chest, and for a moment she didn't know where she was.

A diner off a small highway in Mobile, Alabama?

Or the breakfast nook on Trail Spring Court?

His hand drifted from her cheek to the base of her throat.

She stopped breathing, as though he was already crushing her neck. The last time he'd touched her there . . . A sickening crunch of teeth against teeth. Warm blood filling her mouth.

"You didn't ruin me, Nat," he said. "You tried. You poured out all of my beer and left the empties on the counter, but you didn't ruin me."

Her phone rang from the table. The ringing startled her and loosened her tongue. "Go. Please. If you want to live, you should go."

"Or?"

Her phone kept ringing.

He spun the device around and frowned, seeing a man's face there. "Who's that?"

"A man who wants to kill you almost as much as I do."

His hard eyes searched hers and he grinned. "You better answer it, then."

With her free hand, she picked up the phone. Eyes still on Sean, she said, "Hey. . . . Yes. . . . Yes. . . . He's sitting across the table from me. He has his hand on my—" She paused, then offered Sean the phone.

He snatched it from her and snarled, "Who the

fuck—" Sean smirked as he listened, then said, "Fuck you, bitch." He dropped the phone back on the table.

"You shouldn't have done that."

"I gave you *everything*. You lived like a queen. We could've ruled the world." He released her hand. Sean Dixon was still six three and still weighed more than two hundred pounds. He wasn't scared of *her*; he wasn't scared of Nick; he wasn't even scared of God.

Gray was still five four, heavier but nowhere near his punching class. A halibut fighting a nurse shark was not a fight.

Sean leaned over her plate, parted his lips, and sent a globule of spit from his mouth into her grits. He slid out of the booth and stood over Gray, bending until they were face-to-face. "You better hope your boy kills me."

Gray could smell his breath—the funk of ego and evil. She wrapped her hand around that mug of salted coffee . . . and swung the cup.

Coffee splashed across his face.

Sean grabbed her neck.

Gray wiggled, loosening his grip. She scrambled out of the booth.

He grabbed her shirt collar and yanked her back.

Her head hit the edge of the table and she saw stars. Her hands fluttered around her, and her fingers found tines—*fork!* She grabbed it and jabbed it into his wrist.

Sean loosened his grip.

She grabbed the steak knife.

The waitress shouted, "Whoa whoa whoa!"

The cook, a man bigger than a bear, pulled Sean off of Gray.

Gray grabbed her purse and ran out of the diner and into the rain. It was coming down hard now, but it was still hot. Head throbbing, she stumbled through the weed-choked parking lot to her rental. She looked over her shoulder.

Sean grabbed her arm.

Gray reeled, struck him with a weak blow with her left hand, and then, with her right, jammed the knife into Sean's thigh.

He gaped at her.

She gaped at him. Her breath was hot and rushed, and her hand was slick with rainwater and from the blood now seeping through Sean's track pants.

He leaned into her, and his weight made them sink to the asphalt.

Lower . . . lower . . .

A smile spread across Sean's face.

Gray let go of the knife.

He leaned against the car and wrapped his hand around the hilt of the knife.

She kneeled before him. With a twisted grin, she reached for that knife, ready to pull it out, sink it into his throat, and twist it.

"Don't!" Lottie shouted from behind her. "Let the cops handle him." The waitress pulled Gray away from the fallen man and back into the diner.

The cook guided Gray to a booth and handed her a dish towel to clean off.

Gray swiped and dabbed, and the towel was soon bright with blood. Gray's. Sean's.

Lottie squeaked back behind the counter and returned with a bag of ice for Gray's head and a slice of sweet potato pie for Gray's belly.

It's over. I'm free. If that meant jail, Gray was down for that. She'd explain her case to the jury and maybe, *maybe*, they'd understand.

It didn't take long for two sheriff's deputies to

reach the diner off the highway. Gray told them all that had happened, and the waitress and the fry cook corroborated everything she said.

"Where is this guy?" Deputy Burke had soft brown eyes and resembled Eddie Murphy.

"By the white Chevrolet out in the parking lot," Gray said.

Deputy Burke and blond Deputy Parsons looked out the plate glass window and then at each other. The two left the diner and headed over to the car.

Gray gazed out the window.

There was the parking lot.

There was the white Chevrolet.

But where was Sean Dixon?

56

Even as the cops drove her to the airport, Gray kept scanning the roadsides and highways.

Where had Sean Dixon gone?

As deputies Burke and Parsons escorted her to the Delta ticket desk, her eyes darted around the small terminal.

Was Sean still following her?

She needed to leave Alabama. She needed to leave this case. Finding Isabel or Elyse or whoever she was? Didn't matter anymore. Because what was at stake here? A cardiologist never seeing his dog again? Was Kenny G. worth dying for?

How about Elyse Miller? The *real* Elyse Miller?

What about justice for Ruth and Walter against a con who'd used their dead baby to . . .

Gray muttered, "Shit."

Ian O'Donnell—dirty in all of this—could kick rocks, but the couple she'd met, the couple whose lives had been blessed by a baby girl, only for a riptide to take her away . . .

Isabel Lincoln needed to see the inside of a jail cell.

Gray booked the trip to Oakland, with a layover in Dallas.

Before the security checkpoint, Deputy Burke handed her a business card. "I'll keep you updated.

But you stay safe. Keep your eyes open. Maybe hang out close to security booths until it's time to board."

Gray agreed, and after she'd grabbed a bottled water from the souvenir shop, she found a seat close to airport security. Then she found the Percocet she'd planned to take back at the diner. She needed it now more than ever—pain burst from her head to her ankles.

A few times, she thought about Sean. *Where did he go?*

More than once, she thought about contacting Yvonne Reeves, who was listed as a second cousin in her All of Me report. Gray even opened that report and tapped Send a Message. Soon, her fingers danced over the laptop's keyboard.

> Hi Yvonne. I was born Natalie Kittridge in Oakland on April 25, 1980 but was given up for adoption

Shaking her head, she closed the email window.

On the plane to Dallas, Gray texted Nick. *On board.*

> You should come home.

I will after meeting this woman's family.

She could hear his sigh from across the country and she let herself smile.

You got people in Oakland bigger than Sean?

> Yeah. I got Mike. He'll meet you at car rentals

Gray napped during that flight to Dallas, then woke up in a rush. She made her connection to Oakland seven minutes before the boarding gate closed. Huffing, she plopped into her first-class seat—the only available. Once she caught her breath, she closed her eyes and thought of completing that email to her second cousin. *First cousin to my biological mother.*

Was her birth mother still alive?

What was her name?

Why did she leave me?

There were chocolate chip cookies and champagne—just like those flights she'd taken with Sean "I Only Fly First Class" Dixon—and thanks to time travel, she landed in Oakland a little after nine o'clock. Plenty of time left to work.

Mobile County Sheriff's Deputy Burke had left her a voice mail: "Wanted to see how you were and update you on the case." Gray knew, though, that Burke hadn't found Sean. And that's what the deputy said when she called him back.

At Avis rentals, Gray selected a white Impala. She scanned the faces of other customers in line. No one seemed interested in her.

Nick sent a picture. The bodyguard, Mike, had sandy brown skin, sandy brown hair, a "Semper Fi" tat on his left forearm, and bushy eyebrows. She waited near the desk until a giant man who moved like water stood before her.

He said, "You Victor's daughter?"

Gray paused. *Victor's daughter.* She hadn't been called that in ages. "And you're . . . ?"

"Mike. I'll be driving a blue Charger. You'll see me as soon as you pull out of the lot."

She did see him, and he followed her, and for a moment Gray focused on her mission.

Find the evil Mary Ann.

57

Alicia Kelly didn't answer at the phone number that Jennifer had pulled from Rader Consulting's database. In her driver's license picture, Alicia's cheekbones cut her face just like Isabel's did. Alicia's eyes were smaller, close-set, and freckles sprinkled the bridge of her nose. Now, Alicia parked her Ford Focus in the narrow driveway of a pink bungalow. She wore jeans and pink Nike Huaraches.

Gray opened the door of the white Impala.

The noise of Oakland banged into the car's cabin— squeaking trucks, raggedy mufflers, bad rap blasting from subwoofers, cans and bottles clanging as squeaky shopping carts rattled.

Mike, parked in the space behind her, stayed put in the blue Charger.

Gray called out, "Excuse me . . . Alicia?"

Alicia barely looked back over her shoulder. "Not interested, thanks."

"I'm not selling anything." Gray hustled over to the walkway before the woman retreated behind the bungalow's black-iron security door. "I desperately need your help. I saw your profile on All of Me."

"Oh, so you're a long-lost cousin, too?"

"No. I—"

Alicia turned to face Gray. "You have ten seconds, then you need to kindly get the fuck off my property."

Gray plucked from her purse the creased photo she'd shown to a million people. She now offered it to Alicia Kelly. "Do you know this woman?"

Alicia had formed her mouth to say no, but instead she gasped and plucked the picture from Gray's fingers. "Oh my . . ." Her eyes bugged and her hands shook.

On the outside, Alicia's house was a dreary pink and boasted a scraggly front yard. Inside, though, Alicia had found her inner Martha Stewart. The open floor plan and hardwood floors made the tiny bungalow feel as spacious as Hearst Castle.

Alicia dropped her purse onto the couch. "Who *are* you? What the hell is this about?"

"Grayson Sykes. I'm a private investigator and I'm looking for your cousin." And then Gray told a story about Isabel, Ian, Kenny G., and a check that sat in a safe waiting to be cashed.

Alicia said, "*Isabel.*"

"But that's not her birth name, is it?"

The woman shook her head. "So, she's alive?"

"Depends on what you consider 'alive.'"

Alicia rubbed the bridge of her nose. "Want a drink? Lemonade, soda, water? I'm thinking something with rum is required."

Gray liked Alicia. And as Alicia whipped up a pitcher of hurricanes, Gray wandered the small living room, taking in the prints from Kara Walker's *The Emancipation Approximation*, with those silhouettes of black women being attacked by white swans.

In the kitchen, Alicia talked to someone on the phone. "Auntie, you won't believe this . . . A woman found me on the internet. . . . Yeah, I know, but hey . . . Guess who's alive?"

Isabel Lincoln had been born in Oakland as Deanna Kelly, on November 1, 1972. She was now forty-six years old.

"We were really close," Alicia recalled. "Up until middle school, we were like sisters." She pulled a photo album from a credenza. The pages smelled of old glue and wood smoke.

There was Deanna and Alicia splashing in a wading pool, wearing matching kiddie bikinis, sun reflecting off their squinting faces.

There was Deanna and Alicia in matching majorette uniforms, white boots with green-and-black pompoms bouncing on the laces.

There was Deanna and Alicia wearing stonewashed jeans, posing on the Golden Gate Bridge. Fake Gucci bags. Blow Pops. Frosted hair. Bamboo earrings.

"And then," Alicia said, "she lost her mind. Like something in her just—" She snapped her fingers. "She started running with these badass kids in the eighth grade. Called themselves the Five-Point-Oh Crew cuz they loved that five-liter Mustang? They used to rob us, jump us on the way home from school . . . Bunch of thugs.

"The leader—his name was Xavier Vargas—he was gorgeous. Green eyes. Wavy hair. Everybody thought he was gonna make it to the NBA, but then he raped some girl over in Richmond. He got away with it, though, cuz he played ball.

"Anyway, him and the rest of Five-Point-Oh became Dee's new friends. She started dealing drugs and carrying guns, calling herself the female Scarface and shit like that. Of course, she got nabbed a few times, giving my aunt Carol a fit. So she was in and out of California Youth Authority. And then Dee left and never came back."

Alicia squinted as she sipped her cocktail. "Honestly? The family was kind of glad, cuz we could start breathing and living without her crazy bullshit. I hate to say it, but I wanted her to stay gone." Alicia stared into her glass. "Guess she's still trying to be the female Scarface?"

Before Gray could respond, the doorbell rang.

The woman standing on Alicia's porch was slender and had long silver hair. Her flushed skin was butter yellow and her bloodshot eyes were the color of wheat. As she and Gray exchanged names, Gray heard the lilt in Carol Kelly's voice. She'd heard that same lilt down in Alabama. Those cheekbones, that broad forehead . . . the distressed older woman had the same face as the younger one Gray had hoped to find since July 11.

Alicia brought Carol a glass of 7-Up, along with a plate of pound cake for the room.

"I had no clue where my daughter went." Carol had finally stopped crying and now dried her eyes with a napkin. "I reported her missing the December after she'd graduated from high school. The police told us that, since she was eighteen, I couldn't force her to come home."

"We still searched for her," Alicia added, "even after we realized she wasn't gonna come back. No one's seen her or has heard from her since."

"Tell me," Carol said, squinting at Gray, "who did she become?"

"First, Elyse Miller," Gray said, "and then Isabel Lincoln. She was working at UCLA before she disappeared."

Carol canted her head. "You said Isabel Lincoln? We knew an Isabel . . ." She turned to Alicia. "Youth Ministries . . . The pen pal . . ."

Alicia squinted. "Oh . . . Yeah. I remember her."

Gray sat up. "What? Who is she?"

"There was a moment," Carol said, "that Dee was in and out of juvenile detention, and as part of rehabilitation, there was this pen pal program with a church. Dee's pen pal lived down in Los Angeles. She was only ten or eleven back then . . . Oh, what was the church's name?"

"Mount Gethsemane?" Gray asked, thinking of the church near Dulan's, the soul food joint.

Carol made a face and shrugged. "Anyway, Dee would receive these letters, and eventually she got out of CYA and the letters would come to the house. Dee eventually disappeared, but the letters kept coming. I opened a few, hoping that there was some clue to where she'd gone. But no, nothing. The pen pal, her name was Isabel and she lived—"

"In Inglewood," Gray said, face numb.

"And she wanted to go to UCLA, and in one of the letters she was upset cuz her auntie was going blind and she had to take care of her."

"And then," Carol said, "the letters stopped."

"Isabel disappeared almost twenty-five years ago," Gray said. "She was fifteen."

Alicia cut a look at Carol. "How did she die?"

"Don't know," Gray said. "But after coming back from this trip to Alabama, I don't think it's a coincidence that Deanna used the identity of a missing fifteen-year-old."

Alicia groaned and sank into the couch cushions.

"So, back to Deanna disappearing," Gray said. "She ran off with Xavier?"

"That's what we thought," Carol said.

"You ever meet him?"

"Nope," Alicia said. "He wasn't big on meeting his girls' families."

"And we didn't want to meet him, either," Carol added.

"Dee thought she was the shit," Alicia said. "Nose in the air, like she was better than everybody. Xavier was about twenty-two when they started dating. Dee was only fifteen."

"Already a snake," Carol added. "She drove this souped-up Mustang, had all this jewelry and all this cash. That's what she wanted. Money."

"And Xavier knew that, too," Alicia said. "They were like Bonnie and Clyde. Antony and Cleopatra. Taking over the world, one base-head at a time. But then he went out and got some other young girl pregnant. He dumped Dee, cuz all she wanted was money. I saw him break up with her out there." She pointed toward the scraggly front yard. "She told him that if he didn't change his mind, she'd kill herself. He didn't change his mind, but maybe he should've."

"Xavier was murdered," Carol said, shaking her head. "Shot to death. Police didn't care because he was a drug dealer and a rapist and a thief. Good riddance to bad rubbish."

"My boyfriend at the time knew Xavier," Alicia said. "They were on the same junior high school basketball team. Paul told him to be careful, to watch out for Dee. Told him that she wasn't right in the head. Dee and Xavier had been together for too long for her to just . . . *go away*. And as soon as he dumped her? It was just a matter of time before she got him back."

"When was he killed?" Gray asked.

"Oh . . ." Carol thought for a moment. "I remember it was right before Thanksgiving, 1990. Right before she ran away."

"She seemed . . . *off*," Alicia remembered. "More than usual."

"And the last time you spoke to Deanna was . . . ?"

"A week or so before Xavier was shot," Alicia said.

"And who shot him?"

Carol shrugged.

Alicia drained her glass. "His mom found him at his house in Richmond. His blood was *everywhere*— soaked in the carpet, dried on the door handle, on the light switch . . ."

His mother had followed the blood trail to the bathroom, where Xavier lay dead in the bloody tub. The place had been ransacked.

"He'd hid cash in two safes," Alicia said. "About one hundred seventy-five thousand dollars of drug money. And all of it was gone."

Gray blanched. "Did the cops . . ."

"Suspect Dee?" Carol asked. "No. By then, her juvenile record had been expunged and she hadn't been caught for anything else. They questioned her and that was it. She left Oakland and never came back."

"And no arrests since then?"

Both women shook their heads. "Still unsolved to this day," Alicia said.

She'd been in hiding for two years when she started living as Elyse Miller.

Alicia shook her head. "Can you even imagine the effort to *do* all of this?"

"She used to be on the honor roll," Carol said.

"She played flute and liked Winnie-the-Pooh and . . . Her father lived in the home. I worked, but I took her to practices and . . . Her big brother came out just fine."

Alicia tapped Carol's knee. "It's not your fault. Some people are just *born* that way."

Carol said, "Yeah," but shook her head. "I smoked when I was pregnant—"

"Aunt Carol," Alicia said, words hard. "Stop. Don't." She tossed Gray a look of helplessness. "She does this sometimes."

"If she had used all those smarts for school," Carol continued, "all that energy hustling people and stealing from people, she'd be the president of the United States. But she didn't, and she used a dead baby's name and this other poor girl's name and . . ." Carol looked at Gray with tear-filled eyes. "I don't know who this woman is."

No one did.

DEAD AND ALIVE

The space left by Sean Dixon had been too big to deal with at times, and she found herself crying without even knowing that she was. She'd stand on the deck at Dominick Rader's beachside house and he'd ask, "You okay?" She'd scrunch her eyebrows and say, "Huh?" He'd point at her cheeks and she'd swipe her fingers across her face to find them wet.

Sometimes she and Dominick took walks along the shore. That's when her salty tears would mix with ocean mist.

Hiding in his guest room, she contracted with Rader Consulting to do research on a few cases, and that phenomenon—crying unknowingly—would find her as she determined the birth gender of the prostitute caught with the client's husband.

"I'm going mad," she once told Dominick after dinner. "My mind is decomposing."

Slumped in the Adirondack chair, he had glanced over at her and had then drained his glass of whiskey.

She threw her gaze back out to the ocean. "Not that I want to go back . . ." Her eyes filled with tears. She groaned. She was so tired of crying.

"Maybe you should see someone," he said. "I'll pay for it."

"I have money."

"You don't have to touch it. Not with you planning to change everything. Won't be cheap, getting a brand-new identity. That's what I meant."

"Yeah." She hid her face in her hands and clenched into a tight ball. She took deep breaths to push back the madness at her soul's gate. Two hundred and sixty-seven deep breaths later, she loosened from that ball, then joined Dominick on another walk along the shore.

They took so many walks, they made new sand.

Dominick introduced her to Shonelle Crespin, a psychologist with auburn dreadlocks and perfect white teeth. "What should I call you?" the woman asked. "Besides 'Nick's friend'?"

She'd been thinking about her name, about all those names she'd dreamed about as a kid. Lola, Lucky, Deenie, Scarlett, Jo, Pippi, Leia . . .

"Gray," she said. "Grayson Sykes." And it felt right, coming off her tongue. Sykes—as in "Psych: you thought I was who I was but I'm not anymore." She said it again, and something inside of her wiggled, broke free, and broke apart. Ten minutes into this appointment and parts of her had already healed.

Grayson saw Sean Dixon once during those first months away from him. It had been a random sighting on Sepulveda Boulevard, near UCLA and the federal buildings that housed the State Department. He'd known to look for her in a place that issued new passports. How had he known, though, to hunt for her in Los Angeles?

"A guess," Nick told her. "It's four hours away. He probably looked in Arizona, Utah, and Colorado. Did he see you?"

She shook her head. "I was on the shuttle. It had tinted glass." Her lungs had closed as her husband stalked across the street. He had recovered from her stabbing him and had regained his upright, master-of-the-universe gait. Her knees had sagged, and she was glad that she was holding on to the shuttle's pole.

Twice a week, Gray had nightmares.

Each time, Nick shook her awake.

In one dream, Sean had been strangling her on the beach and his face had transformed into the xenomorph from *Alien*. *Those teeth. That cylindrical skull* . . . The relief of waking up hadn't pushed away that fear. No, she could only clench Nick tighter, tighter still, and wait for time and the strong sunlight to bleach away those images of Sean strangling her.

Gray lived in Nick's guest bedroom for nearly a year. She ate on Nick's dime. Saw the psychologist on Nick's dime. Started the court proceedings to erase who she was and to become who she needed to be—all on Nick's dime.

"I should buy one of those jumpsuits," Gray told him, before the hearing to seal her records. "You know, the ones that race car drivers wear, with all those patches from sponsors sewn on it. You'd be all over me."

His eyes danced, then hardened. "Just a loan. I'm just fronting you until it's safe."

And once she legally became Grayson Faye Sykes, born in November and not in April, Social Security number ending in 0608, she would leave bundles of cash on Nick's dresser, next to his keys or wallet or empty glass that still smelled of whiskey.

On those nights he didn't come home, Gray wondered about the woman he was with. Sometimes she caught a glimpse of him at the nearby Italian place with a blonde named Emma. Or the redhead, Kit or Kate or something. On the weekends, Nick sometimes drove up the coast with a pretty Asian woman he'd brought home once. On one of those weekends, Gray moved into Beaudry Towers. The one-bedroom apartment had enough room for her and gave her enough space from Nick.

Financially, she was now square with her bene-factor. She owed him nothing that could have been deposited at a bank. Those intangible things . . . Well, she could never repay him, so she wouldn't try.

"I'll just live my best life," she told herself as she stood in the solarium.

The muted noise of jammed freeways became the new soundtrack of her life.

And her life with Sean Dixon became as dusty and "wayback" as a video game token left in the middle of the Mojave.

58

Gray was ready to go home. Los Angeles had become Shangri-la, Buckingham Palace, and Paisley Park all mixed up, but without the queen and Prince. She'd left a voice mail for Detective Jake Days, who oversaw Tommy Hampton's case, but he hadn't picked up, and she was glad that he hadn't. If she talked to one more person today, her brain would explode quicker than whatever organ inside of her was still giving her the business.

At Oakland International Airport, she dropped the rental car back at Avis and thanked Mike, her temporary bodyguard. She trudged to the departure gate for a late-night flight to Los Angeles, but a text from Jennifer made her slow her step.

No travel abroad for Elyse Miller.

"Maybe she's using another name," Gray said.

For Deanna Kelly, the world was filled with the unforgotten or the gone-too-soon—the possibilities for new identities were endless. And she'd never stop on her own; she'd been too many people.

And she'd never be satisfied, because stolen identities never settled in like a new nose or a nip/tuck around the neck. Deanna Kelly was Cerberus, except that people didn't know they should be careful around her. Those who hadn't been careful paid with ruined credit and misdemeanors on their previously clean records. Others had paid with their lives. Like Tommy Hampton. Like Xavier Vargas. Like Omar Neville.

Deanna Kelly was a grifter, a thug, a liar, and a thief.

Worse . . .

Deanna Kelly was a serial killer.

And this case was now bigger than ever and needed to be taken over by the police.

On the plane, Gray found her draft email to Yvonne Reeves.

Dear Yvonne.

I was born Natalie Kittridge in Oakland on April 25, 1980 and given up for adoption. Since then, I've never met members of my biological family—but now I see your name listed as a second cousin. And with this test only analyzing maternal DNA, you must be my birth mother's first cousin. Would you be open to talking to me?

Gray pressed Send before she changed her mind.

By the time Gray's plane landed in Los Angeles, Detective Jake Days in Oakland had called and left a voice mail on her phone. She could barely hear his message over the roar of Los Angeles: "*Something, something, Myracle Hampton hope we can close this once and for all Tommy Hampton something something.*"

Gray had answered almost every question she'd come up with at the start of this case, except the original: Where had Deanna Kelly taken the damned dog? That made her heart ache, because her first thought was this: Kenny G. was dead. Deanna didn't care about humans, so why would she care about her ex-boyfriend's Labradoodle?

It was late, but Gray called Ian O'Donnell from the back seat of her cab. "She's worse than we thought. Nothing about her is real. Not the name you knew. Not the name she had before *that* name. She's not in her thirties. She didn't graduate from UCLA, and she may have murdered—well, she *probably* murdered three ex-boyfriends. If identity theft was her only crime, I would've been thrilled, but yeah . . . She's much worse, and until the police find *her*, you should watch your back."

Ian O'Donnell said nothing.

"And I still don't know where she took Kenny G. We looked for recent trips taken by Elyse Miller and didn't find anything. Not sure yet about Deanna Kelly."

Ian said, "I received a call from the medical board and . . . I haven't talked to them, but I'm sure my career is over. I know it. I paid Nick a lot of money for you to stop her and you didn't—you failed. We'll handle *that* later, but . . . the police are involved. That's good, I guess. At least I know *they'll* stop her."

"Like they stopped her back in the nineties? Like they stopped her years ago? Like they stopped her two weeks ago?" She would've chomped Ian in half if he were standing in front of her.

She took a deep breath, then said, "I understand your frustration. You may complain to Nick about my failure to keep your shenanigans in the dark."

She called Nick next.

"You're home," he said. "Mike said there was no sign of Sean."

"The cops in Mobile are still looking for him."

"I'll keep an ear out."

"I still haven't found the dog. Nor have I found *her*." And she told him about meeting Deanna Kelly's mother and cousin.

"What's her long game?" Nick asked.

"There's a mortician down in Belize willing to sell her a body—a car accident victim—for five thousand dollars. Comes with a death certificate and mourners, too. He'll cremate the body and Deanna's hair and nail samples will prove that the body is Isabel Lincoln."

"And then Deanna collects the insurance as Tea Christopher."

"Right," Gray said. "Tea told me that she's joining Deanna in Belize, and I'm thinking Deanna's planning to kill Tea, too."

"For insurance?"

"Yeah."

"But who's the beneficiary on Tea's policy?"

"Don't know," Gray admitted. "Some other stolen identity that I haven't found yet."

"Classic death fraud. Anything else?" Nick asked.

"I have a second cousin in Sacramento and—" Her throat closed.

"You gonna introduce yourself?" Nick asked.

"I emailed her."

"You okay?"

"Kinda feels like I'm betraying them."

He was silent again, but then he said, "Victor always told us, 'The truth is rarely pure and never simple.'"

"Oscar Wilde." She let her forehead rest on the window. "I miss them so much."

"Want me to come over?"

"Oh, how I'd like to say yes, but . . ."

"You're tired."

"Exhausted."

"Tomorrow?"

"Please?"

"Thai?"

"And martinis."

"Dessert?"

She blushed. "Depends."

Like the city, her phone had been buzzing since she'd lumbered off the plane. Text messages from Tea Christopher.

> Where are you?
> I need to talk to you ASAP!
> Please call!! My car's broken down and so I can't drive.

Every message Tea had sent since Saturday night—sixteen—had been similar.

Saturday. Gray had been in Vegas, drinking and hooting. Felt like thirty moons ago.

Gray texted, *Just got home. Coming over to you. Don't let anybody into the house. NO ONE EXCEPT ME! See you soon.*

Gray's apartment was dark, and the light from the living room danced across the couch and carpet. The refrigerator rumbled its usual hello and, as usual, Gray yelped, startled by the sudden booming gruffness made by a simple appliance. Nothing had changed since she'd been gone. The lights, the fridge, the empty vodka bottle in the freezer, the knives, the Mace in the medicine cabinet . . . same as it ever was.

Gray didn't want to sit, didn't want to change clothes. *Just go and be done.* She slipped the knife and Mace into her back pockets and the gun into her battered Liz Claiborne purse.

Maybe she could now convince Tea that she was being had by a con artist.

Maybe Tea Christopher would finally end her carping for Isabel, once she heard the truth.

The truth, though, was rarely pure, and never simple.

59

Tea's raggedy green Altima was parked in the drive-way of the Christopher house. Every bulb burned bright in that rambling ranch, and television light glowed in between the breaks of the closed living room shutters. Gray rang the doorbell, then slumped against the porch railing. Her head and back ached from fighting a crazy man in a greasy spoon down in Alabama.

Why wasn't Tea answering the door?

Had she fallen asleep? Had she let Deanna Kelly in and found herself tied up in a bedroom?

On the other side of midnight, surfing the last mol-ecules of Percocet, Gray's mind couldn't help but come up with terrifying ends for the con's biggest mark.

Gray knocked on the door again.

No answer.

She banged on the door.

Barks came from inside the Christopher house.

Tea never mentioned having a dog. Was that—

"Kenny G.?" Gray squeezed the door's brass handle.

Unlocked.

She pushed open the door.

The smell was more than rot; it was more than trash; it was heavier than shit.

"Oh my . . ." Gray's stomach lurched, and she covered her mouth with the crook of her elbow to block that smell. It was like . . . like . . . She couldn't figure out *what* she was smelling.

"Tea," she shouted, "you here?"

Everybody Loves Raymond played on the television, but no one sat on the white couch.

She scanned the living room.

Fireplace mantel crammed with framed pictures.

Coffee table covered with empty food containers.

Filthy white carpet.

Rotting foot peeking from beneath a green blanket.

"Oh *shit*." Gray flailed backwards, eyes no longer seeing.

The dog started barking again.

That foot was as black as night.

Dead—that's what she was smelling.

Near that foot, beneath the coffee table . . .

A tortoiseshell stem from a pair of glasses.

A small cylinder of burnished gold.

"A bullet casing," Gray whispered.

Tea!

But it couldn't be. She'd just texted Gray less than an hour ago. That foot—and the rest of that person—had been beneath the coffee table for weeks.

Gray swiped her mouth as her stomach rocked, as the liquified fat from this poor soul settled into her nostrils.

The dog was barking, frantic now.

Get the dog and get the fuck out of here.

The barking got louder as she tiptoed down the bright hallway. Gray peeked into the first bedroom she reached. The curtains were drawn, and the stink of dog shit hung on still air. A large dog crate sat in the middle of the room. A big dog with matted chocolate-blond hair pawed at the cage, pawed for release, whined for freedom and to be loved again.

Gray smiled. "Kenny G. Ohmigod, you're still alive."

She slipped over to the cage.

The dog hopped, whined, and circled.

A lock hung from the gate latch.

Shit.

"I need to find a key," Gray cooed. She stuck her hand between the grates to pet the dog. "I'll be back, okay. You're a good, good boy, aren't you? Aren't you?"

"He is the *best* boy," a woman's voice said behind her. "The bestest."

60

Gray pulled the can of Mace from her back pocket and whirled around.

Tea Christopher stood in the doorway.

"You scared me," Gray shouted.

Tea said, "Sorry." She wore that tired lavender tracksuit, and her frizzy bangs looked as dusty as her grungy braids.

"Who is that?" Gray whispered, pointing to the living room. "The foot. Who?"

Tea clenched her hands. Her eyes looked bloodshot behind those thick lenses. "Something's happened and I . . . I don't know where to go. Please, Miss Sykes. I need your help. Kenny G. . . . he needs you, too."

Gray held up a hand. "You *knew* where this dog was. It's obvious that he's been here—"

"I can explain everything." Tea took a step into the room. She smelled sweaty, swampy, like she'd run to Westchester via the Los Angeles River.

"Why didn't you give me the dog?" Gray's voice had pitched toward the heavens. "And why is there a fucking bullet casing—"

"It's Isabel. Not on the floor out there, but she . . . she . . ."

"She *what*?" Gray moved toward Tea.

Kenny G. whined, a plea not to be left alone.

"Isabel's here, in L.A.," Tea whispered, "and she's not who she says she is."

Gray said nothing.

"You know that," Tea said, eyes wide. "That Isabel's lying."

"We need to call the—"

"Who else knows?"

Gray bit her lip and decided not to tell Tea about Oakland Police Detective Jake Days or her conversations with Myracle Hampton or Deanna Kelly's mother and cousin.

"Noelle knows," Tea said, nodding. "I don't know where she is now. I think Bobby beat her up to keep her quiet. Did you tell Ian that you think Isabel's lying?"

"Not yet," Gray lied. "I'm still trying to prove it. I'm still trying to connect some things. It's all one big ball of tangled bullshit after another big ball of tangled bullshit."

Tea slowly exhaled. "I just want it to be over. I just want to breathe again." She slipped off her glasses, then rubbed her eyes. "Don't you?"

She pulled at her hair, and those braids and bangs were now in her hand. Her ponytail—sapphire black and darker than the darkest night—was now free to swing past her shoulders. She dropped the wig and the glasses to the carpet, then pulled off the track jacket and the two sweatshirts she'd worn beneath it. She kicked off her Skechers and tugged off the track pants. She tossed those, and the cushions she'd stuffed around her thighs, onto the heap of clothes.

A new woman stood there, muscled, tattooed, in a white tank top and black leggings. It was the dog thief. The ex-girlfriend. The Mary Ann. She'd hidden a knife with a serrated blade in her discarded disguise and she clutched it now.

Gray took wobbly steps back until she backed against the dog crate. She still clutched a can of Mace, and she prayed that it was ready to spray.

"You . . ." Deanna Kelly pointed the knife at Gray. "You are pretty good. You're still alive. If you were a man, you'd be dead by now."

Instinct kept Gray's tears from tumbling down her cheeks. "Deanna Kelly?"

Deanna's eyes widened, and her lips twisted into a sick grin. "Again, leave it to another woman to get shit done. Same can be said about me. I'm about to do what your psycho ex-husband couldn't do."

The threat of death didn't scare Gray; Sean Dixon had threatened to kill her once a month. No, she was shaking now because she realized that she had never met the real Tea Christopher. Not at Sam Jose's. Not at Post & Beam. Not once. "Where is she?" Gray asked now. "Where's Tea?"

Deanna stepped closer to Gray. "She's out there, watching TV. Well, *technically*, for the last three weeks her soul has been resting in the Lord she never shut up about."

The real Tea Christopher was dead. Bishop Dunlop hadn't seen her in weeks. Neither had Ian. And that was because . . .

"Where is Isabel Lincoln? The *real* Isabel Lincoln?"

"My old pen pal? She's been gone for almost twenty years. Who cares?"

"Her family—"

"Ain't nobody left in Isabel's family except for her blind-ass aunt. Ruby can thank me for keeping her alive—Bobby been wanting to kill that bitch in her sleep. I told him, *Have a heart. Collect your check.* He acts like I don't pay him."

Gray whispered, "Pay him for . . ."

Deanna shrugged. "My Boy Friday shit. He owed me *again*. First, I introduced him to my little pen pal—she was too young for him, but who am I to pass judgment, right? He was grateful once she . . . *disappeared*. And then convincing Ruby to let him be her eyes. Little known fact: I take—a *lot*—but I also give, give, give."

Gray could feel the heat pulsating off the impersonator's body. She could smell the liquor on Deanna's breath. She could smell old blood, too. "Why did you call me here? You could've just left the country. You could've just—"

"You have a check that belongs to me." Deanna took a step. "You're making this more complicated than what it needs to be. I'll be out of your hair soon."

"Why?"

Deanna held out her arms. "I got a funeral to attend. You're looking at the newest resident of Belize City." She held out her arms and posed. "Meet the new Gray Sykes, the worst private investigator in—"

Gray pressed the trigger of the Mace can.

The spray shot out like a snake.

It missed its mark and hit Deanna's neck.

The woman still reeled backwards and out into the hallway.

Gray rushed to the bedroom doorway and darted past her.

Deanna grabbed the tail of Gray's shirt.

Both women stumbled to the carpet.

Deanna climbed atop Gray.

Gray held up her left arm.

Deanna's blade sank into Gray's wrist.

Gray screamed and used all of her anger, resentment, and fear to push Deanna Kelly off of her. With her healthy hand, she reached into her back pocket for her own knife.

She blindly swung the blade.

Deanna cried out and reached for her now bloody forehead.

Gray scrambled to her knees.

Deanna grabbed Gray's leg.

The knife sank into Gray's calf.

Gray donkey-kicked with her healthy leg. Soft cartilage—some part of Deanna Kelly—met the sole of her sneaker. She didn't look back to see which part of Deanna she'd kicked.

She scrambled to the living room as Deanna Kelly rolled on the hallway floor.

In the living room, Gray shoved her hand into her battered purse.

Keys, lipsticks, tissue packets, boarding passes, tweezers, envelopes, wallet, gift cards—*yes!* The purse's torn lining had hidden the prize.

Deanna staggered toward Gray. Blood stained her face and filled her mouth. Her knife glistened red with the blood of two women.

Gray held up the gun. "Stop."

But Deanna Kelly didn't know *how* to stop.

Gray squeezed the trigger.

Deanna Kelly stopped and dropped to her knees. The shock on her face was brighter than the bloom of red spreading across her white tank top. "You . . ." She dropped to her knees.

Then Gray felt herself drifting . . . drifting . . . falling . . .

Big men wearing blue wool or yellow canvas swarmed the Christophers' house. One man in yellow shone a flashlight in Gray's eyes. "What's your name, miss?"

Gray blinked past the tears and croaked, "Name?"

And then she laughed and laughed.

EPILOGUE

The soft, warm winds of Cabo San Lucas drifted past the open windows and lifted the sheer, gauzy curtains. Palm trees rustled as birds called out to each other. Out there, turquoise jewel–colored waters swirled against the sand.

Gray turned over in the king-size bed.

Dominick Rader lay on his back and stared at the slow-turning ceiling fan.

She tugged a lock of his disheveled hair. "You okay?"

"I am now." He smiled at her.

She kissed him. Then she kissed him again and kept her eyes open and let the millions of butterflies flutter around her belly. "Do you think people know?"

Nick shrugged. "People paid to snoop saw us leave together after the reception. They'll think we got drunk and . . ."

"Hooked up."

"Happens all the time at weddings."

Gray had caught Jennifer staring at her and Nick throughout Clarissa's wedding, and she'd noticed how Nick had held Gray on the dance floor. The blonde wasn't dumb.

His finger traced her nose. "I have something for you."

She cocked an eyebrow. "A pony?"

He shook his head, his expression now serious.

She hardened. "What? What's wrong? Did she escape somehow?"

The medical examiner had confirmed that Tea Christopher had been dead in that living room since mid-May. The district attorney had declined to charge Gray for shooting Deanna Kelly. It was over for now. Just in time for Clarissa and Irwin's wedding.

"No, Deanna's still in jail. It's not her." He slipped out of bed and over to his bag.

Nick's scars matched hers, and she had kissed each of them. Then she had closed her eyes as he kissed every one of hers—including the newest ones at her navel.

According to Dr. Messamer, Gray had an intra-abdominal abscess, a complication after her appendectomy.

"Here." He climbed back into bed with an expandable file folder. "For you."

She pulled out a sheet of paper from the folder.

LAST KNOWN ADDRESS AS OF AUGUST 30
FOR . . .

Mouth dry, mind spinning, Gray's eyes darted to Nick's. "Sean. You found him?"

"He's there. Nursing his most recent stab wound, I guess."

"How do you know?"

"Before coming *here*, I found him *there*."

There. Playa del Carmen, Mexico.

"Luxury condo with an ocean view," Nick said. "Four bedrooms, five baths, blond wood floors, quartz countertops. And a dog run."

"Why Mexico?"

"Someone has a little tax problem with Uncle Sam." Nick paused, then amended himself. "No—a *big* tax problem."

Gray's eyes bugged. "Is he evading . . ."

"The feds?" Nick nodded. "But I have friends. Eyes everywhere."

She squinted at him. "I wanna be there when they arrest him. I'll buy the tickets."

Nick said, "We were supposed to go on that booze cruise tomorrow."

"Fuck a watered-down mai tai. I want *this*."

Nick lay back in the pillows. "If I do that for you, what will you do for me?"

Him looking like that . . . looking at her like that . . .

Damn.

The room tilted.

Smiling, Gray straddled Nick's hips and gazed into her lover's eyes.

She'd do anything.

ACKNOWLEDGMENTS

For many reasons, this is one of my most personal stories. It took a moment for me to figure out how to write it and I'm so grateful to those who helped bring it to the world. Thanks to my agent, Jill Marsal, for always being there—your sharp eye and constant encouragement mean so much to me. Thanks to my editor, Kristin Sevick, for believing in this story, and Alexis Saarela and my team at Forge for spreading the word. Thank you, Crystal Patriarche, Tabitha Bailey, and BookSparks, for your great ideas and incredible support.

Special thanks to David Corbett for sharing all that he knows about private investigators—and it's a lot. All mistakes are mine. Also, thank you, Kellye Garrett, Hank Phillippi Ryan, Kristi Belcamino, and Jess Lourey. I cried and whined to you all about this book, and you gave me cocktails, tater tots, or plain ol' love.

Thank you to my family: Gretchen and Jason for driving me around Las Vegas so many years ago as I was conceptualizing this story, and Terence for driving me around Oakland. My mother, Jacqueline, is the glue that holds us all together, who constantly encourages me and reminds me to rest. Thank you, Maya Grace—I am blessed to be your momma. Thank you, David—you have no idea how important your input has been over the last twenty-five years. I love you all.